Eleri

Eleri

IRIS REEVES WILLIAMS

Matador
9 Priory Business Park,
Wistow Road, Kibworth Beauchamp,
Leicestershire. LE8 0RX
Tel: 0116 279 2299
Email: books@troubador.co.uk
Web: www.troubador.co.uk/matador
Twitter: @matadorbooks

ISBN 978 1 80046107 9

British Library Cataloguing in Publication Data.
A catalogue record for this book is available from the British Library.

Printed and bound in Great Britain by 4edge Limited
Typeset in 11pt Minion Pro by Troubador Publishing Ltd, Leicester, UK

Matador is an imprint of Troubador Publishing Ltd

For Ray –
with gratitude for his efforts and successes
and unwavering cheerfulness

CHARACTERS

Mai Madoc Blethyn – matriarch of Pen Melyn
Briende and Eleri – her daughters
Gaston Madoc Blethyn – her son
Sîan – Gaston's wife
Bethan and Selwyn – their children
Gilbert Madoc Blethyn – Mai's brother
Wynn Madoc Blethyn – Gilbert's son
Moya – Wynn's wife
Niamh and Connor – their children
Ralph Weston Maine – Briende's husband
Maeve Marguerite Maine – their daughter
Aunt Marguerite – Ralph's aunt (Preece)
Bridget – friend, maid of Madoc Blethyns
Lady Bettina Garonne – owner of Campions
Mr. Byatt – island conveyor
Rev. Charles Britt – vicar
Janet – his wife

Laurence and Bellan – their sons
Deborah and Editha Madoc – aunts of Eleri
Mr. Day – nursery owner
Rosemary Day – Eleri's childhood friend
Weston and Delphine Maine – Ralph's parents
Malcolm Molyneux – bank manager
Prunie, Venetia, Juliette – Eleri's college friends
Aunt Dinah Blethyn – Mr. Blethyn's sister
Alvar Garonne – future owner of Campions
Wyndham Jolliff – school caretaker
Isabel and Lucy Mason – hotel guests
Royston Garonne Burnette – Alvar's nephew
Mrs. Sullivan – housekeeper at Campions
Abdun – Prunie's husband
Sherene Khalif – Arab doctor friend
Prince Saleem Mahmoud el Eys – guest at Dorchester
Abou el ben Har – Sherene's husband
Abel ben Haran – a Jew in Germany
Hagar, Talal, Barakat – Arabs
Roisin McKenny – an Irish friend of Eleri's
Major Johnstone – travelling companion of Ralph's
Mr. Crispin Penwick – ambassador in Aden
Cecile Garonne Burnette – Alvar's sister
Frieda Rebecca Levi – Jewish refugee
Dr. Amos Skiroski – Jewish refugee
Rachel Mann – housemother at Fentons
Monica and Talbot Bessington – Eleri's friends
Phillip Headingly – architect admirer of Eleri
Saas and Hendryk – Polish airmen
Simon John Peerless – Eleri's husband (2nd)

Ulric – Polish serviceman and friend
Lisa Marsden – Royston's girl
Mrs. Benson – a midwife in Brymadoc
Dolores and Silas Clay – housekeepers
Hazel Corrie – Rosemary Day's daughter
Dominic Witherslea – a former school acquaintance
Brinley Witherslea – his brother
Sefton Maynard – Maeve's Oxford acquaintance
Cynthia Forester and Ceridwen Bowen-Beynon – Maeve's Oxford friends
Percy Edgar Pennistone-Craig (Penn) – an acquaintance of Eleri

PLACES

Brymadoc – a village in llandia
Pen Melyn – the Madoc Blethyn house
Campions – the Garonne mansion
Trevere – a town
Limorrnah – the chief port
Barnshire – Ralph Maine's home county
Madbury – Ralph Maine's school
Dewary – Briende's school
Ondine – School of Art, London
The Hermit – a public house in Brymadoc
St. Petroc – the church in Brymadoc
Myrtle House – the Madoc aunts' home
Brackens – Briende's married home
The Pirate's Haven – an hotel in Limorrnah

Featherstone Heights – Aunt Marguerite's retirement hotel
Saxon's Head – Ralph and Briende's honeymoon hotel
Winthrops – a London gentlemen's club
Marian-lea-Meade – Ralph Maine's home village
Hotel Pompadour, Paris – Eleri and Alvar's honeymoon hotel
Lemons – Maeve and Penn's house

CHAPTER ONE

Ilandia and the Blethyn Family

It was always summer. Or was it? Looking back through the years, wrapped in a haze of memory, there were daffodils along the riverbanks, heather on the hillside, leaves falling and children battling home from school in the sleety gloaming. Evidently, it was not permanently summer, merely a summer of the spirit.

Home was an island, the Southern Island in a land shaped like an elongated, much-fractured figure eight, the southern part joined to its much smaller Northern Island by a narrow isthmus. The whole was called Ilandia.

The inhabitants, though they spoke the English language in a diversity of accents and vocabulary, though established for many generations, were genetically a mixture of Irish, Cornish, Welsh and Breton and if there had existed a nation called Celtia, this would have been the place. Their names echoed these Celtic regions and the gravestones bore the same names as the present inhabitants of the towns and villages in the early twentieth century.

Trevere, the chief centre of administration, was situated in South Island, as was the chief port, Limorrnah, about four miles from the mainland. Around Limorrnah revolved most of the commerce. It was endlessly busy, ferries and ships plying to and from Brittany, Cornwall, Wales and Ireland; fishing boats seemingly loaded, custom houses, warehouses and minor factories lining the docks. Limorrnah was considered affluent and sophisticated compared with the rest of llandia. Apart from fishing and trading, the other activity governing the economy was quarrying at Craigan. Rocks on the West Coast were dynamited, hewn and crushed and the end products sold to huge contractors for road making or building – an economically lucrative enterprise.

The inhabitants not connected with the port or quarry usually farmed the land, bred livestock or worked in smallholdings. A few only were employed in administration.

Our story begins and ends in Brymadoc, a large village near Trevere. It had the usual assemblage of shops; butcher, greengrocer, baker, ironmonger, draper and an innocent-looking bank along the high street. The public house, called The Hermit, was next to the church, in the usual pattern. Legend affirmed that a hermit called Patrick once lived in a stone cairn on the site of the church, the altar of which later encompassed the stones of his humble dwelling, and Patrick, discomfited, left his homeland for Ireland to join his saint and namesake. The church became known as St. Petroc, perhaps a corruption of Patrick or in honour of the real Petroc. The hermit was commemorated in the public house, which, as was customary, once housed the masons during the building of the church.

In Brymadoc lived the Madoc Blethyn family, the present matriarch being Mai Madoc Blethyn, wife of ldwal Blethyn, who had emigrated from North Island to wed the formidable Mai. She was the latest in a long line of maternal ancestors, the Madocs, a matriarchal family where the eldest daughter inherited. They had been domiciled on the island for many generations; some had never left the island. lndeed, most had never seen the mainland, which seemed to belong to some distant planet. Their home, Pen Melyn, was the nucleus of their universe.

The widowed Mai had two beautiful daughters, Briende and Eleri, and a successful son, Gaston, who, with his cousin Wynn, operated a business in Limorrnah. Wynn's father Gilbert lived with Mai, his sister, and helped her manage the remaining estate – land he had always known.

The elder daughter, Briende Madoc Blethyn, was a sweet, untainted product of llandia. Her Dresden china exterior betrayed an inner ambition, a sense of independence, a deep intelligence. Seemingly her fate was to marry a neighbouring landowner. She was considered 'suitable', being quiet, sober and from a respected clan. She was a product of private tutors as a child and then a private school on the mainland, to which she daily travelled by train and ferry, and her mother was appalled when she decided to try some student teaching, just to see if she had a vocation. If so, she hoped to aim for the Charlotte Mason College in Ambleside. To live in Cumbria in Wordsworth Country appealed. She would become a qualified teacher and then return to llandia to open her own school.

Briende was of ancient lineage, folk who had never ventured forth into the wider world, proud people content with their lot. Their substantial granite house, built from the stones of a previous dwelling, which had itself been part of another dwelling, stood stark and majestic on a small hillock, surrounded by its own green fields, hedged in by a preponderance of yellow broom and gorse for several months, the land undulating into a hazy horizon, hence the house being called Pen Melyn, a yellow head or hilltop.

Her grandmother, Anna Madoc Fefyd, had been the wise woman of the village, who concocted her own medicines, poultices, pills and tonics in the uncomplicated, undeveloped days. In a place where a doctor was an unheard-of luxury and had to be summoned from the mainland, if funds permitted, Mother Madoc in her elevated citadel was much esteemed. Her own daughter, Mai Madoc Blethyn, Briende's mother, had inherited many of her qualities, skills and wisdom but her importance had diminished since the acquiring of a doctor on South Island and a small hospital in the North.

As Briende approached adulthood, the transition had begun.

In the old established household religion was much to the fore, the conversation peppered with biblical quotations.

The constant reminders that cleanliness was next to godliness and that the devil found work for idle hands were typical tenets of how life was meant to be lived.

The home itself, dominated by a large lived-in kitchen, spelt security and comfort – the smell of baking ever blending with the smell of carbolic soap, the coal or wood fire ever banked up, an iron oven on one side and hobs on either side, and a brass fender gleaming in the firelight. There were velour tasselled tablecloths, sheepskin rugs on a slate floor, extravagantly looped curtains and holy pictures on the walls: *Come to me all ye that are heavily laden and I will give ye rest* and *The word of the Lord endureth forever* and *God is Love.*

The pictures had cream or white frames and each quotation was wreathed in a garland of flowers – high fashion in those times.

An important personage, such as the vicar or a neighbouring landowner, coming to supper was an occasion for starched tablecloths edged in crocheted lace. Together they were expected to solve all social problems from a lost cat to a wayward youth and no document of importance was signed without consulting either or both.

Mrs. Madoc Blethyn's husband, Idwal, had died young after a noble effort, with other villagers, of rescuing workers at the quarry after a roof collapse. Unfortunately, he ended up a victim and was buried on the same day as the neighbours he had tried to rescue and had since been much honoured among the islanders. Waves of support towards his widow gave her pride and courage to continue, with her widowed brother Gilbert's help, to bring up the family as her husband would have desired.

Their son, Gaston, had already left the home to join his older cousin Wynn in Limorrnah. Gaston managed the fishing vessels and his cousin the processing factories along the quay. Neither had any interest in the older ways, farming or religion. Being business-oriented they dreamed of expansion – purchasing land, establishing warehouses, rearing their children for the modern world. Gaston's Welsh wife, Sîan, and his children, Bethan and Selwyn, were a foil to Wynn's Irish wife, Moya, and their children, Niamh and Connor. Closely knit they were almost one unit and lived in substantial houses close at hand.

The six-year-old Eleri, Mrs. Blethyn's youngest, had merely a hazy recollection of her father and Uncle Gil had been her steadfast male influence. Briende deeply mourned her father. His loss had a reticent effect upon her whole personality, and she, naturally quiet, became more withdrawn for several months.

The pretty, dainty Briende was much admired and promised, as the term went, to a neighbouring landowner, in fact the future owner of the huge mansion known as Campions, sitting in extensive lands. The handsome, smooth Alvar Garonne was, as yet, unmarried but renowned for his sophisticated lifestyle.

One summer's day Briende Madoc Blethyn, as part of her unwelcome training, was scheduled to take her pupils for a school visit to Dewary on the mainland, although for the children it was to be a great experience, as most had never left llandia or felt the need to. Once in Dewary a visit to a museum was on the agenda. There were statues to be looked at and later written about, buildings to be observed then drawn, types of vehicles to be noted, plus observation of the docks at both ends, noting the types of fish caught and boats used. Her brother and cousin had agreed to meet them for a short while and show them around the quay of Limorrnah before they boarded the ferry. To be provided with notebooks and pencils to record all this was an extra-special privilege, as many were from homes where a pencil and paper was a luxury. Each child carrying his or her lunch in a linen napkin or paper bag enjoyed this break from routine.

The barracks at Dewary had been offered for their use during the lunch hour, with young soldiers at hand to supervise the arrangements. For them it was a welcome break from boredom.

Seated at wooden tables, tea provided, sandwiches unwrapped, young recruits in attendance, Miss Blethyn felt proud of her charges and she did not have to chastise any. While the children were busily occupied, she looked around her, and in the doorway, quietly giving orders, she saw the young officer. Tall, blonde, elegant, reserved. He looked towards her. She looked away but for the first time in her life she felt an immediate attraction. Her unease surprised her. A while later he approached her and introduced himself as Ralph Maine and asked if all was well. He knew her name. She thanked him and said they would soon be leaving.

"May I ask you what you propose to do? No doubt you are half-way through your plans."

"We are off to the old part of town to visit the museum and hopefully the Town Hall – with luck, if the mayor is around we could be shown the mayor's parlour – and walk around the old buildings, or so I've been led to believe. Perhaps we can learn something about the administration of the town."

"Don't you think the small aviary and the Botanic Gardens would be more fun on such a fine day – assuming of course that you've made no formal arrangements?"

"I have not, and the gardens sound a far more charming idea. Though at school here, I never ventured far from the school. Can we walk from here?"

She was painfully aware of her shyness and beginning to feel confused, because this man attracted her.

"I'll get some of my recruits to accompany you – they are often bored. I may follow later, when my duties here are over, if you have no objection?"

She uttered a meek thank you and dismissed herself to gather her pupils and graciously thank the young soldiers for their care during the lunch break. Then, led by herself and the young soldiers, they all left the hall.

A while later the officer joined them. The young soldiers respectfully took up their places at the tail end of the group and a small cavalcade walked towards the Park, an uncanny little group of excited children, a shy reluctant student teacher and young men undoubtedly pleased to be free from dull barrack routine on a fine day.

The weather was kind, the sun glinting on the brass buttons of Ralph Maine's uniform. There was a peace about him – gentleness. She could not imagine such a being involved with warfare. Her sentiments may have been evident as she asked him about his work.

"I'm a sort of diplomat, a rolling stone sending back endless bulletins written on the spot, giving as much local colour and information as possible about strange and sometimes inaccessible places."

"More of a writer than a soldier?" she ventured.

"Yes, I sort of prepare the way, if a garrison needs to be sent – then I move on, usually to the next trouble spot to do the same thing over again."

"You have a home and family in England?"

"No, an elderly aunt reared me; my parents died when I was very young. My aunt, the most wonderful person I've known, spent her meagre inheritance and my parents' legacy on my education and upbringing and I now care for her."

Briende conjectured that he had no wife and asked, "Where does your aunt live?"

"In Barnshire, in a small hotel for the elderly – her home had to be sold but it was my home when I went to school."

"So you went to Bambourne School?"

"No, Modbury, and from there to the army. I had no choice."

Too shy to pursue the conversation and sensing his own shyness the conversation ended.

Meantime they had arrived at the park aviary. The children, delighted with the exotic birds, showed their joy in endless questions. Briende was amazed at Captain Maine's knowledge and charmed by his gentle manner when answering the barrage of questions, mentioning his own experiences in foreign lands and his familiarity with some of the species – telling them that cockatoos and toucans in some hot countries were as commonplace as the robins and thrushes here. The young soldiers were as fascinated as the children as the captain also conveyed his knowledge of plants.

Briende thought what a wonderful teacher he would have made and realised that she, herself, was becoming fascinated, and when they reached the maze, something the youngsters had never experienced, there was great excitement permeating the entire group. While they explored the maze, guarded by their young companions, Briende and the captain sat together on a nearby bench.

Briende felt uneasy; she was enamoured of this attractive stranger. This was surely the most wonderful day she had ever known, so natural, so unexpected, but her attraction to the young man beside her was disturbing. Should she have accepted his company? Unknown to her, the nineteen-year-old woman beside him held the same attraction for him. With the first glance he had taken in her soft brown curls and violet eyes, sweet smile and femininity. Her daintiness, so appealing, seemed to plead protectiveness. At the same time, he was aware of her unsophistication – just a sweet, carefully reared, young lady – ever-conscious of her behaviour, in a way poised beyond her years. After a mere five minutes he suggested walking in the vicinity of the maze, as he felt that she was uneasy away from the group. She had about her a loveliness and a vulnerability and he was terrified in case he might frighten or offend her. She appeared like something out of early nineteenth-century fiction and although, he surmised, only a decade older than her, considered that she was a mere child.

The long shadows of the late afternoon were beginning to fall, the tired pupils were reassembled for the walk back to the ship with the young recruits at the tail end and the Captain and Briende at the fore. It was a civilised little group that wandered back to the quay and on to the ferry *Sea Dame*. She shepherded her charges onto the gangplank and instructed them to say thank you to the young soldiers. They then waved and boarded. Briende gave her own thanks to the young men and turned to their officer, holding out her lilac-gloved hand. He held it briefly but before releasing her, quietly asked if he could see her again the following Saturday. Her heart racing uncontrollably, she thought, she said, "There's a twelve-thirty conveyance from Limorrnah. Mr. Byatt meets the boat twice daily."

From the crowded deck they watched the receding coastline and Briende saw that he still waited. Tentatively she gave a demure wave, and all went below for the rest of the crossing.

Reality returned among the bustle of children but, as Briende took a seat among them, she was shaken by the magnitude of what she had agreed to. Her strict upbringing, by a Victorian parent in an undeveloped backwater even for the early twentieth century, had taken its toll – what would people think? Sheer terror overcame her. She had agreed to a strange man visiting her home – a man who had not been introduced to her, a man her people had not heard of and certainly a stranger to llandia. She, Briende Madoc Blethyn, was more or less promised since childhood. Well-bred young ladies were not expected to make their own choice, especially if one came from an old, respected, family in a confined area. In retrospect she marvelled at her own courage, but it all seemed so innocent, so natural. He was quiet, kind, civilised and almost as shy as she. She sensed his attraction to her, and she herself felt very disturbed by him. The feeling frightened her, and she found it impossible to erase him from her thoughts and was strangely, uneasily, prepossessed.

Seagulls were screaming overhead above the mast as the ship sailed westwards towards the dear shore of the only place she had ever really known, apart from schooldays at Dewary, and even then the pattern never varied – she arrived by ferry each morning and returned at the end of the day, unless inclement weather made the crossing too rough. At such times the night was spent with the boarders.

With her usual dignity, on arriving back in Limorrnah, she chaperoned the excited youngsters into the waiting lorry. Mr. Byatt, the island conveyor of people, as his father and grandfather had been before him, would be waiting. With much happy babble they boarded and as evening descended travelled inland, homewards. Briende felt a wave of affection towards the place as Mr. Byatt halted at homes near their destination to unload the precious travellers, and at each gate and doorway there were eager arms waiting. In a cut-off land with few wirelesses or newspapers or motor cars, except at the port, everything was news.

Briende could not help dwelling on what waves her own special news would make on Saturday. Everyone knew everything about the other inhabitants in Brymadoc; the world outside was of little consequence. They thrived on observing other folk and their doings; anything new was of the utmost importance.

Soon the conveyance reached its final stop at the school gate. After seeing the remnants safely deposited to waiting parents or relatives and pleasantly wishing all good night, amid excited chatter and expressions of thanks, Briende quietly made her way home.

Evening was falling, birds sleepily twittering, moths hovering, the very peacefulness a cosseting security. Home was the usual inviting haven when she saw the low firelight, a fire never allowed to go out even in high summer, glinting on the distant windows, competing with the glow from an oil lamp reflected in the window, looming larger as she got closer. In its embracing halo she would have a lot to explain.

The door was open at the end of a long, twisting, narrow driveway, the banked flowers on the large rockeries bordering the path on each side resembling magical clouds of welcome, the sweet scent of the stocks in the evening air adding to the unreality of how she felt. Briende had never been so disturbed and was in turmoil. She did not understand, completely shaken by an emotion hitherto unexperienced, yet strangely outwardly calm, though dreading the family's reaction. Before entering she mentally relived the last few hours as if to recap the actual happening. She had met a quiet, handsome army officer, spent an hour or so with him, while in charge of a group, and agreed to let him visit her in three days' time. This would take explaining. She had to admit that the whole saga sounded bizarre and her dread increased. She actually sympathised with her strong, honest, mother, product of a strict regime; visualised her shocked reaction, and the age-old plaint, *what will people say?* reverberated in her head.

She pushed open the door. The delicious aroma of home baking permeated to the hall as she hung her hat and jacket in the usual place and, vainly trying to be cheerful, made her usual, "Hello, I'm home." All three members of her family, her uncle, mother and sister, appeared from different directions, full of eager expectations for the day's news. Everything was news in Brymadoc. Such was their closeness, each one instinctively knew at a glance that there was news. Mrs. Blethyn busied herself carrying a dish from the oven as they all sat in their usual places at the well-laden table. The pattern never varied; cups and saucers to the mother's right waited to be filled and passed around over the snowy cloth as soon as the bowed heads were raised after Uncle Gil's unvarying prayer.

"For what we are about to receive may the Lord make us truly thankful."

Mrs. Blethyn was the first to speak, as with knife poised, she cut and passed the food around. "You had a fine day – is everything well? Something happened. Did they get home safely?" Direct to the point of being charmless was Mrs. Blethyn's honest manner.

"Of course, all is well. We had a wonderful day."

Brown eyes looked directly into violet eyes as the mother said, "Tell us." Uncle interjected with the old-fashioned dictum, "A trouble shared is a trouble halved."

"I'm in no trouble, Uncle, just very tired."

Her thirteen-year-old sister Eleri pressed her foot gently on her sister's as if to give support but Briende knew she would choke on her words and, though hungry, found it difficult to eat. The others were aware of the uncomfortable tension. Briende knew they were watching her and despised herself for being the cause of their concern. Eventually, feeling hot tears pricking her eyelids, she said, "Forgive me, but I have a pounding headache. It must be the long day. I'll have an early bedtime."

Taking her oil lamp from the alcove, she lit a taper from the low fire, lit the lamp, said a quiet goodnight and went upstairs.

She undressed quickly, folded her clothes with her usual deftness, slipped into her nightgown, moved the lamp to her bedside table, fell on her knees and by its light she prayed, shortly and urgently.

"Please God forgive me if I've been foolish, help me to cope with the way I feel and give me courage to tell my dear people tomorrow." She rarely prayed and had some sort of conscience doing so.

She turned off the light and sank into the security of her own bed, comforted by the familiarity of her neat, sweet room. She listened to the birds tiredly chirping their final goodnight, almost heard the whispering branches of the apple trees sympathising with her plight. She was mentally and physically exhausted as she heard her mother and sister talking in quiet tones in the smaller kitchen, as the tinkling dishes were being cleared away because the maids did not live in. She longed for sleep and was about to drift away when she heard a light tap at her door and the brass latch being gently lifted. It was her sister Eleri. "Mama has made you a posset to help you sleep."

The aroma of lemon, barley, chamomile and chervil reached her in the darkness as Eleri carefully handed her the tumbler and she obediently drank it. As she placed the empty glass on her bedside table Eleri hugged her closely. In the dark they clung to each other and Briende felt the tears fall on her sister's shoulder. In spite of tender affection for each other, they were not normally demonstrative, and the six-year age gap had never lent itself to sisterly confidences. Without any prompting, words tumbled out. "Eleri, I have fallen in love and am so terrified of the suddenness of it all. I'm so upset and confused. I met an attractive army officer today and I have never felt so shaken, so disturbed and I'm confident that the feeling is mutual. When he asked me if he could visit on Saturday I agreed."

She felt her sister start.

"Eleri, you are shocked, rightly so. Am I so terribly, terribly foolish?"

With thirteen-year-old wisdom her sister said, "There's not a foolish bone in you," realising at the same time, that Saturday was a mere three days away, but this was exciting.

"I feel better having told you."

"I shall pray very hard for you tonight, in case there's a God. I know things will work out." Briende appreciated her concern but could hardly imagine Eleri at prayer.

Eleri gently lowered her sister onto the pillows and quietly left, picking up her own small lamp from the landing. Its ray moved in a thin line beneath the door and that was the last thing Briende saw before complete exhaustion or the effects of the posset took over.

Next morning she awoke to birdsong and the happy voices in the garden, where her mother and Bridget, the young maid, were gathering the day's produce while talking in their own patois, fascinating to listen to but they understood each other. The chat was interspersed with English, one blending with the other effortlessly. The sun's rays through the lace curtains danced restlessly as she sat in front of the mirror in her naked purity. She half-expected a different vision of herself from that of the previous morning. So much had happened, she felt a different being. The same violet eyes looked back at her; her small breasts and slender arms looked just as vulnerable, but she felt years older.

She washed and dressed mechanically and descended for breakfast. She was pleased to be alone, Eleri having left early for some school duty or other. She was a prominent member of this art and technical school newly established in Trevere. Snatches of Irish lilt in Bridget's sweet voice reached her as she poured some tea and helped herself to a meagre breakfast. She was not hungry but had a day's work ahead. Then, making her way through the garden door to the back of the house, she called a cheery goodbye to her mother and the maid.

"I see that you are better."

"Yes, must have been the nightcap you kindly sent. I'll tell you tonight all about yesterday."

CHAPTER TWO

Love Hurts

BRIENDE AMBLED HER WAY ALONG THE DEAR FAMILIAR road. The morning was glorious, intoxicated with its own lusciousness, the birds to-ing and fro-ing from tree to hedge and hedge to tree, the yellow corn gleaming in the early light, enough beauty to make the mind grow heavy with languor. Briende's spirits lifted. Oh, to share this land she loved, the dear people and beauteous fields and hills and orchards. She had never been so bewitched by familiar things, and Ralph Maine absorbed her entire being. She could not divorce her thoughts from him.

She arrived early in the classroom and filled the blackboard with numerous words pertaining to the previous day, ready for the written work. The bell rang, pupils arrived and good mornings were exchanged as they stood at their desks until commanded to sit. The register was called, and they filed off to the morning assembly. Briende found her concentration lapsing for every prayer, each hymn emotionally sapped her.

Back in the classroom, the formal rows of desks overlooked by the teacher's iron and wood desk on a raised rostrum, as was the norm in the old schools, she wondered how she would survive the day. Her mind was elsewhere. She climbed into her own eyrie and, while the class worked, she marked previous work. From her elevation she could see the view she had seen so many times before – the constant activity in the cobbled yard of The Hermit, the busy square, the churchyard. The clock in the old church spire looked back at her; its letters, instead of numerals, reading "God be with you" bore a different poignancy. All her life she had known that clock and its legend but had never given it much thought. Inwardly she prayed, *Yes indeed, please be with me.* The day passed, bells interspersed with formal lessons, and it had never been longer.

On her homeward journey everything seemed less lovely, the optimism of the morning having taken flight. Each step seemed heavier than the preceding one. How she dreaded trying to explain to her mother the previous day's wonders. Deep within she knew that she had fallen in love with Ralph Maine and the beauty of his presence would remain with her forever, regardless of the outcome of Saturday's projected visit. She felt secure in her trust, felt she had done no wrong and fervently hoped that what seemed like her rashness would be kindly dealt with.

The dear old house, which had always been her sanctuary, looked inviting as ever, as did the perfumed shrubs and flowers escorting her to the open door. The big iron gate clicked behind her with a sort of finality – no more dithering, but courage.

As she entered the house, with its familiar pungent smell of fresh baking, wood burning, a basket of herbs on the hall desk, the polished hall floor, she was struck anew by the blessings and security she had always known. On entering the large living room, once again, the three members of her family appeared; her uncle, already in his house clothes, was obviously home early from his duties around the estate, her sweet sister with concern in her eyes. Her mother was the first to speak as she busied herself between oven and table in her usual matronly fashion.

"You look better, that's something," as she placed the scones on a glass plate on the table and motioned her family to sit. Uncle intoned the usual short prayer. Mrs. Blethyn presided over the teapot and, as she poured and passed the cups around said, "Well we are all waiting. Something happened yesterday and we should know."

Her uncle's contribution was, "Dear girl, there's sufficient love in this house to cope with any trouble."

"I'm in no trouble, Uncle, but something did happen."

She looked into her mother's brown eyes, full of concern, yes, and love, steady and appealing.

"My daughter, you'd better tell us. We don't want anyone else telling us, tongues do not rest in this place."

"Yesterday was a wonderful day. You know that the school was offered lunch facilities at the barracks. Well, three young soldiers, quiet and bored, were directed by their officer to attend to us."

Once she started, she found the words tumbling out at speed. She stopped for breath.

"Yes?"

"The officer suggested, if we had no definite plans on such a fine day, that we visited the Botanical Gardens and aviary in the Park, and he later joined us. I did not know the way from the barracks, so the young cadets led. The afternoon was so lovely, and time did hang heavily in that dismal building. The officer joined us after a while and the young soldiers then moved to the rear. He was called Ralph Maine."

Briende looked down at her plate and made some attempt at eating her food, though she could barely swallow. She seemed to hear an intake of her mother's breath in the shocked silence, felt a wave of affection as she tried to remind herself of her parent's strict code of behaviour and a life that barely moved outside a five-mile radius.

"You went to the park with a strange man we do not know, you, my well-reared daughter!"

"With the others; we did not sit alone in the park, the rest of them were milling around."

Briende realised that her courage was fading; once again Eleri touched her leg gently beneath the table, a measure of affection and sympathy, as well as stark amusement, Briende guessed, from her lively sister.

The worst shattering news was yet to come.

"Mama, before we boarded the ship he asked if he could come and visit me here on Saturday. I said yes."

A lengthy silence followed; for a few moments Mrs.

Blethyn was speechless, then, “I cannot believe what I'm hearing” – there seemed a croak to her voice – “my daughter meets a stranger on a school outing and asks him home.”

Uncle Gil placed his old hand on his sister's. “Mai, you make it appear far worse than it is. We know Briende is sound and ladylike, she did ask him home and not meet him elsewhere. Think of that.”

Mrs. Blethyn found her voice. “This man, where does he live and what sort of family?”

“He has no house and just one old aunt as family.”

“No house, no family, does he have any money?”

To a stranger, who knew not her goodness and honesty, Mrs. Blethyn's lack of charm was intimidating. “I don't know if he has money, he works all over the world in the army, a sort of writer.”

“I never heard the like, you are more or less promised, my girl – what about Mr. Alvar Garonne, one of the best landowners in the country?”

“Promised to you, mother, maybe, not I.”

Eleri ventured, “Briende does not like Mr. Garonne.”

Mrs. Blethyn snapped, “You keep out of this. I'm not sure you should be listening to such talk or hear of such behaviour.”

For a moment Briende felt the urge of a smile as the tears were beginning to form. Then came the expected, “What will people think? This family never hobnobs with strangers without introduction. We don't want him here.”

Briende declined to answer, she felt too choked to utter one word. Defiance was building within her – if he could not come to her home, she would escape to meet him. Her world, her safe world, was crumbling. She let the tears slowly fall.

Her uncle, with the voice of reason and kindliness, again placed his old hand on his sister's. "Mai, we have as a family been renowned for our hospitality. We will meet Briende's young man with warmth and politeness. It is our way."

"It will be on your head, Gilbert Madoc, if I do wrong in allowing this. May the Lord forgive you. But it shall be so, and we will not say one more word."

The rest of the evening passed as usual. The table was cleared, lamps lit, Mrs. Blethyn took up her needlework from the large basket beside her rocking chair and Uncle Gil, sitting opposite, studied *Farmers Weekly* before getting down to accounts, which he worked at nightly. Mrs. Blethyn ordered Eleri to her music practice in the parlour and her sister to supervise her. Taking up a lamp from the smaller kitchen the girls entered the parlour, sat at twin stools and, one playing bass, the other treble, instead of exercises played favourite songs. Among these were Thomas More's 'Enduring Young Charms' and 'Oft, in the Stilly Night, ere Slumber's Chains have Bound Me' graduating to a selection of Byron's romantic lyrics set to Nathan's music, a recent acquisition as a birthday gift. They seemed unusually close and strangely happy. After an hour or so they joined their elders in the living room, Eleri to do her homework and Briende, as a student teacher, to write up the week's Record Book, usually a Friday night task. It was a serene domestic scene, common to the people they knew and other dwellers in the village, probably throughout the island, the pattern they were used to, with nothing to challenge the contentment. Compared with the previous night Briende was in lighter spirits but each one's thoughts revolved around the Saturday visit. It was to be a momentous occasion; apart from family, people seldom came visiting the staid old families of Ilandia.

Briende glanced across at her parent with love. She knew that her mind was occupied with plans of how to make a good impression on this unwelcome stranger in this beyond the beyond location. Dear, sound, solid, religious, honest and admittedly charmless, Mrs. Blethyn loved her family dearly and hoped not to let them down in any way.

Both girls knew that their mother's brain was in full spate, hoping to do what was right and mentally asking her God to be with her and forgive her if her judgement was at fault.

Saturday at last, and the activity at Pen Melyn, though highly organised, was acute. Each had his or her duty; Briende in charge of floral arrangements, Eleri laying the table, Mrs. Blethyn in charge of the meal, which had to be substantial. Uncle Gil, in the meantime, had to make sure to have the gardens immaculate and the produce conveyed in. True to their breeding they had to make a favourable impression. Briende emphasised, more than once, that they remained natural but Mrs. Blethyn considered being 'natural' to a visitor less than respectable.

CHAPTER THREE

Meeting the Family

HALF AN HOUR BEFORE HIS EXPECTED ARRIVAL Briende had to retire to her room to compose herself. She wore her prettiest lilac-figured dress and heeled shoes, brushed her hair until it gleamed, applied the slightest blush of rouge and lay on her bed trying to relax. In the meantime, she listened for the familiar carriage wheels of Mr. Byatt's big coach. Mr. Byatt had acquired a motorised vehicle in recent months but rarely used it. Undoubtedly, he would meet the ferry in his usual fashion with horse and small coach or the two-horsed large coach, depending on the numbers expected. Today it was likely to be the large-coach because more people travelled on Saturdays.

As Briende lay and listened, at last she heard the approaching conveyance. With pounding heart and immense trepidation, she descended to join the rest of the family already assembled at the entrance. Such was their practice, their idea of welcome and hospitality.

When Ralph Maine alighted at the great gate, she was close to collapse. He was in uniform, poised, calm, attractive and Briende was aware that her people were already seduced. Mrs. Blethyn scrutinised him as he walked towards them and extended his hand and introduced himself, thus sparing Briende this office. One look at her as he held her hand in greeting convinced him that he had not misjudged his instinct, this girl was all he could ever wish for. In a fleeting moment a wave of affection consumed him, and the decision was made. More than anything he wanted this old family, steeped in tradition, to accept him, who had no home, parents or siblings.

Uncle Gil with old-fashioned hospitality welcomed the newcomer; his sister, more reticent, was still on her guard and formally polite. She did, however, direct Briende and her friend to the parlour while she supervised the meal. Eleri was directed to serve them tea and a rare treat, biscuits, from a blue tin decorated by the visages of George V and Queen Mary, a much-venerated gift from Gaston some while ago. Biscuits in a fancy hinged tin box were still a luxury kept for special occasions and this was some occasion.

Alone with Ralph, complete with embroidered tray cloth, best china and rare biscuits, served by Eleri, induced Briende to feel awkward and inadequate. Inwardly, she was excited and disturbed and dreaded to be left alone. What could she talk about? With her usual grace but afraid to look at her companion she poured the tea. As she passed it to him their eyes met.

"Briende, it is delightful to be here and to meet your people. Thank you."

She lowered her eyes. "I do hope you like one another. Mama is overly direct and sometimes seemingly harsh, but she is so good, so good. Living this confined existence has not induced her to cultivate charm." He smiled to reassure her and added, "I know all will be well." They exchanged polite pleasantries, from the charming journey with Mr. Byatt to his travelling companion, the vicar's son, coming home from Cambridge for a short visit. Briende, of course, had known Laurence Britt from childhood, so they already had something in common. Ralph commented on the beauty of the island, the peace, and extended his observation to the gardens and distant hills. He knew the island existed but had never had cause to visit it.

Soon the old brass gong, in use as long as Briende could remember, summoned them to the table.

Mrs. Blethyn, with Bridget's assistance, had a table to be proud of. Normally Bridget did not come on Saturdays, but this Saturday was special. Stiffly, they took their places at the table, Uncle Gil recited 'grace' and Mrs. Blethyn invited Ralph to help himself and make sure he had sufficient to eat. Convinced that nobody could compete with her, when it came to a substantial table, she was proud of her efforts and though not given to self-congratulation, she was confident that the huge roll of roast beef, with its cress bunches and miniature onions surrounding, could not be competed with.

In the meantime, Mrs. Blethyn barely took her eyes off him – she actually approved of this stranger. With his clean, blonde, good looks and perfect manners, his charm and yes, his captivation of her daughter. Her hard-working, religious, common-sensical rearing had not prepared her for polished manners, sophistication and calm bearing and knowledge. She was quite overcome by the conversation during the meal, the extent of his travels and the patient way he responded to her brother's questions and Eleri's curiosity about faraway places.

"I shall see all of them one day."

Briende knew he had passed the scrutiny of her mother's assessment and was secure in the fact that he had been accepted. By the time Mr. Byatt called for Captain Maine late that afternoon, to convey him back to Limorrnah and the ferry, Briende's future was already sealed. Briende, in all her nineteen years, had never experienced such happiness, the aura of which lingered and lightened the whole household for days after his departure, with Mrs. Blethyn's, "Well, that's over with and I fully understand your captivation, but I must see my sisters and give my own version before other embroiderers take them the news."

The embroiderers were the local gossips, fair enough in a place where nothing of consequence happened. The big houses, in particular were closely watched. One could imagine George Eliot or Mrs. Gaskell or even Jane Austen delighting in such ready-made vignettes.

The sisters were Mrs. Blethyn's younger siblings. In a substantial square house, a relic of the earlier large family estate, they conducted a dressmaking and tailoring establishment, where village girls were apprenticed in the trade, spending three years in a hive of activity and the University of Life. Everything which occurred in the village was mulled over on these premises and no newspaper could have amassed more news. Mrs. Blethyn knew she had to see them before Monday's session started in order to give the true picture.

Deborah and Editha Madoc were straight-backed, elegant, cautious, refined, maiden sisters. They had lived together since their father's demise and had inherited that portion of the estate, the larger part, including a substantial farm, having been bequeathed to the eldest sister, as had been the custom in that matriarchal family. Much respected in the church and community and successful in their enterprise, Deborah and Editha were well known for their good sense, low voices, charming manners and integrity. Though handsome and feminine both had declined suitors because it was said nobody had 'measured up' to their expectations. They were proud of their new independence and business acumen. Their imposing home, set back a few yards from the country road, had a large, studded oak door set between two large bay windows. Tubs of geraniums bordered the road throughout the summer to join the spring remnants of daffodils and primroses. These were replaced by tubs of evergreens each autumn. Both geraniums and evergreens had survived endless seasons in storage to reappear again year after year.

To the left of the front door a large room housed four

Singer sewing machines, the hum of the treadles to be heard all day. Behind this was the cutting room, complete with huge cutting table and ironing boards. Here a coal fire kept hot a variety of differently shaped irons for various garment-making jobs – a blunt-ended one for heavy pleats, a long one for frills, a traditional shield-shaped iron for the more ordinary jobs, a huge bar of Puritan soap for smoothing seams and to rub the irons on, huge magnets for picking up pins, drawers of reels and shelves with haberdashery, rolls of cloth, linings, stiffenings and the like, and always activity and chat, endless chat.

Of course, Miss Deborah and Miss Editha never indulged in gossip, but they did listen and nothing happened in the church, Womens' Institute or school without their hearing about it, hence Mrs. Blethyn's cautionary journey, that Saturday night, to see them. Though no more than four hundred yards separated the two households they seldom visited one another. In a crisis of course they 'were there' as each one was keen to point out.

The right-hand half of Myrtle House, in contrast to the left half, was a haven of discretion. Behind the lace curtains, that one could see out from but not into (and this was of the utmost importance) was the parlour. Here clients sat on dainty uncut velvet moquette, horse-hair sofas or matching Victorian chairs to discuss their garments, colours, materials, style or costs. A low fire was kept alight in all seasons, the mantelpiece decorated with a fringed, hand-painted, velvet drape, once the height of fashion but still prevalent in many homes. During discussions tea was usually served by Miss Editha with revered grace in delicate Shelley china, shell-like and exquisite and all part of the elegance.

Behind the parlour was an inner sanctum – the fitting room. One graduated to this after at least a year's apprenticeship. Here no secrets were hidden. The Japanned screen and ebony-framed long mirrors daily witnessed assets and defects. Here in the hushed atmosphere dreams were realised as beautiful creations were adapted to the wearer, with due deference to accessories and practicality for travelling, visiting or dancing.

Briende and Eleri were dearly loved by their aunts and the love was reciprocated. After the age of ten or so the boys never visited, it was an all-female world, but Mrs. Blethyn was determined that on his next visit, Captain Maine was to meet them because this, in her eyes, was correct behaviour.

CHAPTER FOUR

The Whispering Stones

THERE WERE LETTERS OF THANKS TO MRS. BLETHYN and a separate one to Briende before Ralph Maine arrived the following Saturday. This time Briende was instructed to walk abroad with her admirer, accompanied by Eleri in order to keep the proprieties. There was a visit to the vicar in order to put the seal on respectability and a tour around the village and churchyard. The churchyard was almost a park, much used for quiet pleasure, and among the graves of her ancestors Briende was pleased to point out the merits of the conservation area for flora and fauna long before the idea was in common usage. One of the vicar's sons, Bellan, was an accomplished botanist with a first-class academic background and since schooldays had seen the huge churchyard, hundreds of years old, as a conservation area. Some species, already becoming rarer, here found a haven and the constant colour in the heart of the village proved uplifting in every season as old and young relaxed among the aged stones, marking the final rest of forgotten people, and the young fresh vegetation always renewing itself. Sometimes, when precious plants were at rest, even the sheep were allowed to nibble the grassy pathways among the stones.

The young couple walked among the graves of the Madocs and Blethyns, the Madocs in particular, occupying as much space as the Wordsworths' corner in Grasmere, stoutly fenced in with iron curlicues always kept freshly painted. Ralph noted the names and dates with interest, the earliest dates already over four centuries old. Some Madocs would undoubtedly have lived in Brymadoc when the church was built in the early centuries before the Protestant church was dreamt of. One day Ralph planned to delve into any of the known archives, history being a passion he had never had the chance to indulge in. This he anticipated with pleasure. It would be one way to share in Briende's ancestry as he had so little knowledge of his own.

In the church Mrs. Britt, the vicar's wife, was supervising and helping with the floral arrangements, the usual Saturday task. On this week's rota were Miss Mowbray and Mrs. Sullivan. Briende shyly introduced Ralph with quiet pride. As they admired the altar pedestal she wondered if his thoughts were in accord with hers, and sensed that they were, when he gently pressed her hand. Mrs. Britt quickly abandoned the flowers and invited them for tea and to meet the vicar, who happened to be free for an hour.

They found him after much 'coo-ing' as a call by his wife, in the Rectory garden, clad in a battered straw hat and cardigan, doing a spot of pruning, while he wrestled with some problem he was due to confront. He was amiable as ever and he too invited them in for a quick cup of tea. Briende politely declined as she had promised to visit her maiden aunts. Greetings were sent to the worthy ladies, pleasantries exchanged plus a warm invitation not to forget to call in again.

The Reverend Britt was a kind and learned man, his vast scholarship probably wasted in such a backwater which he had considered a challenge. Life was pleasant, the church secure, the Rectory a splendid home and, like his son, the churchyard project in conservation an all-abiding interest. Intellectually, he depended on past friends and acquaintances, who frequently visited, also the occasional scholastic bishop, with a particular interest in some facet of scripture. His library was much envied by those accustomed to such and his sons were also a source of pride because they too were learned.

From thence to aunts Deborah and Editha, surely the afternoon's highlight. Unused to males entering their domain, apart from small nephews or necessary repair men, they awaited this visit with much trepidation. Needless to say they were clad in their best, the sofa table laid with the best lace and Ainsley china, home-made shortbreads and the inevitable cucumber sandwiches, divested of crusts. They seemed quite overawed by accounts of travel in strange lands, promoted of course by Eleri's questions, to keep the conversation light and happy. They were captivated by the charm and gentleness of Briende's intended, for this was their undoubted conclusion; otherwise their respected sister would not have countenanced the relationship. Ralph was as fascinated by the surroundings as by the pristine quality of the aunts, strongly reminding him of his own very dear aunt and he warmed to their honesty, dignity and refinement. As they left with fond goodbyes Ralph longed to tell Briende his own story. He knew she would not ask.

The following Saturday he was again expected. Eleri, in the meantime, overwhelmed by this beautiful stranger her quiet much-adored sister had found, decided to give them a little privacy, knowing full well that she was breaking all the rules of respectability. It appealed to her romantic sense to want to nourish this unexpected love affair and longed for some future day when some man would have the same effect on her as this Ralph had on her sister. With generosity of spirit though, she longed more than anything for Briende's happiness.

That particular day became the most unforgettable day in Briende's life. Eleri suggested passing Mr. Day's vast greenhouses and stopping to admire the innumerable blooms and spectacular foliage. Everything Mr. Day breathed upon flourished and the horticultural establishment was evidence of several generations of effort and success. All weddings, funerals and local celebrations were catered for and most local gardens had their origin in Mr. Day's nurseries.

Eleri's school friend, Rosemary Day, her brothers and cousins, were future inheritors of these fertile acres of gardens and greenhouses and the business had always been family orientated. Rosemary and Eleri spent happy hours in the warm, humid, greenhouses among the tomatoes, cucumbers or cherished flowers. With girlish giggles they clung and whispered and gossiped and learnt much about life via the avenues of school or village life. The girls of the family, from an earlier time all carried nature names; also the boys, where possible. The church register had ample evidence of Oaks, Rowans, Derwyn (the Welsh for oak being 'Derw'), Willow, Berry, even Forest or Brook as middle or Christian names. It had long been a cherished tradition among them to keep the names repeated throughout the generations. The Poppies, Irises, Roses and Heathers predominated among the girls' names. The locals would speculate on what would happen when the names ran out, which sometimes happened. They would then start again, even using foreign nature names if necessary. As a long-established family they held a particular charm but were not considered enlightened, rather lax, in fact, and, if competition ever threatened, the business would soon collapse. Mr. Day was reputed to have a likeness for strong drink; though the providers of flowers for weddings or funerals, they rarely entered St Petroc's church. Sometimes a Catholic priest, his angular cap low on his bushy eyebrows and soutane flapping, would cycle from a neighbouring village to remind them of their duties.

The vivacious Eleri was fascinated by them, her fascination touched with envy as Rosemary, her friend, like the rest of her siblings, did not have to study. They were absorbed into the business in some useful way and usually when young married local partners. They never read books or bothered with homework.

This special Saturday the friends planned to give Ralph and Briende some privacy. They suggested a walk to the Stones, and the girls, of course, hung behind for a while before fading into neighbouring copses bisected with limpid streams along the lower reaches of the hills. Feeling slightly daring, the young couple, hand in hand, climbed the steep path, Briende fervently hoping no word of this reached Mrs. Blethyn. In her eyes this would signify a lack of trust. The young couple knew that though this was only the third day of brief meetings it would herald their engagement. Wrapped up in each other, by the time they reached the Stones, an immunity had set in. The opinions of others mattered not.

The Stones, ancient relics of a bygone age, stood on a bare hill above the neighbouring villages. A great aura of age and superstition had always been connected to them. Few of the older folk ventured near them and children were warned to stay away.

Some were hardly distinguishable from natural stones of great magnitude. Many historians had speculated on their origins, none satisfactorily. Stark, grey, moss-covered, angled in various directions, some bearing Celtic inscriptions, some decorated around the edges with Celtic forest motifs of enigmatic beings entwined. Many were sufficiently weathered to resemble the newly popular modern art creations. All stood silent and secretive, jealously guarding the faded past. Some grew out of mounds, signifying that as much of the rock was beneath the ground as above it, friendly, threatening, ominous or inviting depending on the mood of the weather or onlooker. The locals, the elders in particular treated them with awe. They were also referred to as the Singing Stones. Indeed, on some days, placing one's ear close to them, a music seemed to emanate from them, resembling the sound of a faraway sea in a conch shell, a seductive sound such as long ago lured seamen to their deaths, at the call of mermaids.

Through hundreds of years they had kept their vigil and their secrets and Briende and Ralph's own music of the soul blended in with the agelessness surrounding them. Time present, time past and time future fused together as Ralph held her close for the first time. In the shadow of a great boulder, which seemed to swallow them in its darkness, he held her gently, hesitatingly, half-afraid that the magic of this moment could be ruptured by her timidness. Tentatively, she placed her right hand on his shoulder and slowly, her head on his left shoulder. Not a word was spoken; he bent and kissed her gently. She shuddered, opened her lovely eyes and looked into his. "Briende," he whispered, "more than anything in the world I want you as my wife. Please say yes." She did and as the purple shadows of late afternoon gathered, the dying sun's rays still warm on the stone, they kissed again. Looking westward towards the horizon she saw a dense, dark cloud eclipse the setting sun. Perhaps deep in her psyche lingered the primitive Celtic idea of omen. She clung to him and hoped the same ominous dread had escaped him.

It was not the first time that dread and insecurity had invaded her consciousness. Her love was so intense, had been from the first hour in his presence. Fear hung upon her. Somehow, she felt undeserving of such blissful happiness. Her innermost prayer was to be worthy of him, his goodness, gentleness and manliness, blended into a superb human being. She knew so little about him, yet knew she was not mistaken; her confidence in him was absolute. In that magical moment myriad thoughts swept through her head in the briefest of time.

They dared not linger, the promise was made, both were immeasurably happy. They kissed again, vowed to remember the place and the moment and hand in hand descended the winding path between bracken and heather, past the rambling streams and miniature falls towards the lower levels. Then through the trees and lazy streamlets to where Eleri, without Rosemary, was already waiting.

They knew not for how long she had been awaiting their arrival for time had ceased to be.

There was a light in Eleri's eyes as she beheld the light in her sister's eyes. She gently pressed Briende's hand and the three walked home together along the sleepy main street of Brymadoc. All three knew that the suddenness of this romance was not something Mrs. Blethyn was likely to understand.

After much raising of eyebrows and expressions of shock and the practicalities of finance and dwellings and, "What would your father think?" she calmed down. Should this whole episode not be discussed with someone wiser than she was? Her brother, Gilbert, was too lenient and of little help and so on and so forth. However, she did in her own proud way accept him with, “Since we are going to become relatives we might as well have a glass of wine before you leave.”

Ralph requested Mrs. Blethyn’s and Uncle Gil’s permission to meet Briende in Limorrnah the following Saturday to buy the ring, then known as a ‘keeper’ ring, eat at the hotel and later meet her brother and cousin. This was established amid much trepidation on Mrs. Blethyn’s part, punctuating her permission with, “May God forgive me if I am in the wrong.” Uncle Gilbert smiled a quiet smile and raised his hand in blessing, having comforted his sister Mai by saying that he knew it in his bones that they were not in the wrong. Such was their betrothal day.

CHAPTER FIVE

Briende's Engagement

By the following Saturday, when Briende was scheduled to meet Ralph in Limorrnah, much had already been settled. Uncle Gilbert's large cottage, once his marital home, presently rented to an elderly lady called Mrs. Frame, was to be vacated sooner than anticipated. The woman had for some time been planning to leave, having become too frail to care for herself. Her daughter in North Island had long endeavoured to get her mother to move nearer to her, or with her. The old lady, loath to give up her independence, had clung to the home she had lived in for several years. With slight pressure Uncle Gil requested her leaving the substantial cottage, Uncle Gil's portion of the old estate. In 'Brackens' he had lived with his wife and reared his son and daughter, Wynn and Wenna.

Various outbuildings on the old estate had once been

stables, piggeries, barns and other farm buildings. Many had been sold off and been converted into houses and bungalows. Most of the younger generation of men had departed Brymadoc for good times, customs had rapidly changed since the Great War and all were dimly aware that age-old traditions were fast evaporating, and that the remainder of the old estates would in the next generation be likely to follow the pattern and be sold like the other scattered buildings. The old stone wall, now much fractured to make new entrances, was a reminder of the once extensive estate.

Mrs. Blethyn and her brother accepted that their sons would never return to Brymadoc. They were immersed in exporting to the mainland, buying more warehouse space, processing fish products and actively pursuing trade. Seldom did a ferry leave the port of Limorrnah without a cargo bearing their logo – a fish and shell. With shares in the small channel ferries and fervent ambition the cousins led a far more sophisticated lifestyle.

Dutifully they visited when time permitted, bringing their young families to important family functions, but to them it was the past and, along with the rest of the relatives, visualised the vivacious Eleri projecting herself into realms beyond Ilandia. In fact, they almost wagered on how long the stolid mother would be able to exercise influence.

At thirteen, Eleri gave promise of being more strikingly beautiful than Briende, whose calm, serene, pristine beauty and dainty figure gave the impression of a china ornament. Eleri was more vibrant, livelier in personality and more confident. Her glorious auburn hair, dancing blue eyes and a restlessness of spirit set them apart, though their devotion to each other was deep and abiding.

Bred among beautiful clothes, materials, ribbons, buttons, trimmings on her frequent visits to the aunts, Eleri had, while young, established a skill in art and design and creative attempts with a variety of fabrics. Being a proud inheritor of past fashion books, books of material samples, each precise square with its picot edging, she longed one day to be prominent in the world of art and design and even décor. She possessed what was known as 'flair' and at her exclusive girls' school in Trevere, quite renowned for its artistic proficiency in the creative world, she was almost a star. Though the academic programme was conscientiously adhered to, the specialities were in the Arts and Crafts, Ruskin and William Morris the chief mentors.

The aunts were delighted and wished they had enjoyed a similar experience. In Eleri they frequently saw what they thought they had missed. Her vitality and enthusiasm entranced them and they frequently marvelled that their strict, religious, serious, unromantic sister could have produced this vivacious, often wayward child. They visited every school exhibition of work, never stinted in giving gifts of materials for dramatic productions, supported her in every activity, especially if she was prominent in the stage management of any drama or concert. Their dearest wish was to live long enough to see her triumphant in something or other in the creative arts. Would she become a famous designer like Chanel? Many times they had copied the famous creations.

Eleri's sense of history frequently led her to great paintings for inspiration and the aunts were accustomed to being confronted with a sketch of a garment copied from the Pre-Raphaelites, then coming into some form of prominence, and once a Botticelli type of gown was requested.

They loved Briende dearly but were charmed and fascinated by her sister, who exuded warmth and sweetness as well as exuberance. Strangely, they also respected Eleri's good sense and, with regard to Briende's sudden romance had faith in Eleri's assessment of it.

Saturday dawned as a mild day, calm and autumnal so Ralph and Briende travelled to Limorrnah to Mr. Eli's ancient and quaint establishment to buy a ring. He knew Briende and asked after the family. With no more ado he asked them what ring they had in mind, resembling some Biblical prophet foretelling the future. He led them to the inner room and proceeded to unlock the cases, where they wished to look.

While Mr. Eli was busy, Briende pointed to the immense old ship's bell hanging over the walled garden's door, presumably some form of burglar alarm, and one could imagine the noise it was capable of. The door was partially ajar, allowing some daylight to compete with the spluttering and chortling gas light overhead, which lit the gems in turn with an ethereal light. Ralph was fascinated but longed to be alone in the sweet daylight with Briende. He was happy to choose with her a gold band of pink Welsh gold set with three sapphires. He slipped it on her finger with Mr. Eli's blessing, pocketed the certificate of authentication, paid him and, after thanking him for his good wishes, the lovers departed hand in hand. Both were pleased to escape from the eeriness of the place and marvelled at the quantity and quality of the jewellery he managed to store in such a small area. Lion snarled his farewell as they passed through the entrance chamber. They felt lighter in spirit than at any time since they had met. They took a path along the estuary to a small, sheltered glen Briende had known since school days, when on rare afternoons, usually at term's end, the girls would linger for an hour before boarding the next ferry home.

They were closeted alone among mossy boulders, seagulls lazily whirled and looped overhead, followed by startled wild ducks in strict formation. Swans nonchalantly glided on the water. There was no sound. The sun shone behind downy clouds, its rays now and again glinting on the water, the shiny leaves, the grey stones.

Beneath her dainty little toque hat Briende's soft curls rose in the breeze to catch the sun's rays. The same rays lit his golden lashes as he bent to kiss her.

"Happy engagement day, my darling. May we always remember this moment."

More than anything she longed to be held by him and did not resist when he lowered her onto the smooth turf and sat beside her in this sylvan spot. He kissed her hand, placed his arm around her and drew her to him. This time there was no resistance, she responded happily.

"I hope, Ralph, you feel for me as I do for you. It would break my heart to think otherwise."

"There has never been anyone else for me and there

won't be ever again. I'm as much in a whirl as you – desperately in love and bewilderingly happy."

They were almost sorry when time decreed that they should leave for their special lunch in the harbourside hotel, the Pirate's Haven. The waiter showed them to a side table in its own alcove, overlooking the sea. There was no commercialism on this side, merely the peace of water gently slushing and receding against the rocks on which the hotel stood. In the distance was a lone steamer, seemingly still, almost sad. Ralph had so many times been carried away and would be so again. Sunshine tipped the gentle waves in their slow motion towards the shore. All was perfectly charming, perfectly peaceful. Her first taste of champagne along with the superb lunch transported her to another world. She smiled at him over the rim of the glass, realising as she did so that she knew almost nothing about this man she was going to marry and did not care. He seemed to read her thoughts and gave them utterance. She smiled as she said, "Tell me about yourself. Nothing you say will change the way I feel."

"There is no mystery, nothing of interest, nothing outstanding, nothing of disgrace."

"We have an hour. Please tell me."

With his blend of honesty, tact and sensitivity he started to speak.

CHAPTER SIX

Ralph's Story

RALPH'S OWN STORY WAS AS COMPLICATED AS A novel. The aunt who reared him, Marguerite, and her sister Delphine were the twin daughters of Mr. and Mrs. Preece, who made a modest but adequate living in Beardsley, Barnshire, owning and managing a book shop. They lived contentedly in rooms above the shop, careful and proud of their delightful daughters. Marguerite was studious, reliable and pleasantly handsome. Delphine, vibrant, ambitious, outgoing and bright without being studious. They were a devoted family, much respected in the area, active in church and community and always waiting for a rare or unusual book to turn up among their gatherings from old homes selling up, an old shop being dismantled and ceasing to trade, a market stall or antique shop. Mr. Preece was ever on the alert and more than once had been fortunate in recognising an important book, a first edition or lost manuscript and selling via Sotheby's or equivalent. For the family such a find was a bonus to suffice their needs through several years. Mr. Preece knew and loved his books and Marguerite showed keen interest.

Delphine rejoiced in people, flowers, arts, crafts and hungered for far-off places. She was fascinated by missionaries and their work in distant lands. She delighted in helping at church, whether in the Band of Hope movement, which meant pictures, usually by 'magic' lantern or talks by people who had travelled to strange places. Always eager to help at functions, she was much in demand at bazaars or garden parties, or any fundraising connected with the church and its overseas mission. From what Ralph had gleaned from his aunt, her vitality and indeed fine looks reminded him strongly of Eleri. He had never met anyone remotely like her and thought that, unlike Briende, llandia would not hold her.

To keep the girls at school Mrs. Preece subsidised the family coffers by teaching the piano at home. All helped in the book shop on Saturdays and during holidays.

The girls left school showing much promise. Marguerite prepared to train as a stenographer and Delphine to take a course in horticulture and attach herself to a local florist to learn the business – wreaths, bouquets, decorations for hotels or large country homes for special occasions. Along with horticulture she learnt a fair amount of serious botany, took an interest in herbs and healing plants and planned one day to own her own business involving these interests. She was a very modern young lady for the time, to some, shocking. Her independence of spirit was not considered 'ladylike'.

When aged eighteen Marguerite acquired a secretarial job in a bank in the neighbouring small town of Rolfey. She travelled to and fro by train, as the railway had recently been established in that area. Daily, she travelled from Beardsley to Rolfey. Several times she noticed a quiet, fair man standing on the platform some distance away. His solitariness and immaculate appearance, neat and formal, intrigued her. He always appeared to be alone within his own measured space. He resembled most of the other young businessmen on their way to work but she never saw him talking to anyone else, though it could be surmised that there were other formally dressed young men going to the same place of work. The station platform always seemed a formal sort of place, orderly, quiet, dignified.

One day, quite by accident, because a carriage was removed and the travellers herded, almost, to fill the front carriages, she found herself sitting opposite him. She was fascinated. He was tall, spare and clean-shaven, which was then unusual because most men sported either a moustache and side whiskers or both. He caught her eye as he did the crossword, gave a slight nod of recognition and continued with his clue concentration. This was their first meeting, but a well-bred young lady would have to be introduced before speaking to a strange young man.

A day or two later, again on the platform, an acquaintance of her father, a Mr. Wharton and a colleague of the stranger from the same bank, happened to be standing nearby. The young man raised his hat to his senior in the bank and Mr. Wharton introduced the young people. It was all very natural and within the bounds of propriety. After that Marguerite and Weston Maine, for that was his name, shared the same compartment and after a few days ventured to speak. They became cautiously but sweetly friendly, discussed the news, traded crossword answers and talked briefly of local events, as they came from the same village, though Weston lived about a mile from the village on a country road. He knew her parents' book shop and he attended the church infrequently. The independent churches interested him far more and on Sundays he frequently attended one of these in order to get another viewpoint. Unitarianism attracted him most, where Beauty, Truth and Goodness seemed to be of more consequence than accepted doctrine. Marguerite decided that he was what some called a 'free-thinker' and this she admired.

One autumn evening when the train arrived back at Beardsley it was already getting dark, there was a storm brewing and Marguerite had almost expected one of her parents to meet her with a rainproof cape and umbrella, as had happened several times before. Such was the care to which she had become accustomed. Instead young Mr. Maine offered to walk her home. She was completely overcome, flattered, delighted. How she wanted her parents to meet him and perhaps allow her to see him alone!

When they reached the house, Mrs. Preece was at the door, waiting. Marguerite introduced them and her mother thanked him for seeing her daughter home and bid him farewell. However, the ice had been broken and when the young couple met next day both were more at ease. He walked her home that evening and on being invited inside asked Mr. and Mrs. Preece's permission for Marguerite to come to tea with his mother the following Sunday. Knowing the widowed woman slightly and cognisant of her respectability, the permission was given.

How Marguerite longed for that Sunday. She planned her dress, even her conversation. She knew that Mrs. Maine was a keen gardener, so she had an inkling of what to talk about. She longed to make the proper impression on his mother. His father had recently died.

That Sunday was the happiest day of her young life. She was in love with Weston Maine and felt convinced that he was deeply attached to her. His mother was kind and charming, the garden delightful, the tea in the parlour pleasant and relaxed. She was so happy, so delighted, so optimistic. Money would be in short supply as banks did not pay generous salaries to their trainees, but she felt confident that things would work out and that they would end together.

She asked her parents to return the invitation the following Sunday, which they did.

The following week, though she daily saw him while travelling, was an exercise in patience. She longed for Sunday, so that her dear parents could meet him properly and accept him.

Sunday emerged as a lovely autumnal day, a slight nip in the air, leaves already beginning to turn, the bright flowers of summer already fading but bravely facing the coming blast. The Preece household, like many others, had already stocked up with firewood, which was being daily delivered on laden carts. Mrs. Preece honoured their guest with the first log fire of the season. The girls returned from church radiant with preparations for the coming Harvest Festival though Marguerite was unduly anxious about the coming afternoon.

Tea was already laid when Weston Maine arrived, correctly punctual. He made a very good impression with his neat appearance, and brought his hostess a bunch of late chrysanthemums from his mother's fine garden. The parents and Delphine chatted amicably with him while they awaited Marguerite, who nervously lingered upstairs, building up courage to descend.

When Marguerite came downstairs to greet him, he had already met Delphine. The same pattern emerged. Delphine, with her vibrant good looks and confident personality, already held the young man in thrall. He could not take his eyes off her. Politeness reigned but the message to the sensitive Marguerite was quite clear. Once more her sister had the upper hand; she could not help being the conqueror in any situation. Marguerite's hurt and disappointment was acute. She calmly withdrew from the conversation, deeply wounded but on the surface sweet, quiet, poised as usual. She longed for the visit to be over and when he left, promising to take both to the last summer fête at the municipal park (the proceeds to local charities, led by the churches), Marguerite knew that politeness alone dictated this and knew in her heart that she would appear and disappear, when the following Saturday arrived.

She loved her sister dearly but her own nature was not the competitive kind and her hopes were shattered.

That Sunday night she cried herself to sleep. She had decided that, if possible, she would avoid travelling with Weston Maine henceforth. If she had to, she would try not to sit opposite or beside him. Delphine would win him of that she had no doubt. Her parents, not aware of how seriously involved Marguerite felt herself to be, welcomed Weston Maine into the family and accepted that Delphine would marry him.

A few short months later the wedding was solemnised quietly and tastefully. Marguerite did not attend. Delphine accepted that she had probably captured the young man to whom her sister was devoted but no words were exchanged. As far as she was concerned, Weston loved her and she him and she felt grateful that Marguerite had brought him into her life.

Delphine and Weston went to live in his mother's home, which would one day be theirs. They led an exemplary life, Weston gradually being promoted at his bank and Delphine studying part-time and working occasionally at the florist's, then an unusual thing to do but she needed spare money for her lessons. In between she took great interest in Mrs. Maine's superb garden, still being maintained by her mother-in-law, and when their first child was expected the rejoicing was shared by Delphine's parents and Mrs. Maine. The conscientious young couple continued with their work and interests and the future held every promise.

Marguerite never forgot that first attraction but behaved impeccably and loved Delphine as much as ever, meekly accepting that she possessed a magnetism she herself lacked. When Ralph Preece Maine arrived, Marguerite, along with her parents, adored him. They were so proud of the vivacious Delphine and hoped her son would inherit her vibrance rather than his father's stolid calmness and reserve.

Two years after the wedding Mrs. Maine died, leaving all she owned to her son. Their grief was inconsolable, as she had been a much-respected person and the whole neighbourhood mourned her. She was what they termed, a very useful individual, much appreciated in local life from flower clubs and gardens to church and charities. The child was their solace and the young parents were thankful for the joy he had brought his grandmother.

A short while after her death Weston was chosen to accompany a senior manager at the bank to India, with the view to opening a branch in Bombay. Delphine, excited and appalled, could not visualise being without him even for a short time. She, being adventurous, wished to accompany him, a thing unheard of among rising young managers. The more she dwelt on the idea, the more determined she became.

During the past few years, she had been active via the church with Overseas Missions, a health and educational organisation, which was operated from this country. Delphine had organised garden fêtes, something called 'sale of work' whereby people gave their creations to be sold, concerts and tea parties in the wealthier homes to gather funds for her chosen charity.

Her efforts had not been in vain. Overseas Missions

offered a modest stipend to help towards her journey. Accommodation had been arranged by the bank; she would share cramped quarters with Weston. Delphine was to attend daily the charity institution operated by the nuns. She was to liaise with the nuns in the poorest quarter of Bombay and bring back first-hand observations. Delphine was delighted and, along with her meagre savings and some help, thought she could manage. She looked forward to sincerely applying herself to doing all she could and returning home with graphic accounts after first-hand experience. The days would be hers to give of her best and gain experience, while her husband was at his work. Ralph would go to his Aunt Marguerite and his grandparents in the village. She had no fears regarding his well-being.

The day of departure was sad and jubilant, but Delphine's spirit was not easily quenched. The voyage was a splendid undreamt-of adventure and she eagerly anticipated working to her utmost. Life, to her, had always been kind, a cosseted existence, loving parents, adoring husband and child. How she longed to give something back to the less fortunate; what a chastening effect poverty and neglect would have on her. Something in her psyche made her feel that seeing the exact opposite of what she had taken for granted would be good for her soul. Ever the optimist she really imagined that she could be of immense help.

From the beginning her weeks in Bombay were highly interesting and constantly stimulating. In her wildest imagination she had not realised such poverty and human degradation possible. She found a superb relationship with the nuns and other charity personnel, and her deep sympathy with the underprivileged and ignored manifested in her unstinting efforts day after day to do what she could to shine one weak ray of light in such utter blackness. The nuns and helpers were an inspiration – the ugliness and suffering which so staggered Delphine was what the Ladies of Charity had always known, day after day, year after year, with no alleviation in sight. To them it was commonplace, but the shock to Delphine considerable.

Her sheltered upbringing in a tranquil English village had not prepared her for this but had instilled in her a sense of service. It was devastating but after one agonising day and a sleepless night she took the good nuns as her beacon and braced herself for the task in hand. She adapted, loved and gave of her best. Weston, who saw her at the end of each long day, was proud of his lovely wife and felt grateful that she was with him and that the experience would somehow enhance their future life. It could be the key to something Delphine would achieve once home again in an England which, from here, seemed Paradise. Their first-hand knowledge would do more for the unfortunates whose lives they had touched. They would speak to groups, write to the press, anything to create more awareness in England of what was happening within the empire. England had her own social problems, especially in the cities, but these were as nothing compared with what Delphine had experienced in the slums of Bombay. The children deliberately crippled and used as begging pawns, the filth, the hopelessness, the almost subhuman inhabitants, victims of their environment, huddled in alcoves or under temporary coverings. The putrid pavements or what served as such, the dilapidated houses or rooming hostels (some charities had made an effort), the frequent corpses encountered with no claimants and, most disturbing of all, the acceptance of the 'them' and 'us' philosophy among the privileged was a kind of shock. To enter a reception in a palatial house but having to step over the sick or dying to get there, only to be assured that it was 'Allah's will', was deeply distressing. The wealthy citizens of Bombay seemed unaffected.

By the end of the sixth week Weston, and Mr. Malcolm Molyneaux, his superior, had completed their research and established a foundation for a business deal for the company. With shining eyes and a new jauntiness in his step, he headed for their humble hotel for the last time, with a gold bracelet for his wife as a mark of his affection and appreciation for her stamina and yes, goodness. He also carried a brand-new travelling case, a gift from his business hosts. Delphine was already packing but in tears at leaving the nuns and their charitable institution, feeling almost guilty to be leaving but delighted at the prospect of seeing her beloved child again and breathing the seemingly innocent air of England. Yet her fragile conscience gave her unrest; she could see the value of what good Christian people projected and realised the worthwhileness of giving of oneself.

On the morning of the last day, Delphine was distinctly feverish, her head aching, her throat sore. The air seemed more oppressive than usual, the foul street odours, more pronounced. With effort she wrote her family a loving letter.

In the afternoon they departed for the ship and settled into what was to be their cabin for the long sail home. Weston, agitated, was trying to make her comfortable in the crowded ship. She was by now relieved to be travelling homewards. Weston sensed that his wife was more seriously sick than she admitted to being and summoned the ship's doctor. He was familiar with tropical fevers and could only recommend cool drinks galore and rest. There seemed no treatment available. Three days later she was beyond recovery and against advice Weston lay beside her through the following days. By then she was comatose, and Weston was also beginning to feel very ill. As there were other cases of fever aboard, little attention was paid to their plight, for nothing could be done. Delphine died late on the fifth day and Weston early on the sixth day, by then convulsed with grief as well as sickness. They were buried at sea in a dignified ceremony.

Several weeks later, about the time the young couple were excitedly expected home, several letters arrived by the same post. This, in itself was ominous as the family perceived the strange handwriting on the envelopes. The first letter, headed by the bank's logo, had Mr. Molyneaux's name, whom they knew was Weston's superior and travelling with him; another was from the bank's headquarters; one was from the shipping line; and one headed by the captain's name. There was also one from the padre. All had been mailed from London two days after the ship docked.

There was silence in the homely room. Until her death Marguerite was haunted by the ticking of the grandfather clock during that unearthly silence. Even the child sensed some great disaster and moved to sit on his aunt's lap. Mr. Preece bravely opened the envelope headed by the name they knew. The shock was immeasurable. As Mr. Molyneaux was still ill from the voyage he referred them to the captain's letter for full details. Mrs. Preece collapsed; all were stunned. A kindly neighbour was summoned to take the child from the grief-stricken atmosphere as Marguerite had to take control of her parents.

It was some time before the other letters could be opened. The captain spoke of Weston and Delphine's popularity with crew and passengers on the outward journey. He wrote of her vitality and beauty and her enthusiasm for the new venture she was determined to undertake. Her husband's anxiety was evident but his attempts to dissuade her were futile. He had spoken to him once, during the voyage out, when he voiced his fears. The chaplain's letter spoke of their quiet death and dignified burial service. He also promised to call upon the family soon, as he had become attached to the handsome, honest, young people. The shipping line sent formal condolences and death certificates and again mentioned the burial and where it took place.

News of the tragedy soon passed though the village, and support from school, church, friends and neighbours spoke of the high regard in which they were held.

*

Marguerite never completely recovered. Hers was a deep and sensitive nature with a strong sense of duty. It was many weeks before she received their belongings, which had probably been in quarantine. The laws on this she did not know. It took several weeks before she could cope with the unpacking, which sadly revealed Delphine's last two letters. Should she, or should she not, let her parents read them? She decided that they were more cheering than depressing because Delphine had been happy at her work and her love for her family was evident. There was an optimism about her intentions and what she would do on arriving home and through it all shone her indomitable spirit. Her parents, being religious, would be comforted by her seeming indestructibility. Yes, she would show them.

In the meantime, Marguerite would need all the courage she could muster. Not only had she elderly parents to morally support and, in some measure, financially; she also had the lovely child to rear. She herself had lost the two people she had loved most, and they had bequeathed her the child she had always coveted. Being in Weston's presence had never ceased to be painful; seeing Delphine's happiness her only comfort – and then the child. That child was now her life's mission. She dried her tears and faced up to her responsibilities.

Gradually the Maines' house was sold, and the furniture distributed, the private books and papers kept. Bred among books, Marguerite had a particular reverence for them. The money from the Maine house sale was invested for young Ralph's education. Later on the elderly parents had to sell their business and move to a substantial cottage near the church and school in Marian-lea-Meade, a nearby village. With her time employed ministering to elderly parents and a young child, her life became one of service. Ralph, after early years in the village school, was sent to a nearby preparatory school, from where he gained a scholarship to Madbury. Aunt Marguerite's efforts were unstinting. Like her mother she taught piano and prepared accounts and typed business letters at her home to subsidise the meagre funds available. The company which had employed her mother were pleased to send her work, though not regularly. No mother could have given more care and affection than she gave Ralph but she had, early on, become aware that after her father's death, no masculine example had influenced the boy; hence her decision to send him to a school in a neighbouring town.

After Madbury the church or army seemed the only choice for a boy without influence in the commercial world. Being honest, his doubts regarding Christianity made the army a sensible option. Luckily, his skill in writing, blended with his love of history and geography, placed him in the type of work he came to accept and enjoy, his only regret being the long absences from England and his beloved aunt.

When the time came for her to vacate the cottage, sell up once again and enter a hotel for the elderly, Ralph took over in conscientiously caring for her well-being.

When, over lunch on their engagement day, he told his beautiful fiancée his bitter-sweet story, Briende was entranced, though now and again close to tears. He related his history without embellishment, but she felt she had never heard a more poignant story, and as she looked across at him with eyes full of love, she knew she had found someone very special. She resolved to meet his aunt and be kind to her, and deeply sympathised with her youthful lost love. Being so much in love herself she felt that long-ago agony, and in her imagination saw herself and Eleri competing for Ralph and ached with sympathy for Marguerite. The child Ralph had become her only blessing, and Briende longed to love Marguerite and care for her until her days were done.

She reached across the table to grasp his hands and smile at him with eyes tinged with tears. A tender moment for both and certainly an unforgettable one. Once more they toasted each other, each with the same fervent desire that Fate would smile on them. The strange but happy meal over, they dutifully departed to meet the family.

Gaston, Briende's brother, and his Welsh wife Sîan lived comfortably in a substantial house overlooking the bay. Their two children, her cousin Wynn and his Irish wife Moya and two young children joined them for a celebratory tea to greet Briende and her betrothed. Wynn's unmarried sister Wenna joined them also. After the small gifts of paints and jigsaws and an illustrated atlas had been distributed to the children, all gathered around a specially laid table for a well-thought-out tea, complete with an iced cake bearing the word 'congratulations'. After the excited chatter and questions, endless questions, as to future plans and wedding arrangements peace was restored, while Sîan played the harp and Moya sang. The children bounced around to merry choruses and Briende and Ralph bathed in their own happiness. Ralph rejoiced in his new-found family, something he seemed never to have experienced. Sheer exuberance was new to him, his blend of Welsh and Irish merriment, sentiment and Celtic emotions both amused and delighted him. The young fathers seemed at ease with their world, knowing how to enjoy themselves and work excruciatingly hard – business deals daily, managing men and equipment and constantly planning future expansion. How Ralph envied them their security and ambition. They were indeed splendid young men and he looked forward to becoming their friend as well as relative.

This special day over, Ralph and Briende, after fond farewells, departed for the quay where he had arranged that Mr. Byatt would meet Briende in his new motor car. Loath to part they clung to each other before Ralph handed her into Mr. Byatt's care and announced their engagement. Mr. Byatt, who by then knew Ralph, gave a hearty handshake and asked permission to spread the news in the village. He was ecstatic at being the bearer of news, enjoying the role immensely. On the back seat awaiting Briende was an enormous bunch of red roses and in their midst Ralph's mother's pearl choker necklace, her own wedding gift from his father, for Briende to wear on their own wedding day.

Leaving him was painful. Not wanting him to see her tears she did not turn around to wave at him, merely raised her hand in farewell.

CHAPTER SEVEN

Briende's Wedding

On arriving home there seemed more jocularity than usual emanating from the house. There were no carriages or pony traps, yet there seemed to be movement within. There was music playing and as she entered bearing her flowers, a cheer went up and congratulations were offered. The large dining table had been laid in full splendour and dear ones had gathered for her own special engagement supper – all arranged by Ralph as a surprise. The vicar and his wife and sons, her maiden aunts, her father's sister Dinah, who had been summoned from North Island, Uncle Gilbert, her mother and Eleri. This was Briende's day and the excitement permeated the entire gathering. Briende was quite overcome by Ralph's thoughtfulness and stunned that he had shown such imagination. How she wished for him to be there!

She had guessed that there was some plan afoot in his headquarters and some important duty pending.

She went to her room to freshen up and change, arranged her roses and conveyed them downstairs. The necklace she wrapped up in a silk handkerchief. Ralph would have to be present when she wore it.

The meal was happy and plenteousness was much in evidence. Mrs. Blethyn was in her element, Uncle Gil at his most genial, Eleri excited and the vicar's sons charming. Having heard something of Ralph's strange history she looked at Eleri through new eyes and wondered if Ralph's mother had possessed the same vitality, confidence and beauty. Briende was aware that the Britt boys were enamoured of her and for the first time Briende realised her budding beauty and its power. Her red hair hung smooth and glossy, one side swept behind one ear, one side hanging loose. She had adapted an emerald-green dress to a sophisticated new style, almost off the shoulder but held on one side by a dramatic shiny clasp – no doubt cajoled from her aunts' boxes of dress trimmings. They rarely refused her anything. Mrs. Blethyn had already protested about the dress, but as Eleri only appeared at the last minute, there was no time to change. Unused to wine she sparkled more than the bubbles in the one glass she had been allocated for this occasion and her flip repartee with the boys invited a sharp kick from her mother beneath the extravagant cloth. Briende, for the first time, became aware of her sister's attraction to men and half-feared for her undoubted sexuality.

The conversation ranged from world events to

university to church and village. The Reverend Britt mentioned that Mr. Garonne was selling some infertile land for development and likely to make a great deal of money. Mrs. Blethyn and the aunts wondered why he had not yet wed. They calculated that he must be around twenty-seven years old. Eleri piped up, "It was hoped that he'd marry Briende but she would not have him." Mrs. Blethyn paled with shock and could have slapped her. Young Bellan Britt sensed Briende's embarrassment and, poised gentleman that he was, quickly interrupted with, "Perhaps he's waiting for Eleri," and everyone laughed. Briende's gratitude showed in her face but did she, or did she not, for a fraction of a second catch a fleeting idea crossing Eleri's lovely face? From that moment, Briende knew that her pretty little sister was no longer a little girl. She gave promise of being a ravishing beauty and a confident lady – and the vicar's scholarly sons would not be within her orbit.

With fond goodnights exchanged and good wishes for Briende's future happiness from all quarters the evening ended and the small family sat together around the fading fire, as Bridget cleared the remnants of a grand supper and busied herself in the kitchen. For once the girls were excused from helping – there was information to be divulged to Briende. Mrs. Blethyn and Uncle Gil endeavoured to be kind when they informed her that Ralph was to spend the following month in Gibraltar, preparing the troops for India, where there were frequent skirmishes. It was a land he knew well, and he was considered the right man for the task. Not wanting to ruin Briende's day he had requested the supper and arranged the calling of wedding banns beforehand. He was leaving early next morning.

Briende paled at the news, though Uncle Gil gently reminded her that Ralph was a soldier. Though dejected, Briende could not but realise his thoughtfulness and quiet planning.

The following week completed the arrangements. Mrs. Frame was to hasten her departure from Uncle Gil's old house, which she had rented for ten years, and move to North Island to be near her kinsfolk as planned. This particular family considered money discussions a vulgarity but each offspring had absolute faith in the elders' decisions; honesty was a creed Mrs. Blethyn had always lived by. The planning of the home was meant to be Briende's diversion until Ralph joined her at weekends once his present duties were accomplished. Eleri cheered her up with ideas regarding décor and felt excited at the prospect of helping her sister with shopping and planning.

The wedding was set for the Saturday before Christmas, when the church would be decked in swathes of green. The wedding reception was to be at Pen Melyn, in the large dining room which had witnessed so many family occasions, happy and sad, during the long years of its history. After the gathering the young couple would depart for Aunt Dinah's home in North Island before crossing to the mainland to visit Aunt Marguerite, Ralph's only surviving relative. The main honeymoon was to be at the ancient Saxon's Head, a few hundred yards from his aunt's retirement hotel, Featherstone Heights. Ralph's other surprise was revealed; the acquisition of a car, a

Riley, and Briende's new experience was to include driving instruction. She felt truly liberated at the idea, as there were very few cars in Ilandia and certainly no woman driver. Mrs. Blethyn was horrified at this unexpected development – to her, cars were fearsome machines, noisy and smelly and quite unnecessary. A handsome coach and pair represented more elegance and refinement. People would talk! There was no greater horror than the latter. Her secure predictable world was crumbling, events moving so fast; Briende engaged to marry a man on their fourth day of meeting, Briende already with the assured understanding of the war years she had heard so much about. In her present state she could never read Edward Thomas, Siegfried Sassoon or Wilfrid Owen's work as she once did at school. Did everyone in love experience the fears and black premonitions she was subject to? Was it a condition of love?

Comforting herself with remembered poems and songs and great scenes from fiction and drama, one after another, until sleep's healing wand passed over her, she slipped into unconsciousness.

The next day and the following days rolled by in the usual pattern. Excitement, a condition foreign to Mrs. Blethyn, infected the aunts and friends. There was a current of interest in Brymadoc and in the school. A registry office marriage would have suited the pair involved but would have been greeted with suspicion and, with many, non-acceptance, as this was not the sophisticated world. Ralph Maine would not have suggested such an unorthodox union in this very orthodox family. Regardless of how each felt neither could be cruel enough to Mrs. Blethyn to ignore her feelings on such an important event; tradition would once more have to be observed. One day they hoped to have the courage to follow their own instincts in religion, education of children, politics.

From Gibraltar letters arrived almost daily, stating his deep love and outlining his ambitions when his army days were over. Briende seemed to be undergoing an education such as she had never known. Ralph, in conversation, had already hinted at some of his ambitions. llandia had few schools of any merit, an ill-equipped hospital, no military academy, art gallery or library and just a local newspaper. The world was changing more rapidly than ever before and this paradisical backwater would not remain unaffected.

Ralph realised that he had found something he barely knew existed; an almost unpolluted small western nation, tenuously linked to Britain, with its own culture and history, home for a mixture of Celtic people, inhabitants almost remote from the fast-developing world. Ralph foresaw many Limorrnahs along the length and breadth of both islands, with tourist trade, transport and industry. To be at the forefront, hoping to help retain the best of these delightful islands and protect them from the worst elements of modern times became an all-abiding ambition.

In short, he hoped to serve in a civic capacity when his military career ended in a year's time.

With a splendid old family and charming wife, the future seemed an intoxicating challenge. He craved not for wealth or recognition, such was not his nature, but to work and achieve would be consolation enough. His facility with the pen, the military discipline of his early training, his travels, would surely prove an advantage. The future gleamed ahead of him, domestic happiness marching hand in hand with all the energy and effort he was prepared to offer. More than anything his present expectations revolved around marriage to his lovely Briende. To him also, four months seemed like a century. His love for her was overwhelming; he had never expected to find such a being. Dreams of domestic happiness had often occupied his mind in strange, distant, inhospitable places. Loneliness had almost been a condition of his childhood and adult life and he, more than most, realised one could be lonely in a crowd, especially when ill-matched companions were often the norm in army life.

He hoped that he had held on to his serenity and dignity without appearing to be a loner or judgmental. He had always been more inclined to feel sorry for a person than to dislike him. Each human being was a victim of sorts; beneath the surface most were more alike than unalike.

Gibraltar could be the last but one posting before the army part of his career ended. Life in the austere garrison was unsettling; so much of his writing depended on rumour or set bulletins from the Army Intelligence Department for which he worked. He hinted at the unrest and prophesied the Spanish War. The Rock seemed under a permanent martial law and he disliked the place. There would be no wrench when he left the army, just absolute delight at the prospect of a settled home with Briende constantly beside him. Though his career had been successful, his personal life had been sadly lacking. How he longed for peace, participation in local life, being part of a community, caring for dear ones. He longed to give his utmost to that new life, the beginning of which had so strangely come to pass. He saw her still, the demure little student teacher, careful, conscientious, reticent, vulnerable and so sweetly pretty. He ached at the thought of her, ached to be with her, re-read her treasured letters at every opportunity, realised her timidness about expressing herself. He smiled as he thought of her 'correctness' – yes, that was the word. What forces could have formed this delightful creature, so fay, so warm, but so afraid? He reached for his pen and started another letter.

Fevered preparations pertaining to the new house kept Briende and the family occupied. Her notice of cessation of employment had been given, as married women were not expected to keep student teaching posts. Advice and offers of help came in plenitude, summer passed into autumn and Ralph came home to England and travelled to Brymadoc each weekend, staying at The Hermit each Saturday night, returning to base each Sunday afternoon. The weeks became continuous weekends, three days to savour the past weekend, two days to anticipate the next. Wrapped in happiness she conscientiously continued her daily work and spent joyful evenings preparing her home, accepting gifts of family furniture, buying and choosing the rest. Time ceased to hang heavily, there was so much to accomplish.

The wedding was planned by the relatives; she cared

not. If it pleased them then the old lace wedding gown could be rescued from the attic, where, wrapped in a sheet, it had forlornly hung for years. In its day it had been worn with a hoop and without, with a corset and without, altered at the seams, shortened or lengthened for Madoc brides. The lace was exquisite Honiton lace and Mona Lamoine alone knew how to whiten and freshen it, skills she had once learnt as a lady's maid in Paris, or so it was rumoured. Some vowed she used cornflour, some said she used salt, but when Mona had finished with it the garment looked new, with its tight long sleeves ending in a point below the wrist, a tight bodice, high neck and voluminous skirt. Both Briende and Eleri considered a veil rather silly and both bride and bridesmaid opted for a circlet of white blooms on bouncing curls with a matching bouquet, made by Rosemary, aged sixteen but already married, as her wedding gift. December gave little choice for white blooms but miniature winter pansies, Christmas roses, winter white jasmine and maiden's hair fern would suffice. Eleri would create her bridesmaid dress to her own design based on the Pre-Raphaelites, her current interest. The romantic paintings were, as yet barely appreciated in the art world but Eleri was always ahead of accepted trends. The aunts provided blue panne velvet, which exactly matched Eleri's eyes, the tight bodice complete with lacings up the centre back and along the length of the long sleeves. Like the bride, she wore the circlet of white winter blooms and carried a matching spray.

*

The bitter cold of the dull December morning hindered not the villagers. The church was full to capacity, the path to the west door, lined with school children bearing evergreens and any flowers they managed to find. The congregation, each clad in Sunday best attire, had jostled for seats long before the appointed time and quietly whispered their comments on the church décor and special carpet. Scores of them had helped with the preparations and quietly congratulated one another. Goodwill and affection spiced the atmosphere in the ancient building, the flames from a hundred candles danced in the chilly air, competing with the sparkling brasses and silver. Shooting shadows played merrily on the polished pews, resting on many a shiny pate or rug-covered lap. The many-feathered hat of Mrs. Doran, the organist, could be seen above the organ, nodding and gently circling to the glorious music filling the very air with joy and expectation. There was calm, warmth, closeness, belonging and a murmur of recognition and respect when the family arrived together and proceeded to their pews surrounded by their closest friends. Brymadoc's world was the only world most of them knew and they shared in the family's joy. Ralph, resplendent in full uniform, his best man beside him, gave the family a nod of welcome.

As flecks of snow began to appear at the great windows, as if pleading to be admitted, the bride arrived to a swelling crescendo of triumphant glory, all eyes upon her – many of the men diverted by the taller, wand-like Eleri, who looked magnificent in the blue velvet. Briende, dainty and doll-like on her Uncle Gil's arm, looked ethereally fragile in the exquisite dress, worn many times before at the same altar. When Ralph rose to stand beside her, there was a consciousness of emotion, blending with the now-subdued music. Even Mrs. Blethyn seemed affected, visibly taking an intake of breath and swallowing to ward away the tears which seemed to be gathering. There was many a tear because the girls looked so beautiful in the church, more beautiful than ever before.

As the vows were exchanged soft flakes of snow began to build along the window ledges, settling on the old lead panes. Christmas being close at hand, it was quite apt for the choir to sing 'In the Bleak Midwinter' as the pair had requested, as one of the lovely hymns. The congregation joined in perfect harmony. The happiness was infectious.

Fashionable village weddings demanded Mr. Byatt's handsome Victorian coach, bedecked with available flowers. Wrapped in a fur-lined silk cape with Ralph beside her holding her hand, the couple departed for Pen Melyn for the wedding breakfast. A variety of carriages and the occasional motor car, looking invasive, were soon parked in a continuous line down the driveway, spilling onto the lawn and along the road. It was some time since Pen Melyn had known an event of such splendour, the fashions would be talked about for months. Aunt Editha in mauve, Aunt Deborah in dove grey, were particularly handsome, enjoying their special importance on this special day. The laden tables, happy chatter and constant good wishes continued for several hours. Before the young couple left for their wedding journey Sîan played a haunting melody on the harp and Moya sang in her clear, pure, voice an old Irish love song. It was a touching moment before their departure.

CHAPTER EIGHT

Joy and Hope

Snugly clad in a long grey coat with a Persian lamb hat and muff and long boots, Ralph in heavy tweeds against the inclement mid-winter weather, to a chorus of good wishes, they walked hand in hand down the winding driveway to where Ralph's newly acquired car was specially parked near the gates. They turned, smiled, waved and drove away.

Alone at last, their happiness seemed the culmination of a dream. They drove northwards, ever northwards, in snow, sleet, light rain and weak flashes of the late afternoon sun, each bright ray resembling a promise, then fading again to be replaced by clouds and sleet. As they followed the winding roads no human or animal seemed abroad. There was a brooding unreality in the silence of the wintry hills, the scrub, the brown heather, sparse trees and floating clouds their only companions.

After several hours mist-shrouded hamlets set in the hollows became apparent. Soon they would reach Coombe Ecton where Aunt Dinah lived. As a child, Briende's journey by carriage had taken much longer but the warmth of her aunt's welcome was fondly remembered. Tonight, her aunt was still at Pen Melyn and her sweet cottage was to be their honeymoon destination for a while.

At last, a few hundred yards outside the village a light beckoned from the undrawn curtains. Drawing closer they saw the firelight glinting on the panes – someone had prepared for their comfort. The little gate closed with a friendly click behind them as they trudged up the path bearing their luggage, laughing as they slipped on the crazy paving, already smeared with a light frost. Ralph rested the cases on the doorstep before lifting her over the threshold and through the open door, the door which was never locked in those halcyon days.

They scrambled out of their heavy coats and, clinging together, reached the fireside. Though some kindly neighbour had arranged for their coming an appetising supper, complete with a miniature wedding cake and bottle of champagne, their hunger was otherwise. Ralph swiftly drew the curtains and within seconds they were in each other's arms and in one graceful motion slid onto the sheepskin rug on the hearth. Time ceased to exist as they discovered each other; each thought the other the most beautiful vision ever beheld. Briende abandoned all claims to herself, she was his, his to possess for ever. She would be selfless, completely so; this wonderful being was hers and her joy in him measureless. To him she seemed a vision in a confused and compromised world, an ethereal possession, a delicate, intelligent, unsullied, young and beautiful girl. Both marvelled, each in the other, and felt blessed beyond human experience and overawed by the exquisite joy they had found.

Neither knew for how long they had slept when a chill dawn woke them. Ralph gently disentangled himself, reached for their gowns, which were still packed, and after banking the fire, they smiled at each other as they realised that it was a very long time since their wedding breakfast.

Leading her to the table, he uncorked the champagne and, devouring the supper left for them, made it their first breakfast. Never had routine been so sweetly disrupted, all was unreal, almost deliciously wicked, dawn breaking and champagne for breakfast in a borrowed cottage in a bleak, silent, landscape. The world seemed elsewhere; they were all that mattered. Each seemed to read the other's identical thoughts. Was it possible that humans could experience such absolute happiness?

They felt unique and very blessed in each other, both overwhelmed by the way they had found each other, newly bewildered that their wedding day was merely the ninth day of their association, their engagement day having been the fourth. Had all this been prophesied by some oracle, neither would have believed. Words could not convey their turbulent emotions but if all life ceased at this moment both would feel that they had lived.

Footsteps in the crinkly snow and a friendly clink – the country milkman. Her aunt had thought of everything. This friendly disturbance jolted them back to reality.

There was a world outside. Ralph kissed her hand and saw to mundane household tasks, while she went upstairs to soak luxuriously in the spacious tub with its enormous brass taps. She felt strangely tired, emotionally weary, everything had happened at an alarming pace. With a rough towel she rubbed herself dry, allowing her damp curls to settle as they would. Donning a nightdress, that she had respectably brought with her, she climbed into bed. Ralph laughed when he found her and ten minutes later followed the same pattern with greater speed as he eagerly hastened to join her.

Day ran into night and night into day in the same happy pattern, both radiant with joy, not wanting the delight to end. On the third and fourth day, or was it the fifth and sixth, they trampled across the heathland, over the hills and along the river, the wind whipping at their faces, the frost crunching underfoot. Ralph remembered his childhood in Barnshire and tried to block out the ugliness of so much of what he had seen in distant lands. Briende had never known anything except the beauty of her own island, the love of her family and her ladylike school in Dewary. She was so precious, he wished her never to know any place which did not match her loveliness. One more year and his military life would be over, and they would be together always. He wished to live on Islandia and again conveyed to her some of his ideas and hopes. He would give of himself to this idyllic place, Briende beside him being all the inspiration he needed to do so much.

She listened and encouraged; yes, he would use his considerable talent. With his intellectual vigour she visualised him in every facet of public life from education, to local government, to writing, even perhaps starting a newspaper – her homeland had been asleep for so long. People tended to leave rather than arrive, once trained in any field. She longed for their active life together in the beloved island, working for what was worthwhile.

But for the moment after her youthful baptism into adult experience in a humble cottage in a frosty Christmas landscape, the morning seemed an exquisite brush with unreality. All was pure, noble, luminous, immense and ambling through this wintry landscape, pristine in its beauty, under a leaden sky, sliding over frozen puddles, brushing through the crispy dead heather, rejoicing in the world and in each other. They were intoxicated with unimaginable joy. When they came upon a regular formation of half-submerged stones and saw a bough of winter jasmine, its little golden stars gleaming, they speculated on the little homes which had once stood on this patch of heather, gorse and bracken, all keeping their secrets. Alas, whoever planted that jasmine against the wall was long gone. The plant gave pleasure still. Like an omen of promise, green and gold, fresh and young, regiment. One year after this and he would be free, with time enough for everything.

Early next morning, in the bleak greyness, no sun to add sparkle to the waiting frost, they departed on the long journey to visit his aunt Marguerite at Featherstone Heights, the hotel for ageing gentlefolk. Briende was anxious to meet his only relative, Ralph all eagerness to introduce his sweet bride. More than once they stopped to embrace and revel in the delight of it all – mile after mile of unsullied countryside. Once on the other side – mountains, valleys, the occasional village with a brand-new petrol pump and a crumbling public house. It would take some hours to reach Barnshire via Plymshire, the Vale of Morden, the Wolds of Byre and a quiet country road to Modbury and Beardsley and Marian-lea-Meade. His spirits lifted as he reached home territory. The next two days would be spent sharing his past with his wife. Briende excitedly felt that she already knew him better and was eager to arrive at the Saxon's Head, where they were to stay. After unloading and lunching they were to meet Marguerite.

Briende, again that Celtic instinct at work, recognised her immediately from about a dozen others relaxing in the lounge. White hair swept back in soft waves, blue eyes and flawless skin, white hands wrestling with a hank of wool, busily occupying time as she awaited their arrival. They moved towards each other and, gracious as ever, she embraced Briende before Ralph. "My dear, you are so young!"

Ralph smiled as she hugged him. "I am so happy for you," then with arm around each she introduced them with pride. There was a spontaneous clapping and "Good luck to you", "May you be happy" and even "Merry Christmas" reached them in waves. The matron arrived, their coats were removed, and tea ordered. There was also a surprise – a photographer had been arranged. They posed self-consciously, while he ducked under a black cloth and appeared and reappeared like a Jack in the box. This occasioned much merriment. A posy of flowers arrived miraculously, probably from around the house, and there was more clicking and hiding.

The pleasure was shared as the couple relaxed. Marguerite was delighted and proud. "Tell me about the wedding. Will you please send a photograph?"

"Of course. Briende wore a dress over one hundred and twenty years old and I my best uniform. It snowed lightly for us and the old country church was filled to overflowing."

"How I wish I could have been there. I never saw your mother married you know. My courage failed me as she won the man I loved."

"Yes, Marguerite," (he never called her aunt) "I remember the sad story. I outlined it to Briende on our engagement day. Never mind, you had me. I knew no other mother. Briende will write to you and give full details of our day, far better than I could do it. They were all her people."

Briende promised that she would.

There was more happy gossip, talk of the forthcoming Christmas celebrations, comments on the weather and questions regarding Ralph's next posting. They circled among the old folk, chatting here and sympathising there, laughing at some past reminiscences and staying for longer than they had intended. Marguerite, true to her own gracious self, had made a silk nightdress case for Briende, beautifully embroidered and appliqued with pink roses and a dewdrop of pear. For the pair she had crocheted a white bedspread, the whole company present having monitored its progress over several months that late summer and autumn. It was a big moment of esteem and a sad farewell to follow. None knew when they would meet again, though Ralph corresponded with regularity wherever he was stationed.

The Saxon's Head proved comfortable and hospitable. Many of the regulars and a sprinkling of guests guessed their honeymoon status. Perhaps they glowed; their eyes were certainly alight. "Here's a couple in the seventh heaven," remarked a cheeky waiter. He meant well and showed much favouritism. They let the remark pass for this was a crude country hotel, not the Ritz, and they both desired nothing better. The warmth and food compensated for the lack of style.

Next morning was to be a day Ralph had often dreamt about in faraway places, mosquito-ridden and scruffy, humid and ugly. To at last be taking his new bride to see the places he had loved and been nurtured in, his old home, his school, his grandparents' homes, the church, the village and hopefully just one person from his formative years. Already the clock had reverted to school days. The familiar countryside closed around him as he hugged her to him before entering the car.

Briende watched his eyes as he gazed once more on those fields, those hills, cottages and barns, along the way. Soon they reached the environs of Madbury. "Look, that's the chapel steeple, the school is behind it."

He alighted at the scrolled iron gates with the gold embellishments, spelling "Madbury 1767", the gates creaked open and he drove slowly into the courtyard.

Their first visit was to the chapel, to read the memorial stone, names in gold leaf, line after line. He held her against him. He knew her thoughts for he too was a soldier – *may it never happen again.* "Do you remember any?" she ventured sadly.

"Oh yes, Johnson was the wildest thing ever – could not wait to enlist. The award for valour for him would have been the 'derring-do' of the gymnasium or game field." He smiled with affection. "And Jacob here, thought he'd show the generals how… many is the time he mocked Kitchener of the pointing finger, 'Your country needs you', and here's the pebble-rimmed, thick-bespectacled overweight Saunders, who during rifle practice in the cadet squad dropped the gun on his big toe and ended up in sick bay."

She kissed him. "Such lads," he said. "I have been lucky – just missed the fray, you know, the war was just ending."

He looked again at the memorial stone, eyes sad with memories. "Wilkin's there, fine Greek scholar, wasted in the trenches – would have seen the last wounded private out of hell. A fine athlete also." He quoted Isaac Rosenberg's lines, which Briende knew:

"Strong eyes, fine limbs, haughty athletes,
Less chanced than you for life,
Bonds to the whims of murder,
Sprawled in the bowels of the earth,
The torn fields of France."

"Strong eyes, fine limbs, haughty athletes Sprawled in the bowels of the earth The Torn fields of France."

"We'd better move on to more cheerful things." She grasped his hands; they were icy cold.

In the weak winter sun, they walked around the old walls. The crack in the opaque glass of the shower room had never been mended. Ralph smiled as he recollected the day – "Throw my boots over, Dandy, old Spike is waiting, about to explode." Dandy did and hit the glass.

"You'll be billed for that." He was not. The jollity of the changing rooms before and after matches was part of the scene. Something was always amiss – water too hot, water too cold, tap washer worn, shirts mixed up, soap being thrown, suds splashed, towels hidden. As much tension was released there as on the field itself.

Next the classrooms. Ralph had to show her his name carved on the oak panel along with many others. He showed where he sat and when bored counted the conkers on a nearby conker tree, on the branch which touched the window. They roamed the corridors and visited the main hall. "Maine, is that you? Can it possibly be you? They said you were in India." It was Jolliff, the caretaker, janitor, psychologist, counsellor, stand-in parent, repairer of punctures, confidante, excuse maker, cigarette concealer and lots more. Ralph's face lit up like a child's; he was a boy again.

"Good old Jolliff, you are still here and not a day older. If I had known you'd have cigarettes you would not need to hide!" They laughed at the memory. They were invited for tea in his house on the grounds, solid, grey stone to match the parent building, a fine, neat garden and spacious office, the walls of which were covered with cards, notes, mementoes of far-off places from far-off pupils of yesteryear.

"Jolliff, may I peruse? Please?"

"Of course, the latest are on the right, including your last from Gibraltar – would I like some apes for the grounds indeed!" They laughed again. Briende was happy to see him relive days when she had not known of him or dreamt of him.

"May I also read some of the cards? I have done so little travelling. I almost envy them."

"Please do but I apologise in advance if some are too saucy for a pretty new bride like you."

They drank tea, the two men swapped memories and asked questions along the lines of "Have you news of…?" Men such as Wyndham Jolliff certainly held a place in the lives of so many boys, as did the kindly matrons, who had cared for their physical welfare and between scolds comforted them. The present talk was about one of these, a Martha Mainwaring, who loathed to be called Sister Mattie, which she was often addressed as, just to tease.

"She married you know."

"Never!"

"Yes, the retired Latin master, a widower, after your time."

"Good on her!"

There was sadness also, remembering the sixth-formers who had gone off to die in the trenches, leaving a mere name on a stone, some never reaching their twenties. Some were wealthy, well-married, secure; some were divorced and two had over-reached themselves on the Stock Exchange. Quite a few came back with their families, especially if they were visiting from abroad, and all were welcomed. Some of their sons already had their names down for Madbury, some sons were already here.

Promising to come again, Ralph and Briende drove away, light in spirits, hands waving, horn tooting. Wyndham Jolliff waited until they were out of sight.

"Ralph, you are no longer a stranger to me – I saw you as a boy. Your laugh was young and I love you even more, if that is possible. I thought Jolliff splendid. With many parents abroad he was needed."

"Thank you." He squeezed her hand, gave a fleeting kiss and they continued back to the Saxon's Head.

"We will visit again?" she asked.

"Most definitely. There were times when we felt he was all we had. He never failed us, hence the fact that so many keep in touch."

With evening grimly advancing upon them, through sleet, along rutted roads, escorted by ghostly avenues of tall hedges, they whirred their way towards the distant lights of the small town, to arrive in time for a quick change and supper.

Over the meal, they relived the tumbling reflections of the past day. So much had happened, Briende had so much to learn. She wanted to learn more of his childhood and school, tried to remember the names of his long-lost friends.

"Was Jolliff always there?"

"Always, as far as any of my acquaintances could remember. He always seemed to be on our side against the foe, which of course meant the headmaster and staff. He had been known to help with junior Latin but they gave up hoping after the second year."

"Did he have a family?"

"Oh yes, a cosy wife and two sons, both at a distant school, each having won a place. Sometimes when our holidays overlapped by two or three days, they became a popular novelty. I think they made most of it up, but we were impressed. Sometimes they brought cigarettes and we smoked surreptitiously behind the bicycle sheds, like hundreds of boys before and since."

"I missed out in my prissy ladylike school, living on gossip, while waiting for the train or ferry. Gossip usually centred on the teachers or senior girls. There was no outside world."

They both laughed into each other's eyes; the same thought occurring to both, they were married but still strangers learning about their past. This was only the fifteenth day of their relationship and both were in a whirl of disbelief, their world revolving at too fast a pace for them to stand and take breath.

As newly-weds they discussed their new home, Briende's progress in the planning, Eleri's artistry, Uncle Gil's gardening, Mama's endless help with domestic necessities. The wedding presents had yet to be sorted, together.

How they dreamt and planned and revelled in the sharing of their future! How they loved each other! How unbelievable it all was! Tomorrow they would start on their homeward journey and suddenly, they hungered to be home.

Christmas Eve at last, after a journey which had at times been treacherous, thwarted by inclement weather and anxiety in case they would not arrive in time for the family gathering.

They found Brackens alive with lights, artistically decorated by Eleri with all manner of evergreens, cones and Christmas roses. The blazing fire lit the shiny evergreens with myriad points of light; the brass table lamp with its green glass shade on a white cloth seemed part of the décor. A light supper was laid for later because they were expected to join everyone else for the midnight service.

In the church they were joyously greeted, their wedding day atmosphere almost recaptured. Afterwards, a quick call at Pen Melyn where the rest of the clan were already gathered for the traditional Christmas repast of punch and mince pies. As usual all the children and grandchildren were staying for Christmas Day and Briende, eager to leave with Ralph, was on the first step of her journey to a new life. On the morrow they would gather at the big house for the most memorable Christmas Day ever.

Mrs. Blethyn was in her element, the large dining room resounded with happy voices. She was queen of her universe, with sixteen members of her dear family seated at the long table. Wenna alone failed to come. Each would always have that last happy gathering sealed in the memory.

Ralph had accumulated leave because of his overseas service and had a full month to adapt to his new status, a lovely wife and for the first time ever a home of his own. Each day was an adventure, a dream from which one never awoke. He delighted in his new-found family, the countryside, the traditions, at times the quaintness of the language, the warmth and hospitality. To be free from discipline and disciplining others, to be away from cramped uninviting army quarters, to wait for no bell except the church clock chime, to know contentment such as he had never known. They walked in the sleety rain, trod the hillsides in the snow and on a cold, frosty, dawn climbed the steep, craggy path to the Singing Stones to watch the sun rise across the incoming sea, almost close enough to hear as it lapped the pebble-spangled shores; that endless expanse of sea and sky encircling the great rocks, seemingly at the entrance to eternity. They descended towards it till they heard the sifting of the sea, rasping on the pebbles, tasted the salt on their lips, lulled by the whirr of the breeze. The great Stones above them became reflections, like ghosts hovering around their foundations. With the sounds of the sea rinsing through their heads, they clung together, vowing to remember that moment if ever Fate played a cruel hand. Clinging together they climbed again to the Stones, listened to the weird music in the cracks and hollows and wished them to keep their secrets always.

CHAPTER NINE

Ralph's Death, Maeve's Birth

BEFORE THE END OF JANUARY BRIENDE WAS WITH child. Though delighted, she was overwhelmed by the speed of events and Ralph's excitement was infectious. That spring and summer would be etched on their mind forever. The weeks grew longer as each waited for the weekend when Ralph travelled home from duty. With joy they discovered the length and breadth of both North and South Island, camped in woods, had picnics in caves along the shoreline, slept in the car on some warm nights, explored valleys, followed streams and climbed to the Stones, where in these lichened monsters the essence of memory lay trapped. Ralph speculated whether they could have been tombs, once erected with solemn rites, for a passage to some underworld for long forgotten kings, queens or priests.

Or were they parts of a weird temple for a faith long extinct? They found trenches and mounds smothered in heather and bracken and there was ever present the haunting quality of a special stillness. Wherever they went those Stones on the horizon seemed ever-dominating. Briende related some of the superstitions they engendered. "Mama used to say God had frozen a number of evil people for desecrating the Sabbath but she emphasised that she disbelieved this as her God would not be so merciless." They laughed at the idea. "One day, Briende, we'll compile a book gathering all these beliefs and superstitions. Each must have some origin, don't you think?"

Briende smiled. "llandia's superstitions would fill a library."

"What about the Devil, had he no hand in all this?"

"Some say he threw up the blocks of granite from his kingdom to prove his defiance."

"Now they defy the centuries, weather-beaten, tilted, hollowed, cracked, yet mighty."

In the meantime, Briende had become a competent driver, occasioning more raising of eyebrows, for a lady driver in llandia was a rare novelty, unladylike in the extreme.

Because of Marguerite's failing health, they made two further journeys to see her. She shared their joy. Precious as time together was, both felt they owed her that kindness. Their happiness ignited all around them and they were still bedazzled by each other. The nine-month wait seemed like an eternity as they planned and daily celebrated this new miracle.

So many things were accomplished that summer, the car, like a magic arrow, shooting them to the family in Limorrnah, to the aunt in North Island, to Briende's old school across the water, the ferry crossing without the car a poignant reminder of her schooldays, such a short time ago, when the daily crossing was part of the timetable. They'd revised their French verbs, swapped notes, completed essays and gossiped. Briende marvelled that so much had happened in less than three years. She shared something of her reverie with Ralph. "I too feel intoxicated with it all. You are my world and will ever be so." He held her to him as the disciplined waves hugged the sides of the ship on a calm late summer afternoon. Soon Briende's life would have to become more stationary as her time drew near.

In late August Ralph was recalled unexpectedly half-way through another blissful weekend. He was to sail to India on the Tuesday, replacing the officer who should have gone. Some disaster had struck the latter and instead of Gibraltar once more, as Ralph had hoped, it was to be India.

Briende remembered her uncle's dire warning on her engagement night that her husband was a soldier. Her agony that night was a mere shadow of what she now felt. Ralph reminded her that it was his last posting, a mere three weeks, doing the same sort of work he had done on his last duty, nothing arduous, nothing new. He would be home for their child's birth.

"Six weekends without you – I cannot bear it."

"Keep occupied, keep writing, start a journal, think how our child will one day enjoy it."

"Write every day, please, even on the journey."

"Of course, I will leave a letter at every port to be forwarded. It will be a quick journey this time. I understand we will only leave government papers en route. We will not be staying anywhere."

"So letters will come in packages, not individually."

"That's right. by the time you have reread them all, I will be home."

She released him, stood on the quay to wave him off as he had done seemingly so long ago. Then, her tears, competing with the rain which beat on the windscreen, this welcome shower at the end of a warm day, seemed an offer of sympathy in her sadness. His face, his voice, his sweetness travelled with her. She could almost feel him beside her, and her child stirred within.

"Please, if there's a God, bring him safely home."

That night she went home to Pen Melyn. She could not bear to be alone, the old house enveloped her. His inspirational letters began next day, each an extension to her education. All subjects were touched upon. His religion or religious feelings bordered not on the orthodox beliefs of any creed. He seemed to accept the best tenets of each, the sensible, the acceptable. Beauty, Truth and Goodness would always be representative of what he thought of as God. Briende lived for his letters and the unimaginable joy of their reunion just before their child's birth. She had endeavoured to enjoy her pregnancy, read copiously, directed by him to his splendid library and even the remembered reference books. She worked at improving her piano playing, walked daily, perfected her home and glowed with health and happiness until the first gentle fall of autumn leaves served to remind her that her time was drawing near.

On a mellow afternoon, a slight autumnal nip in the air, sunshine weakly striving to warm the remaining flowers of summer and coax the last hardy rosebuds to unfold, she lay on her bed listening to the faint twitterings of the birds in the eaves, watching the sun's rays fall on the few apples still clinging to the huge tree, making several appear like balls of gold, like some image in a long-ago fairy tale book. Vaguely uncomfortable, she tried to rest but sleep eluded her. Then a patter of feet on the front path, a gentle tap of the knocker, sounds which came as an assault on her reverie. Who could it be? Family members never knocked.

Pulling her loose gown around her, she descended. Her mother and Eleri, pale-faced and silent, stepped in and, arms around Briende, led her to the sofa.

Words were unnecessary. Seeing tears roll down Eleri's lovely face, for the first time ever, Briende instinctively knew that Ralph Maine would not be coming home – ever. All became a blur, unreal forms and faces hovered over her. The doctor, already summoned, arrived and Eleri was dispatched to the vicarage in Bridget's care.

The news had reached Pen Melyn from the barracks at Dewary. There, the communication had arrived from headquarters. Two fellow officers brought the dire news. With a touch of humanity, the commanding officer had directed them to the family home, knowing of Briende's condition. Full details, in a formal military document, told of Ralph Maine's death. It was one day of sickness and exhaustion followed by a rapid fever, which lasted a mere three hours before the final coma. His last message to his wife, delivered in a lucid moment, was, "Be brave, rear our child as we…" then, "tell of our love." The rest became unintelligible as he sank into his final sleep.

For the remaining day and two more days Briende slipped in and out of consciousness. There were fears for the child, whose birth had been prematurely induced, though the child seemed strong and lusty in spite of the mother's suffering. At more than one stage the unborn child seemed likely to be born an orphan. As violet evening fell on the second day, Maeve Marguerite Maine made her appearance. Too exhausted or traumatised to cry lustily, a squeal announced her delivery, but she was a survivor, six pounds of white flesh and flaxen hair, a miracle to all present. Too weak to nurse her and devoid of speech, her mother would take several days before registering her existence. Mrs. Blethyn's ministrations would once more have to be relied on. The modern doctor had no fears; he had lived just long enough on llandia to realise that some of the old country women were at times remarkable in their wisdom. The child was healthy, his fears were for the young mother, who had undergone a severe shock followed by cruel suffering. Her youth would bolster her recovery and no doubt her speech would return as her body healed and her mind found acceptance of the catastrophic misfortune. There was a lot of healing ahead. The condition was known as aphonia. It could take months. These facts he divulged to the family.

Mrs. Blethyn's own reasoning had reached the same conclusions; her intelligence told her all she needed to know and do.

On the evening of the second day, Briende faintly motioned her desire to hold the child. As she surveyed her, she saw Ralph Maine in the plateaux of her face, the sweet expression already manifest. She so strongly resembled him that her tears began to flow, copiously, seemingly never ending. An onlooker might have become alarmed but not Mrs. Blethyn. These were cathartic tears; her daughter would recover.

Gradually the immensity of her loss mingled with a bewildering acceptance of this priceless gift – now her future project and all-abiding reason for existing. Maeve was still Ralph's and hers, their creation, and she would try to honour his memory in the conscientious sincerity of her efforts. At each crisis she would try to act as she thought he would have reacted. The future with this daughter was already mapped.

She raised her eyes to her concerned parent – eyes of gratitude. Henceforth her family would be of prime importance. Maeve would know love, care and security and, she hoped, happiness.

Exhausted, she sank back into her pillows and the flimsy bundle became as a heavy load. Mrs. Blethyn removed the child, placed her in the cradle, gently brushed Briende's hair from her face, rearranged the bedding and left her.

As she moved carefully and slowly around the much-loved house, she gathered up mementoes of him, which were far too invasive for her healing process. The silver-framed wedding photograph, the large one of Ralph in full uniform, were to be too painful as daily companions. In a special large drawer these would be wrapped and placed along with his superb letters, wearable gifts and personal possessions. His clothes she had already arranged to be packed and given to Mrs. Britt for charity. His beloved books would remain, where she had arranged them, while lonely for him in their earliest days. It would take courage to first open them, but she would. She had already, in between cruel attacks of grief, taken stock of her life; she was twenty years of age, not properly trained in anything, as few women were. She had a child to rear and house to maintain. Being suffocated by a blanket of irremediable grief was not conducive to being a good mother. She would henceforth conduct her life with the courage he would have expected of her. Deep within her would always lie the memory, delight and gratitude of having known such a being as Ralph Maine, a happiness seemingly as short as a butterfly's life, and for a short measure life had been perfect bliss. In spite of present pain, it was a glory she would not have missed. "In short measures life may perfect be," as the poet had stated.

Tears coursed down her face as she went about her excruciatingly painful tasks, in between gazing with wonder at the perfect infant, as if sent in replacement. She would tell Maeve about her father, of course, and answer each question uttered. She hoped to rear her with an awareness of her parents' love for each other and when asked would tell her of his sad, lonely, death.

Footsteps at the door, her mother bringing a tray of nourishment, alarmed at finding Briende recumbent. "I'm all right," tortured-sounding, a stranger's voice and almost her first words.

"I believe you should come home for a while."

"No." She shook her head.

"Then I'll send Bridget again for a few nights."

Briende agreed, half-relieved because she had disposed of Bridget's help but admitted to herself that the nights were not easy if Maeve awoke more than twice. Briende had a genuine fear of collapsing. But she would heal, her malaise was more spiritual than physical. She now forced herself to listen to religious broadcasts, thinking the well-known words of familiar hymns would induce speech – something she could practice alone with no embarrassment.

A few days later, after three weeks, she did push the old wicker perambulator the half-mile or so to Pen Melyn. Cheerful noises from the kitchen informed her that Bridget was there with her mother and both came at once. Briende noted the warmth and relief in her mother's face; a feeling of gratitude flooded over her. She was going to be dependent on her family for succour, support and sharing in the rearing of her infant. Mrs. Blethyn checked on her granddaughter.

"She's ready for nourishment, you'll take a jar of rose-hip syrup home with you." Mrs. Blethyn had not yet heard the word 'vitamin'; her word was 'nourishment'. Briende felt that she had a lot to learn.

Small domestic incidents and the duties of a well-reared girl had occupied her spare time, which was still interspersed with spasms of grief. Mr. Jolliff, the caretaker and friend, the Madbury headmaster, Ralph's old school friend in Malta, were among the recipients of the sad news. She could not put her life together, as she thought, until these tasks were completed.

Not least among her preoccupations were Mrs. Blethyn's and Reverend Britt's plans regarding a memorial service. This formality the young widow could not bear. There were fewer than twelve people in Brymadoc who had known him, and Ralph would never have condoned such distress for Briende.

Another sleepless night was occupied by thoughts of what she should do. The man she had loved was buried thousands of miles away in alien territory, a quiet soldier, too modest to have ever considered himself important enough to merit a special service. Yet a coldness came upon her as she realised that there had been no funeral with loved ones present; that sweet being had faded into nothingness, not having been properly mourned by those who loved him and those who knew his worth.

Distress seized her. Who could guide her? What should she do? Before morning she had decided alone to have him remembered within the usual Sunday morning service, the family present, her brother to read the lesson, Moyah, in her lovely voice, to read Rupert Brooke's already famous lines: "That there's some corner of a foreign field, that is forever England".

Nobody could be more English than Ralph Maine.

Sîan would render a gentle melody on the harp and the Reverend Britt would lead the prayers. The warm-hearted worshippers in that close-knit community could not object, indeed most would be moved to join in. The wedding was still remembered, the sudden joy, the swift bereavement. Gifts and flowers galore had arrived at Brackens. These were good people and Ralph Maine had planned to spend his life among them.

Surprisingly, Mrs. Blethyn and the vicar thought Briende had done the right thing, the sensible thing, and again their sympathy reached out to her. It would be another ordeal to endure but the young woman accepted that nobody was excluded from pain, anger, loss. Nobody was immune. Uncle Gil's words reverberated during that long night of decision – "Ralph is a soldier, this, you must accept".

He had not died in action as they euphemistically write. Like many other serving men, he had died of a fever. Briende nevertheless allied herself with the war widows of the Great War. Her beloved lay in a far-off grave and there was a child he had not seen. Grief, once more, clogged her thinking process, tears, more tears, a sense of having been cheated and a deep love, deeper than she could ever have imagined, suffused her.

So each day followed another, a sorting out of emotions, some planning for her future. During the deepest agony she had reasoned that hers was not be a nun-like existence, a martyr to memory. There was a child to rear. Her parent, aunts and uncle were ageing, her brother and cousin had their own lives to lead and Heaven alone knew where or what would be her sister's fate. In one brief year of knowing Ralph Maine she had realised her deficiencies. They were to be filled, gaps in knowledge and experience in life. She had determined that as soon as she was physically strong her tasks would begin. The child would spend two days with her grandmother, one day with the great-aunts, one day with Bridget at home, while she, as a young mother, would pursue a secretarial course in Limorrnah. In the meantime, for relaxation, she would embark on external studies, involving guided reading in literature. She had seen such courses advertised in sober publications. She had a wealth of books available and would buy any volume she did not possess. Work would be the best antidote and reading could be pleasurably pursued in bed at night as she would undoubtedly retire at the same time as the child. All this would claim time and energy, involving daily driving to her studies and assignments to be completed at home. Constant demands would consume her days. Recognising that the discipline would be overwhelmingly demanding, she had nevertheless decided her future course.

With experience, confidence and advanced education many avenues would be opened. She would perhaps become involved with local government, or any other project offering what she could to the betterment of life for ordinary people. At each progressive juncture, she would ponder on what her husband would have suggested. She felt his influence, sensed his presence. Perhaps this was her way of coping with grief; without this sort of willpower she would be consumed by it and completely ruined.

Feeling somewhat comforted after making her

decisions, she would concentrate her efforts on getting well. Recovery was slow, her demeanour easily shaken, but her speech was returning and sessions of physical activity daily lengthening, when her peace was shattered by another blow. Barely five weeks after Maeve's arrival, news came of Marguerite's death. Briende's mixed emotions at this news proved a further setback. Marguerite would never see her great-niece and namesake but would not have to be told of Ralph's death. After a harrowing hour or so Briende did the sensible thing and walked home to Pen Melyn. Company, the diversion of the baby, Uncle Gil's homely philosophy and comfort, were essentials of the moment. At least Marguerite died believing her beloved Ralph a happily married husband and father.

CHAPTER TEN

Eleri Leaves Art School

THREE YEARS LATER BRIENDE HAD MORE THAN fulfilled her promises to herself, having followed her commercial course in Limorrnah and her home studies in literature. She had emerged as confident, cool, sophisticated and attractive and several upstanding and successful men had sought her and tried to court her. Charming and independent was the usual impression, removed, reserved, self-possessed.

Maeve, a lively flaxen-haired, fairy-like child, was the pride of her existence. The child's fatherless situation seemed not to have affected her. Frequent associations with the Madoc and Blethyn family and friends, in a settled environment, had created a well-adjusted infant. Livelier and more talkative than either of her parents, she was a constant amazement to her grandmother, who considered her unusually bright; the delight of her now-ageing Uncle Gil and Eleri's toy.

There were many days when Briende's pride in her daughter evoked a great longing for her father – how he would have enjoyed her – what a great emptiness was still evident.

Mrs. Blethyn had again been approached by Alvar Garonne, and once, when out riding, he had pulled up alongside Briende's mount and exercised his considerable charm. His strong-willed mother, who lived in the west wing of Campions, their large mansion, had always hoped for 'the Blethyn girl' as she voiced it. The Garonne family had always amassed land and property adjacent to the Honourable Bettina Garonne's land was something she understood above all else. Mrs. Blethyn, also ambitious, would have encouraged the union but to no avail, as Briende had no intention of linking herself to another man. Recently elected as the first lady councillor in Trevere, having instigated a department of the environment, she was beginning to feel fulfilled. By some spiritual osmosis, Ralph Maine seemed to be guiding her. Once established she had ideas of a permanent town library as well as a mobile library. Later on, a health centre perhaps, or a maternity unit. The wheels turned slowly in llandia but they were turning.

Eleri, now at Ondine School of Art, writing regular letters from London, encouraged her to live untrammelled by circumstance: "spread your wings and fly into the blue". Eleri was always as a plant with its head inclined to the light, not welded into the stuff of family history as

Briende's tended to be. Briende, pretty, dainty and with a sweet nature, lacked Eleri's vivid personality and striking beauty. However, there was between them an affection implicit and unquestioned. Too unalike in their ways to be complementary, yet in a sense they were never parted. A copious correspondence united them whenever they were parted, and each smiled at the other. Brymadoc never ceased to marvel at Eleri's daring fashion sense and lightness of spirit – a breath from some alien territory each time she returned home for the vacation.

Ondine School of Art, which Eleri had insisted upon – nothing else would do – was the epitome of modernity in the London scene, which suited her effervescence. Sharing a Chelsea house with the Hon. Prunella Winterton, known as Prunie, Venetia Barton-Kendish and Juliette Corby, was an adventure of the highest order. Each was breaking the family mould, each felt as, or more, daring than the other. Freedom of spirit was the term they used for any excesses, whether connected with late nights or champagne for every minor celebration. Prunie's free artistic style never ceased to fascinate Eleri and one of her creations had been accepted for the Summer Show at the Academy, to the envy of her peers. Juliette's chinless wonder from Eton, who visited at weekends, was a constant source of amusement, yet all knew that she would marry him. Prunie, on the other hand, was much envied. Her admirer, Abdun, a rich Egyptian diplomat's son, seemed to offer all one could possibly desire, charm, looks and fairy-tale promises. As foreign as something from *The Arabian Nights* or *Desert Prince* he was swooned over and admired.

Girlish gossip, usually past midnight, revolved around the Horaces, Ruperts, Jonathans and Nigels of the next weekend's escapades. The London scene, the country weekends, the visits to theatres and art galleries, the quick trip to the continent, the giggles, laughter, sighs and sleep. Eleri, through it all, hoped to make her own way, know some sort of success. Never hindered by the restrictions of lslandia, she blended in superbly with this new sophisticated existence. Indeed, when sleep eluded them, she often regaled them with stories of llandia's crippling influences but her talent, vivacity and superb looks equipped her for anything. Her room-mates and some of the other students reminded her of the young women she had frequently seen visiting Alvar Garonne's great house, the debutantes from England likely to have 'a season', the gay young things talked about in the magazines. Eleri would be almost convulsed with laughter at the idea of Mrs. Blethyn giving her 'a season'. Financially Mrs. Blethyn would have managed splendidly but her stern Christian outlook would never lend itself to such frivolity!

Eleri was undoubtedly popular and a natural leader and raconteur. All this she related in letters to Briende.

Tramping around London in way-out garb, visiting Thameside pubs or sometimes disreputable Soho basements, in a group as released in spirits as herself, art became not something they studied or reproduced in paintings or sculptures, read about and wrote about, but the whole study of humanity in all its facets. After two years she felt twenty years older in experience.

By the conclusion of the third year Eleri had fallen in

love. From the age of sixteen, almost from the moment she first met him, she had been fascinated by the fine artist and art history tutor, though, at first he seldom taught her. Fascination evolved into infatuation, the pain of which became at times unbearable. Friends and acquaintances became aware of the mutual attraction; without exception all warned her of the hopelessness of the situation. Traditional gossip from the past few years certainly verified that Spenser S. Fortesque's appeal was legendary.

Female students automatically fell in love with him, as one year followed the next. Yet, there was never a hint of scandal or criticism. He was well-known to be happily married to a charmer who had once been his student, and that he was the proud father of three lively children.

Eleri, in her pride and beauty, had never considered herself as another ordinary student. Instead of Time's healing process, her passion grew stronger. Day and night, night and day, her dreams and desires revolved around him. In fairness to herself she realised her own sensuality and could remember the appeal of her sister's husband and the excitement Alvar Garonne aroused in her each time she saw beautiful women descend on Campions. But she was then so young, nothing seriously registered. This was different. There was arousal, and the attraction mutual, though no words were spoken. Many became aware of the electricity between them yet neither made an undignified move. Her room-mates sympathised but tried to discourage and divert her. She was 'different', much admired and considered delightful. Outings to theatres, restaurants and country weekends, introductions to other men brought along by her friends' suitors, more work at college, more time in libraries, completing assignments on schedule, were all part of the programme. Nothing could divorce her mind from Spenser Fortesque. Almost every man she met became enamoured of her and many young women considered her a threat, but those who best knew her, knew that she was completely engrossed in S.S. Fortesque.

Though popular, a relationship within her age group was not to be considered. The situation seemed quite serious. It was obviously noted that he was trying to avoid temptation, never allowing himself near her or alone with her. Eleri's artistic creations became more bizarre but interestingly so; her work output increased to please him. The malaise which came upon her curtailed her sociability and for the first time she became a serious student. She emerged as the best student of the year but with clipped wings. Eleri Madoc Blethyn, for once, felt a loser; for the first time ever, things were not going her way.

On the surface life continued as usual in that world of theirs in their bleak flat. Conversation in the bedroom, from their respective beds, followed the same pattern, their situation wittily equated with Gray's Elegy "each in her narrow bed" or the biblical "Take up thy bed and walk" when boredom suggested moving the positions. This space one week, that space the next. Happy, healthy, unattached young females, conversations usually revolving around life, marriage, sex, the role of women, contribution of the suffragettes, women in power, their own hopes and ambitions. The age-old arguments were endlessly discussed.

Eleri was quite definite about sexual freedom; women were sexual beings as much as men. She often quoted and agreed with Shelley; sex was sordid without love and she had decided that her first experience would have to be with a man she was engrossed in. Infatuation maybe? What was the difference if the agony and the ecstasy were identical? Infatuation could grow into a quiet all-abiding love once the violent, tempestuous, extreme joy was fading but a quiet friendly love to begin with would never amount to anything. That early bliss had to be experienced.

They agreed, they disagreed, they doubted, they half-believed. So passed the late nights before sleep overcame them, only to repeat the same arguments the following night.

Eleri was exasperated by the passive acceptance of some of the girls, clinging to their suitable boyfriends, emphasising the belief that the social bracket counted as much as anything. Where was the tumult, the protest, the craving for fulfilment? Why accept what society tossed their way? Personally, she would give up suitability for one mad fling with a man she desired. This attitude both shocked and amused the friends. Not ruthless enough to destroy a marriage, she nevertheless had no conscience about one lapse… what the eye does not see, and so forth, a secret to hug to oneself.

Sometimes they teased her, comparing her with the artists, musicians and poets who littered our culture with meaning. They vowed they expected such great creations from her. She laughed with them – merriment was a fine tonic and she never bottled it. In one thing her friends were correct; her tastes ran to older men, experienced, worldly men. With this she agreed. It had ever been so; she remembered how, aged thirteen, she had envied her sister's capture of Ralph Maine and how desirable Alvar Garonne had seemed when she and Rosemary, huddled together in the steamy greenhouse, discussed his women and lifestyle. She smiled at the memory. She shared the memories with her friends, and all found it excruciatingly amusing. Occasionally one of them, disappointed in a grade, a falling-out with a boyfriend, or even simple homesickness after a gruelling spate of studying for an examination, would ask her to talk of llandia with its religion and restrictions. She reiterated wise sayings: 'One can only be judged by how one looks' when she had sported a hand-painted shirt and shorts, 'Respectability has its price' or even 'I hope you ask for guidance in your prayers'. The favourite was 'You cannot turn the clock back'. With all this she regaled them until their spirits were once more lifted.

"You should write your own book, Eleri – nobody would believe such a place exists," from Prunie or, "They'd go in search of it and develop a tourist trade," from Juliette.

Sometimes they thought her imagination was at work and disbelieved her, but she vowed the truth of it and invited them to visit and find out for themselves. She realised, though, that with the passing of Mrs. Blethyn and her ilk, the beloved place would lose its pristine quality and become an extension of the mainland.

The last term ended and the three years, which had become a lifestyle were coming to a close. With mixed feelings, they speculated on what the future held for them. Prunie, with new Arab wealth and old family connections, dreamt of having her own gallery – displaying what was fresh and new, exhibiting such work as she had become appreciative of among her year group. Juliette, like Eleri, hoped to opt for design, clothes, film, theatre – almost anything. Venetia hoped to manage a future husband's country house, plan its redecoration true to period and maybe open it to the public. The parties and excitements of the last week, the sad goodbyes and well-wishing, were typical of any graduation scene anywhere.

Individually, students said their goodbyes and expressed thanks to the principal tutor, as was customary. Eleri both dreaded and excitedly anticipated her last meeting with Spenser S. Fortesque.

CHAPTER ELEVEN

The Seduction

It was late afternoon on a Thursday in early July; a hot unfriendly afternoon when most students felt jaded and ready to leave, an anticlimactic sort of afternoon, the end of a surfeit of experiences, people and places.

Fortesque was in his study, seated at his untidy desk, when she entered. She automatically shut the open door; he in one smooth move opened it. Was it the heat of the day? Or was it nervousness? Eleri was no fool. He motioned her to the seat at the other side of his desk, casting quick glances at the door.

"I've come to say goodbye, and thank you."

His head remained bowed and she noted yet again his unruly shock of brown curls, straight eyebrows, long lashes. He lifted his eyes to hers and extended his hand across the desk. Somehow their palms lingered as he tried to withdraw his hand. At the same time, he noted Eleri's large tears falling helplessly on the debris of his work. Then, in a quietly measured tone, "You are nineteen, Eleri, a beautiful creature. The world can be your oyster."

"I need no oyster, I'm in love with you."

There, she'd said it. Too emotionally upset to accuse herself of boldness, which he knew she was not guilty of, she dried her eyes and tried to take hold of her dignity.

"I'm sorry. No, I am not sorry. I spoke the truth."

"No man could fail to be attracted to you, you have looks, brains and presence. You will do far better than a thirty-seven-year-old art lecturer."

He tried to smile but she could see that he was affected. Not daring to touch him again she merely whispered, "Goodbye then," and quietly left the room, closing the door behind her.

She left the college by the back way, the first time she had ever avoided people. Her emotions, like a swirling tempest, would have blinded her to a familiar face had she encountered one.

Spenser Fortesque was a good man, a noble man, a strong man, and it made him all the more desirable. He was now probably mastering his own emotions because she was sure that the attraction was mutual.

The hot sun outside annoyed her, the hum of traffic and sticky pavements were ugly reminders that the world was not always beautiful, as her world had once seemed to be. She wished with all her heart that Spenser Fortesque had not disturbed her equilibrium, "put rancours in the vessel of my peace" as the Bard had written.

Hardly knowing where she was going, she kept thinking to herself, *it's mutual, he is also suffering and just one mad interlude of giving in to temptation would harm nobody.* It was settled.

Her steps took her towards Harrods; it was quite near. A cool drink in the basement bar of fruit or carrot juice, new clothes, her last shopping spree before leaving London. The coffee-coloured lacy slip and French knickers she'd seen, a few days ago and considered too extravagant, a change in their exquisite rest rooms and yes, it was to his studio. They all knew where it was, but it was his private domain, not even his family ever entered it. She did not feel wicked; selfish, perhaps, but too genuinely stricken to allow such beauty, yes beauty, be unfulfilled. Nobody need ever know, the decision was made.

About two hours later, clad in her drop-waisted sleeveless dress with accordion-pleated skirt, cream Cuban-heeled shoes and a saucy little cream straw hat with its creamy organdie rose beneath the brim, she hailed a taxi to Chamber Street, Kensington.

Her heart beat rapidly, as she ascended the steep narrow staircase and timidly knocked. No reply but she sensed movement inside – a slight rustle. As she placed her hand on the doorknob, there came a faint, "Enter." He did not come to the door.

She stood inside leaning on the door; he stepped towards her and in the blink of a second, she'd thrown herself into his arms. It was abandon, it was a temptation he found irresistible. No words were spoken, he merely led her to the unkempt bed and disappeared. She lay back, hypnotised, confused, expectant, she knew not what.

A brief glance around the chaotic studio revealed a half-finished portrait of her on an easel, many pictures leaning against the far wall, a portrait of an exotic Eurasian-type woman on the mantelpiece, a sort of curtained alcove at the far end of the room – a lavatory, bath, shower, or what? Her mind in a whirl, nothing seemed to register clearly, in fact the whole unsavoury room seemed hazy. With difficulty she removed her slip of a dress and threw the hat across the room to land on the corner of the easel, which made her own portrait appear to be wearing it. Her sweet dress she carefully dropped on a nearby box, its pleats fanning as if arranged. She closed her eyes and waited, seemingly every nerve end now raw and twitching.

She felt him beside her, his weight upon her, his hand on her thigh. She gasped. Never before intimately touched, it was like an electric current about to consume her. His hand reached upwards beneath the gossamer lace to touch her breast, then abdomen, his shudder, then collapse.

She opened her eyes. The room was spinning, his moist chestnut curls mingling with her auburn tresses, his face buried in her neck, his weight crushing her. No words had been spoken. He released himself and kissed her tenderly as she turned her face to the wall, then after gently covering her, moved away.

Retrieving her dress and shaking out her hair, she tidied herself and, still feeling giddy, she raised herself to a sitting position and looked around. Her own image looked back at her, as if to rebuke her, or sit in judgement. She noticed one thing only; the portrait on the mantelpiece was no longer there. The only real thing in that sordid room seemed to be the portrait of herself.

Spenser returned, spruced up and fully dressed. He sat beside her, placed his hands on her waist, bent her across his lap, loosened the strands of her hair from the confines of her dress, hooked up the back of her dress then with his foot found her shoes beneath the bed and, lifting each slender leg, placed them on her feet.

Throughout this pantomime she was as helpless as a rag doll. Holding both her hands, he looked into her eyes.

"Eleri, it was your first time?"

"Yes."

"It should have been better than this. Your beauty and intelligence deserved a better baptism. I'm sorry. I have never before been unfaithful to my wife."

"And I seduced you."

"No man could have resisted you but…"

"We must never meet again, and nobody need ever know of this. I promise. Do you believe me?"

"I do."

They both rose. He reached for her hat, placed it on her head, just so. She knew she need not refer to a mirror. He indicated the bathroom, or whatever sufficed as such – she declined.

As he led her to the door he placed his hands on her shoulders, turned her towards him, looked into her eyes and said, "I have seen how men and boys look at you – please take care of yourself."

"I am fully aware of my sexual power but, as yet, you

alone have attracted me." Her eyes swept over her portrait.

"Get rid of that. I don't wish you to have a conscience."

"Would you like it?"

"No, please leave it unfinished, wrap it and leave it in Nations Bank. In five years, on this day, I'll pick it up. It will grace my walls unfinished."

He smiled – the first ray of happiness in that entire afternoon. Then, on opening the door she realised how reticent he was about seeing her out. She kissed him lightly on the cheek. "Goodbye, Spenser, and I mean goodbye. Don't come down the stairs."

She shut the door quietly and descended into the hot sultry street. Every noise seemed an affront, the steamy pavements became abhorrent, the passing citizens ugly phantoms. For the first time she longed for the peace and freshness of her island home as she trudged to the nearest bus stop at the end of the road. She would take any number, even if it went in the wrong direction. Eventually, she would get to Primrose Avenue and the, by now, inhospitable shared flat.

No.22 down Sloane Street took her part of the way, she cared not. As she squeezed beside a fat man in a bowler hat and pinstripes, who carefully removed his briefcase from between his feet, she thought, *Ugh, convention! So British in this sweltering heat.* The bus seemed crowded with similar types. Nevertheless, she felt herself a disturbing force, as her thigh inadvertently touched his substantial one. He moved away a fraction of an inch. *If he only knew*, she thought, *if he only knew.*

The flat seemed deserted. The doctors downstairs had already departed. She let herself into her shared domain to find it dark and empty. Somebody had drawn the blinds to block out the sun. A note on the door from Juliette. She left her love and an invitation to her wedding in August, a formal invitation to follow. Her Claude had come to claim her, her trunk awaited collection. *A cold bath*, thought Eleri, *a cotton dress and underwear, tomorrow's clothes for travelling. A wide-brimmed hat and crocheted bag for small essentials on the ferry. The new finery to be put in her trunk, more shock tactics for llandia*, she surmised, *if they could but see it.*

Lying on her single bed in a brown and white striped dress, hair tied on top of her head, she experienced a great weariness. Was she sorry? No, merely honest. Selfish, perhaps, but fulfilled. One day Spenser Fortesque would be out of her system. The old proverb, 'time heals', was some sort of comfort. It would never occur to her to destroy a marriage; at the height of her infatuation, if that is what it was, she had no desire to cause misery. In this she was genuine. An overpowering sexual desire was but a fleeting agony according to her belief.

It was a relief to hear a key in the door and hear Prunie's cheerful voice. "Gracious, what's up? Are you all right?"

"Of course, where have you been?"

"With Abdun, at the embassy. Such luxury! I wish I were not in love with an Arab but I am." She glanced at her recumbent friend.

"You are all right, you never keep still in daytime? Oh... I'm sorry, it is Spenser, isn't it? You went and said goodbye. We all asked you not to."

"I had to... just had to."

"And?"

"I told him how I felt." Prunie looked alarmed.

"I knew he'd left early – he sees the rest in the morning."

She flung off her silk printed dress. Eleri had a swift whiff of expensive scent and faintly sweet sweat, then, sitting beside her, she whispered, "Eleri, I wish you had not. I love you dearly, but have to point out that it is hopeless. We have told you – he adores his wife and children, was besotted by her as a student and married her. They say she's lusciously beautiful, dark, almost foreign."

Eleri remembered the removed portrait and – well – her guess had been correct. "I never had any desire to upset things. Do you believe me?"

"I do. You will have offers galore coming your way. Is there nobody at home to divert you? Even temporarily, I mean. Nothing to look forward to?"

"Bellan Britt, the vicar's son, is twenty-three in August. There is to be a candle-lit dinner party at the rectory. Both brothers will be home from university."

"Well?"

"He's studying botany, grows rare plants in the churchyard, keen on preservation and the environment."

Prunie smiled. "His brother, what of him?"

"He's studying classics and ancient history and if you cannot relate the twelve tasks of Hercules or know exactly where Troy was, he's appalled."

"No interest in you?"

"On the contrary, both are spellbound by me, have been since I was thirteen. Even then I was in command, but they think modern art decadent and art students, me in particular, even more so. They consider me the most released being that ever existed. But how they desire me!"

They clung together and laughed, young again, devoted and vulnerable.

A key turned in the lock and Venetia entered, flushed, excited, exasperated but her usual sweet self.

"What's up with you two? Isn't it hot enough that you have to lie together?"

"Confession time. How about you?"

"I've been shopping with my mother. We had to get the dress and as usual we disagreed. I was asked to make a list for my dance and half are crossed out as unsuitable. Who'd be a deb?"

"Tell us about the dress," said Prunie.

"Oh, organdie, white of course, huge puff sleeves and scoop neckline… oh, and a shower of pink silk roses from waist to hem, graduating from buds to full blooms."

"Sounds lovely," said Eleri. "Remove the pink roses and you have your wedding gown ready." She threw a pillow at her friend.

"Eleri, you have none of these pressures!"

Eleri was amused. She tried to visualise Mrs. Blethyn believing in the 'coming-out season'. Mrs. Blethyn just chose, did not believe in putting her daughter on display. Eleri said something about this and all laughed. They had heard it all before.

"You have no sort of 'being released into society' celebration? None?" asked Venetia.

Prunie enlightened her with accounts of the vicar's sons. They agreed that they sounded like Juliette's Claude.

It was their last night and they decided on what they

called a 'slap-up' meal at Antonio's Italian hangout. They would meet up with other late-leaving students and they knew Antonio would 'do them proud'.

The final-year students entered in small and large groups and came and went throughout the evening. There was much consumption of cheap wine, merriment, reliving the highlights, some gossip, some trepidation creeping in, the buoyancy as political news from Europe seemed unsettling.

At midnight there were fond goodbyes, promises to keep in touch and shouts of good luck as the three friends left to walk home to their flat, bemoaning the fact that Juliette was not sharing their night. Once there they moved their beds closer as a last ritual and wearily whispered goodnights.

Eleri, in a blurred state, relived the astounding events of the afternoon, until they became enmeshed in a sort of dream, as she slipped into dreamland.

Next morning more hugs and tears, before Eleri and Prunie raced down the narrow stairs for the last time to where Abdun and his driver waited to take Eleri to Wellington Station for the long journey home. Diplomatic immunity allowed the vehicle almost to the platform. There, from a vendor, Abdun, with typical Arab generosity, purchased an armful of papers for Eleri.

She boarded the train and settled in a corner seat in order to wave at them, only to find them obscured by an enormous cloud of smoke from the monstrous engine. She closed her eyes and, for her the closest she could get to a prayer, she wished Abdun and Prunie every happiness.

Then without speculating on what lay ahead she settled to her reading, confident that she could cope with whatever fate could fling at her. The time was ten-thirty in the morning. By ten-thirty tonight she would be home.

Two or three days to unwind, then serious action. She must plan her life. Unlike her sister, she was minus responsibilities with no memory of tragedy. She was free to do as she wished. Briende she much admired, because she had embarked on an everyday course to make her employable, and a serious correspondence course to direct her reading and add cultural awareness. Maeve was delightful, seemingly unaffected by the disciplined road her mother had pursued. Uncle Gil was gently ageing, Mama as implacable as ever. Briende she thought more beautiful and more confident. Not only was she a representative for their own local council, she had been elected to Trevere's regional council, the ideas beginning to take hold. The environment was now a department, as was tourism. No doubt health care and a new more advanced library, complete with a reference centre pertaining to the old islands' history and language, were on schedule. News of Briende's own tragedy had spread beyond Brymadoc and this had undoubtedly facilitated her entry into local life. Facing an adult audience was now no ordeal to her; she was far removed from the nineteen-year-old who had married Ralph Maine, seemingly so long ago. There would, of course, be nobody to compare with him – ever. She craved for no man and had become adept at politely declining attentions. The great-aunts, though continuing in business, had drastically curtailed it. Their main interests remained engrossed in their nieces and throughout the three years of Briende's emergence into public life she had been exceptionally smartly dressed, always in the greatest taste.

Eleri, in the meantime, abandoned her art school fashions and reverted to what was considered respectable. She speculated on her ex-flatmates, wondering if they too had adapted. Letters seemed to suggest that this was so. She had decided on dress designing, and if this would mean branching forth into other ideas comprising period décor or equivalent, then that was splendid. The weeks of July and August were spent perfecting her French, or rather improving it. As a special concession she attended evening classes at her old school, meant for the summer examination failures. In this way she was furthering her own background in art history. In view of her years in a famous London school of art she was even allowed to give an occasional illustrated lecture. This she appreciated and enjoyed but accepted that her future lay in creating rather than in teaching.

Her own excellent training and firm friendships were a recipe for success. What's more all knew that she had beauty and talent. She could model her own creations and market them. She recognised, however reluctantly, that it was a man's world and occasionally she envied the protection offered by marriage. Nevertheless, she convinced herself that a marriage of convenience was not for her. Venetia and Juliette appeared content to let their parents use their influence concerning associating in the 'correct' circles. Having been sexually aroused she could not imagine any Heaven to remotely compare with initial animal attraction followed by fulfilment and marriage. It could mature into a delightful friendship, loyalty, serenity. The fairy-tale idea of falling in love and living happily in bliss forever and anon was something she scoffed at.

But physical attraction was of the utmost importance, however tempestuous or extreme or extravagant; for such as herself it was imperative. Sophistication in the form of social confidence and experience was also an important expectation. At nineteen she could afford to wait and search. An inner glow convinced her that she would find what she sought. Added to all this, a career of her own was not something she intended to sacrifice. Juliette, she considered, was in an enviable situation and Eleri wished her all the luck and happiness possible. She would not have exchanged the last three years of warm friendships for early romance and sweet domesticity. The pages of her life were just beginning to turn, and the book was to be a long one.

CHAPTER TWELVE

The Marriage

AN EARLY MORNING IN AUGUST, CRISP, STILL, SILENT. Eleri in a tweed divided skirt and beige ribbed jumper, Camus on his best behaviour, elegantly trotting through the Dell – no leaping over streams or fallen tree trunks with his usual gusto. Perhaps he was in tune with his rider's pensive state. Her world was green, her hopes were high as she cogitated on her future plans.

Camus jerked his head and sniffed. There was another horse approaching. Soon they were almost colliding on the narrow woodland path, the horses head to flank as the newcomer reined alongside.

"Good morning. Miss Eleri Madoc Blethyn, I believe." (*As if he didn't know*, she thought.)

"Yes, and you are Mr. Alvar Garonne."

"I heard that you were in London. You were but a little girl when I last saw you."

"Little girls grow up, Mr. Garonne." She hoped she had not smiled.

"Enjoy your vacation."

He half-saluted and rode on, the horses bumping as he passed on but not before she'd noticed the long dimples when he smiled, the pointed eyebrows and dark eyes, the slim thighs in white whipcord, the sort of garb she'd seen on the privileged men riding in Rotten Row, Jermyn Street, she thought.

And auburn curls, lifting in the breeze as she rode, the pointed breasts and heavy leather belt on her slender waist had not passed unnoticed. Each went onwards in different directions with a complete mental assessment.

Eleri understood his attraction to women, had been aware of him even as a schoolgirl as she and Rosemary had comfortably gossiped in the humid greenhouse. She pondered on why he had not married, as he must be thirty-two, she calculated, if not more. She rode in the Dell almost every morning yet had never encountered a single rider. She abandoned her ride and went home, not to Pen Melyn but to Briende.

She tied Camus to the iron ring at the gate, giving him ample rein for grazing on the succulent grass behind the wall.

Briende was at breakfast with Maeve, who delightedly ran to her aunt. Eleri swept up the flimsy blonde child before catching Briende's eye. "Finish your breakfast, Maeve, and gather some ripe raspberries for Aunt Eleri – only the red ones," as she fetched a deep basin. Not usually allowed to pick fruit, the child was all eagerness to begin.

The sisters sat opposite each other, Briende's instinct already primed. "What is it? You are positively aglow. Where have you been?"

"Riding. I came back early."

Briende looked directly at her. "In the Dell and you met Alvar Garonne."

"How did you know? You are a witch, Briende."

Briende smiled. "He is an attractive man."

"Yes, very. Why do you think he is unmarried?"

"He has not had to, women swarm to him."

"Seriously Briende – why?"

"Lady Bettina Styles, his mother, who is one of the Lancashire Styles, lives in the west wing of Campions. Anything that happens is her decision. I do not give much credence to gossip, as you know, but dismissed maids do talk. He is in no hurry to marry."

"But you have been approached Briende – twice."

"Did you not know, I'm the Blethyn girl? Lady Bettina hungers for land, more land and a sober daughter-in-law to go with it would be a bonus."

"I've never seen his mother. Does she leave the tower?"

"She travels, the wealth is hers. She is from the Lancashire cotton family and reputedly finds Brymadoc stifling."

"Why stay?"

"She is a good businesswoman, always on the look-out for dilapidated farm buildings or any waste land and guards her son's inheritance."

"Carry on..."

"I will not say any more. You know my situation locally. I glean information from what comes my way."

"What brought her here?"

"Marriage to Garonne, who came from Brittany. His father sold land for the extension of Brest Harbour. To people like Mama they are newcomers. Our grandmother remembered Campions being built."

Eleri smiled. "She probably envies the Madoc Blethyns. From my brush with history our cotton manufacturers were dependent, long ago, on the slave trade."

"Careful what you say, though you are probably correct. The Madocs always looked after their farm hands and domestics and have earned enormous respect over many generations."

"Tell me, Briende, do you know anything of him? Why, why, why, has he not married?"

"I do not know, but there were some rumours of a child by some spoilt but not wealthy titled lady. An army officer was paid handsomely to marry her."

"I seem to remember that he was in the newspapers – Rosemary and I were too young to bother."

"He was named as co-respondent in some society divorce case."

Eleri gasped. Having a past made him more interesting. Her sister knew her thoroughly.

"Tread carefully, Eleri – I know your impetuosity. No doubt you'll go riding in the Dell each morning."

"I resent that. If I wanted him, I'd get him without the Dell."

They both laughed, knowing the statement to be true. They both rose, and holding hands went to check on Maeve.

One further unplanned encounter in the Dell led to some innocuous conversation followed by an invitation to accompany him to an agricultural show in North Island. It was not exactly his kind of interest any more than hers, but as a landowner he was on the committee and he did own a fine flock of sheep. There would be more rosettes for his collection though his two fine hunters were of far more interest to him. However, a long drive in his new Jensen would more than compensate for any boredom he was likely to undergo. Eleri knew how to spread happiness, chat to farmers, wear stylish country clothes, admire the children and share the warmth of her personality. Eleri was happy. Memories of Spenser Fortesque were blending into some distant past. The agony of being confronted with him, on a daily basis, was fading and certainly served to make her more equipped to deal with this new fascination. It was electric being near each other, even when driving or riding. His experience and sophistication enthralled her, though she was aware of her superior intelligence and breadth of interests. Boredom, which he quickly manifested, was unknown to her; patience, which he lacked, was something she naturally had an abundance of. Both accepted that they did not delight in the same things or enjoy the same types of people. Though physically attracted, both accepted that they had a casualness about their relationship, accepted that they were vastly different species but acknowledged the overwhelming sexual attraction which inflamed them. Both were honest, neither bad-tempered nor vindictive; each was a 'taker' in the relationship, each knew what was being embraced. Fortunately, they liked each other as people but accepted that they were unlikely to do anything together except socialise.

The first socialising was at Juliette's wedding in late August. These were people he understood, felt easy with, and Eleri presented him to her friends with pride. He resembled an illustration for a Regency romance – cool, dark, fashionable, charming, appreciating the attractive young women as they appreciated him. Eleri made the usual stunning impact but only two men had ever attracted her. Alvar delightedly met an older gentleman from his old school and even met a member of his own club – Winthrops.

It was exciting to see her friends again: Venetia, dizzy as ever, pawn of her mother's ambitions; Juliette, with financial help from her own family and Claude's, had set up her establishment in Kensington, while Claude continued with a junior position at the Foreign Office. Prunie, with her delightful Abdun, was to marry in London and Cairo. Eleri also had a career in mind. She had her contacts. Venetia's 'coming-out ball' would no doubt add more. She discussed this with Alvar.

Eleri decided on a quiet wedding in Brymadoc church, family and a few friends only as guests. The fripperies and insincerities attendant on large affairs, the numerous guests, few of whom they were interested in, or likely to frequently meet, the planning, unnecessary expense, to her seemed – well – immature. She did not need it.

Mrs. Blethyn would have liked a grand local affair, Lady Bettina would not, but Mrs. Blethyn was somewhat chastened by the staggering turn of events. Belatedly her dream was becoming fact; an older man would be suitable for Eleri and she was more suited to him than her sister could ever have been. Though Mrs. Blethyn had a nodding acquaintance with Lady Bettina she was, to Mrs. Blethyn, a newcomer who had never really managed an estate, directed the foremen at harvest time, supervised the dairy, the brewing, or taught a shepherd to treat a sick sheep. The ancient skills in Mrs. Blethyn, incorporating generations of learning, practical common sense, strong leadership, were all gleaned from ancestors who had always managed the land. When had Lady Bettina witnessed huge harvest suppers or seen her mother's cast-off hat and dress on a corn dolly atop the hayrick? What did she know of sorting out the produce, which to dry, to use, give to the poor? What did she know of balms, possets, or poultices? Her ostentatious home and cool hospitality were as nothing, compared with that the Madocs or Blethyns had always offered. Modern music and dancing and brittle fashionable girls were what she had seen, and most of the time disapproved of, from what was heard. Well, her modern Eleri would cope and with her presence make Campions less false and add more substance. Though her daughter was a great enigma in many ways, Mrs. Blethyn recognised that she was educated and intelligent. Alvar Garonne would have something to reckon with. Added to all this was the thought that she was to settle in a grand house near her old home. There was no point in interfering with wedding plans. Eleri, as ever, would do things her way.

It was, therefore, on the Saturday of Harvest Festival

in mid-November that she became Mrs. Alvar Garonne. Not for Eleri the Honiton lace dress hanging forlornly in the attic, to be adapted once again. Her aunts made an emerald-green silk velvet creation in Eleri's still favoured Pre-Raphaelite style, with lacings up the back and along the sleeves. Maeve was the only bridesmaid and an identical dress had been made for her. The bride and her miniature attendant carried a long triangular bouquet of white blooms and wore coronets of similar blooms as a headdress.

Eleri, after much discussion, had allowed her brother to give her away, a practice she considered stupid and antiquated. To have Uncle Gil doing this duty would have been too reminiscent of Briende's wedding, as would the reception at Pen Melyn. So Campions was decided upon, with hired caterers and no speeches, or music; the buffet was to be a splendid one. Christmas time would have given them more planning time but again Briende had to be considered. The day was a great contrast, a glowing sunny autumn day, the rich blooms at their best, the trees decked in autumn finery, the gaudy leaves already fallen making a crisp path to the church door. Most of the villagers had joined the congregation; the Garonnes, though inhabitants, seldom involved in village affairs, were a source of curiosity. There was no Edwardian coach for Eleri; she was to be conveyed in Mr. Byatt's new Rover. Alvar would drive with his best man and school friend, Aubrey St. John, in his own Jensen.

Mrs. Blethyn, overwhelmed by the speed of events, was delighted, as presumably was Lady Bettina, though the two women had virtually nothing in common. Politeness alone would make them acknowledge each other. Briende would have been more malleable but Lady Bettina was delighted to see her beloved son arriving at some semblance of responsibility. She liked Eleri a great deal, admired her vivacity and definite approach. Over the years she had despaired at the baa-a-ing and mewing shallow fashion icons and pseudo-sophisticates who had often invaded her home, along with their limpid escorts. There were innumerable times when she had harshly quarrelled with her son over his choice of females, his general laxity about the estate and days of dissolute pleasures with his army of friends, either in London or on some country estate. His daring on the field was also a constant source of anxiety, particularly as his brother and father had been killed in hunting accidents – the former drowning after being thrown in a stream.

As she watched the handsome couple exchanging vows, she prayed, for what her prayers were worth, that they would settle down and beget an heir and be happy.

Mrs. Blethyn, who knew her daughter, wished them well, though never for a moment could she visualise Eleri settling for domesticity. Unlike Lady Bettina, she prayed fervently to the God she respected, in whose shadow she confidently walked. She prayed that Eleri would never know Briende's cruel fate, that the love the couple had for each other would increase and not wane and that the years ahead would be many. She dared not look Briende's way – dared not – because the tears would flow and Mrs. Blethyn was proud and controlled, without being hard or grasping, which was her view of Lady Bettina. At this juncture she prayed for God's forgiveness for her uncharitable thoughts.

Her mind reverted to Briende's wedding, six years ago. The myriad candles lighting up the dark mid-winter day, the patient snowflakes dancing on the ancient panes. Today was sun and promise, strong rays shooting through the stained-glass windows carrying regular lines of crimson, violet, green and gold, bending as they reached the emerald of Eleri's gown, emphasising her slenderness and rich hair. The altar silver gleamed, as did the lectern and crucifix, the restless sunbeams moved as if searching for a resting place, lighting the edges of the gold-leafed Bible and forming a halo around the ring. Mrs. Blethyn and Briende, their Celtic instincts at their most receptive, took this as an omen and each knew how the other thought. Eleri was radiant, her clear voice intoning the vows as she looked directly into Alvar's eyes. Both glowed but each knew what the other had undertaken. Like a caress the sunbeams hovered around them in a magical dance on that glorious autumn day. "Season of mists and mellow fruitfulness" – ah yes, but today was sharp sun and ripeness – the rich autumnal shades of the chrysanthemums and berries and fruit bathed in light.

The Reverend Britt pronounced them man and wife and Alvar Garonne raised his wife's hand and kissed it in a very un-Brymadoc gesture. It was not an arm in arm walk down the aisle. Royally he held up her hand at shoulder height as he led her to the West Door. Maeve mentally measured the precise distance, before falling in step behind the bride, inviting comments, comparing her with her mother's poise. The music rose triumphantly as if competing with the sun's rays, until the couple reached the great West Door. The beauty was infectious as family and friends gathered around the handsome couple, seemingly blessed with everything.

They honeymooned in Paris as expected, Eleri carrying, in her luggage, painting essentials. With luck a fine day on the Left Bank and a joyful painting would result. What better memento of a honeymoon!

The Pompadour Hotel was all that it professed to be, and the wide boulevards were magnificently bordered by glowing trees. Alvar faithfully followed the tourist trail, bathing in the splendour of the garden, days in the parks and along the Seine and the velvet nights in romantic restaurants, to return in a beautifully frivolous mood to the luxurious bedroom. This was heady stuff and the inflationary excitement of being together in the loveliest of cities, a joyful experience, but in spite of the rapturous nights, the wine, the food, the lovemaking, the days, to Alvar, began to offer a sort of cultural indigestion. As a final gesture he condescended to visit La Vallée-aux-Loups – Chataubriand's home not too far from Paris. Eleri, as a girl, had been fascinated by the romantic-looking politician and longed to see his celebrated house, where he had entertained his friends and mistresses. She hungered to see his amassed treasures, in particular the paintings, especially the one depicting Madame Juliette Récamier. So reminiscent of Josephine, the chaise longue on which she reposed was still there, as were many other artefacts Eleri was familiar with. In the exquisite grounds they made love on the dewy grass, in a sheltered arbour, birds singing around them, the kind autumn sun an unexpected bonus as the russet leaves clung to the remaining green of the rustling merrily in the slight breeze as if rejoicing with them.

A few days' sightseeing in comfort were pleasant, his much-admired wife a source of pride. He felt himself the envy of all men, whatever their age. He did enjoy the famous Folies Bergère, as did Eleri, the artistry much appreciated. Enthralled by the tall beauties, Alvar compared his wife with the best of them. Some memorable acts captured their imagination. Both were transfixed by a tall, thin girl, clad in what seemed like snakeskin, writhing across the stage, pulsating energy. They were close enough to almost hear her quick, sharp breathing, and the deadly hush, as the dulled lights alighted on her, while the rest of the nude cast stood statue-still, was an eerie experience, almost primitive. This could explain the same unattached men who nightly seemed to occupy the front stalls. Sad yet amusing was their verdict.

Twice Alva accompanied her to the Louvre, but a third gallery visit to see the Impressionist exhibition resulted in a definite 'no'. Good-naturedly Eleri kissed him in full view of everyone; she would never insist. Her world was not his world and this they both accepted.

At the hotel, a family of four had fascinated them for days – their wealth was evident, yet the beautiful daughters seemed bored. Judging by the overheard conversation they had become satiated by sightseeing and the topic of conversation appeared to be bridge. They had many friends and acquaintances in Paris, either living there or visiting, and rejoiced in afternoon bridge parties at the hotel. During coffee in the lounge was heard:

"I am not playing anymore," from the elder girl.

"Paris is wasted on you, Lucy, one would never believe that you work in an art gallery."

"I am only a part-time receptionist until I find something more interesting or someone marries me."

"Typical! You could come with me to the gallery."

"It's all right for you, you've 'done' art history. I find it boring."

Lisa, the younger, took a deep breath in exasperation. "Well, I'll go myself. Find somebody else for bridge, Mother."

"Isobel, I consider this rude and thoughtless of you. There are sixteen people expected, including us; without you we are one short."

Eleri, eyes alight, looked their way; Alvar's eyes had already feasted on the bored-looking Lucy, half-shielded by giant planters.

Mrs. Mason, for such was her name, in a cultured voice calmly apologised. "Sorry, we did not realise we were not alone. The plants obscured you. We were so engrossed in our own arguing."

From the bright uninhibited Eleri, "It's all right, I was fascinated by the art history mention. It is my own field – I too hate bridge."

She smiled at Isobel. "My husband is a splendid player and bored with art."

Everyone laughed. "Well, there's no more to discuss!

Perhaps your husband would join us if you could spare him, of course."

"I am planning to see the Impressionists exhibition; perhaps your daughter would join me."

There were introductions all round, Lucy's eyes fixed admiringly on Alvar. Isobel seemed delighted to be free.

It emerged that Isobel had studied at St. Martin's School of Art so had much in common with Eleri. Together they left the hotel. They delighted in each other's company, drank steaming coffee from clumsy basins in a scruffy café off the main thoroughfare, savoured the croissants, had a brandy and discussed art; what they had studied, what they had seen, before returning refreshed to the hotel.

Hungry and eager as if they had been parted for weeks, Eleri and Alvar delightedly met up in the early evening. Happily, they dressed for dinner. They loved each other but the sixth day of their honeymoon was a semblance of what was to come. The nights were still theirs, their passion insatiable, their delight in each other and their sumptuous surroundings was enough. Their polarity of interests mattered not in the least. In their own particular way they would be happy and content, revelling in each other's beauty and good nature, conscious of being admired wherever they went, seemingly blessed with everything as if the gods had been present at their christenings.

CHAPTER THIRTEEN

Eleri's Fashion Venture

By the time they arrived home Eleri was pregnant, excitedly and blissfully happy, her creative instinct enhanced by this new condition, her health, vitality, mental process and energy stimulated beyond belief. She would not waste the waiting months – the old kitchens would be cleared, the huge wooden tables scrubbed, the walls painted in cool pastels. Two of her aunts' best-qualified apprentices would be employed and Eleri would begin with her own establishment. The location, though remote from the thoroughfares of fashion and commerce, had much to offer and she had the utmost faith in the talent available, the quality of work as emphasised by the aunts, the loyalty and decency of the country girls employed. She would do her own designing and pattern making, something she had excelled at while training. At first, she would use Juliette's label, having decided to be in personal monthly contact, the rest of the time by telephone. Juliette was already establishing a clientele and would eagerly feed work to Eleri.

The rest was left to Hannah and Annette, who worked with her, and through her had entered a new world. Having never left the island, to be taken in turn to London, was beyond all expectation. Their workmanship could be compared with any from the Royal School of Needlework, and Eleri had absolute confidence in their efforts. Their initial skills had been practised on a black silk-velvet gown Eleri had designed for herself, while still slim, something to look forward to wearing – an elegant creation which merited a splendid baptism. She could wait, the opportunity would arise. Its splendour she did not share with Juliette; this would carry her own label. In the meantime, Juliette would continue to send measurements, Eleri create a style, material samples exchanged and lovely frocks result. An adjustable model was acquired and both young newly established designers were fired with ambition. Alvar, who indulged in country sports and meeting up with old friends, gave her free rein. His mother agreed with Eleri's industry and imagination – the old house needed an influx of energy and organising. The old kitchens had been in disuse for years and the old equipment disposed of. She encouraged her daughter-in-law, realising that she was clever and accomplished; she also loved that precious, easy-going, handsome, indolent son of hers. The fates had smiled at last and Campions would have an heir to displace Royston, that appalling grandson of hers, her daughter's child, so unfeeling, conceited and smug. Perhaps Alvar would begin to recognise his faults; he had always more or less treated him as an equal, which resulted in young Royston being even more unappealing.

Towards the closing months of her pregnancy, requiring a fresh interest became an obsession. A new fashion, based on sun and sea holiday styles to capture the partakers of the new prevalent trend of luscious, exotic holidays, especially on the French Riviera, seemed promising. Eleri had decided to market under her own label – why share inspiration! Wrestling with a name she pondered on the beautiful people she had encountered, Spenser S. Fortesque among them, but her imaginative self found no difficulty in coining a designer tag. Ralph Maine had captured her imagination as a girl, could she conjure up something from that? Suddenly, a flash of inspiration and she alighted on Ra-Maine. That was it; she became excited by the idea. 'Ra', the sun god of ancient Egypt – 'maine', the sea. She would have rays emanating from the prefix 'Ra'. With Briende's permission, this was going to be her trademark.

Alvar, in the meantime, had become bored with her pregnancy, but Eleri realised his low threshold when it came to patience or denial of any kind. His parties had recommenced, his seemingly shallow friends from the upper echelons of society were again gathering, fairly frequently. He now missed the charming, easy personality of his beautiful wife, her brightness and freshness as she moved from group to group, quickly assessing and adapting, admired by his friends, a figure of envy and suspicion to many wives or girlfriends. Overwhelmed by his pride in her during those first blissful weeks of marriage, he now felt deprived. His hunting parties became once more a success, the late suppers, loud music and puerile behaviour were again in vogue.

Eleri, to begin with, did her utmost to be pleasant, lively, warm and hospitable but, by the seventh month, had abandoned all socialising efforts to concentrate on exercise, interests, creativity. She had also taken to her own bedroom; his late nights and often intoxicated state were more than she wished to tolerate. Nevertheless, as yet she considered him faithful and devoted to her and happily expectant of the coming birth. His mother, lamenting what she considered his neglect, spent many happy hours with Eleri and wondered at her daughter-in-law's patience, but they shared the adoration of the handsome, charming, light-spirited man so precious to both.

One day, during the latter part of the seventh month, walking around the estate, almost the only exercise now undertaken, she wandered towards the stables. Much to everyone's concern, until then she had continued riding over the entire island. She loved horses above all animals, considered them beautiful and noble and had always been a conscientious owner of fine mounts.

During the latter part of her pregnancy she had also become acquainted with Royston Garonne Burnette, Alvar's only sister's only son and Lady Bettina's only legitimate grandchild. Fourteen years of age and at Eton, Eleri's only experience of him had been confined to the school vacation, and on short acquaintance, had considered that he was in need of guidance. She had witnessed his treatment of the stable hands and his harshness to horses; she had also learnt that Lady Bettina did not love him but that Alvar almost adored him, laughed at his arrogance, admired his prowess at hunting and shooting, was amused at his precocity and envied his excellence at several sports. Considered academically lacking, this too seemed something to be admired; "He's all man, just wait how the fairer sex will crumble around him," followed by guffaws of laughter.

Amused though his uncle appeared to be, his father, chief partner in Burnette, Adair and Toms, the foremost legal practice in Limorrnah, despaired at the thought of his son joining them. Alvar's sister, handsome and dominant, had no empathy with her mother and had, according to hearsay, spoilt Royston, her only son. By criticising his attitude from an early age, Lady Bettina had made herself unpopular.

When, after first meeting young Royston, Eleri had heard herself referred to as 'some filly' she complained to her husband. He had merely laughed, commenting that he had 'great taste'.

Though feeling heavy, lethargic and impatient at the hindrance of pregnancy on that hot July day, minus her usual optimism and bright spirits, Eleri walked to the stables to visit her much loved horse Comus, to find him being harshly treated and yelled at by young Royston. Comus was renowned for his strength and spirit. It was thought that no woman could handle him; highly bred and temperamental he had, even to Eleri at first, proved unmanageable. Any other rider was resented, and a battle of wills ensued if any other rider tried to mount him. Young Royston accepted this as a challenge while Eleri was indisposed and he turned up frequently at his uncle's stables with no task in mind beyond mastering Comus with the same assurance as his newly acquired aunt.

That particular morning having already heard a dog yelp after a kick, she loitered outside while another horse neighed and stamped in a sort of panic. Comus, after much protest was led outside, to be unexpectedly grabbed by a sympathetic Eleri. Speaking reassuringly, she patted his head and breathed down his nostrils to calm him, then held him still.

"Royston, you should be ashamed of the way you panic animals. Try kindness, just try, you could have better results."

He threw back his head and laughed. "They have to know who is master. A soppy woman can ruin a good beast." With this comment, he slapped the horse hard, sending it galloping at speed across the paddock before Eleri could release the reins.

She was dragged, then fell, hitting her head. With a yell of Shakespearean flair, "Look to the lady", to one of the grooms, he laughingly went in pursuit of the horse.

On an old door which had leant against the wall, Eleri, unconscious, was conveyed to the house by four of the estate employees. In her advanced state of pregnancy this they deemed the most dignified way of carrying her. Word had already been sent to Lady Bettina; the doctor had already been summoned and Mrs. Blethyn and the local midwife informed.

For two days Eleri lay in agony with a severe headache, something she had never experienced, pains in her legs and an excruciating pain in her back and abdomen. The baby was alive, exceedingly active, as if in discomfort, Eleri's heart pounding, her mouth dry, a ringing in her ears. She was very ill and about *compos mentis* enough, to realise this. They hovered around her, anxious and well-meaning, appearing and disappearing as she seemed to drift in and out of consciousness. In lucid moments she longed for the child to be saved, requested her mother's wisdom and medication but the modern doctor had no use for country concoctions and had also brought his own nurse. Mrs. Blethyn had never been confronted with such a complication as this and this was her own beloved daughter. In heaviness of spirit she left the room, to wait along with Lady Bettina, Bridget and Briende in an anteroom nearby. Temporarily the older women felt relatively close.

Alvar came and went. Unpleasantness did not suit him; this sort of situation was not something he could cope with. Why were things so complicated? He merely wanted a son and could not bear his lovely wife suffering. Of course, that young imp Royston had not anticipated this, but it was annoying, nonetheless. What could he do about it? He'd probably forgotten the whole quick incident or thought it of little consequence.

In his own agitated state Alvar fetched the family jewels from the safe, a traditional gift to the mother of the first-born. He thought to encourage her, cheer her up. He placed them on the chest beside the bed to gleam in the lamplight, as if his wife could possibly be interested. How could a birth drag on so? Eleri had never been ill, why this? He stooped over his wife, kissed her as he felt his own eyes brimming and disappeared again, in the meantime having summoned a staunch friend to come and champion him. They played billiards in the small library and attacked the brandy, until he made a further visit to his exhausted wife.

At seven-thirty that evening a tiny girl was born, perfectly formed, fragile. She was breathing but barely moved, having consumed her energy before birth. Eleri held her, though in spite of her weakness, almost accepted that the child would not live. A glow of love suffused her; she felt apologetic for not having managed to give her a better chance.

For the first time in her own life she emerged a failure. Dr. Phillpot now allowed Mrs. Blethyn to do what she could but already Mrs. Blethyn's instincts told her that there was no hope. She knew that Eleri and Alvar were not religious in the usual sense, or in the way she was, and asked that the Reverend Britt be sent for. Eleri was beyond caring; there was a blackness streaked with crimson in the pain in her head. As Alvar was unavailable, Lady Bettina agreed. Eleri was asked to name the child, which was meaningless as far as she was concerned, but the little girl had breathed, therefore deserved a name. Bleakly she said, "Call her Faye, a fairy child, just lent."

She sank into an exhausted sleep – a sleep of defeat.

The child died as she was being baptised. Mrs. Blethyn ordered Briende home – she would spare her this sorrow, but she was commanded to ask Uncle Gil to dig the tiny grave on the family plot. It was night; Mrs. Blethyn did not relish a brigade of sympathetic villagers in the morning. News travelled fast in Brymadoc and the matriarch, stalwart as ever, took over the arrangements, believing it best to get it over with, with the least distress.

The servants were sent in search of a box. Lady Bettina remembered that new books had been delivered to the library that week. Wrapped in a silk scarf, a white rose from the dining-room arrangement beside her, the little being was laid in the box, which was tied with a pale blue ribbon, another white rose in the knot and her name Faye Madoc Garonne written on the lid by Lady Bettina. A solemn little procession by torchlight, through the gardens to the churchyard, attended by the Reverend Britt and Mrs. Britt, the two grandmothers, Bridget and Mrs. Sullivan, the housekeeper, marked the end of the fragile life. There was no church service, just the evergreen words intoned over the tiny grave, after which the sad little group wended their way back to the house and with ladylike grace and her well-trained self-control Lady Bettina ordered brandy and some sustenance.

When Eleri woke towards dawn it was all over, masterly arranged by Mrs. Blethyn, with the least agony for all concerned. Eleri also noticed that Alvar had reclaimed the traditional gift given to the wife on the birth of the first-born. It was of no consequence. She sympathised with his disappointment and probably, bewilderment. He disliked anything unpleasant or emotionally taxing – things usually went as he desired and to feel cheated was alien to him. Eleri reasoned that they would both have to adapt and cope with this disappointment and perhaps be stronger for it.

She buried her face in the pillow, red hair tumbling around her like a pall, and quietly wept. Being sad was to her a new emotion.

CHAPTER FOURTEEN

Eleri's Foreign Adventures

A mere three weeks later and Eleri was regaining her staunchness of spirit. Feeling older, seared by experience and less strong physically, she accepted that she had undergone a horrific experience. Her tenderness enveloped her husband, who still appeared bewildered. She actually encouraged him to have friends staying; tried to help him plan the September shooting party, even suggested a few days in London with her, to meet some of her old friends and colleagues and spend some time with his own associates at the club. She had determined to visit her friend, hopefully attend a function and wear the splendid frock. Lovely as Campions appeared this summer, overwhelmed with kindness from friends and family, she still considered that a brief respite from familiar things, even a while away from Alvar, would help her adapt. She wished her headaches would disappear. These were to her a hitherto unknown malady.

Alvar dutifully spent quiet hours walking with her in the surrounding countryside; they even walked to the Stones, but for them, these held no magic, no romance. She knew that Alvar was endeavouring to be kind and companionable and loved him for it, though she realised that neither mentioned their shattering experience. It was as if the whole trauma had not occurred; they were merely 'toned down', more placid, more mature. Eleri was confident that the essence of their relationship was still intact; each was still deeply attached to the other, though both realised that theirs was a tumultuous love affair rather than a friendship. There was a canker somewhere.

Eleri found that she still had to rest but understood that the malaise was spiritual rather than physical. She spent more hours reading and resting than ever before. She made every effort to eat sensibly, exercise daily and consume large quantities of water. Unconsciously she was responding to some sort of natural healing.

It was in this unsettled state that she left for London alone, as her husband wanted to stay at home; some old friends were visiting. Normally he was content to accompany her to the city, either driving over the new bridge or using the ferry and train. Usually they stayed at the Alberry Park, sometimes with friends, or he would stay at Winthrops, his club, and Eleri with Juliette. On the whole the waiting months had been pleasant, exciting and expectant of much happiness and fulfilment in this sort of pattern.

Before leaving Alvar, on this particular weekend she made one request, that Royston was not welcome at the stables. This Alvar refused, though he promised to supervise the boy's behaviour to the staff and animals. Uneasy at the thought of leaving Camus to his ministrations she calmly rode him to join Briende's horse at the Pen Melyn stables, believing that this would be a permanent situation.

There were always small rifts between Eleri and Alvar and these seemed to be widening, yet the physical attraction of each to the other was still magnetic. Present trials were a mere setback; optimistic as ever she thought they would recapture the early bliss. Her headaches remained but were less severe. She would recover.

Feeling slightly wan but excited, Eleri arrived in Juliette's London home to be greeted warmly by her and Claude. They were expecting their first child and were particularly sympathetic towards Eleri and her recent loss. Anticipating her arrival, Juliette and Claude had requested that Prunie and Abdun include an invitation for Eleri to a dinner at the Baronchester, where funds were being raised for the Sudan Famine Appeal after the recent much publicised natural disaster. Enthralled by her friend's black velvet creation, Juliette requested that she wore it. In the meantime, Juliette would unearth a zircon tiara and choker necklace. Such accessories Juliette was now apt at acquiring, having recently started showing designer frocks at various venues, and was already beginning to establish a clientele. As Juliette planned to show her own works, suitably modelled, along with the creations of two or three other new designers, during the short interval, she hoped Eleri would join them. The whole exercise was meant as a dramatic relief from the dancing and socialising, a proportion of any ensuing orders to go to the Famine appeal. Eleri's tall slenderness, red hair and white skin would be a perfect foil for the silky black velvet and Juliette was confident of orders ensuing. If so, Eleri did not mind passing the design on to Juliette to use as she wished. The day would come when she would jealously guard her creations, but temporarily she was non-competitive.

Juliette was happy and contented and resented not Claude's fulsome appreciation of Eleri's magnificence. At the dawn of the Hollywood style of glamour Eleri was something to be noted.

As Juliette had foreseen, all eyes were on Eleri as she entered the splendid ballroom; the narrow fold of black velvet over one shoulder, the long bodice, low back and a fantail silk pleated back insertion, gracefully opening as she moved, was new and unusual. She appeared poised, regal, distinguished; she was as Prunie and Juliette had envisaged. All longed for Venetia's presence, as well, but Venetia was travelling abroad. More than anything Eleri longed for Alvar; this sort of occasion was one they could have comfortably shared. His admiration mattered greatly to her and she wistfully remembered their evenings in Paris a mere nine months ago, the attention they commanded when her high spirits seemingly flew in feathers, compared with the recent heaviness.

Abdun proudly presented her to his superiors from the embassy, gathered some more from the London Arab community and all shared a table with some of Claude's friends from the Foreign Office. The flowers, the décor, the music, the food, were a level beyond that which Eleri had previously experienced and again she wished for Alvar's presence. In the heat of the excitement one of the headaches, which still plagued her, returned. Sensibly she relegated these attacks to the severe fall before the confinement.

Imperceptibly, after the dance ended, she moved to a curtained alcove in a wide corridor off the ballroom. A very beautiful young Arab woman, earlier introduced to her observed Eleri quietly withdrawing and after charmingly extricating herself from her dancing partner, followed Eleri and joined her. Each of the young women had been fascinated by the other, so different but so strikingly attractive, almost a foil to each other. In the cool alcove they became acquainted.

"You do not mind if I join you? We met earlier. My name is—"

"Sherene Khalif, I remember."

"And you are Eleri Garonne." She pronounced it, "El-er-ee," which sounded charming.

"I hear that you have also been asked to walk the catwalk; next to you I will seem too fat."

"Curvaceous and beautiful in that exotic dress."

(Eleri wondered whether it was one of Juliette's creations – rich royal blue, peacock green, cerise, shot with gold thread.)

Both smiled. A beautiful woman knows she is beautiful. It is false modesty to pretend otherwise.

"Will your husband mind? I am on my final dance

with freedom. I am returning to be married. In my country displaying one's feminine charms is the greatest vulgarity, almost a sin."

"My husband would be delighted. The more men admire me the happier he is – knowing of course that I am faithful to him. Have you been living in London for long?"

"Yes, six years. I am a doctor, just qualified. I love my work and am loath to leave it."

"Why should you? Do they not require doctors in your country?"

"They certainly do but I will be relegated to treating women or children – maybe work in a maternity hospital. With oil wealth my people are gradually, very gradually, becoming Westernised."

"If I were a doctor nobody would stop me. Incidentally, should we not be returning to the others?"

Sherene touched her arm. "Of course, though I must confess that I am enjoying talking to you."

There was an expectant hush at the table. Prince Saleem Mahmoud el Eys had just entered. Sherene knew him but being a woman, had to allow Abdun's boss to do the introductions. Eleri thought the prince the handsomest man she had ever beheld; no doubt other women thought likewise. He was a taller, darker replica of Alvar and as he bowed formally to her, he even appeared to have a similar suave attraction.

Supper was served as soon as he joined the party. During the supper about two dozen models were to parade before joining their respective groups for their own meal. From their table Sherene and Eleri were the only two.

The frocks were a great success. Eleri made the usual impact, sufficient for film producer Simon L. Seznick to approach her later after seeking an introduction. Charmingly she made it clear that acting did not appeal to her. She knew herself well enough to know that she could never be other than she was. What she knew of the shallow world of Hollywood was not a world she wished to emulate. In accepting his card, she wondered whether someday, behind the scenes, she could become involved – costume, adaptation of books for the screen, décor, research – yes, there were avenues. One day perhaps? But there was time enough.

Back at the table, noting the excitement and variety of the other diners, Eleri was reinvigorated. Her high spirits, responsiveness, charming self-effacement and sweetness, all combined in a beautiful woman, added to everyone's enjoyment. She knew that she was recovering, her natural responsiveness with people in full sway. 'Enchantment' was the word some used. Juliette smiled inwardly, remembering Eleri's raconteuring in the students' flat and was pleased to see some of the old colourful charm returning. Juliette also noticed that her friend did not touch wine. Eleri had already reasoned that the recent assault to her mind and body would perhaps render her physical state intolerant to any stimulant.

The highlight of the evening was one dance with Prince Saleem el Eys, who was in London on business. He spoke English, with effort, but was more relaxed speaking French. In a happy mixture of both languages they communicated adequately. He gradually relaxed as the dance progressed and mentioned that Sherene had told him that Eleri had been ill and with typical Arab generosity he invited her to a sea journey, as he phrased it; his yacht was moored near Greenwich.

In spite of dire warnings hammering in her head she was tempted, but wisely said she'd think about it. And still thinking she returned to the others. He had said that Sherene would be returning home in the yacht and Eleri thought he had said 'tomorrow'.

Her old adventurous self seemed to be taking command, but this man was too attractive, even for her, in her present state of not being interested in any man. She reminded herself that she was married and tonight had revived her spirits; she knew that the healing process had begun, she had recovered 'tone'.

Consumed with excitement she surveyed the assembled company – international, successful, wealthy, the mixture of languages and customs intoxicating. This was her type of society, so much colour, experiences, diversity of occupation and a general confusion, as if each was endeavouring to become established in a shrinking and competitive world. Aware of her own luminosity and how much she enjoyed the pulse of life, she planned, before long, to become established in London, directing her own business, her own retreat, utilising her own irrepressible energy.

When Sherene extricated herself from the goodbyes and politenesses at the closing of a superb function, Eleri did likewise, leaving with her to collect their wraps; a chance to talk while waiting. "Sherene, are you really returning tomorrow? Or did I not hear correctly?"

"Yes, I have to. The ship sails home and what pleasanter way of travelling! It has to return because Prince Saleem is sailing to America on the *Mauritania*. He is always travelling on business."

Conscious of her own heart thumping, Eleri immediately decided to accept the offered holiday. Never again would such an opportunity arise. "Sherene, I will accept the prince's offer if you are not averse to my company."

As they accepted their wraps Sherene squeezed Eleri's hand. "Of course, it will be pleasant for us both, it will be less lonely. I have sailed before without a companion. The staff will be returning with us, eager to get home, but apart from looking after me, they are far more content with one another."

"What about clothes for Arabia? Cotton or what?"

Sherene laughed. "Dear Eleree you must be hidden. You will wear a chador, as I will. I have a spare one. You will also cover your glorious head."

She laughed again. "Pack that gorgeous frock in case there's a Westernised dinner-dance at one of the embassies. Sometimes there is and the excitement of make-up and smart clothes is beyond imagining. Phone me in the morning, here's my card. I'II tell you when I can collect you. We sail in the evening – something to do with tides." Another squeeze of Eleri's hand and she was gone.

Later, snug in dressing gowns, sipping cocoa around the elaborate electric fire, Claude, Eleri and Juliette relived the supper dance, discussed the people, the fashions, the food. Socially and financially the function had been an outstanding success. Several orders had materialised and the ticket sales had exceeded expectations. Eleri's invitation to the Middle East crowned everything and her friends encouraged her to make the most of such an unusual opportunity. The prince was enormously rich; they speculated on his palace, way of life plus domestic life. Juliette had asked whether he was married and learnt that he had two wives but never took them outside their environment. They all laughed at the spectacle of Eleri in a chador in the middle of all this, wondering how she would cope and having no fear that she would fail to cope. At the same time, all three hoped that Sherene would not desert her. With inferior French and no Arabic, and clueless with regard to customs, there could be problems. Claude wisely suggested that Eleri accompany him when he left for his office in the morning and on the way equip herself with foreign currency from Thomas Cook, just in case matters became complicated. She would also purchase toiletries and cotton and woollen garments while in the West End in case she got an opportunity to wear them.

CHAPTER FIFTEEN

To the Unknown

THEY EMBARKED IN THE EARLY EVENING THE following day, Sherene having collected Eleri as arranged. The accommodation on the yacht was luxurious. In the hour before sailing, using the ship's stationery, Eleri wrote to her husband and then her sister.

Dear Alvar

With thoughts of you occupying my mind during this hour before I sail, I want you to know that I am not being overtaken by my restlessness and sense of adventure. This is no whim. I need to be alone, to think, even perhaps to dream and experiencing a real journey by sea, for the first time, will be a fine way to heal in body and spirit.

I am travelling with an Arab girl, a doctor

trained at Guy's. Her name is Sherene Khalif, and we met for the first time last night when I attended a charity function at the Baronchester with Claude, Juliette and an assemblage of people, British and foreign, mainly Arabs.

This yacht is owned by Prince Saleem Mahmoud el Eys and is returning to its home berth. The prince is not on it but many of his servants are. They are all in long cotton shirts, men and women, and the women being Moslem have their heads covered. Sherene and I will do likewise when we arrive at our destination. Cannot you just see me?

Last night I wished you had been there; you would have enjoyed it immensely. Sherene, intelligent, glamorous, educated and thoroughly Westernised, is returning home to be a dutiful, submissive Arab wife, her charms hidden beneath a chador, but she is in love.

I have no idea what the mailing system is, or whether there is one, but you know I will keep in constant touch. This letter will be posted before I sail. My warmest regards to your mother and a happy season to you. I hope you will miss me.

My love,

E.

P.S. The prince is as handsome as you are but has two wives and is allowed four.

A similar letter was sent to Briende with a few more sisterly details. There was no point in explaining anything to her dear mother who had despaired of her many times over. She sent her mother her warmest love and thanks and appreciation via Briende, with orders to stress her gratitude for all she had done during the unhappy period. She also promised to purchase sandals and a chador for Maeve to wear to the Christmas fancy dress party at school.

After some further farewells along the quay, Sherene rejoined her in tears – full of mixed emotions. Her ex-fellow student friends had loaded her with gifts and flowers and entreated her not to waste her medical studies, but also to do what she could for the sad state of women in her new domain.

As they sat together eating their evening meal Sherene instructed Eleri on what to expect. She emphasised that conforming was important; life would otherwise be intolerable. She told her of the heat of the day and acute cold of the nights, the sounds to expect, the poverty and riches, the contrast between modern wealth and acquisitions and the age-old ways of the indigent people. Many had been Bedouins before the onset of oil wealth. She was not to express opinions or be confident and always keep eyes lowered when talking to men.

At intervals both enlightened young women would laugh then appreciate the seriousness of it all. Conversation led to the prince. "Tell me, Sherene, what do you know of the prince?"

"I have known him for years. His father's new-found wealth enabled him to be educated in France."

"I cannot help but speculate on why he invited me to

accept this holiday. He is very attractive and found me so."

"I understand the drift of your thinking but the Arab male, in spite of opportunity, is far less sophisticated than his counterpart in the West. He found you beautiful, a novelty, something different on his arm, if there's a function. He is also kindly, can afford to be generous and I had told him you had been ill."

"Is he married? Or was I being teased by Claude?"

"Have no fear on that score. He has two wives I know of and several children, but the wives never accompany him anywhere."

Eleri laughed. "Surely physical attraction is basic enough in all men; I wonder if he remains faithful."

"I doubt it, but he is a Moslem and any third marriage would be to a Moslem."

The intriguing situation appealed to Eleri. "But, Sherene, you said he would possibly take me to a function when he returns."

"He would, it would be a status thing, a lovely Western lady as an accessory." They again laughed.

Eleri was beginning to look forward to her Arabian sojourn.

It had been a warm and pleasant interlude. Once more Eleri found joy in a female friend. She longed to tell Sherene her recent sad story. She felt that some of it was known and Sherene was a doctor and would listen, maybe advise, certainly help to unravel the tangled thoughts which plagued her.

Eleri rejoiced in this new friendship and hoped that it would continue, even after they went their separate ways.

As she lay in her elegant, rather ornate, cabin that first night at sea, Eleri had time to reflect on what had happened in the past three days. Carried on a wave, leading she knew not where, to placid or rocky shores, she nevertheless tried to remain sane and strong. Events seemed to have overtaken her at an alarming rate, but now alone, desire kept her awake.

She thought of Alvar, the impact of her letter and tried to contemplate his reaction. She had been genuine and wrote as she felt – kindly. Was she infuriating or interesting, she wondered? Would her character prove a strong enough bastion for the temptations her beauty could invite? Alvar would not reason it as succinctly but Briende would. Her heart was with them at this lonely moment as the sea broke gently against the porthole, with precise, accurate, timing between each splash; the stars, hanging low on invisible threads, peered in between each heaving motion, like some never-ending monotonous game aiming for the unobtainable.

In the quiet and isolation, while resisting sleep, she tried to marshal her thoughts.

As her lids grew heavy she mentally recited the names of all the people she knew and loved, or had loved, or merely brushed with along the way, mentally naming them lovingly one by one, including the sweet baby she never knew. Such was her usual sleep potion. On this contented note she fell into the sweetest sleep she had known for several weeks.

She awoke early but in that interlude between sleeping and waking she seemed suffused by a clarity of vision, as if a mist had been lifted from her overcast mind. It was as if some unseen hand had grasped her befuddled emotions and disentangled the chaos. In her recent confusion it had not occurred to her that Lady Bettina's hopes and the future of Campions rested with Alvar and his issue. Eleri reasoned, for the first time, that young Royston would otherwise one day inherit Campions as well as his father's established law practice. Lady Bettina would desire the estate to survive, as so much of it was her creation, mostly her money and her energy. Much as she disapproved of her grandson's unappealing attitude and manner, as yet, he was after Alvar, sole heir.

In that quiet and isolation in the middle of the Mediterranean Sea Eleri's decision was made. She would return to her husband, do her utmost to accept him with his inadequacies. They were just 'different'. The physical attraction was intact, he was not evil or cruel, merely spoilt and weak. She was not aware of any hidden depths, but nobody really knew anyone; that's what made life poignant, interesting, dangerous and intriguing. Her sense of fair play always surfaced.

On this happy note she greeted the new day, swiftly changing into cool cottons and a long soft cardigan, to clamber onto the deck, look at the never-ending sea, sniff the pure air and consider that 'all's right with the world'.

She longed to join her new friend for early breakfast, tell her the full story, weigh her judgement. Women do communicate and an intelligent, educated woman's opinion was worthwhile.

Eleri returned to her cabin to write another letter to

Alvar; she would mail it at the next port. With no idea of where she was, she imagined the next port to be Gibraltar, unless the ship had passed the Straits during the night – she would have to check, being such a novice when it came to sea journeys. She wondered whether there was a map or time zone displayed somewhere. For the first time she really understood the expression 'I'm all at sea'!

An hour or so later she entered the dining salon to find Sherene already there.

"Good morning, Eleri, I thought I was early."

"I've been on deck for half an hour and written a letter, I'll have you know." Eleri smiled.

"You slept well? I certainly did once I settled. It took a long while because this is a momentous step," said Sherene.

"I too lay awake trying to marshal my emotions into some sort of logical pattern."

"Tell me."

"I've a feeling you know something of my recent trauma, from Juliette."

"She told me you had been ill, had a horrendous accident and lost a much-wanted baby."

"Is that all? Did she mention that I was in a serious dilemma regarding my marriage?"

"No – just asked me to look after you, said you had much talent but could be impetuous."

Eleri smiled, thinking any impetuosity was usually laced with a dollop of common sense.

"Well, what are your plans? Nobody can deny that you need a 'space' to sort things out."

"I am grateful to you and the prince but frankly I

don't know where I am going or how I am going to cope. Without you I would be lost in a place I know nothing about."

"Have no fear, I will see that all is well. You will find a strange land. I can accept both cultures. Reared in one, education of another, about to marry into another."

"Is your husband from Saudi Arabia?"

"No, educated in Cairo but from Dubai."

"And you will live…?"

"In Dubai. That is where we are heading but after the Suez Canal we'll stop along a Red Sea port for a while. It's a godforsaken place – desert behind and around but do not worry, we will be safely catered for."

Eleri had to accept this without further enquiries.

Suddenly both laughed, Sherene at Eleri for her absolute adventurousness, Eleri at Sherene for giving up a promising career and sophisticated existence for love. In a way both were victims of circumstance, and each accepted this.

"Would you like to tell me what happened, Eleri? I am a doctor. Try me."

Eleri told her story between sips of orange juice, sticky buns, scrambled eggs and coffee.

She succinctly related Royston's appalling behaviour and her first taste of disliking a human being. She mentioned Alvar's predictable behaviour, taking away the gifts and inviting a friend to console him during the crisis. She skimmed over her suffering and barely mentioned the child, except for her mother's prompt disposal of the small being, late that night. She told of her encouraging Alvar to gather some old friends for the shooting season and yes, hinted at the shallowness of many of his friends – the women who seemed false and brittle though glamorous, the men clubby and shallow, relying on their own kind as props. 'Puerile' was the most appropriate word.

"These women – are they likely to divert your husband?"

"Probably. They offer no challenge; they have nothing to say but say it constantly."

Sherene laughed merrily. "I've met them."

"I take it that your husband is very attractive."

"Desperately so and, in case you ask, physically we are extremely compatible. He is also suave, polished, perfectly mannered, easily bored. Life must be a sensation. And you – is not life also a sensation? Or just a part of life?"

"It is a part of life. I am eager to learn and experience more, more, more but I have a strong work ethic, imagination and energy and, dare I say it – honesty. Also I have no desire to be anyone other than I am. Acting ,for instance, was never for me in spite of a recent offer." Eleri smiled again. "Judge me."

"I conclude that he is more contented than you are."

"Certainly, as long as nothing disturbs his equilibrium. He hates any inconvenience and is not good at facing up to adversity."

"A sort of immaturity?" ventured Sherene.

"I suppose that is correct. I wonder what you really think. I hardly know you yet feel as if I had known you forever."

A waiter approached to remove the used crockery.

For a few moments, the young women were silent and thoughtful, as if digesting what had already been touched upon. Sherene then raised her eyes to Eleri's. "Your career? Does your husband object to your independence?"

"Not in the least, as long as I'm available socially and sexually. Actually, he is rather proud of me. When I do flit to London, he is ever disposed to accompany me, though, once there, we frequently go our own ways. Then we meet up for dinner or theatre or a party. We seldom fail to spend the night together. We have had a delightful year."

"You have obviously considered that a child of yours was meant to inherit. I understand that there's an estate."

"Believe me, until I awoke early this morning, with a mind clearer than it had been for some weeks, this realisation had not occurred."

"And now that you have thought about it you will return to him and embark on a baby straight away."

"You read my thoughts, Sherene. I can barely wait to be back with my husband."

"Even if he proves unfaithful, considering the long reins you seem to have given him? The Anglo-Saxon male is meant to be monogamous. An Arab wife has no choice."

"Yes, even if he has been unfaithful. While I am available, he will be mine alone."

"You are in love with him."

"One can be 'in love' without loving but still hopelessly attracted."

"In a way, Eleree, I envy you. I am in that hopeless situation, but I feel crippled by the thought of my lost career."

"Once the first overpowering flush of deep,

immeasurable attraction is over, when common sense begins to reign, you will – unhesitatingly will – become immersed in the opportunities offered, in that newly-rich land. My Celtic instinct or common sense stipulates this." Eleri laughed. "I mean it. I am convinced, absolutely, certain. I can see you establishing clinics, holding a post in a new hospital, bringing enlightenment and modern Western practices, all instigated by your cajoling. You will not remain a docile, hopeless, appendage."

"I hope you will be proved correct."

"I will."

On this happy note they left to stroll on deck before the sun became unbearable, before Sherene returned to her books. Currently her interest revolved around the more common diseases attacking children in the region she was about to live in. At the momen, preventive medicine seemed the better approach. There was immeasurable ignorance, little idea of diet or basic hygiene. The women in particular, were in dire need of training.

"Do you anticipate prejudice, Sherene? Serious blocking of anything you attempt?"

"I certainly do – unquestionable suspicion. I will be considered a modern virago tainted by the West. Marie Stopes or Elizabeth Anderson would not stand a hope where I am going. But once settled, I will try. I will take courage from the likes of Mrs Gaskell, George Eliot or Charles Dickens, who did their best to reveal the ills of society." Sherene laughed at her own audacity but continued, "Eventually, I hope to have my well-qualified friends coming to assist me. Watch the headlines!"

Eleri too laughed, visualising the conflicts ahead.

They became silent for a while, each imprisoned in her own conflict. The seemingly never-ending ocean offered no answers. To Eleri it was not Byron's ocean, its "breast gently heaving, as an infant's asleep" but an impatient sea, a constant turmoil beneath it. To Sherene it was distancing her from all she had learnt to accept, the advancing world, a contrast to the less developed world of her immediate future.

Next morning, before they awoke they had entered the Suez Canal. Soon after breakfast the young women on deck tried to absorb all they saw and heard. To Sherene, it was not a new experience; sharing it with a friend made it more interesting. To Eleri, it was magical. Nothing she had read or heard about it matched the reality. The first surprise was its narrowness, the second the weird terrain around it – the wadis – some with Bedouin encampments, the scrub, the heat and in parts the silence. Eleri could not help reflecting on Disraeli's foresight and imagination in persuading the young Queen Victoria to become involved with a strong stake in its construction. His patient, studious clarification to the young Queen, as with map on desk he outlined its importance in simplifying the passage to India and the Far East. Eleri fondly visualised the two bent over maps or charts, in the library, at Windsor or Kensington Palace, the stolid young Queen hanging on his every word.

When they eventually reached the port of Suez another excitement awaited them. Eleri had never witnessed such activity or noise. The odours, the clamour, the combination of port sounds and human voices shouting in a strange language, the absolute strangeness of it all, was intoxicating.

Suddenly Sherene leapt in the air, crying, "It is Abou, my beloved Abou," and with a quick leap across the gangplank he was on deck, embracing Sherene, before she joyfully introduced them, her friend and her lover.

Abou el ben Har, clad in a tailored linen short-sleeved shirt and matching trousers, but with Arab headdress, seemed exotic and fascinating. Eleri understood Sherene's captivation. About six feet tall, with very dark deepset eyes, straight brows and a long narrow nose almost in line with his forehead. From her classical studies Eleri seemed to recollect that this signified beauty. Yet he was Semitic in appearance. His smile revealed small, square gleaming teeth. A narrow moustache and one canine tooth, unaligned with the rest, gave him a saturnine appearance when he smiled. *A man to contend with* was Eleri's first thought. Charm and kindness seemed to emanate from him; one look at them told Eleri that they were in love and she excused herself on the pretence of some errand or other and doubted whether she would join Sherene for the evening meal. She minded not – in fact, she shared their joy.

Eleri returned to her cabin and wished for one person to talk to in her own language. She understood the loneliness of the dumb and the deaf. Not being able to communicate was the saddest human condition, like a constant mental pain with no applicable medication. She decided to read the *Tatler* or *Homes of Beauty*, not being inclined to the novels about doughty dissatisfied females depicted in the few chosen books hurriedly packed by Juliette. No doubt her friend intended her to take courage if the situation became difficult, as she felt it now was. How could she survive without Sherene; had she been abandoned? Her optimism returned. Of course not, such thinking was unworthy of her.

Several hours later, when the boring, endless sea had seemingly become an irritant, a note arrived from Sherene. "I apologise for my deserting you for such a long while, but I know you are happy for me. Join us for supper as Abou has a staggering story to relate. Affectionately, Sherene."

During the meal that evening Abou certainly had an extraordinary tale to relate, which he did with much drama in a charming manner, in his quaint English interspersed with French for effect.

An architect by training and education he was a partner in a large Dubai-owned enterprise operating mainly from Cairo, but with most work coming from the new oil states and Germany. Currently, they were employed building new government offices in Hamburg, chosen after the usual tendering and flattered at having been chosen above the French and Americans, though most of the teaching in Cairo had been by the French.

On arriving in Hamburg at his hotel, the Brunhilde, and presenting himself at the desk, to claim his pre-booked room, doors shut, and bells rang and within seconds, police appeared. Without ceremony he was bundled into a heavy vehicle and driven to a police station, in the meantime being roughly handled and treated like a criminal. Having no German, he could not defend himself or ask for explanation. The questions, however, were waiting for him and as these were in German he could not answer. His wallet and papers had already been confiscated. They took his lack of German to be strategy, part of his training and the papers part of the espionage plans. He wrote in French, in block capitals, to request to see his employer, whom he named. To no avail. Thrust into a cell and left overnight, he lost sense of time, without his watch and there being no clock in view. His only hope was that somebody would miss his presence at a meeting and start enquiries, or even if somebody in authority would check with the name given and hope he could be identified. There had to be some mistake.

There was. His Semitic features had led the authorities to believe him to be a Jew named Abel ben Haran, who had strong business interests in Poland and Germany but who, aware of what was beginning to happen to the Jews, had been instrumental for some time in clearing his investments and transferring money to Switzerland, where 'J' was beginning to be put on Jewish passports to distinguish German Jews, securing their money, from ordinary German holidaymakers. His name, so similar, to that of Abel ben Haran, carelessly telegraphed to Hamburg police after tracing the bookings for train and hotel, led to Abou's wrongful arrest. In fact, Abel ben Haran had been observed for months and his movements noted. The previous day he had been on Abou's train, as it journeyed northward.

Abou had on previous visits to Germany been aware of what was happening to the Jews; like other foreigners in Germany he had noted the wearing of yellow stars, had heard of pogroms and confiscation of Jewish wealth but had never become involved or given it any thought. It would pass. At the moment, in Germany an excitable man called Adolf Hitler was firing the people to a new patriotism. Of course, nothing would come of it. Now he thought differently. Not being overly sympathetic towards the Jews, he still seethed with the insult to his proud person and had already, while waiting for his friend's yacht to arrive, written to *The Times* and *New York Times* and was intending to do the same to several papers in Cairo and Paris. He considered it his duty to mankind. His firm was considering moving out of Germany once the present commitments were completed.

A few short years later Eleri was to remember this story, told with passion and bewilderment. Abou was convinced that a new war was brewing and he was one of the few, outside Germany, with the first-hand experience of that undercurrent of aggression; young men in uniforms exercising in the small town squares and villages, a militaristic climate everywhere and a new pride and confidence absorbing the whole nation.

CHAPTER SIXTEEN

Eleri Embarks on a Long Journey

EARLY NEXT MORNING THE YACHT DOCKED IN A seldom-used harbour at a remote settlement along the long Red Sea coast. Ushered ashore, insisting on carrying her single holdall, in case of loss of documents, along with Sherene, Abou and some of the ship's staff, Eleri stepped on land. A more inhospitable location could not be imagined. In the short walk between ship and town Eleri witnessed poverty and human degradation hitherto unimagined. Accosted by odours and hectic shouts in a language she did not understand, seeing the squalor, the poverty, the half-starved dogs and mangy cats, was an uncomfortable experience. Where the path from the boat met what served as a road, she found people, adults and children, stoning a sick and dying dog, who according to them, had 'the evil eye' as Sherene explained. Eleri's sweet nature was affronted: she drew the hideous scarf over most of her face, rather than appear squeamish to her escorts. The others seemed unaffected; they were products of these seemingly barbaric lands.

Outside each miserable hovel, lining the road, no more than a track, covered-up women, seated on cane-type chairs, crocheted and gossiped. Soon the heat of the day would send them indoors.

They reached a sort of square, merely an open stretch, where Abou summoned a decrepit human creature to find him transport. The lined face, encrusted with dirt or sand, yellow teeth and greasy turban was enough to alienate any visitor. With exaggerated obsequiousness and many compliments, grovelling and gesticulating, he led them to a dilapidated vehicle. With no ceremony Abou virtually pushed him into the driver's seat and they drove off, the driver being completely ignored, in spite of his veracity. Eleri could not help comparing him with the chatty cockney cab drivers she had so much enjoyed, with their colour, humour and knowledge of London and such a contrast to this sad sample of humanity.

In half an hour or so they arrived at their destination; it seemed to be known to the driver as he did not have to be directed. They arrived at a castellated huge, white-stuccoed (or so it seemed) flat-roofed expanse, entered via huge much-scrolled iron gates complete with Arabic symbols and a name. None of it meant anything to Eleri but Sherene obviously knew the place as she greeted the gatekeeper, lshid, by name. Abou half-frowned at her, a reminder that he should do any talking. Sherene nudged

Eleri, as if to say, "See what I mean?" After driving up a scrubby driveway, no gardens as one would expect, they entered a cool dark porch-way, to be met by one of the most beautiful middle-aged women Eleri had ever seen. Attired in a chador and scarf, there was a grace about her; the kindness in her eyes and the sweetest smile could not diminish what Eleri immediately thought as an inner beauty. The attraction to each other was immediate. Abou introduced them, though he did not venture inside; he gave a sort of half-salute by raising his hand and walked towards the other end of the complex.

Hagar, for such was her name, with extended arms pressed Sherene to her. She then held Eleri's offered hand and placed it between both her hands in a gracious welcome. Hagar was in charge of the women's quarters, in the vast edifice. The three women walked together along a dark tile-floored corridor reminiscent of an abbey. When they reached a far door Hagar, advised by Sherene, demonstrated her special knock – knock, knock – pause – knock, "Hagar." The door, when opened, revealed a room appealing in its simplicity, richly embroidered white bed-hangings on a low bed, embroidered cotton pillow slips, a brass elaborately-scrolled bedhead. The window shutters were almost closed against the heat and these were surrounded by snow-white muslin curtains. The floor was of marble, as was that of the bathroom plus water closet off the bedroom. The bath was a hip bath ascended by steps; the taps were of gold. The huge wall mirror had an elaborately scrolled frame. Eleri was charmed and smiled her thanks to the departing women and surveyed the bedroom in detail.

Soon she seated herself in a white cane chair, on cushions of intricately embroidered and appliqued silk. There were few ornaments and no pictures. The bed cover was hand-crocheted lace. Eleri hoped to be able to purchase such exquisite accessories, her trained eye able to appreciate such creative efforts.

She washed in lukewarm water. There seemed to be some sort of plumbing but there was no electricity; the metal lamp on the bedside table, with its beaded shade around a glass funnel, had a leather-covered box of matches conveniently placed beside it. There was no timepiece if time meant anything. Ever eager for adventure she stepped into another world. Truly, this was *Arabian Nights* territory. Even the pot holding a dismal palm she seemed to have seen before in her *Arabian Nights* story book, Ali Baba suddenly seemed real. As she gazed around the room, she spied a small black lizard, absolutely motionless in the far corner, as if glued to the wall. Sherene had warned her, knowing the horror of some Europeans of such creatures, but Eleri was not squeamish and it had its own jewel-like beauty – quite fascinating. How could a living thing remain so still?

After a brief rest, a sudden loneliness descended on her. Ever in need of people, solitary confinement to her seemed the ultimate punishment. She would write up her journal, write yet another letter, then in the half-gloom try to read. Perhaps she could open the shutters just a fraction more. The ever-present merciless sun was something she could grow to loathe.

After an hour or so, Hagar gently knocked her special

knock and announced herself. Eleri was so happy to see her and longed to talk to this sweet being. She smiled as she gratefully accepted the silver tea tray, bearing a, by now, familiar long-spouted, pot-bellied teapot and a woven metal dish of honeyed cakes; there were also dates and slices of lemon and some milk, probably goat's milk. There was a nanny goat tethered somewhere, she had heard it bleating.

She consumed the strange repast and tried to fend off her loneliness, remembering the happy occasions she had known her usual way of lulling herself. She reached for her sketch book, paints and charcoal, her ever-present salve. Sherene was undoubtedly with Abou and would remain with him for the rest of the day. She was happy for her, her delight and surprise at meeting him was memorable. She glowed with love.

Eleri must have slept, for Hagar's knock aroused her. There was a note from Sherene asking her to join her for the evening meal. Feeling overjoyed, she tidied herself and within seconds, it seemed, joined her friend.

"Sherene, I thought you would dine with Abou."

"No, custom again I'm afraid. It is politeness to spend the first night of a reunion with your hosts, in this case, the male cousins. He met them today."

"You had the day together, I hope."

"Some of it. There were people he had to greet and business to discuss, their affairs rather than his. They like word-of-mouth accounts of places and likely trade outlets."

Eleri felt compelled to ask how the time would be spent

before they rejoined the ship. "There's only tomorrow. The men are planning to go inland. Barakat, that's the cousin, has to visit a far oasis."

"You mean they are going into the desert? How I would love just one glimpse of the inner desert! How far is it?"

Sherene laughed. "It is two hours' driving at least to get there and two hours to get back, providing there is no hindrance like a sandstorm. It can be very frightening."

"Have you seen the real desert?"

"Many times. I'll see how they feel about it; they may consider us a liability. Hagar would have to come, of course. Talal wilI drive, he has some English. I'll try to charm them, tell them it is a politeness to an eager guest. It will mean excess preparation, but Hagar knows the routine; I'll send you a message."

"I'm so excited. I could not bear to be shut in all day and you told me that it would be a breach of etiquette to wander out alone."

"Indeed it would be brazen and shocking. One never sees a woman alone. But I'll be around."

After a pleasant evening meal which seemed to have lasted a long time, they bid each other goodnight.

As promised, later that evening a note came from Sherene; mission accomplished. "Hagar will call at dawn. She will bring all essentials."

Another adventure to look forward to. Before the sudden darkness she would open the shutters sufficiently to watch the bustling activity close at hand. She saw water skins being filled and much to-ing and fro-ing, plus much argument it seemed. A group of Arabs were obviously preparing for a journey by night. She distinctly heard the camels complaining, a strange sort of braying. The contrast between this scene and the gleaming Cadillac and Mercedes, near what looked like the front entrance, was staggering.

The largest stars were already visible in a slate-blue, cloudless sky. A level plain appeared to lie ahead in the fast-fading light, blackened by millions of pebbles. Moonbeams gleamed white on little patches of sand. There seemed to be yellowish streaks of scrubby grass. Or was it an illusion? Without the excitable chatter, as the travellers loaded their beasts, the silence would have been eerie.

Almost too excited to sleep, she tried to remember what she had read of the desert, particularly William Gifford Palgrave's account. It had been compulsory reading before painting in oils (three colours only allowed, the extra shades created) an atmospheric desert scene. The resulting picture, an examination requirement, now hung in Alvar's study. She never expected to compare the imagination with reality. How inspired she and others had been with William Gifford Palgrave's words – he the son of the founder of the Public Records Office and brother of Francis, compiler of the *Golden Treasury of English Songs and Lyrics*, so familiar to thousands of students.

In the morning she would experience more of this strange land.

She seemed to have barely slept when Hagar's knock woke her and she entered with gesticulations, advising her to hurry before the sun awoke. Even so, Hagar appeared gracious and kind. She helped Eleri get organised then smiled her exit.

The old and young, loading what looked like a clumsy elongated van, talked endlessly. Talal, the young driver and one of the family, asked Barakat to sit beside him. Behind sat Abou and Hagar, then Sherene and Eleri. The substantial place behind was occupied by boxes and sacks and baskets of food. The water skins and spare can of petrol were covered with bales of dried grass, then a tarpaulin – a shade from the rapid evaporation. Any desert journey could lead to disaster and any speed depended on the prevailing wind or the prevalence of sandstorms, always a hindrance.

As the sun rose the distance seemed a vast sea of fire, the near distance seemed an immense ocean of loose reddish sand, unlimited to the eye. The whole scene reminded her of Holman Hunt's terrifying painting of 'The Scapegoat', or biblical pictures from her Sunday School book, *A Child's Bible Stories*.

Soon they reached enormous ridges running parallel to one another. Capricious winds flirted with the summits, an awesome sight to behold. A surreal experience seemed the most apt description. Around them were countless pebbles of basalt and flint, now and then patches of withered grass. Talal had enough English to keep Eleri informed, but in the deep silence even he spoke in whispers as he pointed out Venus, looking immense in a deep, blue velvet sky. Everything was harsh and monotonous and cold; the searing day was yet to come.

A couple of hours later they entered a settlement,

around a meagre pool. They alighted and followed Barakat, as if in formation; she seemed known to the assembled inhabitants. They were greeted with tremendous hospitality and flowery compliments. Talal said that the people were mostly Bedouins, with a sprinkling of Uzbeks or Kirghiz among them.

Extravagant greetings and gestures of welcome were politely responded to, to mark their arrival. Talal, enamoured of the Bedouins, explained to Eleri something of their way of life. Before the onset of oil wealth in those areas, the Bedouin was a rather contented, fatalistic being. There was no civil or religious strife, as he cared not for such. He fought over a brackish well or a desire to get a horse or camel into his possession, or a piece of miserable pasture, as his only object in war. They were also puritanical regarding morals.

The truck was unloaded and leather goods like bags, sandals and belts, carved boxes, dates in large plain boxes, items of metalwork and, strangely enough, what looked like bales of silk, were loaded onto the vacated space. Eleri realised that Barakat was trading and these purchases would be enhanced in factories somewhere. Barakat's contribution amounted to hard fruits, tea, coffee, biscuits – some with the English manufacturer's name in evidence, Jacobs or Crawfords.

He had also brought crockery and cheap gaudy jewellery and other products too well packed to identify. She saw no exchange of money.

After consuming treacly coffee and small, hard, sweet cakes, with much ceremony they departed for the uncomfortable journey homewards as the punishing sun rose higher. They would be back near the coast before the red-hot blasts of air and sand foamed around them. Talal said a simoon was expected. Eleri could not imagine how any human being could choose to live in such hostile territory.

As they returned to the truck, Barakat in the lead, Hagar, who was behind, beside Eleri, pointed a slender finger at Barakat, then lifted the finger in the air, as if in warning, as she faced Eleri and looked directly into her eyes. The message was clear even without the medium of speech. Her quick imagination alerted her to any danger.

After returning and consuming a meagre meal, Sherene suggested that they both rested for the remainder of the day as the next day would mean another early departure to the ship for the continuation of their voyage.

It was late afternoon. The sudden nightfall would soon be upon them. Both were tired and ready for rest, as they wished each other a fond goodnight. The heat on the homeward journey had been unbearable.

Once in bed, though immeasurably weary, Eleri found that sleep eluded her. She was pleased to be leaving at dawn. Remembering Hagar's warning, which she did not take lightly, she slipped out of bed and secured the huge iron bolt on her door. Against what, she wondered; there were no men in this area of the complex. She was not a nervous person and was usually ready for any contingency; her attractiveness had always supplied her with a measure of caution – common sense, she called it. Even when dashing around London she kept a constant vigil, and also when travelling across the country alone before boarding the ferry to Ilandia.

In the darkness and silence, she experienced an acute loneliness; not loneliness as in a bath or walking in the woods but the loneliness of the soul in unfamiliar surroundings, minus the ability to communicate.

She did not know for how long she had slept when she was awakened by a knock on her door. Light but insistent, it was not Hagar's precise knock and it was not Sherene, who would have announced herself. It must be the middle of the night. She could not see her watch. She remained perfectly still but alert and distinctly heard the doorknob tried. The bolt, of course, held and she heard soft footsteps move away. Her heart raced wildly and there was an old convulsion of her insides; she was bathed in sweat.

She was not as brave or worldly as she had hitherto thought herself to be. In her own land she could cope but not in this remote, foreign domain. She suddenly determined not to continue to the other side of the peninsula. She would go home – but how? Perhaps she could ask Talal how he went to school in Cairo. Once there, using her contact with Prunie's Abdun, known at the embassy, she would somehow get home. Alone, from here, the situation seemed fraught with danger.

Having made this decision, she napped spasmodically until startled by a knock – pause – knock, knock; when Hagar's welcome summons aroused her at dawn.

She quickly packed her meagre possessions except for her sketch book and charcoal. She tucked the sketch book under her arm. Thus, she greeted Sherene, who was already seated at the low breakfast table in a corner of a huge room. All was dark and silent except for a newly lit great lamp, almost opposite, flickering away before settling to a steady flame.

A long narrow window to the left of this would soon admit the rays of sunrise. Between the lamp and window Hagar sat, motionless and almost sad. Did she regret the young women's imminent departure?

Eleri had determined to sketch this lovely woman; her serenity, sweet smile, kind eyes, had made their impression. She asked Sherene to ask her permission for Eleri to sketch her. She so resembled the saints and nuns in some of her art books that she was determined to portray her, then work her sketch into a splendid painting executed with love, a copy of which she would, by some means or other, have conveyed to her.

Hagar nodded her permission. As she did so one sharp ray of dawn sun stabbed into the space between lamp and window, giving a surreal image. Excitedly, Eleri worked rapidly, producing two images, one full-face and one a three-quarter face sketch. Her friend was impressed by her accuracy and speed. On being shown the sketches Hagar smiled the widest smile they had yet seen produced, as Sherene explained Eleri's purpose. What a picture she would paint!

This done Eleri found the courage to tell Sherene of the night's fear and her determination to abandon the journey and try and find her way home.

"Eleree, we both know who the likely visitor was.

In fact, he resented taking us yesterday. To him, a fair-skinned married lady, travelling without her husband, is an invitation."

"I never even looked at him. I kept my eyes down as you advised."

Sherene laughed. "I too was only half-respectable, though escorted by Abou, because we are not yet married. Even so, the women rarely accompany them. Anyway, how do you propose to get home from this back of beyond place? It is more than I would attempt, and I've been reared in these lands."

"I thought perhaps Talal would accompany me to Cairo today. He knows a way, he's at school there. Once there I could contact Abdun. I could pay Talal for his company and for the journey."

"That they would certainly not understand! You are – what do you say in English? Clutching at straws. Talal will next go to Cairo, when he returns to school, at least two weeks from now. He will not leave from here but from Jeddah, where Barakat has a trading ship and some workshops. Only private yachts stop here and then but rarely. In case you don't realise it, there's a very long desert journey, through inhospitable regions, to get there by truck. Even you would be alarmed."

The idea of being left without Sherene and possibly having to meet up with Barakat on the ship terrified her. Pale as she was, she became paler, even in that gloom. Sherene quickly noted this.

With tears of disappointment Sherene looked at her friend. "I did so want you at my wedding. Dubai is not as primitive as this place. Are you quite sure? You would find an English sector there and would not feel so isolated."

It was Eleri's turn to moan. "What can I do? I seem so far away from normal shipping lines or even railways."

Sherene thought quickly. "Come with us as far as Aden. There's a thriving city and there is a British garrison. The consulate there will take up your case and arrange a journey home. You have money to stay there for two or three days if necessary?"

"Yes, Claude saw to that. Even so I'm sure they have a bank, which could contact my bank. I won't be a liability."

"I would see you cared for; you know that."

"How long will it take to reach Aden?"

"About one and a half to two days, depending on whether the yacht anchors at Jeddah; I believe we are not stopping anywhere along this coast. Do you feel better?"

They held hands, vowing to be always in touch.

Suddenly, a small boy entered, a child they had not before seen. He advised hurrying; the men were impatient. He felt very important being entrusted with a message. He almost shooed the young women in his eagerness. He then ran to Hagar, telling her to make them hurry. With her arm around him she came to the women. She hugged Sherene and clasped Eleri's hands in both her own. There were tears in her eyes. It was a sad moment for the three women – and without words Eleri and Hagar had communicated warmly. Eleri would never forget this hauntingly lovely woman.

CHAPTER SEVENTEEN

The Adventure Ahead

THE JOURNEY TO ADEN WAS UNEVENTFUL, A REPEAT of their earlier journey. Eleri tactfully allowed the betrothed couple to be together. Now lighter in spirit, she minded not being alone, and her old optimism returned. That night she joined them for the evening meal in order to plan Eleri's passage home from Aden; it was likely that she would have to be in Aden for a few days.

Abou had one day's business to conduct. It was then to be a sad parting for the friends. Eleri could not help but muse on whether she'd have continued to Dubai, had not the strange trespasser tried her door. She now wore her scarf and chador with triumph, like some academic or clerical garb, a mark of hard-won accomplishment. She felt confident that a passage home from Aden would be easily acquired. She could also telegraph messages home and maybe do some shopping in a real casbah.

After disembarking and clearing customs of some sort, Abou hailed a cab and they delivered Eleri at the consulate. Abou made his elegant departure, kissed Sherene chastely and arranged to meet her that evening. He emphasised the need for care. She was to stay at the consulate doorway at six o'clock until this particular driver arrived to convey her to the yacht.

Ah, English at last! Her request to see the consul, after much deliberation, was granted and with Sherene beside her, she explained her plight. Her education and bearing were evident, and she was politely listened to. A secretary was sent for to see if anyone from the army or diplomatic service was about to sail for Britain.

The minor secretary was an Irish girl, Roisin McKenny, and she was in charge of such items. The bubbly fresh brown-haired, blue-eyed young lady came armed with papers. Yes, Major Johnstone and family were returning in four days' time on the *Lancastria*. She could quickly arrange a berth for Mrs. Garonne and she could travel with them if this was acceptable. She could not promise a comfortable top-deck berth, but she could possibly arrange something. Mr. Crispin Fenwick thanked her, dismissed her and told her to try.

Sherene approached the question of accommodation for Eleri in the strange city. This Roisin heard as she reached the far door and she chirpily announced, "She can stay with me for two or three days," adding, "if she wishes, sir."

Her Irish lilt reminded Eleri of Bridget; she felt a touch of homesickness and quickly said, "Yes, please let me come with you."

Mr. Fenwick shook hands with both women and smiled as he said, "That's settled, then. Miss McKenny will make the arrangements. Things seem to have worked out for you." He politely added, "It has been a pleasure to meet you both and I wish you a pleasant journey in your different directions."

"Now that is English smoothness," said Sherene, as they emerged into the relentless sun.

"And this is Irish charm," said Eleri, as Roisin breathlessly joined them.

Arrangements were made to meet outside the consulate at six o'clock – Sherene and Eleri to say goodbye, Roisin to escort Eleri to her meagre flat a short distance away.

The rest of the day the two women shopped with delight, had a meal, had another meal, drank coffee and speculated hugely on what lay ahead. Time too soon dictated their return to the consulate, Sherene to the waiting cab as arranged by Abou and Eleri to meet Roisin.

It was a particularly sad parting, and both were overcome. They had known each other for a mere three weeks, yet their initial attraction seemed to have forecast a great bond. They had shared experiences, emotions, confessions, opinions and a warm friendship. They would meet again; of this they were positive. Sherene entered the cab, Eleri was left with Roisin.

They walked to Roisin McKenny's flat. The dirty busy streets were crowded with an amalgam of nationalities – Orientals, Indians, mixed Asians and a variety of Arabs. The varied styles of turban and clothing, the rough transport public and private, the hawkers outside each bazaar or shouting their wares outside their own shops; some mere cavities in walls or parts of collapsed buildings. The mixed voices and odours, the strange food displayed, the furtive glances or beaming smiles, added to the unfamiliarity. Arm in arm they trudged quickly through the teeming throngs to where Roisin lived. She seemed quite confident as she negotiated the way she daily went to and from work.

Her abode was a plain concrete block consisting of four apartments, two on one side of the entrance, one above the other, two on the other side. There was a scrubby walled back yard for hanging out washing and two sinks made of stone, which were somehow plumbed for cold water. Hot water had to be boiled on a sort of Primus stove.

Roisin's apartment was on the upper floor to the left of the entrance and reached via an uncarpeted staircase. She lived alone. In the other three apartments dwelt an Indian couple, a French family and an Arab family. There was no sign of children. It seemed amazingly quiet for such a city, though the building was some distance behind the main thoroughfare.

Roisin chatted prettily. Her story was a typical one. Convent bred, she and her friend sought adventure by answering an advertisement in *The Lady*. A military family in Aden, with four young children, required two nannies. What an adventure if they were accepted! They would be together with a British family. After an interview by a Dublin agency, they were accepted.

After two weeks Roisin's friend, Cathy Ann Callahan,

was homesick. Their employer spent most of her time partying at the base or with friends and referred to her children as sprogs; she could hardly wait to pack them off to boarding school in England. The children were undisciplined, wilful and rude. Cathy Ann hated them, but Roisin had some measure of pity and tried to be kind and instil some pattern to their lives.

Cathy Ann saved her earnings for two months to pay for her passage home. She pined for Ireland and her boyfriend, Dermot O'Hara, who had a new farming job in County Wicklow. With luck he hoped to manage the farm later, as the owner was ailing and his only son, at university in Dublin, was not remotely interested in farming. She crossed off each day on the wall calendar – each day a step nearer home.

Roisin on the other hand, more canny, read the advertisements in the local English bulletins and watched for a secretarial post, however minor, for this was a way to save. Eventually, she acquired her present post at the consulate and was thrilled to be independent.

Eleri found Roisin delightful. Her simple apartment was spruce and fresh, her domestic planning faultless, each day's menu and tasks carefully planned. The sisters had trained her in thrift and instilled order and much wisdom. She faithfully said her prayers and attended a nearby Catholic church and dutifully went to confession.

She made Eleri welcome in the sweetest way, preparing a fresh bed on a couch and quickly providing a simple meal using a primitive stove, all the time chatting amicably, her speech interspersed with homespun philosophy.

"One has to remember this is not a Catholic land. Decent Irish girls must be constantly alert. Tomorrow, I will take you to the casbah. It would be foolish to go home without seeing a real Arabian market. Alone I would not venture."

"You go to church alone?"

"To be sure, though I wonder why because Father Costello is not like Father O'Brien. Oh no – he is sour and gallops through mass. I cannot believe that Our Lord approves. He also smells of liquor and that's one good thing about the Moslems – they are supposed to disapprove of strong drink."

"What nationality is this unappealing priest?"

"Could be Spanish or Italian or a mixture, nobody seems to know or care."

"And yet you dutifully attend?"

"A lifetime of habit I suppose, it takes hold of one. I feel sinful if I do not attend, though I ask forgiveness for my unkind thoughts."

"When do you think you will return to Ireland?"

"I am aiming to save one thousand pounds and my fare, then home to all I care about."

"After working abroad in a consulate, you will easily find work in Dublin."

"I have no doubt, though I will go to evening class and improve my speeds. The work here is too easy and not offering much challenge to improve any skills. It is a very minor position."

"And then you will search for a husband?"

"Indeed, I will not have to; Kevin McFadden will be

waiting." She opened a drawer and produced a sheaf of letters. "He writes twice a week."

"He must be in love to be so conscientious."

"He sure is and has been for two years. He blushed like the rose of Shannon when he first clapped eyes on me, and it has been ever thus."

"Did you meet while at school?"

"Oh never! The Holy Sisters would have been appalled. We were taught to avert our eyes when passing the boys' school in the town. We met during the last holidays. We were both on Christian youth work, helping the underprivileged of the city. I taught catechism and he taught carpentry. It was our last year at school and he wanted to get married the following year. That is one reason my dear parents did not object to my coming here, so far away. Mind you, I have not told them that Cathy Ann is no longer with me; is that deceit on my part, do you think?"

Eleri listened, transfixed. Roisin's freshness and warmth eased some of the sadness of her parting from Sherene. She did not care if she waited a whole week for a passage. Roisin was also charmed by Eleri; it was wonderful to have someone to talk to, someone so worldly. "Tell me about Kevin. What does he do?"

"Oh, I should have mentioned it. He has been hired by Father O'Brien to renovate pews at St. Mary Magdalen. He already has two assistants and he only nineteen; he plans to have his own business in the future. Even my parents approved. Unknown to him they have paid a secret visit to the church and surreptitiously looked at his workshop in the town. They believe he has a fine future and will be better off than they are owning a small grocery store in Coreyhaven, though it is the only one there."

"You are an only child. They were brave to let you come so far."

"They are good people. It was a financial sacrifice to send me to the Convent of Our Lady, but they wanted me trained to be independent. I was only ten when I left home. I heard that they both cried for days. Now why am I talking about myself? What brought you here?"

Without detail, Eleri told her of her accident and disappointment and how she accepted a holiday from a rich Arabian prince, friend of a friend, a lady doctor. She said that, like Cathy Ann, she became homesick, mainly because of being unable to communicate, and how she longed to return to Alvar. Eleri considered her story too complicated to elaborate and she did not want to install a wedge into this sweet new friendship. She was just two years older than this girl but by comparison seemed to have lived an entire lifespan. She recognised Roisin's courage and careful demeanour; how she wore calf-length skirts for work and fresh short-sleeved blouses; how she threw a light scarf over her head when passing a group of building workers, when walking home. She had an in-built common sense, as well as a quick intelligence, and would tread carefully.

"Well tomorrow, after work we will go to the casbah. I will finish at three. They will not complain, I'm sure, as I frequently work overtime because it is less lonely than being here for a long night. I do not go out alone. But you must cover your bright hair all the time as you will frighten the donkeys. They won't have seen red hair."

Eleri laughed. "Don't you worry, I am as cautious as you are. I have already been well-instructed by a real Arab lady. I feel safer here than at the last place I stayed at where the women barely existed; I wondered that they had the daring to breathe."

"It may sound smug, but the office seems a haven of security each day once I turn in from the street. There is a sort of order, some rules and regulations. I sometimes wonder whether the multitudes here know anything of order or security."

"I suppose we are all victims of our heritage. They probably consider us strange as well as unchaste."

Roisin agreed.

Eleri slept beautifully that night on her makeshift bed. Had she been religious she would have given thanks for her good fortune in finding Roisin and Sherene, each so different but knowing both an unforgettable and uplifting experience.

Next day they did go to the market and Eleri's shopping carried a comparable bliss to a good day at Harrods. She now smiled as she recollected her last foray there and could barely imagine how she could have been so bewitched.

If only Roisin knew, she thought, *the pure Irish girl would be rightly shocked.*

The noise, odours of coffee, stale or over-ripe fruit, perfume, sweat, sweating canvas and wool, animal smells, even people's breath. Such was the casbah.

There was a hyped excitement, strange music and thousands of voices it seemed, all yelling their wares or communicating across stalls to one another. Many had their goods on the floor around them. The variety of wares was amazing. She knew that Aden, as a trading post, collected and sold all manner of goods.

She purchased a chador and beaded sandals for Maeve and embroidered linen for the young relatives in Limorrnah, shawls, handbags, silk ties and waistcoats. For Uncle Gil there was a splendid wallet and silk tie.

All these necessitated a new leather suitcase, which could itself be a gift. Eleri felt immeasurably happy.

Next day, when Roisin returned from the office, Eleri's travel documents were handed over. Two days later Eleri met up with the Johnstones at the consulate to travel with them to the ship, as had been kindly arranged.

They were to be tenuous companions but at least they had been introduced. On the homeward voyage Mrs. Johnstone emerged as a brittle, over-dressed, over-indulged colonial wife, having experienced many enviable postings. She was bored, unopinionated and demanding, constantly smoking and sighing her impatience. She was averse to Eleri conducting a conversation with the major but Eleri, even with the chador, would intimidate any insecure or unintelligent woman. This, Eleri accepted and understood, and she behaved accordingly, avoiding them whenever she could, even arriving late at meals and abandoning coffee, in order to shorten the time with them. She felt sorry for the major.

She did, however, while on deck one day, accidentally

meet the major. His wife was either resting or pouting. Her children's nanny had given her notice and decided that during the journey home her duties were over with. This was surmise on Eleri's part after gleaning bits of information as they stiltedly conversed at the table. Judging from the major's moodiness something of this kind had emerged.

On deck, the major sat nearby and thoughtfully threw his cigar overboard, as he patted the deck chair beside him. She moved a yard or two closer.

"We may be going in the right direction," he said. "I've a feeling we won't be returning to Aden. My duties will take me elsewhere."

Eleri understood immediately. Several times on that ship, she had overheard similar observations.

"You believe that Britain is heading for conflict with Germany."

"Yes. I was on a mission in Germany last month, staying at a schloss in the Hartz mountains. The old owners were Jewish, refugees from Russia. Their grandchildren had no idea of their Jewishness and the parents and grandparents were non-practising Jews. Having escaped a pogrom in their youth, they had decided not to reveal their origins. However, while I was there, I experienced the arrogance of what is known as Hitler Youth. Athletic young men, aggressive in behaviour, ordered drinks, sang patriotic songs, kicked over chairs and marched out without paying, shouting 'Heil Hitler'. It won't be long."

Eleri remembered Abou's story and related it. Major Johnstone showed no surprise.

Eleri was to remember the relating of these two incidents. She would be among the very few, in her own country, who had heard at first hand.

The major excused himself before his wife appeared in search of him. To be found in conversation with Eleri would precipitate unpleasantness.

Elei had never, before, approached England alone from abroad. To see the gleaming cliffs of Dover in weak sunshine, to feel the sharp breeze, aroused in her a sentiment she did not consider herself to possess. There was even a hint of a rainbow in the intermittent drizzle on the breeze. What a welcome! Her favourite Bible story, as a child, had been God's promise in the rainbow. It made more of an impact than much else with which she had been indoctrinated. Later on Iris, the messenger, running along the rainbow linking the gods to men, had also captured her imagination. Once when she had to illustrate something from the ancient myths, this is what she chose to depict. The finished work had a delicate airiness, which still delighted her, when she gave it thought.

Oh, the order on the dockside, the uniforms, the checking-off sheets; each to his allotted task. The discipline of the arriving guests, patiently queuing. What a contrast to what she had recently seen!

The Johnstones, who had a military car waiting, offered to take her to London, but she politely declined by telling a white lie, that she had to visit someone nearby. She did not wish to further impose upon them. Civilised handshakes were exchanged and good wishes for the future uttered. Eleri retied a loose label on the major's suitcase. She did not then know that she would next see his name on a wartime casualty list.

After the first train to Victoria, then the underground to Wellington, she made her usual way home. Blake's green and pleasant land had never appeared pleasanter. She had certainly gained something from her sojourn in a desert land. Safely ensconced in a corner seat, her roomy, comfortable cardigan and headscarf worn for comfort rather than modesty, she slept for the last couple of hours. She entered into no conversation; she had had a surfeit of talking on the ship and with Roisin. Instead she would relish her own thoughts and dwell on the joy of reunion, feel intoxicated by her myriad blessings, not the least of them, being a native of a blessed Western island.

Her first task on arriving at Dewary was to telephone her brother and extract a promise that they keep her return a secret, as she herself wanted to meet Alvar at Campions. Gaston could deliver her from Limorrnah next morning.

Gaston was breathless on hearing her voice. She sensed the excitement. Yes, they would meet *Sea Dame* at ten-thirty that night and yes, he would take her home in the morning. They had received her letter from Aden, but she had then been unable to give them a date or time.

Ten-thirty on a cold September night and dear familiar *Sea Dame* chugged into harbour. The four children had been spared the usual bedtime and eight loving faces in the dim light greeted her as she came down the gangplank – pale, they thought, and thinner in the eerie lights but with the same glowing hair and wide smile; the same delightful spontaneous Eleri, who dropped her luggage and ran to their waiting arms. Throughout she had managed her own luggage, but it was now of no importance.

Gaston and Wynn retrieved the bag and case, stowed them and with the women and girls in one car, the men and boys in the other, they convoyed home. They had a prepared supper around the fire, gifts were unpacked, and the conversation was unceasing. So many questions, so much news, so much excitement.

Even after Wynn's family had departed, Sîan, with her practical Welsh outlook, was concerned for Eleri's debut next day. Did she have something pretty to wear? Were all her clothes crumpled?

When Eleri awoke next morning her own pale-blue linen dress, much the worse for wear after travelling, was hanging newly laundered and pressed outside her bedroom door. Sîan had decided that this was the dress to wear for the reunion with Alvar.

Later that morning Gaston, after a brief telephone call to Alvar, delivered Eleri at her door; Lady Bettina and Alvar were waiting. He then left abruptly to convey the news to his mother and sister. Mrs. Blethyn had convinced herself that her daughter had gone forever. Gaston felt privileged to be the messenger of such thrilling news, hoping, at the same time, that his fascinating, mercurial sister had had her fill of adventure.

CHAPTER EIGHTEEN

Eden Regained

ELERI GASPED. THEIR BEDROOM DOOR, PUSHED OPEN by Alvar, revealed a room exquisite in its beauty. Eleri's practised eye, at a glance took in the silver and blue striped wall covering, brocaded bed cover to tone, lavish window drapes in pale blue silk, a blue carpet and Chinese rug. Lady Bettina's own Louis Quartz reproduction furniture replaced their carved oak furniture. Oval framed pictures of the same period hung on the east wall. The vista of the park from the huge west window was as before. On hearing that Eleri was definitely returning Alvar and his mother feverishly planned to refurbish that room. They hoped to erase the sad memories. Before Eleri could utter one word, Alvar's lips were upon hers. The convulsive shudder overcame them; the electricity was as charged as ever. All became a void except their own selves, suspended in some primeval force. The magic was intact.

Several hours later they awoke simultaneously. The whole room was bathed in the rosiness of the setting sun, its restless beams alighting on the mirror, the pictures, the ornaments, the patient clock on the mantelpiece. The manic dance continued, onto Eleri's tangled curls, like restless jewels, then touching Alvar's nose, ears, hands, as they proceeded in their mad whirl.

The lovers sat up, gazing into each other's eyes with a slow intimate smile, such as they had exchanged at the altar less than a year before. The odds remained the same, but they had regained their Eden.

A quick bath and fresh clothes and they were ready to join Lady Bettina, for a special supper. Elegant in grey and white she came towards them. Her fine dark eyes radiated relief and love – the beautiful, chameleon, intelligent and charming daughter-in-law had returned. Her handsome, insouciant son needed such a magnet and anchor.

It was a delightful supper. Both had news to impart. Eleri regaled them with some of her adventures; Alvar enlightened them with some of his recent successes. He had achieved two coveted awards at the annual show, one for sheep and one for his matchless bull, Samson. He had also been car racing and came third.

Eleri remembered Samson and asked after his well-being. They had chosen him together.

"Actually, he is imprisoned. He deserted his own herd and leapt over the fence to Farmer Conlan's field. The argument now ensuing revolves around who actually owns the fence. In the past we have shared its maintenance."

Eleri asked what the problem was.

"Oh, Farmer Conlan found Samson asleep, the herd munching contentedly around him. It is now a matter of time to find out how many he impregnated. It is not funny."

Eleri thought it was and could not resist implying that he could not be a Christian bull, she herself having just arrived from a land where the males were not monogamous. Her own mother would have been shocked but Alvar's mother laughed.

"Consider also what it would have cost Mr. Conlan if you'd hired him out," she added. There was much merriment and warmth.

Alvar also mentioned how the environment department in Trevere had thwarted his building ambition of converting old stables into homes for his staff. Briende was, of course, the instigator of any refusal pertaining to new buildings. Henceforth the environment was the primary consideration. Even the Madocs had shown restraint regarding further conversions. Briende was now head of the department and had certainly found her niche.

Early next morning, the breeze a trifle sharp, the young couple wandered hand in hand or arms entwined throughout the estate to announce her arrival home and respond to the warmth of many welcomes. She had a word, or a question, for each, congratulations here for the awards, praise there for the crops, enquiries pertaining to their families and expressions of delight at being among them again, her quick sympathy for another's pain on hearing of any sadness, and rejoicing in any happy news.

Alvar never ceased to be amazed by her memory and charm. This morning she was snugly clad in the beige ribbed jumper, leather belt and divided skirt she had worn the day they had met in the Dell, just over a year ago, and both about to embark on the throes of entrapment and with fervid reasons for meeting again.

A visit to Pen Melyn was next on the agenda. Alvar accompanied her but she wished to be alone with her sister afterwards. "A sisterly exchange of confidences is my only indulgence," she told him, "apart from finding you irresistible. I have no other sin. In any case I'll be riding Comus home." She understood that young Royston had been banned from the stable because of his arrogance and the discomfiture caused by his presence. With ill grace he had accepted but the whole situation had caused estrangement between Lady Bettina and her daughter, Cecile.

The dear old house looked inviting as ever. Her mother placed both hands on Eleri's shoulders and looked deeply into her eyes, a combined look of love and disbelief. Mrs. Blethyn had actually accepted that her daughter had gone forever. Uncle Gil, wreathed in smiles, tears coursing down the hollows of his dear face, put his arms around her and the spontaneity of his greeting was as always. Mrs. Blethyn looked across at her. She was certainly beautiful, but she could not see an iota of herself or her husband in her; something of her sister Editha's delicate face and her husband's sister, Dinah, perhaps? In her youth she had the same rich hair colour.

From a brown carrier bag with string handles the gifts were produced. Mrs. Blethyn unwrapped the shawl, and commented that she ought not to have been so extravagant. Uncle Gil said the silk tie and wallet were the best he had ever seen. The exact reactions expected. Sitting on the arm of his chair Eleri deftly undid his tweed tie and replaced it with the silk one. While he examined the wallet's many pockets in detail, she ordered, "Throw your old one away, Uncle. The cow who grew it went to paradise ages ago." She then moved over to her seated mother, still overcome by the fine gift, and draped it over her shoulders, pecking her on the forehead as she did so. "Now you'll wear it, not put it in a drawer for special occasions."

"Now that you've decided to come home, my girl, it calls for a family celebration." She was obviously planning to wear the shawl.

"I don't want a gathering, there is nothing to celebrate. Lady Bettina also offered me a party."

Regardless of Alvar's presence, "That would be outside caterers and chosen guests. It is not our way. In any case even the Prodigal Son was given a welcome-home feast."

"You are indefatigable, Mama. I have not frittered away my inheritance and I did not disappear for years," Eleri quickly retorted.

Uncle Gil looked upon them with amusement. She had descended like a bolt from some unknown source, a bewilderment to her mother, a delight to him, a foil to

Briende and a wellspring of joy to all who knew her. She was home; that was all that mattered.

The remaining itinerary meant a visit to Briende – to be listened to, not judged. Alvar shook hands with the old folk and left.

Briende's gentleness and calm welcome had its usual impact. If Eleri could be marginally influenced by anyone, it was Briende. Briende's instinct now told her that Eleri would settle contentedly, as long as she was not thwarted. She encouraged her in her designing ambitions, advised her to cherish her marriage, even suggested that she had a child as soon as possible. Eleri countered that she had already decided on the latter.

An hour later the dignified Camus made a sprightly dash towards her, placed his muzzle on her shoulder and snorted. He showed his welcome.

As she harnessed him herself, he danced impatiently. Anxious to demonstrate his true form, he galloped at speed across the familiar fields, and Eleri's world was complete.

Lunch time. A quick sandwich and a glass of milk and a smile at Alvar's note propped against the flowers. "Did not wait for you. You know what would have happened to my afternoon had I done so."

Organised as ever, elated, restless, she had three duties to accomplish. The first was to visit her beloved aunts and Maeve, who had been granted an afternoon off from school in order to greet Eleri, with them. Afterwards a check on her old workrooms and setting up her easel for the morrow. Hagar's portrait would be her first task while the image was still fresh in her mind. The last pleasurable duty was a telephone call to Juliette.

She packed the assorted gifts in tissue paper and placed them in the brown carrier bag, which she tied on Comus's saddle. She had identical soft leather handbags for her aunts, one in light grey, the other of a darker shade. They could sort out which was for whom. Perhaps they would take a toss for Maeve's amusement.

As expected, the apprentices had been given a free afternoon and the parlour table was daintily laid for tea. The child was thrilled with her strange presents, which she examined with care. While far away, lonely and vulnerable, Eleri had comforted herself with this sort of scene. They questioned, listened and marvelled at her courage and were filled with awe at her daring. How they loved this delightful young woman! What a spell she had always cast upon them!

Eleri told of her plans. She intended establishing herself in fashion design, rather than in painting or interior décor. The aunts gave themselves sole credit for being her mentors.

Maeve studied the shirt-like garment in disbelief. "Do little girls really wear such things?"

"Yes, almost all of them, and even in the city the girls covered themselves up, arms, legs and heads, even if the garment is not a shirt like this one."

After an hour or more Eleri announced that she had to leave. "Comus will eat up all the lawn and he is becoming bored."

At last a chance to telephone her friend. She gave the operator the number. "Juliette, I'm home. Are you well?"

"Telepathy. I have just sent you a letter. Thank you for the exquisite presents. Claude was thrilled with his embroidered waistcoat. How was your adventure? Please...?"

"It was fascinating, strange and frightening. I'll spare all details until I see you. Your news?"

"There are two main things – exciting, actually. The Hon. Priscilla Fentone-Burke noticed you at the supper. She thought the black dress a dream and wants you to make her wedding dress. She is to marry a Portuguese nobleman and wants something slinky, classic. She's about your build, actually. She will carry one long-stemmed red rose, their custom apparently. She wants no veil or hat. Now are you not thrilled?"

Eleri was almost speechless. "I cannot believe it. I see heavy ribbed satin and a medieval circlet with jewelled earpieces descending – very Queen Guinevere. Thank you, Juliette. And the second news?"

"Venetia got married. We went to her coming-out dance. She looked exquisite in that Harrods dress but glum in spite of the 'suitables' in her wake, but she had recently gone to the village dance with the maids and fell in love with a young trainee pilot in the R.A.F. The coming out was a waste of time."

"And the airman was not invited?"

"Of course not. There has been much discord in the family, and he was barred from the house. So, imagine what she did? She got herself pregnant and married by special licence. I would not have such courage."

"I would. My heart goes out to her."

"Eleri, you are incorrigible."

"Tomorrow I will buy her a divine gift and it won't be china or linen."

"Of course not, it will be from Eleri. I must go for my boring pregnant-mum rest. Lovely to have you back."

"Goodbye, Juliette, and thank you. I long for that letter." She replaced the receiver.

Being alone she excitedly swirled around and around. Tomorrow she would ask Alvar to accompany her to Limorrnah. They would have a full day together, have a romantic lunch at the Pirate's Haven on the harbour and choose Venetia's gift together. Work could be postponed for a day.

She trembled with delight as she heard his car on the driveway and ran to meet him. Ecstatically they clung together, and he suggested an intimate supper by candlelight in his study, then an early night.

During the meal she conveyed her news and mentioned her plans for the next day. Calmly he stated, "Sorry, darling. Randolph St. Mears has a shooting party. It's our annual reunion. Come with me, several are bringing their womenfolk."

Womenfolk, she thought. "Cannot you cancel it?"

"I promised weeks ago. I did not know when you'd be home. Please come."

"You know I dislike cold and drizzle and tramping through soggy heather to shoot a few hapless birds."

"You eat them. I'll bring you a brace and one for your mother. Lewis the butcher will take any spares. We expect a good bag."

She looked across at him in the flickering candlelight. The attraction was still there but so was the chasm.

Hands behind her head, her whole body relaxed between the silky sheets, she impatiently waited for Alvar to emerge from the steamy bathroom while she planned the next day. Before an early breakfast she would telephone and arrange to take her nieces shopping, let them help choose Venetia's gift, or make a pretence that they had, then take them to Nello's for a sundae. That would give her more pleasure than a country shoot and the children would be delighted.

Sitting opposite their aunt in the fish tank-lined room, which they enjoyed so much, she observed them. Niamh, dark-eyed with dark curls, like Moya in manner and speech with her Irish sibilance and easy charm, Bethan, with her neat Welsh face, high cheekbones, blue eyes and soft brown hair, small and neat, Maeve, with white skin and flaxen hair, thin, long-legged and quieter. There was so much of her father in her eyes and expression that it made Eleri feel quite sad. She wondered, whether Maeve's resemblance to him was the reason for Briende's complete lack of interest in any other man. With this child around nobody could cease to be reminded of Ralph Maine and Briende knew she would never find another remotely like him.

One more walk around to admire the fish, listen to the girls' chatter, smile at some of their comments, before the bill was paid.

They left, to be driven home along the shore in order to count the ships. At seven, eight and nine years of age this was a ritual.

By early afternoon Eleri was home. Several hours would elapse before she saw Alvar. So, a quick change into her working gear, hair tied in a scarf, Eleri set to work with energy and inspiration. She would consider no other work until the portrait was completed but would accept the undreamt of commission to create the wedding dress and actually decided on the date of commencing the order, even deciding the dates for the fittings at Alberry Park Hotel. Three or four such commissions and she would have her own London address, to be purchased without touching normal finances. Her indomitable sense of independence was a part of her character.

CHAPTER NINETEEN

Eleri's Plans

THREE WEEKS LATER ELERI WAS POSITIVE THAT SHE was pregnant. She announced the fact as soon as Alvar appeared for breakfast. He actually turned pale. Never before had she seen such a reaction in him, pertaining to anything at all. For a few seconds he was speechless, then grabbed her, swung her around and said, "Let's go to Mother. You are sure?" He sounded hoarse.

"Of course, let us go." Hand in hand they sped away. Normally they never went unannounced to Lady Bettina's apartments, but this was special. If she were still in bed it mattered not.

She was but minded not. She called for her wrap and, thus clad, joined them for breakfast. This was a departure from her usual stylish behaviour. She had never appeared happier. There was talk, of course, of acquiring the best medical care, but Eleri dismissed all that.

"I am young and healthy; it is not an illness. I'll have the midwife all the others have."

Needless to say all three remembered the last birth but Eleri quickly announced, "This time no horse is likely to drag me, so I'll sail through, as any gypsy or peasant. No more to be said."

They knew better than to argue.

Alvar cancelled all the morning appointments and accompanied his wife to Pen Melyn. They rode through the Dell, through the fast-falling leaves, silent and happy, the crunching leaves underfoot the only sound except when they whispered as they sailed down.

Mrs. Blethyn, of course, agreed with Eleri's plans. Who needed fashionable doctors? Women managed very well before men doctors at a birth became fashionable. It was women's work. Nothing more.

"And if there's a complication?" Alvar timidly ventured.

"Old Dr. Philpott will do his usual best," she retorted.

It was the end of the discussion except for admonitions to eat well and exercise. "Now have a glass of wine. I suppose this is an occasion, but it will be my own brew, not some stuff from France with a fancy label."

Mrs. Blethyn never felt at ease with her son-in-law, considered him – well – insubstantial. It was a splendid match, of course, as she had wished. As long as he cared for her daughter, she did not have to like him. She now realised this daughter would manage him. If a stanchion was needed Eleri would be the one to provide it. He smiled at Eleri and accepted the proffered glass. Then all three went in search of Uncle Gil. This was flattering as Mrs. Blethyn seldom broke from routine.

Briende was telephoned at her place of work before they rode home through the woods then around the estate, feeling very close, very fulfilled. Observing her husband somewhat pensive, "I know what you are thinking, that I won't give up riding, that I will overwork and be irresponsible, and in general overdo things. Well, I won't. I am not exactly foolish. Sometimes impetuous but never rash!"

She looked at him again. "I promise."

That day they did go to the Pirate's Haven for lunch and took a boat around the harbour although there was a chill wind and some drizzle. They walked along the shore, then drove to inform the two families in Limorrnah. This was Alvar's first visit to them. This day Alvar was remarkably docile, overwhelmed, she thought. These people were unlike any he'd met, and their homes cocoons of music, crafts, warmth.

The following weeks necessitated much planning and much hard work. The portrait was finished within a month and if self-assessment meant anything, Eleri considered it a masterpiece. She planned to enter it for the Royal Academy Summer Exhibition and felt reasonably confident that it would be accepted. She envisaged a lot of interest because the subject was unusual and the woman depicted, beautiful, though past middle age. There was no intention of selling it.

The Hon. Priscilla Fentone-Burke dutifully chose the material from samples sent by Eleri, who had spent most of a whole day at John Lewis's Oxford Street, requesting a snip of this, a snip of that. These she mounted, priced and labelled before sending the file to her client.

The procedures were explained: she would need four fittings but in the meantime Jemima, the adjustable dressmaker's model, would be permanently set in the corner of the workroom until the work was completed. Eleri's client could meet with her in London or feel welcome to make the journey to llandia, which was not onerous and quite interesting. She also explained that her two helpers were perfectly trained and had worked with her in the past. A third, recently qualified, apprentice would also be at hand. All this was agreed before they lunched together in order to get to know each other. Fortunately, the young women liked each other. Their fashion sense was similar and good relations were established. This was of the utmost importance.

While this commission was in progress Eleri had also been searching for modest London premises and constantly studied data sent from various estate agents. Her aunts were retiring from business and not taking on more trainees and anything considered useful was passed on to Eleri. This included their dainty Victorian parlour furniture, special china, tall mirror and so forth. They were excited about Eleri's ambitions and envied her her freedom and confidence. Needless to state, they gave her every encouragement.

*

Later, in early spring, Alvar and Eleri attended Priscilla Fentone-Burke's wedding in Lisbon. Eleri considered she could possibly make herself presentable if cleverly attired.

She would delight in seeing the beautiful wedding dress worn on this special day.

Completed a month ahead of schedule, it was a splendid creation. It was made of heavy white satin with a barely perceptible raised stripe, cut on the bias, stark in its simplicity but with a long train. The medieval-style sleeves were closely fitted to the elbow but wide at the wrist and gracefully drooping to points at hip level. The inner tightly fitted sleeve was of lace, the headdress was a silver filigree circlet with a shower of white gems, seed pearls and diamante falling below ear level in a shimmering cascade.

The single rose was exactly correct for such a garment and there was an audible gasp as the bride descended from her husband's family carriage. The cathedral in Lisbon was overflowing with rich and fascinating guests from all over Europe.

Alvar, who had been attentive throughout the winter and spring, had accompanied her to London several times. They enjoyed the amalgam of people Eleri constantly managed to find, attended shows, dinner engagements and functions at the country houses of some of Alvar's friends. Together they attended Prunie's marriage to Abdun and he, being an Arab, had two ceremonies; a civil one in London followed by breakfast at the Savoy and the other in Cairo, which the Garonnes did not attend.

The sixth month of pregnancy dictated a slowing down of an ultra-active lifestyle. Eleri's final task, namely acquiring premises in the Kensington area, known as Abbots' Walk, commanded her interest.

A narrow street, lined with small businesses, led

to a small open space; an old garden encompassing the large shapeless remains of a seminary dotted here and there. Seats had been placed among the shrubs and the communal private garden was for the residents' use. Here Eleri escaped for many a lunch break to consume fruit or sandwiches, sketching or making notes, while supervising the work in progress on her property.

Alone and with Alvar she had attended auctions and antique shops and cajoled demolition workers to supply her with interesting pieces from buildings in the process of being demolished. Sometimes she merely paid the men for delivery, as the objects were heading for demolition anyway. She figured that she was maybe preserving a part of history.

Her premises, half of a narrow Georgian three-storey house, were opposite a delicatessen and next door to a firm of accountants. There were also on the street a tiny interior decoration studio, an exclusive shoe shop, a small Swiss baker's shop and a cool elegant French restaurant. There was also a gift shop and a stationer. It was an ideal location, quiet, ablaze with tubbed flowers and window boxes, brightly painted doorways and no traffic. There was no space for cars and the road led nowhere. The inhabitants of the street, forced to walk, became familiar to one another. Naturally contacts were made, and clients acquired.

Eleri delighted in her carefully planned abode. A sitting room was walled off at one end to create a fitting room. A bathroom and kitchen were designed for the first floor and a double bedroom above that.

The flocked wallpaper was in cream and white. There was the spindly Victorian suite and a desk, purchased at an auction, with a splendid marble top from a Victorian dressing table. The carpet was purple, as was the imposing Georgian front door with its brass fixtures. The scarlet geranium tubs on each side made an unusual colour scheme.

The plaque on the outside wall read, "Ra-Maine designs" and underneath, "Eleri Garonne".

Eleri was happy and Alvar was becoming more inclined to stay with her than at his club or an hotel. It became their retreat during the months of inconvenience.

The bright yellow kitchen, compact and neat, had white curtains with enormous sunflowers, an ever-smiling welcome. The stark cool bedroom above had an antique brass bed purchased at a second-hand shop and polished by Eleri and a crocheted white bedspread reminiscent of Portugal or France.

By mid-summer Eleri had her business well-established and her treasured son, Quellyn Madoc Garonne, had made his entrance. The birth was natural, and no doctor was summoned. When he was first placed in her arms, tears of joy intermingled with tears of merriment. He was a miniature replica of his father – a slash of black hair, pointed eyebrows and long dimples. His look of cool aloofness had also been inherited – that look Eleri had found irresistible as well as a challenge. She was overwhelmed and asked the midwife to summon his father immediately. He, in his turn, was completely stunned with disbelief; his voice was barely audible as he kissed his wife and asked permission to send for his mother.

Gracious, as expected, Lady Bettina first crossed the room to kiss her daughter-in-law, whose arms were held out to engulf her. There was a muffled, "Thank you." She then went to see the child.

As father and grandmother leant over the cradle, Eleri sensed anew their close bond.

Mrs. Brécard, the midwife, forbade more visitors, in spite of the new mother's wish to call in the whole household and her relatives. She also instructed the midwife to open wide the great windows. There was no better moment than this to enjoy the velvet perfume of roses and newly mown grass. Her midsummer day baby, an early arrival at that, would share the fragrance.

Mrs. Brécard insisted that she rested, as she would not answer for the consequences if she were not obeyed.

As soon as Eleri lay back a sudden overpowering tiredness consumed her. When she awoke, around her neck was an antique choker in seed pearls and sapphires. While she had been delving in auction rooms or second-hand markets shopping for her premises, Alvar had been to antique jewellery markets. Eleri was touched but also delighted.

Next morning, a rare event; the two grandmothers met and commiserated over her choice of name. For once the two women were in agreement.

"I believe Eleri met somebody on that ship, last year, a wine merchant from Chester, whose name was Quellyn."

"Believe me, Lady Bettina, it's a corruption of the Welsh

name, Llewellyn. The English found it unpronounceable."

"Then it is not a real name?"

"No but try getting Eleri to do anything other than she wills." However, both were delighted and proud. The sturdy youngster was a great new important chapter in all their lives.

Two days later Eleri was afire with her usual energy. The elders were appalled. "Stop fretting. What about the gypsies? I saw a new-born babe washed in a stream by its mother."

"You are not a gypsy. You've had a sheltered, cosseted lifestyle."

"What about the Chinese peasants? They take a break to have a child then go back in an hour or so, to till the land, or plant rice."

She met with opposition from all quarters but still went back to the workroom, her baby in his basket alongside her. She had refused a nursemaid; with Mrs. Sullivan and Bridget to help all would be splendidly managed. He was to spend as much time as possible in the workroom, with people around him. Once toddling he would accompany his father around the estate, again to be talked to by a variety of people. The Garonnes' usual arrangements of a resident tutor when young then away to school at a tender age, did not enter into his mother's plans. Later on, she would seriously consider education of a formal kind, but the early years were to be with parents, in a settled home. If he went to his father's school, Peak House in Sussex, he would be close enough to spend one weekend per month in London, when she was at her duties there.

Eleri had clear-cut ideas and never doubted her own instincts. The idea of a seven-year-old departing for a faraway school she found abhorrent. Those early years would embrace learning in all its manifestations, observation, reasoning, wonder, every day had to be a journey, the young learnt so quickly. She found herself excited at the whole prospect ahead. How she would enjoy him!

CHAPTER TWENTY

War Clouds Looming

If "in short measures, life may perfect be" the second half of 1938 was an outstandingly happy period.

The child, plump, lusty, alert, thrived, the mother worked, and the father became conscientious regarding his duties. In a baby basket, the child was comfortably conveyed to London, where with his mother and Bridget he was resident for one weekend in four, in the Kensington house.

Much of the dinner party conversations embraced the current political scene in Germany. Several refugees penetrated Eleri's circle and the experiences related were sad and riveting. It was difficult to accept that, in modern times, in a cultured nation, such an abuse of human rights could possibly take place.

The discussions among the enlightened classes

hovered on the immense spectrum between pacifism and conflict. Some thought pacifism the mature approach, some thought that armed conflict was inevitable. The nation seemed geared to war; the atmosphere among thinking people was electric, each gathering providing yet another opinion. There was no doubt that excitement prevailed as well as gloom.

London seemed a city preparing for war although civilian life continued with an excess of zeal, as if this could thwart the political machinations. *Under your Hat* was on at the Palace, the Crazy Gang at the Palladium. Plays by Shaw, Emlyn Williams and Terence Rattigan were performed to full houses. *Charlie's Aunt* was on at the Haymarket, *Me and my Girl* at the Victoria Palace. All these and many more were attended by the Garonnes and their friends, mostly in parties. Later they would dine in favourite restaurants or at somebody's house.

To be in fashion meant reading current publications. *The Letters of T.E. Lawrence* and Margaret Lane's biography of Edgar Wallace were much in vogue. The Nobel Prize for Literature had been awarded to Pearl Buck, an American, and it became important to acquire a copy, as these quickly sold.

Spare hours, which were few in number found Eleri at the Royal Academy, surveying each new exhibition. She even met Edwin Lutyens, the president, who talked of his house in the west country, as well as remembering the picture of Hagar which Eleri had submitted in the summer. Though everything appeared a froth of excitement, there was also unease among informed people. Snatches of unsavoury happenings in Germany seeped into English society. Jews were being moved to concentration camps. There were pogroms in the cities and much looting and arson. Jews in some parts were not allowed to drive cars or own retail businesses. Eleri had herself spoken to people who had escaped and heard first-hand of their vanished husbands, sons and daughters.

One wet summer's day, on one of her weekends in London, a Mrs. Frieda Rebecca Levi contacted Eleri. A client of the neighbouring accountants, she had been directed to the dress designer next door, when she requested advice regarding somebody who could make her entire winter wardrobe.

Mrs. Levi was of medium height, large-busted, with a squarish frame, balanced on thin legs. Her bright eyes, husky voice and white skin, though not pertaining to beauty, had a sort of luminosity. The eyes were clear, the skin flawless and her husky voice, in spite of the fractured English which she was still learning, quite fascinating. Eleri sensed a particular quality in her. The clothes she wore were made in very fine fabric, though the style seemed out of date. Not blessed with good looks the woman still appeared to have substance, a zest for living, an optimism.

Eleri's first reaction was negative. She had until the present created garments for the slim and elegant, the successful or fashionable. A part of her warned that this person would not be the right image for her creations.

Yet, she was intrigued and invited her to join her for tea. During the tea was heard, once again, a typical German story.

Mrs. Levi had, in her youth, been an opera singer, trained in Berlin and very much in demand. She possessed a magnificent voice and on stage managed an overpowering presence. She attracted and married a rich industrialist, a cloth manufacturer.

As Chancellor Hitler became more and more prominent, everything changed; subtly at first, then with arrogant confidence. Her husband was requested to manufacture flags and banners bearing the swastika. At first, he refused and was then so ordered. A German manager was installed to make sure orders were obeyed yet this was Mr. Levi's own business.

For a few months, though in agony of spirit, he thought it advisable to collaborate. In the meantime, his wife and relatives transferred money to her sister in Austria, to be banked in Switzerland. The sister was married to a Gentile, a Swiss, and the family was aware that this arrangement could not continue.

One day Mr. Esekiel Levi was sent to a northern factory, presumably to give advice and pass on his experience, then to another city to do likewise. Each time he found himself not needed. In the meantime, he was being relieved of the reins of his own private business.

Mrs. Levi, after much searching, telephoned some of these factories and spoke to him on several occasions. He sounded a broken man. One day she telephoned to be told that he was not there, and nobody knew where he was.

A communication from an unknown person, genuine or not, informed her that he had died of a heart attack. Her two daughters, both opera singers, were much in demand entertaining the upper echelons of the armed forces. Their letters became stilted.

As an intelligent woman she knew that escape was imperative. Using her skill at make-up, learnt in theatrical days, she bought clothes from a poor woman, wore a St. Christopher medallion, clutched a walking stick and donned a greasy headscarf and worn shoes and travelled south, south, south as far as she could get. Day and night, night and day she kept moving by tram, bus, train, farm truck; any transport until she arrived in Vienna. From here, with her sister Miriam's husband's connivance she left for Switzerland, a quick decision after a Jewish child, who lived nearby, had been beaten badly at school.

Gathering as much as she could of her wealth and transferring it to London, selling the jewellery sewn into her petticoats, writing farewell letters to her daughters, hoping against hope that these would reach them, she left for England.

Her spirit was indomitable and Eleri admired her but was doubtful whether she could take on the assignment. The lady was not easy to dress. She promised to give it consideration, using pressure of work as an excuse.

That night in bed, Alvar beside her, Bridget and the baby in the fitting room, which converted into a bedroom at night, Eleri lay awake, her conscience troubled. She thought of her label, Ra-Maine, and the man who had inspired it. This was sufficient to make her accept Mrs. Levi as a client. Satisfied, she slept. One day she would tell Briende of this.

Next day she set to work immediately. Other work

was abandoned. The cloth, styles, price, were decided upon. There were to be a coat, two jackets, two skirts and a dress; the dress was to be in wool georgette, the rest in barathea, all in a shade of aquamarine and completely interchangeable.

In the meantime, Mrs. Levi was becoming known in music circles, her fine voice much appreciated. Sometimes she sang in lunch-time charity concerts, sometimes she was hired and well paid for classical musical performances in London and the Home Counties. She conscientiously attended English lessons and kept up her singing exercises with a well-known teacher. Undoubtedly, she would become established in London. Her warmth and personality were also assets.

It took a mere few weeks before she met Constantia Bolero, who had been invited to appear at the Royal Command Performance. Constantia was to sing two arias from her favourite opera, *Carmen*. Bizet himself could not have chosen a more apt Carmen. Tall, dark, fiery, with glossy curls and flashing eyes and a temperament to match, she became completely absorbed in preparing for the great evening.

After searching all over London for the exact crimson satin dress she had in mind for herself and failing to find it, Mrs. Levi casually mentioned, when both were appearing on the same programme, that she should have it made.

"Made, made, who could make as I want. There must be a shawl collar, just so, low front and tight waist and miles of skirt."

Such was the dress Eleri found herself chosen to make

in the autumn of 1938. Once more she had a powerful new friend from the artistic world. She could visualise her work becoming recognised and her label accepted. Success was with her, a confidence in herself and her creativity. She felt decidedly launched in the world of fashion, offering quality and dedication in her work.

The social life continued uninterrupted. Of Hitler's influence in Austria she heard at first hand, from a Mr. Zui Eli Schloss. Eleri had heard a similar story from Mrs. Levi. An astounded party at a St. John's Wood gathering heard first-hand about Kristallnacht in November 1938. Some refused to believe what they heard about the pogroms, the arson and looting of Jewish houses and businesses.

There was excitement combined with uneasiness that autumn. Trenches had been dug in Hyde Park and Queen Mary came to see them. Gas masks were beginning to appear, and America had provided twenty million pounds for shelters. The Chamberlain broadcast on September the 27th had not comforted the majority. On the eighth of December the air raid sirens were tested but the nation still hoped a war could be avoided, although young men were rapidly enlisting.

The theatres and restaurants continued to be well-patronised. Eleri and her friends met for frequent theatre outings and discussed the productions at dinner parties. They read the critics' reviews and exchanged opinions. Hollywood film stars became household names and people connected with broadcasting of the utmost social importance.

That Christmas Alvar, Eleri and their child were in

London. Alvar, unused to a family Christmas, usually visited friends or had his own house party. He never felt quite at ease with the Blethyns and was unsentimental about family gatherings. His own mother usually joined a friend for the popular Sunshine Cruise.

In England that Christmas was one to remember. There were four inches of snow on Trafalgar Square on Christmas Day and while the city was white and deserted people swarmed to Hampstead Heath for skating and sledging. For the Garonnes, with their young friends and their children, this was to be remembered as the happiest and last carefree Christmas. The Garonnes shared Juliette's nanny.

Political gloom deepened throughout the winter, yet there was a suppressed excitement, as if waiting for the inevitable. By the end of March Germany had invaded Bohemia and Moravia and facts became inseparable from rumours. Threats of shortages led to hoarding and the entire nation seemed poised on the brink of some impending disaster.

Throughout the spring and summer Eleri's business venture blossomed. It became a discipline to spend a mere one weekend in four in London. The main work, as ever, continued at Campions.

With her irrepressible energy she managed to entertain their many friends at Campions, which to most was a novelty. She continued her correspondence with distant friends and was overjoyed when letters began to arrive from Sherene and more often from Roisin. Both had settled to married life and Sherene had a son. She, nevertheless, after much persuading, had been manageress of a pre-natal clinic at the newly built hospital. Even the women mistrusted women doctors and her task was an uphill one.

Prunie was happy in Cairo and had two infants; Venetia had a daughter and was still unreconciled with her family. Eleri met Juliette regularly, who her closest contact with the world she understood. The Ra-Maine label was becoming known, after some of Eleri's creations had appeared in the more expensive periodicals, well-advertised by young socialites and the occasional bride. Eleri foresaw a future where she would have to curtail orders, in order to keep the fashion house small and exclusive. She was energetic but not overly ambitious.

Alvar, as ever, interfered not at all. He was content, more conscientious about his estate and adored his son. The marital relationship remained intact. It was more biological than spiritual, but the attraction remained. Once in his embrace, the explicit alchemy began in her toes and rocketed throughout her entire body. She was confident that the sensation was mutual.

CHAPTER TWENTY-ONE

Dark Days Looming

An eerie expectancy hung over the nation throughout the early months of the following year. A nation not at war seemed to be preparing for war.

In America daily bulletins about the impending catastrophe in Europe punctuated the domestic news. Lady Bettina heard once or twice a year from an old admirer, one she was once attached to. He had emigrated to Florida after being repulsed. He had lately written, urgently asking her to visit him while the luxury liners were still crossing the Atlantic. Rupert Grayling, from Lancashire, had been her first love affair, which, as the poets tell us, is never forgotten, but in the early part of the century a mere builder was not considered a suitable match. Heartbroken, he went to America, married and flourished. The simple building business he started mushroomed into a residential complex for the retired. A whole village grew from a simple, single-storey house on a large piece of land.

His wife, after a long and successful marriage, had died and he once more invited his old girlfriend. He now had wealth and social standing and would never again be intimidated. Alvar and Eleri persuaded her to accept his invitation.

Lady Bettina sailed on the *Queen Elizabeth*, on almost her last journey as a liner. By the time war broke out in September, Lady Bettina had embraced her new life with pleasure. It was expected that they would marry.

Alvar and Eleri were happy for her. The only cloud on their horizon was that she would not see young Quellyn growing up, but both were delighted that this attractive stylish woman would have a new lease of life. She had never blended in with Brymadoc.

In Britain there was a fever, a now-or-never fever, permeating everything; there was an indulgence while one could indulge. Everything seemed perched at the end of a precipice, which could topple at any minute. The number of uniformed men on the streets from a variety of nations seemed to daily increase; those with money spent wildly. The number of weddings increased and Eleri's designs continued to be in demand. Clubs of all kinds flourished, and London was a hive of restless activity. In spite of this Eleri's rapidly expanding venture seemed poised for disaster. Emergency exercises of all kinds, throughout that summer, commanded time and provided excitement. Uniforms became more popular than ball gowns and drilling more important than dancing or partying as the season approached its climax.

At a quarter past eleven, on a beautiful Sunday morning, on the third of September, the bubble, which had fed on rumours, fears and expectancy, finally burst. There was mingled relief and intolerable grief. Peace was dead at last. The Prime Minister's sombre tone of defeat, followed later in the day by the King's broadcast, concluded the last chapter of a tedious, unsettling saga. Nothing would ever again remotely compare with what had been. The pattern of life changed completely. The banks and Stock Exchange closed for two days; theatres, cinemas and most restaurants closed.

The following day saw the *Athenia* torpedoed, bringing danger foremost into the minds of people. Conversation revolved around blackout, rationing and evacuation. Resolution and togetherness took precedence over pleasure and selfishness. Everywhere there was a spirit of purpose and dogged patriotism. There was a surge of change as people moved from menial jobs to munitions factories, doubling their wages. Guns sprang like plants from hitherto quiet reaches along the Thames. Heavy and light high-angle guns were mounted on pre-selected sites around the docks. Barrage balloons grew like fungi; these were to deter dive bombers from pinpointing locks or bridges or other vital targets. Liners disappeared to become troop carriers or hospital ships. Pleasure cruises ceased, boats and houses were requisitioned.

Eleri reasoned that an established couturier like Norman Hartnell was likely to continue throughout the war but saw little hope for the newer, younger, creative people such as herself. She would complete the work in hand before serious rationing of fabrics was introduced, then remove herself to Ilandia; she had a child to rear. A monthly visit to London would involve risks and inconvenience. To believe that London would not be attacked from the air was escaping reality. Everyone knew what had happened in Spain; air raids would become routine. She would remove to safety some items dear to her from her Abbots' Walk house and rent it for the duration, hopefully returning to it when hostilities were over. Once this decision was made, she embarked on planning the next stage of her life. With the accountants next door acting as agents, her property was rented to Mrs. Levi, whose humble terraced house lodging in Deptford was too near the river for comfort. She was delighted at the idea of renting from Eleri, sharing expenses with Zara Lichter, a French Jewish girl of great talent, daughter of a French music teacher. She had completed three years of study at the Royal College of Music. An only child, her parents were nervous of her returning home, and in fact hoped, a faint hope, to somehow join her in England. Having lost touch with her own talented daughters, Mrs. Levi, with warmth and sympathy, had determined to cherish and encourage another talented youngster deprived of parents, as she had been deprived of her children.

In the late summer before leaving London, a farewell dinner was given for Eleri by Juliette, before she removed herself and her young child to her parents' country home. Claude enlisted in the 11th Hussars, his father's old regiment, reasoning that by joining before call-up, which seemed inevitable, he had more choice of regiment, without lengthy formalities, and quicker promotion.

That night Eleri met one who was to figure strongly in the years ahead. He was Amos Skiroski-Goldstein, a small, delicately built Jewish doctor. His kind eyes behind tortoiseshell-rimmed spectacles, long delicate hands and low voice spelt a sensitivity and vulnerability of which Eleri immediately became aware. She knew before he spoke that he had a story to tell. Indeed, his experience closely resembled that of Mrs. Levi.

Using a genuine envelope with stamps, which had held a letter to his mother Anna S. Goldstein from a friend in Pittsburgh, he concocted a job in Pennsylvania. The 'offer' was expertly typed in English by his mother, using a fictional clinic and address in Pittsburgh. Waving this with delight to his young fellow hospital colleagues and pretending to go home to his family to say goodbye before booking a passage, he managed to escape. To make it more authentic he promised to return next day for a beery farewell party; at the same time, if things worked out to his future advantage, promising to ask friends to join him.

Clad in his normal suit, a file under his arm, no luggage and money in a body belt, he sailed from Rotterdam to England on the *Heron* three days later. He did not feel at ease until he had boarded.

After gentle prompting, as they sat in a quiet corner, he told Eleri his story.

His father, who owned a factory in the Ruhr, making industrial tools, had, like Mrs. Levi's husband, been ordered to change production. Instead of tools he had to manufacture small armaments, or parts thereof.

One day his father did not come home. On making enquiries his mother was told that he'd left a message saying he had to go to Leipzig on business. Anna Goldstein knew immediately that her devoted husband would not have left so suddenly, and immediately started plans to facilitate her son's escape. Sadly, he did not know what had become of his mother, sister or small brother, though he sent a letter, a brief one, via the friends in America. (He was supposed to be there and was wary of any suspicions against his family.) He specialised in thoracic diseases, his main field of interest being industrial diseases such as pneumoconiosis; hence his ruse about going to the coal fields of Pennsylvania.

His other sadness on leaving Germany was saying a temporary goodbye to his adored girlfriend, Sonia, who had promised to follow him wherever he went. From England he sent German money for her voyage, even found out the sailings from Holland. She returned the money to his humble lodgings in Stepney, East London, where he had settled in a Jewish community, many far poorer than he was, since his family, anticipating trouble, had for years sent money to London and Geneva. Here he met many educated refugees who were doing menial jobs in shops or public laundries or sharing stalls in London markets. Sonia had not joined them, because her mother had become very ill and was scared of going to hospital. The Jews were too afraid to enter the hospitals. And this was before the outbreak of war.

By 1939 Guy's Hospital had accepted Dr. Skiroski without demur; one interview was sufficient to emphasise his brilliance and excellent training in Berlin. He apologised for his inadequate English but made it clear that he was taking lessons. He agreed to work long hours and to undertake further study.

After the war he planned to emigrate to America, the farther from Europe the better. In the meantime he desired to purchase a large quiet estate in a backwater for holidays and occasional weekends, not primarily for himself but as a home for six or seven or eight orphaned Jewish girls from Germany, and maybe a rest home for Free Polish wounded soldiers before they were discharged or returned to duty. In the meantime, he'd dropped the Goldstein and reverted to his mother's Polish name.

Eleri sensed injury, bitterness and goodness. Alvar, who was with her listening to this, remembered Fentons on North Island. It was large and peaceful and inexpensive, as the old people had left for Cumbria. Their only son, who was English and an old school friend of Alvar's, Randolph St. Mears, had become one of a new breed of daring young pilots. He had been killed when his plane hit a mine as he landed near Tilbury. It was the first of many such accidents connected with these mines. Suddenly the war was becoming a reality, to a few, in spite of the first quiet months.

That first autumn of the war Eleri continued with the work in hand, once again using a room at the Alberry for fittings. She did not visualise further orders; she had not become sufficiently established. She accepted that all are victims of time or circumstance.

In January 1940 rationing was introduced. This ended the availability of lovely materials and somewhat curtailed restaurant parties. Air-raid warnings began to sound. To find oneself at the Dorchester during a function, sitting on dainty gilt chairs in the underground apartments because of a raid, was a strange experience. Evening dress continued to be worn by the minority. The theatres, which reopened very quickly after a brief closure, continued as usual. Lupino Lane continued at the Victoria Palace in *Me and My Girl* and 'The Lambeth Walk' or 'Knees up Mother Brown' were the popular songs sung at many gatherings. 'Pack up Your Troubles in your Old Kit Bag' became a popular marching song. There seemed to be swarms of people everywhere.

Eleri had left London heavy in spirit and arranged for periodicals like the *New Statesman* and *The Spectator* to be forwarded to her in Ilandia.

Homeward bound she had a sense of guilt at her own peaceful existence and while travelling in darkness and discomfort tried to solidify her plans for helping the deprived or afflicted.

Her obvious link was Amos Skiroski. She worked tirelessly to make Fentons, which he had purchased, into a practical habitation. Much of the kitchen equipment and furniture had been left. Bereft of their only son, the St. Mears had not been sentimental about possessions left behind. The charity 'Temple Wall' provided beds and made a monthly allowance for food.

For the managing of Fentons Dr. Skiroski employed a German woman, almost a fully qualified doctor, as matron, housekeeper, teacher and mother figure. Her name was Rachel Mann, another refugee, and they had met in Stepney, when he had first arrived there. Delightedly she accepted his offer and the charity agreed to pay her a meagre salary. She was consumed with gratitude, even hoping one day to complete her studies and repay.

Eleri's dear aunts, now fading into old age, provided enough grey suiting to make into six uniforms as the Fenton girls, all orphans, had left Germany with just one change of clothing. In the days when mourning was a part of respectability, grey was known as second mourning. For some reason, a large family had not gone into second mourning, hence the availability of the excess material.

Dr. Skiroski was delighted at the idea of a uniform. It simplified the clothes situation. Eleri, helped by her assistants, attired the young girls in tunic dresses, bib-fronted, with flared skirts with capacious pockets. Underneath they wore yellow blouses in summer and grey jumpers in winter. The bodice had a logo worked into a yellow pattern. Eleri's first idea was for a star with rays, but this was too reminiscent of the insults in Germany, when yellow stars had to be worn to denote Jewishness. The girls, in broken English, pointed this out. Indeed, some became emotionally upset, pained by their memories. Eleri devised a candle design instead – the flame emanating from the candle to form a broken sphere.

Dr. Skiroski was delighted, his agony of spirit somewhat abated by the kindnesses he now experienced. He became a friend of the Blethyns, particularly Briende, whom he never failed to visit on his rare weekends away from hospital duties.

Romance was out of the question. Each seemed that rare type who falls in love once and viewed a second romance as a desecration of the first, souls seemingly too sensitive to face a second loss, each inoculated forever against sexual commitment.

He returned to llandia at every opportunity, to find the good woman Rachel Mann in full control, the girls at a local school and helping at Claire Vale Hospital whenever they could find transport. He felt sure that some of the girls would study medicine. Sometimes, when present, he would do some teaching, as did Miss Mann. Briende, Eleri, Mrs. Britt and even young Maeve came to help with English lessons. The scriptures were ignored. The good doctor desired no Hebrew taught or any emphasis on Judaism. If they desired to keep their culture active at Purim or any other festival, he would not prevent them or provide for it. The charity did not challenge this, though it was one of their aims to keep their heritage. Fentons was owned by Dr. Skiroski and, as they paid no rent, they interfered as little as possible.

Once more, with Alvar's encouragement, Eleri embarked on the closure of Campions and made their home at the lodge at the gate, which was nearer the village and easier to manage. Mrs. Sullivan would move with them. Precious furniture would be stored in their own attics, Lady Bettina's wing locked, and the large dining room partitioned into three rooms. These were to be made into pleasant units to house victims of the London bombing raids, which had not started in earnest, although there were interruptions and shortages and anguish. Many of the menfolk were away. Families, their fares paid by the British charity Friends War Victims Relief Committee, would spend two weeks in peace together before the menfolk left for overseas duties, especially if their homes had been damaged or if members of the family were recuperating from injuries.

The charity did the choosing and controlling but Dr. Skiroski had for some while been on the board of this particular charity, which worked closely with the hospitals. It was completely separate from Temple Wall, which contributed to Fentons.

Eleri had never worked so hard; she of the limitless energy felt that she was doing something worthwhile when compared with creating beautiful garments for rich people.

Work on the estate continued as usual. More crops were grown, more meat exported to the mainland. Limorrnah was still primarily a fishing port but there was some increase in export. The ferries continued uninterrupted but fewer people travelled. The schools at Dewary on the mainland, with evacuees from the cities swelling their numbers, continued almost as before. Since that stretch of coast was mainly rural it was considered safe. The barracks had been abandoned and converted into classrooms for evacuated schools, mainly from the Midlands, and the troops from the old barracks moved closer to the North Sea and Channel ports. Here blackout and shortages became the norm as in the rest of the country. Briende's school continued with virtually the same staff and headmistress and the academic results were as good as they had always been. Briende was still attached to her old teacher. Several were still there. She visited whenever she could, taking Maeve with her.

CHAPTER TWENTY-TWO

Establishing a Refuge

BUSTLE, ENDLESS BUSTLE, WHERE PEACE AND BOREDOM had once reigned. The Lodge at the gate enabled the Garonnes to be more part of the village. Suitable furniture was brought from the big house and Eleri soon recreated the blue and silver bedroom so lovingly planned by Alvar and his mother almost three years before. In the large attic, divided into two rooms, she placed her studio next door to Quellyn's nursery. She still insisted on keeping him near her as much as possible. Though Alvar retained his estate office at Campions, his overseer, Ryan Cordell, acted as supervisor and caretaker of the large dwelling. Eleri placed her own desk in an alcove, in her studio at The Lodge, and from here she supervised her charity work, and planned concerts to be held in the erstwhile drawing room at Campions. She organised the visits of various small families, which she expected to come and go for the duration. No group could stay for more than two weeks. Travel documents were distributed accordingly by the charity. Each little unit had its private accommodation but the kitchens, supervised by Mrs. Sullivan most of the time, were communal, as was the large games room or playroom, which had once been Eleri's precious workroom.

Between bouts of organising functions and relief, Eleri's creativity was confined to painting, mostly in snatched hours, while the child slept or traversed the estate with his father. Her rigid discipline had not deserted her; the excess work and unsettling news fired her imagination more than usual.

One facet of her discipline was letter writing. In a thick file she gathered letters from several parts of the world, personal records of the war's effects on the most unlikely places. She also encouraged Maeve to keep a scrapbook of cuttings from newspapers or magazines.

Venetia wrote of her life in what she called a government house, along with other young airmen's wives from a variety of backgrounds. Occasionally, a censored letter would arrive from Prunie in Cairo and a more heavily censored one from Laurence Britt in Greece. Before the outbreak of war, as a classical scholar he had accepted a post in Athens University to teach English and Classics and now Greece seemed on the brink of disaster. His brother Bellan was in Manaus on the Amazon, where, as the recipient of a grant from Cambridge University, he was to study the Indian tribes and their use of medicinal plants.

Both the vicar's sons had always been in love with Eleri. Alvar knew, of course, as did everyone else, but he had the utmost confidence in his wife's attraction to him and jealousy was to him an alien instinct.

Occasionally a letter from Sherene made its tortuous route; some were undoubtedly lost, as were those from Greece. Letters from Lady Bettina arrived more regularly but many of these were lost as the Atlantic was frequently a cauldron of warfare; hardly a week passed without a ship or ships being bombed or torpedoed.

Eleri had no ambition to write a book but perhaps Maeve, or Quellyn, or even Briende, would one day appreciate this human catalogue.

Venetia's parents' home had been requisitioned and her parents had moved to the nearest town. Juliette and her parents had likewise given up their home and now lived in cramped conditions in a wing of the old house. Yes, she would keep her records, including the constant notes from Amos Skiroski, detailing the circumstances or injuries of the people coming to Campions for relief from air raids and entrusting his project for the Fenton girls to her capable hands.

Letters from Mrs. Levi told of air raid warnings and dogfights in the air above London and the South East, the queuing and food shortages. She wrote of a past acquaintance who had managed to leave Germany, then Belgium, then Holland after the German invasion. She heard that Jews had to be in their houses by eight o'clock at night and were not allowed in cinemas, concerts or theatres, or to use trains or trams. They also had to shop between three and five in the afternoon. Some in hiding had been betrayed for money and treated with appalling indignity by the ruling masters. All this made her conscious of her good fortune in escaping. She had no news of her sister in Vienna or her daughters. It was common knowledge that many Jews had been conveyed to detention camps. Mrs. Levi agonised about her daughters, wondering if they would ever meet again. Zara Lichter was still with her and both were reasonably fortunate in the amount of work which came their way. Letters from Zara's parents had ceased as their part of France was in occupied territory. The last letter had arrived in June 1940.

These letters in fractured English were much appreciated but each letter became more fluent. Eleri longed to meet her again and invited her and Zara Lichter to stay for a while, when and if they had spare time. Mrs. Levi considered that once she had mastered English sufficiently she would give singing lessons when the conflict was over. She would never return to Germany, whatever the outcome.

Eleri wrote of the concerts at Campions, giving details of the entire programme. Though she no longer required evening dress she and Alvar made an effort to dress formally for the concerts at Campions; this encouraged everyone to make an effort and added 'tone' to the proceedings. Many who had never worn formal dress delighted in these occasions. The Garonnes, and the sophisticated tastes of Amos Skiroski and some of the people he sometimes brought along, were bringing changes to llandia.

Eleri missed London, as she knew Alvar did, and both

remembered the relaxed dinner parties and the sparkling conversation ensuing before the outbreak of war, the variety of people and opinions, the cultured Europeans who had fled, the rapid political changes affecting nation after nation. Both had felt part of the real world.

The backwater known as llandia, an almost forgotten domain, now had outsiders galore invading its seemingly impregnable shell, but all did not take kindly to these changes. Sometimes Eleri was amused by the snippets of conversation relating to her. "The Blethyn girl was always different. She never belonged – perhaps it was that art school. We could see this coming." Or "I wonder Garonne puts up with it. That little Jewish doctor she brought in is above himself. Fancy bringing all those girls. They are not even English or Irish."

Others rejoiced in the changes and when a London preparatory school arrived and brought with it much needed local revenue in Morvennah on South Island, some were pleased. Among these was Eleri herself. She now had a school of repute for Quellyn, without sending him away. It was a boys' school but along with Briende she had ideas about this. Why not have a girls' section? If she got to know the principal – and why not – perhaps it could expand. As ever she was looking beyond, and her husband usually followed.

Dr. Skiroski became fluent in English after a lot of conscientious work. Because of prejudice among the less enlightened, she would soon ask him to give talks when at home, talks about his own experiences. When Mrs. Levi's English was adequate she would invite her to do the same. As an introduction she herself could relate her own first-hand knowledge, remembering Major Johnstone's story and that of Abou. She had never been an isolationist, appreciating the security of her charming childhood and the natural beauty of her own island, which she relished in sharing, but had never felt that it was the most beautiful or the most unsullied place. There was always a world outside beckoning, a world she felt she belonged to.

However, like myriads of others she had been trapped. Travelling, except for goods and troops, had diminished to a trickle. Posters all over Britain advised one to 'stay put' in order to keep communications open in case of invasion. 'Go by Shanks' Pony', which meant walking instead of using public transport, blazed from many posters, as did 'Remember Walls have Ears' as a warning for loose talk.

The full horrors of the retreat from Dunkirk in June filtered through to llandia. Claude Havilland had a serious knee injury but had been fortunate enough to reach a humble Thames barge, to which he was conveyed in agony, and certainly owed his life to a handful of men he did not even know but would like to know. They were not from his own regiment. In that chaos they were all united, helping one another, whatever their rank or regiment.

He was home, unlikely to walk properly again and hoping to help the war effort from a desk job, or be discharged and return to his old job in the Foreign Office, thereby braving the heavy bombing which would undoubtedly come.

This news was soon followed by news of a former student friend, who basked in his daring exploits in

Fighter Command. He relished self-reliance, daring, independence, one's own skill in close combat the surest weapon, almost mythical in its fatalism. However, this romantic, one of thousands, was lost over Hellfire Corner, as the South-East projection of England was called. On that particular day, his was one of 161 planes downed.

She had barely absorbed the two pieces of sad news when a telephone call from Juliette informed her of the death of Venetia's young husband, shot down in his beloved Blenheim, one of ten fighters lost in the latter half of June. The previous day he had scribbled a pencilled note to Venetia between sorties, boasting that he had that day brought down a Heinkel bomber. He had enclosed a snapshot of himself leaning against the plane.

That same night there was a much-planned concert at Campions. Though devastated, Alvar and she would make an extra effort to be glamorous, charming and encouraging. They would even arrange, at short notice, some refreshments during the interval – not a usual inclusion because of the extra work involved. They would also load more flowers onto the stage, as if in celebratory mood, and provide buttonholes for the performers. At the end of the evening they would provide wine and canapés for the artists. It had to be an occasion.

In the grimness of that July Eleri longed for another child. Her work for the displaced, and economically deprived would continue; she would work throughout her pregnancy as she had three years ago – but what a difference in outlook and aspirations.

A clear and beautiful summer evening after the

saddest news, the Campions concert that night had been particularly poignant, the music heartrending.

After the praises and goodnights, the large empty drawing room, which had once witnessed Alvar's lively, irresponsible parties, seemed to hold the echoes of a tomb. Hand in hand the young couple ambled out into the stillness and happier sounds of the gardens, a sweet rustle of leaves barely touching, the occasional sleepy twitterings of the birds at prayer, the almost imperceptible sound of their own footsteps on the grassy paths. That 'lamp of heaven' seemed to be alight just for them. They were still in love, working together, adoring their child, living for the moment. Grief for lost friends hovered around their consciousness and made them envelop themselves, more so in each other. Wrapped in the intoxicating beauty of the night, the pearly white globules on a wand of broom were like spangles in the moonlight, the iris leaves like silver-edged swords, the faint perfume of late viburnum, blending in with that of cushions of carnations, added to the magic. The radiant stars hovered around the moon, their queen, and seemed to twinkle their approval of the lovers in the garden. She thought of T.S. Eliot's line, "humankind cannot bear too much reality" – there had to be pleasure and laughter to make life bearable. She conveyed her thoughts to Alvar, who held her closer. For the moment they seemed to be breathing the same breath of life; they would create, in this closeness, a beautiful new life.

The soft earth beneath became a bed strewn with rose petals, suspended in some ethereal cloud. Her white skin and rich hair, his darkness and paleness, fused into the splendour of the night. They were a part of creation, another link in the mystery of life, the tumbling cataract and ever-sounding timbrel, the ever-rushing stream, the constant moon and bejewelled sky. They would remember the moment.

The ease and softness of her voice, when she spoke, suggested they return to the Lodge. The woods, ponds, coppices and glades echoed their peace. Morning was approaching, its onset heralded in the mother-of-pearl sky. The chimneys of Campions were towers in the haze, the church spire beyond spearing the silent sky.

In a dream-like haze they crept into bed, in their own silvered room, to wake a mere three hours later to the happy demands of a lively child and Bridget's sweet voice enticing them to rest.

The days following immersed Eleri into a different consciousness; Claude's crippled dependence on Juliette, Venetia's widowhood and her co-student's death, leaving a young wife to fend for herself and children. What if there were no Alvar? Inwardly she convinced herself that there was another child conceived. Celtic instinct? She did not know – yet she knew. She was alive with a new impetus, a swirl of activity dominating her thinking and doing. She would henceforth work alongside her husband and learn to run the estate. Her normal energetic efforts would continue; the concerts at Campions, the fundraising, her interests at Fentons. She would even continue with her painting. However, this day was going to be different from the usual routine.

After breakfast, she dressed Quellyn herself and Bridget returned to her family. Quellyn wondered where the moon had gone. The previous night he had admired it with Bridget and this morning she had concocted the story of its being stolen. He seemed upset.

"It will be back tonight, darling. I promise." He seemed satisfied. She then placed him among his toys, while she wrote to Venetia, shortly, with warmth and love, reminding her gently that she was still young and attractive with a lovely child and was happy for her, for having found such love, so spontaneously, so fulfilling. She asked her to visit with her child, for two weeks, when she felt ready.

Having done this, she drove with Quellyn to surprise her husband, already at his work. Surprised, he raised an eyebrow. "What bringeth forth my lady in her morning beauty?" he teased her as he cuddled his son. "What plan hath she afoot?"

She told him of her plans regarding the estate. He lowered the child and took her in his arms. "Don't you think you do enough? You may be pregnant again. Is this wise?"

He knew her well enough to know that she could not be turned from her intentions. "I've written to Venetia."

"I understand, but I am not likely to be called to war."

"Neither was your father or mine. Both our mothers had to take the reins."

She teasingly reminded him that he was thirteen years her senior. He held an imaginary mirror. "I see no grey hairs." Bearing in mind his vanity, "Those would only add distinction and make you even more devastatingly attractive to women."

As usual she had hit the right note. "Shall we start?"

The three left to walk around the property. This was to be a new routine. With her quick understanding she absorbed all she heard and saw. When she left to return home, he handed her a bundle of letters in a rubber band, marked in order of importance. "Start with these, we'll talk tonight." Warmly embracing they parted until the evening. She had made a start.

July breathed into a lush August. In Alvar's office on a radiant morning, her eloquent eyes gave him the news.

"Brilliant, absolutely brilliant." He was delighted. Knowing what a trial it was to him she would go herself and inform her mother.

An hour or so later, "Mama, I have good news," she shouted to her parent who was upstairs.

Uncannily her mother said, "You're expecting. I am pleased," as she descended the wide staircase. "I thought on your mad escapades to London you were seeing that Marie Stopes woman. I do read and know what goes on. I wouldn't be surprised if you knew her personally."

"She's a good woman, Mama, and a doctor."

"It's a personal matter, nobody else's business."

Eleri sighed. "Think of all the poor women in the slums."

"What would you know of the slums, my privileged girl?"

"In art school we were sent out to sketch humanity in all its facets and it's not all garden party ladies in flowered hats. We learnt to recognise hundreds of works of art depicting poverty, degradation, humiliation including tramps and prostitutes."

Mrs. Blethyn gasped. "It's the first time I've heard that word beneath my roof." As usual Eleri over-reached herself. "Your religion made a saint of one."

"Don't you desecrate the scriptures in my hearing. Thank God for your beauty, it softens your… well, free thinking, but beauty can fade—" Eleri interrupted with, "I give up, we'll never agree."

"Certainly not. I cannot comprehend how someone supposedly so artistic could be so averse to cooking or gardening. It is unnatural, the time you devote to voluntary work. Normal domesticity or even supervising should be of some consequence, but God be praised you have purposefully embarked on another child."

Momentarily Eleri slipped back to the drab flat of student days and how she entertained her friends at bedtime with such repartee. To think they thought she made it all up!

"Actually I am doing serious work, learning to run the place – as you had to and Alvar's mother."

"That's not work, it is common sense – know what you buy, what you pay, what's left over and treat your staff with kindness and honesty. You will keep them forever." Uncle Gil suppressed a smile.

At this, Mrs. Blethyn left for the kitchen, bringing back a tray with cups of tea and cake for herself and her brother and a glass of milk and a stoned halved peach for her daughter. "You had better eat this, I don't suppose you had a proper breakfast."

Eleri obeyed with a smile. She then crossed to her seated parent, put her arms around her and kissed her cheek. Then a bear hug for her uncle before leaving.

As she left, she heard her mother announce, "I blame my sisters. They always treated her as an adult."

She untied Camus and deftly mounted. Learning forward she placed her face on his powerful neck. "At least I don't irritate you. Home we get." Another episode had ended.

Awaiting her was a letter from Venetia, thanking her and promising to visit soon. She described in detail the snapshot Robin had enclosed with the last scribbled note. It was of himself in flying gear smoking a cigarette as he leant on the damaged plane and how she could not stop gazing at it. Eleri had never seen him but Juliette's description of the shock of corn-coloured hair, stocky build and devil-may-care smile fired her imagination.

Her easel was always her escape when her normal high spirits were somewhat dented. She would, while Quellyn slept, start another picture. She saw it so vividly. The image would remain throughout her lunch with Mrs. Sullivan and the child then work.

She hurriedly sketched the golden-haired youth in a flying suit, nonchalantly smoking a cigarette. She saw the torn wing and scraped runway, the damaged trees.

Beneath the dominating wing across the page she painted in scorched earth. The row of trees on the distant right fully foliaged on one side, scraped almost bare on the airfield side. In the far distance she placed two crippled planes; the foreground was dominated by the attractive youth leaning on his conquered German machine, as he smiled with triumph or bravado, the cigarette smoke curling around him.

The picture excited her. It had something, so typical of many such pictures, but the youth to her seemed as real as if she had known him. She tinted in sufficiently to suggest a completed work and mailed it that evening to Wannaker and Sons, the publishers of postcards and calendars. If they accepted it, any royalties could be given to the R.A.F. Benevolent Fund. Surely there must be one. Venetia would undoubtedly be cared for by her people. This done, she rested briefly, as if emotionally exhausted, then went to meet Alvar by walking the drive with Quellyn, as an angry red sunset seemed to be railing against the earth. She held her son's hand tightly. One's whole existence seemed such a fragile state, a mere blip on the scales of eternity.

Together, the trio arrived home a short while later to find a letter from Prunie. Battered and almost illegible, it seemed to have seen much travelling. Postage delivery times were of little consequence in llandia and this must have been a late afternoon delivery.

Delightedly she read of a third child and a happy marriage, also that Abdun, in an official capacity, had visited Talal's school in Cairo for a prize-giving function. Talal, as an ex-student, was present. He had been contacted in the past when Eleri's portrait of Hagar had been sent to his school, in his care. Talal had heard from Sherene and learnt of Eleri's contacts at the embassy in Cairo and asked Abdun if he knew her when he realised Abdun's wife was English. Prunie was overjoyed to hear from Talal of the delivery of the replica portrait to Hagar and how it was her most precious possession. He was much peeved that Eleri had not thanked him since he had informed her of his having accomplished his honourable duty. It was another example of lost communications. Prunie assured him of Eleri's honour and integrity; his letter had never reached her. He seemed consoled and there were promises of further letters from both sides. Talal now worked with his father and the youth's marriage was being arranged.

Eleri's evening no longer seemed sad. The rosy sky took on a brighter aspect and became an omen of promise, beauty, contentment.

CHAPTER TWENTY-THREE

Eleri Visits London

LATE SUMMER FADED INTO A MELLOW SEPTEMBER and a slight pause in hostilities after the debacle of Dunkirk and the fall of France and harrowing air battles over London and the South East with the ensuing sombre news. Venetia and Juliette were meeting in London and contacted Eleri, requesting her to join them. They would go to their old students' cheap restaurant, hoping after so much destruction along the river it still stood. Both her friends were at a low ebb compared with herself, who seemed to be thriving even more than usual, feverishly working, executing her plans, encouragingly succeeding in understanding the management of an estate, writing constant letters, succouring her old aunts, enjoying Maeve and Quellyn.

Alvar considered that she would gain from the visit

to London now that things seemed quieter. He had never spent so many months in isolation and had declined several invitations and felt aggrieved at not meeting old friends. He had ceased hunting; his last promise to his mother, who had constantly agonised over his powers in the field, remembering his father's and brother's deaths.

September the 7th was a day as lovely as any early autumn day could possibly be, the trees in the royal parks beginning to deck themselves for their last dance as if defying the scarred ugliness and drabness surrounding them. The morning nip in the air was like a new beginning, relieving the Londoners from the anxiety and constant alertness of the past months. People were ready for a change even if a change only in the weather. Most looked tired and shabby, there were queues everywhere among boarded-up shop windows. This was not the London she had left. The pulse seemed weaker the pallor greyer, in spite of that sunny autumn day. Her London had gone.

Venetia looked pretty but fragile; Juliette appeared distinctly older, her face bearing the strain of anxiety over Claude. At first, he was listed missing, then there was no news at all, then a sudden message to come and visit him in a military hospital near Oxford. He had been grievously ill for several days and communications had gone astray, mainly because of address change; they had been living in London when he enlisted.

Venetia had not come to terms with Robin's death; she had accepted the fact but had not adapted. Her parents had been bastions, in spite of their early disapproval, and the child was a great salvation.

The young women decided to walk arm in arm as of yore, negotiating the much changed or eroded side streets which had once been their 'shortcuts'. They seemed to be in a different city. They walked toward the north bank and found their favourite, now sad-looking, restaurant. Dark and boarded, teeming with dockers and still some students, the cheeriness within was almost as it used to be. There were endless cups of tea and spam sandwiches, dry uninteresting cakes and no choice. Yet it thrived. Apart from the large West End establishments, this echoed almost every other small eating place. The girls, happy to be together, soon revived in spirits, even managing to buy good wine from 'under the counter' at an exorbitant price, but they cared not. They were so happy to have chosen such a place for their reminiscences and some hope of recapturing more carefree days, when their humble abode had been a paradise of learning and planning, when life ahead seemed an untrodden carpet, pristine and smooth and delicate. They remembered the laughter over Eleri's sedate upbringing, so different from theirs, her colourful anecdotes and her casual acceptance of her remarkable beauty and how any other might have used it as a weapon, a demand. They dared laugh again at her infatuation for Spenser S. Fortesque; Eleri laughed with them but did not tell. He now had more children and was still at the school but was also employed with military duties externally – maps or charts or similar. They had no details.

The saddest note was the fate of Nigel Selkirk, one of the medical students who lodged below them. His wartime service took him into the River Emergency Service. Each ambulance vessel carried one doctor, ten V.A.D.s, two nurses and two orderlies. All on his vessel were killed in June 1940 during the bombardment of the Thames; Juliette had heard of this during a previous London visit.

They soon revived in spite of a daily dose of bad news to contend with. Eleri told them of her pregnancy and the latest altercation with her mother concerning the interfering evil of Dr. Stopes. Aided by the wine, the brightness and hope of youth returned to their faces; Eleri had not lost the glory of personality and all became exhilarated.

Then a wailing siren, which shocked them out of their merriment. Terrified, they watched the dock workers vacate the place, to return to their duties. The nearby dwellers departed for their homes. the few uniformed customers also disappeared. The friends found themselves ushered to a miserable cellar, dingy, damp and furnished with a few camp beds, old sofas and emergency rations ready for distribution. Clinging together, surrounded by strangers, each though the same thought – *Oh to be at home with loved ones* – as the walls shook and the bombs whined and exploded close by. It was the first experience of fear to each though others around spoke of previous bombings, the June bombardment in particular. It was a prolonged raid. Refreshments miraculously appeared after about two hours, the proprietor having braved surrounding chaos to help his uninvited guests. He returned with news of immense fires along the river, numerous fire engines arriving from all directions and several ships and barges on fire. The drone of aircraft overhead was unceasing;

this was a major raid. The brilliant sun of that Saturday afternoon was obliterated by smoke.

The strain and anxiety to the non-seasoned, such as themselves, was terrifying, yet they sensed that many were blasé about it, as if they lived with daily danger. In addition, the strain of what they might find on re-emergence added to the fear.

When the 'All Clear' sounded there was a sense of unity among the large group of the shelter as they endeavoured to give courage to one another. Somehow, they all had to make their way home or to a nightshift of duty somewhere.

*

The young women walked through silent streets, many houses still burning, fire engines still racing, and there were mobile canteens dotted here and there as well as blood transfusion centres. There were warning notices of unexploded bombs and many small fires caused by incendiaries still being doused. Air raid wardens were directing people, and some were digging in smouldering debris. Around the canteens was a contrived cheeriness, a sort of 'thank you' prayer for having been spared. Sloane Square seemed the best station to aim for unless, with luck, a bus might appear. Each would have gone anywhere outside the metropolis and hope to find a way home in their various directions.

Venetia and Juliette risked the underground, though hold-ups were inevitable. Eleri opted to walk, hoping for a bus or taxi to Wellington Station. Subdued and scared, they hugged and parted, feeling even closer for having endured the horrendous experience together.

In the dim light of early evening Eleri noted evidence of destruction as she walked, hopefully in the right direction, as so many streets were closed. She passed basements rapidly becoming lakes and skeletal rooms, where she had once dined in this erstwhile lovely section of London. Her trained eye noticed fine mosaic floors, probably unseen since Roman times but unlikely to be rescued in the present mayhem. The smoke was everywhere, strange odours and ghostly noises, as masonry or wood continued to crack and fall. There was no hope of a taxi and the one bus which passed was filled to overflowing and did not stop, its hooded lights ominous and strange. When a solitary taxi did appear she had to share it with two cheerful ladies returning to dockland duties; they were heading for 'the river' as they called it and in order to claim that taxi for her own use to the station, she first accompanied them.

What she saw made an indelible imprint on her mind. Warehouses more than a century old were aflame on St. Katharine's Docks, the fires in the warehouses had ignited barges and paraffin wax floated on the water, or so she was informed. The basin was a cauldron of flames resembling pictures of Dante's inferno.

Her companions seemed to accept it all. They were members of the Women's Legion and always helped in mobile canteens, from which they served tea and coffee to the fire workers and first aid teams. On more than one occasion they had served tea in jamjars from milk churns. The memory still amused them. Their job was arduous, dangerous and exposed but they considered it their war effort.

Eleri wished them the best in the task ahead. She would remember them. Her fear had abated; they had left a warm glow and an idea germinating in her mind. She would start a voluntary organisation in llandia.

Later that night in a cold, crowded station, like others, hoping that a train would eventually arrive, she planned the work in hand.

Later still that Sunday night, guided by the smoke of earlier bombing, following the trail of fires the onslaught started again and for nine and a half hours they rained their destruction. Would-be passengers huddled in a tunnel leading to the station. In the melee she heard of further devastation along the Thames; they talked of an unbroken wall of flames three miles long. All trains were late because of delayed action bombs. She longed to be home to embrace her husband and child and felt guilty about her peaceful existence.

Trapped in a confined space, people felt amazingly friendly and kind. All barriers were down; a feeling of dependence on one another pervaded. She gathered more information about the Women's Legion and their work throughout the severest raids. She remembered the V.A.D.s she had met at the Cavendish Club, Marble Arch, and knowing of the work of the W.R.V.S. in England she determined to use the Fenton girls as a core and start up something similar at home. This was to be her new project, carefully planned during this forced incarceration. She would call them VAL (Voluntary Aid Legion) – Vals for short.

When she eventually arrived home next day after a tedious, long, uncomfortable journey, her plan was already formulated. The bliss of husband, child and home was enervating. After a much-needed sleep and with a deep sense of gratitude she set to work. The idea spread. Based on the Fenton girls and their uniform, many women joined and provided their own uniforms. They organised jumble sales, tea parties, outings, competitions and a weekly stall to raise funds for charity. Jams, cakes, good used clothing, garden produce and plants were usually on offer. The village hall and church hall were in constant use. Fine days would find market stalls in the square. Eleri's ex-assistants, no longer employees, worked alongside her and within two weeks a committee was formed. Excitedly Eleri could visualise the movement growing. Alvar championed her but never ceased to be amazed by his energetic wife.

CHAPTER TWENTY-FOUR

Briende Visits the Stones

THE YEAR 1940 WAS DRAWING TOWARDS ITS AUTUMN, as the political news became grimmer and a pall of gloom was spread over Western Europe.

The late summer had a particular significance for Briende; the tenth anniversary of her first meeting with Ralph Maine.

As Eleri was excitedly looking forward to her ill-fated London reunion with friends, Briende, on the tenth anniversary of her first climb to the stones with her beloved, decided to recapture, if possible, the memory, alone. Since his death she had not been near the magical place.

As she slowly toiled up the craggy slopes, and over the stones, the almost knotty fossilised roots of bracken, impeded now and again with invading gorse or bramble, she felt his presence. The breeze lifted her hair and breathed past her face as it had long ago. The birds sang the same song and the nearby sea echoed the same sounds as it rasped against the pebbled shore. There was the same lapping of the waves, the same distant forests and timeless hills, holding for her as ever, the voices of her ancestors. They too had sworn allegiance to each other aeons ago and she felt a part of all that had gone before and Ralph's touch, like the down of Rosebay or thistle, was ever present, as she watched these delicate particles swarm in the breeze around her.

She had been a pretty girl, hardly more than a child, no ambition beyond finding contentment, but since his death his spirit had urged her onwards, ever onwards. After the initial shock she had allowed herself to be guided as she thought he would have guided her, to training, to reading, to professional success.

She composed as she walked, as if some unforeseen presence was aiding her:

"We climbed the craggy footpath, you and I
Hand in hand or arms entwined up the steep
mountainside
while the sun sank red in the western sky
We parted the tall bracken, you and I
To reach our green haven by the murmuring stream
Where we lay and loved and planned
But we were parted you and I, you and I."

On reaching the stone of their secret betrothal day, she

sank to lean on it and listen to the quaint music they had heard long ago. The Stone was warm to the cheek, the springy grass at its base an obliging cushion. Were it not for her beautiful daughter the whole episode of her romance would seem a dream. She gave thanks for the unimaginable bliss of the brief time they had spent together.

Taking hold of her emotions she decided that it would not be wise to linger. The mist was encircling the hilltop, the stillness and loneliness were not inducive to comfort. She felt removed from the world though llandia, in spite of strangers from without, was still a gentle world, divorced from turmoil.

As the shadows of the evening were rapidly gathering, she descended over the same craggy way, feeling a calm, a sense of communication, a commitment to continue working at what she hoped he'd have aimed for. It was as if some divine plan had been laid for her and trustingly, she followed it. And in today, as the poet tells us, already walks tomorrow.

For Christmas that year Mrs. Blethyn, as was her usual practice, decided to gather the family together and inject the political gloom of that winter with warmth and joy. This meant 'family' to include Alvar.

The attractive, intelligent Madoc Blethyn clan wearied him. Why did such beautiful women have to be so agonisingly vivacious and informed, as well as talented? They talked of films and books and theatre, politics and passions. Briende alone had a repose about her. At almost thirty years old she was still lovely and fragile and had, of course, influenced by his mother, been his first intention. Their eyes never met. From the point of view of age, she would have been more suitable and by now there would have been several children, and this thought drew his eyes to nine-year-old Maeve. She was so exquisitely lovely; long straight silvery-blonde hair, tall and lithe. Was there not a queen or mistress once with hair like that? An unsuitable liaison – Edward IV, he thought? He would not ask this lot; they would tell him plus accompanying data. He watched Maeve watching him. She was unlike her cousins, more pensive, uncannily sensitive to the nuances of other people's thoughts.

The gong rang for dinner and broke his reverie. Seated between a niece and Sîan, his gaze took in the assortment of kin round that table. The women were lovely yet Eleri's striking beauty and luminosity surpassed them all. Moya, opposite, with laughing Irish eyes, Sîan beside him with her seductive Welsh sibilance, Eleri animatedly charming her companions, her maiden aunts watching her with love. To them she gave the perfume to the rose and the sparkle to the stars and represented what they would have wished to be.

They all toasted Eleri's expected baby, led by Cousin Wynn, causing a ripple of excitement among the children, including Quellyn, who decided to clap without understanding why. This brought laughter.

Knowing that Alvar felt an outsider, as soon as the sumptuous feast had ended, Eleri charmingly suggested driving to Fentons. The good doctor and Anya, the eldest girl, home from Cardiff University where she was studying medicine, would be home for the holiday, as well as two Polish airmen, now R.A.F. They had been wounded when their crippled plane had made a forced landing. The doctor had met them at the hospital soon afterwards. She told the assembled family that a visit from her would be expected. Alvar's usually impassive expression showed relief.

The family understood and quietly admired Eleri's tact. Mrs. Blethyn rose and calmly returned with a basket of confections, jams, wine, dainty cakes and mince pies and handed it to Eleri with a, "Wish them all Christmas joy. We'll hold Quellyn here." A woman of few words but the few usually pithy.

His spirits lifted as soon as they were alone, speeding towards the hills, with Pen Melyn in the car mirror fading into the background.

In the silence of Christmas afternoon, they met no human, beast or vehicle, as they sped northwards. There was no sound either except the hypnotic hum of the car engine.

Half-way across the moors he saw not but sensed her gaze upon him, studying him, and consumed with longing. He felt her power, the scent of her hair, her magnetism. There was between them a sort of silken cord, each echoing the other's desire. She dwelt on the idea that passion was to him like slithering into the deep lake at Campions on a sweltering afternoon, swimming under water then emerging on the other side triumphant and exhausted. Desire, to her, went along with her artistic temperament – a selfishness, a need.

He stopped the car, grabbed the travel rug, alighted,

crossed to her side and, holding her hand, pulled her with urgency. He placed the rug on a piece of ground half-surrounded by brown, twig-covered boulders and with a leaden sky as witness and the lacy pattern of frost on sleeping hedges, they made love. A contrast to their midsummer moon and hazy intoxicating perfume was this bleak midwinter madness but she smiled her enigmatic smile as they rose to return to the car. There was a hint of mischief in their irrepressible attraction to each other, a sort of defiance, a sense of greed.

He tucked the heavy rug around her, brushed her forehead with a kiss and turned his attention to the wheel. They would soon arrive at Fentons.

Young women found Alvar devastatingly attractive and he bathed in their admiration. The joyous arrival at Fentons called forth blushes from the older girls, Anya in particular. Her eyes were alight and Eleri actually caught a grin from the good doctor, for him a frivolous gesture as he noted the girls' excitement. Anya, at eighteen, was comely and susceptible; Liesel, her younger friend or foster-sister, herself aware of the same feelings. The pilots, hitherto a novelty, faded into insignificance when Alvar Garonne was present. Each time young women admired him Eleri remembered herself at nineteen, bewitched in a wood, on an August morning. And he was hers; as long as she was around, he was hers.

At the same time, carrying his much wanted second child, she knew that as her slenderness became a fast-growing bulk, his ardour would decrease at a corresponding rate. His woman had to remain beautiful and inviting and, as Eleri reasoned, there lay his incompleteness and unreality. She dismissed such thoughts and concentrated on the warmth of their welcome.

Leah, aged nine, interested her, and she always felt flattered when the girl voluntarily edged herself beside her. Leah's story was typical of many, but she was the only Fenton child without a surname or exact birth date.

One market day, in the small town of Schleiden near the Belgian border, a youth of about fourteen years had cast the weeping child onto a horse-drawn cart with the plea, "Take her, please take her, she will be killed."

The old ignorant farmer and his wife were left with a sobbing girl aged around seven years crying, "Humbert, don't leave me." He had quickly disappeared. He had not sounded like a country boy.

Both youngsters wore the yellow star. The innocent farmers understood, quickly removed the horrid stigma and took her home to their sons, who were unwelcoming and uncharitable. They too had been infected with anti-Semitism.

Neighbours began to talk, and the simple old couple felt threatened and ostracised. The child was a bed-wetter, a poor eater and already disciplined to a Kosher diet. Her clothes were of superior quality but what she wore were all she possessed. She was also clean regarding washing her hands before and after eating anything and her manners were refined. She wrote her name 'Leah' carefully and clearly but never wrote a surname. Was she blaming her Jewish surname on her family's misfortunes, or had she been told not to use it? They knew not. She could already read and write German and Hebrew and labelled things in her room in Hebrew. She was also terrified of all uniforms.

One night, after a few weeks, the old couple took her by train to Ostende, to them an enormous journey. They bought her a ticket at the ferry office and threw her among a horde of Jewish refugees, youngsters of all ages, where she quickly blended into harbour-side crowds and disappeared in tears.

The child arrived with others at a Jewish orphanage in England, having attached herself to a fourteen-year-old boy she insisted on calling 'Humbert'. He was embarrassed and inconvenienced and constantly rejected her.

Child psychologists learnt very little from her. Asked to draw a house, she drew a building with tall walls and a large round window and flames rising from it. Asked to draw a man, the figure wore a dark hat and a side curl. Could the house have been a synagogue and her father a rabbi? If so, the punishment meted out would have been extremely severe. Aachen and Bonn, the nearest cities, had once held well-attended Jewish synagogues.

Dr. Skiroski was seduced by the child's story. She felt thrice rejected and was slow to react to him. He gave her his name and placed her in Rachel Mann's wise care. He would follow her development with interest. Was the horror of her experiences buried within her? Would she forget or refuse to remember?

Eleri was attached to the girl. She coaxed her to school, one day a week at first, then suggested she be put in charge of Friedel, a new, younger refugee who had joined them. This proved the antidote required; things were improving.

Too soon yet to uproot her and have her at The Lodge for a visit but it would come. Amos Skiroski had her welfare at heart, as he had for all of them and he was grateful to Eleri for her help, her warmth, her intelligence. This beautiful woman had renewed his faith in mankind, supported his project and embraced them into her family, and if she should ever need a devoted friend he hoped to be at hand.

*

Throughout the winter the air raids on the cities seemed unrelenting. The doctor seldom came home; the pressure of work increased as more people were injured and several hospitals, including his own, were damaged by bombing. In his drab room, during allocated rest periods, he never failed to write detailed letters about his experiences, as he wanted them recorded in case he did not survive .The casualty wards, in basements where practicable, operated like assembly lines in a factory, an endless supply of bewildered humans coming and going day and night. As well as injuries, serious and superficial, there were cases of impetigo, scabies and lice. The courage of the people boosted his own efforts when he considered their adaptation to shortages, damaged homes, disturbed nights, disrupted transport.

That same winter Ryan Cordell, the foreman at Campions, contracted pneumonia. This increased the workload on everyone else, including Alvar, who spent more time than ever before managing. Gradually he became appreciative of his wife's grasp on the business.

She had by now taken over almost all correspondence, pleased to do anything useful in her hindered condition.

Another January invitation tempted Alvar to London. A good friend of long standing was about to be posted to Egypt. He thought little of his chances – the journey alone around the Cape, of course, was not something to be anticipated with pleasure. Eleri actually thought he would benefit from a break in routine but asked him to stay outside London just in case. She had not forgotten her own experience of a raid and, in her vulnerable state, she wished him to be safe. He met a number of his friends near Croydon and came back rejuvenated. He had even contacted Dr. Skiroski and invited him for a meal, but a new influx of burn victims, after a cable collapsed in the East End during a raid, kept him at his work. Eleri appreciated her husband's kind intentions, as the two men were very different.

Another tempting invitation came in March. Ryan Cordell had recovered and Alvar considered that a brief escape was in order. Eleri, the least selfish person, begged him to stay home. She had felt uneasy all morning. Mrs. Britt had telephoned asking if she had recent news of Laurence. The last letter had come from Thermopylae, which was holding out as gloriously as it ever did, but Greece was on the brink of falling. The two women exchanged thoughts and hopes. The political news was dire as ever.

Alvar succumbed to his wife's unease and stayed at home. By the end of the week they had heard that the Café Royal, where the celebration was held, had received a direct hit during the party. It was crowded with officers on leave with their wives and girlfriends. The bomb fell as they danced and laughed. The band leader, and a large number of the revellers were killed, including the daughter of a leading politician. Alvar felt that he owed his life to his wife's uncanny mood that day. His friend was one of those killed.

In the midst of this gloom a happy letter from Lady Bettina announced her marriage and delightful lifestyle. There was also a list of instructions, charmingly rendered, regarding putting some of her favourite possessions into safe storage until the war had ended. She asked that certain personal items be sent to her daughter but her most treasured pieces were to be for Eleri. The other favour requested was that they call the coming child Miranda, if a girl; her husband's choice for a child she had miscarried. She sounded happy, longed to see them but was delighted for them.

Miranda was born easily at the end of April. Alvar was overjoyed at having a daughter and impatient to repossess his wife, who would regain her fascination and beauty. The path ahead was bright and bestrewn with flowers, the sun ever shining, no cloud on the horizon. He had two beautiful children, the loveliest wife in the world, prosperity and health. Together they were working for the less fortunate and making meaningful use of their country home as well as enriching local life.

A mere three weeks later they were to attend a London wedding. Alvar's closest school friend and ex-hunting companion was marrying a rich divorcée. Eleri had promised earlier in the year to accompany her husband to the nuptials and both looked forward to a splendid event.

It was early May, an unusually lovely May day, and the golden couple walked to his office in the big house. They made a partial tour of the estate as they had many times before. The land still appeared to be at rest, the quiet hills, the sheep, the long-stemmed daisies budding, the fragrant wind and promising sky. Eleri, tuned in to natural beauty, was content. He, she knew, was eagerly anticipating his drive to London. To him, it seemed years, not months since he had been there. She did not destroy the morning by conveying her fears to him, but she had decided not to accompany him. His disappointment was going to be acute, but the softness of motherhood was not something he could appreciate, and fear for her children being left motherless, if she became a victim in a raid, was gnawing at her. She had experienced a serious raid, but he had not, and hardly expected a repeat of the Café Royal direct hit such a short while ago.

The day before they were due to leave, she informed him of her decision. For the first time ever, she detected his possession of a temper, something she did not know existed. He turned pale and his dark eyes resembled deep pools as the irises and pupils became one dark hue. How could she be so selfish, he exploded! How he had longed for his friends to meet her! They had all become so scattered and this was a long-planned reunion. It would have been a second honeymoon, and the children were safely and lovingly cared for! Completely baffled, he failed to find words of condemnation. After the terrifying outburst he was silent, then stared and remained motionless. The baby suddenly awakened, crying, and his wife responded in one swift motion and ran upstairs, relieved to remove herself from an unpleasant situation.

Her heart thumped as she picked up Miranda. Devastated, she tried to comfort herself that two and a half weeks after a birth was too soon to go partying at such a distance, that she was not being difficult or illogical. She felt sorry for him but convinced herself that she was right. The question plaguing her was how she could possibly make amends; she wanted so much to make him happy. She lay on the bed, her baby beside her, and her heart raced uncontrollably. To her this sort of panic was a rare experience. She often laughed her mother's 'cures' but at this moment, had there been one at hand, she would have gratefully swallowed it.

Early next morning she heard him stir after having spent the night on a couch in his dressing room. Quickly donning a robe, she rushed downstairs to reach him as he reached his car. He still wore his mask of unforgiveness, but she wrenched the door open, placing her arms around his neck. "Please do not leave me in such a mood!" He vaguely responded, "You broke a promise. For months I've seen you in a black dress for the evening dinner and in something striking for the ceremony. My old crowd and my stunning wife – bliss!" He began to shake with renewed anger.

"There will be other times. We'll plan a splendid function at Campions, the next time you are all together. I love you, love you."

This mellowed him somewhat. "I may never see them again – they are all over the globe. All right, I'll look forward to coming home to you."

It was not said with any warmth, but her spirits revived. When it came to relationships, pride should always take second place. She was relieved that she had managed to reach him before he left. She spent the rest of the day planning some special reunion for him, to make amends. It had been their first serious quarrel and she would never forget that day in May.

She accomplished her usual chores, telephoning, writing, visiting the baby every hour, talking to Mrs. Sullivan, taking Quellyn for a romp, writing her journal. By nightfall, tired physically and emotionally, after settling the children and dismissing Mrs. Sullivan early, she retired to bed.

Mrs. Sullivan had her attic flat, above the nursery, especially converted for her and this she considered her domain, far more so than her village home. She liked to read and listen to her wireless and Mr. Sullivan, a builder, preferred early nights and lights out. He also arose very early and expected breakfast. To have separate bedrooms, in his view, was tantamount to divorce, an unheard-of state, utterly unrespectable. Much argument regularly ensued, so she was always delighted to stay, which she had done for most of the nights since Miranda's birth.

Eleri tried to read but could not concentrate; she tried listening to music, but her mind wandered; she tried adding to her journal but in this she also failed. She could not bear the thought of making Alvar unhappy. She longed to charm and sparkle for him among the friends he so admired, attend his favourite haunts, buy him a handsome present like a superb hand-crafted saddle – anything different, showing much thought.

Feeling easier next day, work, as usual, became her escape. She began to plan a concert on his birthday, when a full audience could share the celebration. She listed his favourite pieces of music and proceeded to plan the programme. A lot of revenue had already poured in and the hard-working committee had sent a great deal to charity, mainly refugee charities, including some help with the visiting families who came and went with regularity. It had all been very worthwhile, that idea of hers, which had germinated that horrendous night the previous autumn. She decided against listening to the wireless; any report of a London bombing would be too unnerving.

The second night sleep did not elude her. An extremely exhausting day had guaranteed a readiness for rewarding sleep. One day more and he would be home.

CHAPTER TWENTY-FIVE

Death of Garonne

A SHARP RINGING OF THE BEDSIDE TELEPHONE–insistent. Was she dreaming? Her watch showed half past three. Startled from a deep sleep she reached for the phone.

"Is that Mrs. Alvar Garonne?" The voice was kind but tired.

"It is. What has happened?" She was immediately alert.

"I'm sorry to have to inform you but Mr. Garonne has been severely injured in a raid. It would be best if you could come here to St. Bernard's as soon as practicable unless you have someone in London."

"I'll come; I should be with you by midday." Her voice was barely audible.

"Are you still there? Yes? You know where St. Bernard's is?"

"I do. I take it he is—" and was interrupted.

"I can say no more. Report to Sister Martin in Parker Ward below. Bypass reception. Sorry." She hung up.

Alvar was dead. She knew that he was dead or dying. She replaced the phone.

She found herself shivering uncontrollably, the bed hitting against the wall, her hands ineffectively trying to gather the quilt around her. Her brain was clear, slotting actions into compartments. She was in shock. What would her mother do? Hot milk laced with honey and brandy was the best idea she could conjure. Brandy she hated. She had to keep in control, think straight, be sensible. With difficulty she struggled into her dressing gown and slippers and, holding on with care to walls and banister, descended into the kitchen. He was dead. She knew that he was dead.

She leant on the range, poured milk into a saucepan, retrieved a notebook and pencil from a drawer. She endeavoured to think clearly; numbered her priorities. The milk boiled over.

Stirring honey into a cup of hot milk she took deep breaths as if to take hold of herself, placed her head on the table and waited for the milk to cool. She was still unsteady.

The kitchen seemed large, clinical, unfriendly; the big clock ticked loudly, each tick a knell. She began to sip her milk and calmed somewhat. She proceeded to shakily write; Briende's number first.

Please could Miranda, with essentials, be taken to her grandmother. Could Bridget be brought for Quellyn. She noted that she had been called to London urgently.

Was there anything else pending? There was. Another sheet of paper informed Ryan Cordell that the surveyor was expected at three o'clock for the annual check-up. Would he see to him at Campions and note any items needing attention?

Her brain was still clear, but her body seemed to be working independently of her mind. She felt cold and was still shaking but not as much. Three hours before morning, the sensible thing would be to return to bed. She would not sleep.

Curled up in the foetal position, bedding wrapped tightly around her, she tried to assemble her thoughts. Alvar was dead. She knew that he was dead. Miranda would be fatherless as Maeve had been and Quellyn had lost his friend and hero. Her burdens lay heavily upon her; the estate, the children, the war efforts at Campions, the VAL project and all its implications. He was dead, she was certain. Everything was quiet as if Death walked.

She was so very relieved that she had seen him the morning he left, so happy to have parted amicably. In a fevered jumble of thoughts, past and present, an emptiness within, she awaited the dreaded light. At six o'clock she got up.

She decided to wear the VAL uniform, most sensible for wartime travel, the navy cloak made by the aunts and the peaked beret – very uniform-like. Her capacious shoulder bag would carry toiletries, essentials, address book and money. She would get the first train from the village at seven o'clock. Driving to Limorrnah would be a mistake in her present agitation. She knew not what lay ahead, her condition on returning or even when she would be home. Her own car would be at the local stationmaster's house. Her thoughts were galloping ahead, her practical self, trying to take control.

Mrs. Sullivan, on hearing movement downstairs, quickly appeared in her great dressing gown. Alarmed, she enquired, "Madam what is it?" on seeing Eleri so pale and already dressed.

"I have to go to London urgently, there are notes on the table."

'Will Mr. Garonne be back today?"

"No, I will let you know when I'll be home."

"It is not for me to say but you had a baby less than three weeks ago. You must eat something. It's a long way."

She bustled to make tea and toast. Gratefully, Eleri drank the tea and mechanically tried to eat toast. She failed. Mrs. Sullivan quickly placed apples, bread buns, cheese, tomatoes in a white paper bag and placed them above Eleri's open bag. She helped her on with her cloak, even slipped the bag on her shoulder. Inwardly, she was most concerned, and sensed that this vivacious young woman must be in some dire trouble. There was something not quite right.

"Make sure the children are all right. I entrust them to you. If you need more help, please call my sister. She will arrange things. Thank you for your kindness." She seemed a stranger.

The early train was warm and relatively empty. The ferry left on time. The journey on the mainland train was slow, crowded, alternately stuffy or chilly, innumerable stops, blanked out station names, troops in a variety of uniforms boarding or alighting, smoking, talking. Country women with baskets on their way to some market, pushing their way in, sad-looking wives or girlfriends seeing their men off at several small stations. A WVS lady pushed a trolley from window to window at the larger stations. Eleri watched and listened, wishing she could sleep; her mind was still racing, the ache inside her unrelenting. The train would be late and she would not reach St. Bernard's by midday.

She must have dozed.

London at last.

Wellington was teeming as usual, some exits blocked, some escalators not functioning. Some platforms were closed. She heard snatches of conversation pertaining to damaged lines, so she made no attempt to use the Underground. On reaching the street she waited for a taxi. Not one appeared unoccupied, so she boarded a crowded bus going in the right direction. She would walk the rest of the way if she could not get a connection. In this she was fortunate.

Everywhere there was evidence of heavy bombing, disrupted traffic and knots of bewildered people. The forecourt of the hospital, when she arrived, was a maze of cars, ambulances and at least three makeshift fire engines, which meant old cars painted grey and adapted. There were teams of helmeted workmen around the building.

She walked past reception as directed and went down to the basement ward. She had never felt so lonely, so lost, so vulnerable. Alvar was dead. She knew that he was dead and waited to be told.

At last she found the ward. Sister Martin was very busy. There were people on stretchers and in wheelchairs. Some looked shocked, including the so-young, and weary, porters moving among the dead and dying on the floor.

Taking her chance at the first pause, she presented herself to Sister Martin.

"Step into the office, Mrs. Garonne, here in the back. I'll see you presently." Eleri wanted it over with. She was ready. She sat and waited.

"Mrs. Garonne. Sorry, so sorry about all this chaos. You realise your husband was gravely injured?"

She held her hands and sat beside her. "I'm afraid he died soon after I phoned."

"Tell me, if you can, how was he?"

"Unconscious, neck and chest injuries, also serious damage from flying glass. He did not suffer."

Inexplicably, she found herself asking, "Was he in one piece? Was his face damaged?"

She could not bear the thought of the exquisite Alvar Garonne being disfigured. She remembered his poise, his charm, his pride.

"The neck wound was patched up. He looks very peaceful."

She waited a moment, though her phone was ringing and red lights flickering above the door. "Are you prepared to see him?"

"Yes, will you take me?"

"My dear, I cannot."

A nurse appeared and took Eleri's arm.

It seemed a long way, a nightmare journey along

endless corridors and through swing doors galore. She hoped she would not falter.

Courage, she thought. *Courage, Eleri, there are children at home, there will be enough time for tears, grief, loneliness.*

There were several sheeted bodies in the large mortuary, but all was a blur except the one at which a green-coated figure stood. He turned back the sheet. The handsome sleeping face was unmarked, the black hair sleekly combed. She bent and kissed his forehead as an outward show of affection. It was icy cold.

She did not feel the ground beneath her feet as, with the nurse, she left the room. In an outside anteroom she asked whether she could sit. There was a bare wooden bench against the wall. In the corner a white-coated youth sat on the floor, his head on his knees. He was asleep.

The green-coated figure came to the swing doors and said, "Leave him, nurse, he has been on duty all night. Will you please wait?"

The young man, one of the porters, now overcome with exhaustion, had escorted a middle-aged couple and was meant to escort them back to the ward. Very soon the couple re-emerged, the man inadequately supporting his wife. The nurse with Eleri would guide them back, then have the task of escorting more shocked and grieving relatives for the same grisly task.

Back in the anteroom off the ward, waiting to sign forms, the three bereaved people became acquainted, the woman weeping uncontrollably, her husband trying to be supportive. He looked at Eleri, pale and still as a statue, and realised that she had also lost someone. During the seemingly long walk back they had each been trapped in personal grief, barely aware of anyone else. Now they sat together and waited while screams and crying ensued from outside.

"I am Talbot Bessington. This is my wife, Monica. We lost Serena, our only child, in last night's raid."

"I am Eleri Garonne. My husband was killed."

At the name Garonne both reacted. That was the name which had been mentioned as the other victim who was with their daughter. This beautiful young woman must be his wife.

The situation was delicate, but sensitivity was overpowered by grief on the part of them all. Did she know, he wondered? She did not, at that point, but almost immediately that inexplicable instinct of hers told her that they had been together. Some indefinable contact had been made between this couple and herself and she felt that it was forever.

Sister Martin called Eleri into her inner office and at her questioning gave a brief account. The couple were in a taxi, on their way to the city. The woman was killed immediately, and Mr. Garonne brought in unconscious. The driver, less badly injured, was in another ward with arm, shoulder and back injuries. He had been thrown clear; the passengers took the main blast. They came in along with many other casualties about three o'clock. Some were still coming in. She indicated with her arm. She produced from a drawer Alvar's battered wallet and broken watch and one cufflink. His clothes were ruined. She said the woman had been quickly identified because she wore a gold identity disc, though her handbag was found later.

"Her name was—"

"I know her name. May I visit the driver?"

"He's in Gifford Ward – a Mr. Bower. Ask the sister on duty, I'm sorry, I have to go. There are others to see. I'm so sorry."

"Thank you for your kindness, and also the nurse who took me down. Her name, please? I'll write."

"Jane Smithers. Her husband died in action two weeks ago."

"Thank you for telling me. May I say goodbye to the Bessingtons after you have seen them?"

"I'll ask them to wait for you in the foyer."

"Thank you."

Gifford Ward was quieter; all had been seen to. Eleri asked for Mr. Bower. The sister on duty waved her through. "Five minutes, no more. Bed number six."

His head was bandaged, he was pale and one arm, heavily bandaged, was suspended in a sort of hoist.

She introduced herself and told him why she was there. She could almost see him thinking. He was being kind. She liked the man. "People share taxis these days, they often don't know each other." She respected his sensitivity.

"That's all right. Don't distress yourself. Where did you pick them up? I'd like to know."

"Outside the Park Lane. There was a big party. The lady wanted to go over Tower Bridge. A fancy, I thought, she was a bit, well…"

'Yes. They had been drinking. Don't worry, please tell me."

"The warning sounded but she said not to stop but take them straight to the city. That is all. I remember no more, except coming in here. I heard that she was dead on arrival and he almost dead. I'm sorry."

The nurse came. "Sorry. Time's up."

Eleri pressed his good hand. "Thank you, Mr. Bower."

She returned to the foyer, planning to send him a gift. The Bessingtons were waiting for her. In a way they sensed a responsibility.

Eleri, on finding them, was immediately uplifted. "Thank you," she whispered.

"Where are you staying? We wondered..." His voice faded off.

"I don't know. All was too rushed, but I have a friend in Kensington. The hotels are probably full."

"We live in Chelsea. Come home with us." The tears rolled down his cheeks. His wife murmured, "Please."

Outside in the fog and rain, a typical, dismal day, when London has such days, they waited. Every taxi was full, the rain unceasing. At last a taxi with one elderly passenger drew up and the driver's brusque voice volunteered, "We are going as far as Sloane Square. Any good?"

"Thank you." They gladly entered, the elderly passenger in the front and the Bessingtons with Eleri behind.

The driver chatted on, not expecting a reply. He had worked for eight hours at a stretch, the night had been hell. He wondered why people came to London if they did not have to; he was planning to get out. The army had refused him, this was no life and so on. Sloane Square at last. Mr. Bessington paid and they waited for further transport.

As if by magic a private car stopped. A young man and his girlfriend were going to Battersea. 'We are going through Chelsea – any help?" They accepted with gratitude. He was on leave, had not been home for two years, could not believe what had happened to London. They briefly told their story of the past few hours.

In Cheyne Walk Mr. Bessington offered a note but he refused. They wished him luck and he sympathised with them. A very warm memory for all.

The noble house, which had once been beautiful, appeared cold and forbidding. At one glance, once inside the imposing front door with panels of stained glass heavily taped over, she sensed an elegance now in eclipse. Talbot Bessington drew the heavy blackout curtains before switching on the lights, then turned on the three-bar electric fire now sitting in the classic marble fireplace. He tenderly draped his wife in a shawl from the sofa and offered Eleri a plaid rug. She declined; she had her cloak.

She noted the magnificent furniture and silk curtains, the ornate ceilings, now cracked, and the Turkish rugs covering the floor. Huddled around the inadequate fire they attempted to make contact. Monica Bessington still seemed buried in grief; her crying did not cease. Mr. Talbot said he'd make some tea and find something to eat depending on what they had. Eleri offered to help.

The cheerless kitchen had cupboards galore. As he searched for something to eat, she noticed that most were virtually empty. What a contrast with her home! Rationing was a serious business, she realised. At last a tin of corned beef and a stale loaf! He decided to make toast, so Eleri cut the bread.

"I fear my wife will completely collapse. I must try and get her to eat something." He found some trays and placed exquisite Royal Albert plates upon them. Eleri recognised the pattern and knew them to be rare. On each he placed a meagre portion. Eleri remembered the uneaten food in her bag and fetched some. She had not eaten on the journey. Her spirit, heavily laden, had had no thought of food.

As they ate, she told them of her home and children, the sad telephone call, the long journey, her refusal to accompany her husband as the baby was only two and a half weeks old.

They spoke of Serena, her charmed life before the war, her marriage to a soldier last heard of in January 1941 in Egypt. He'd been promoted soon after the wedding and she was so proud of him. They talked of the big wedding, the parties, her love of life, her job at Trinity House before it was bombed, her flat in the city. All three guessed that it was where they had been heading. Unspoken words seemed to unite them – their good-time daughter and Eleri's unfaithful husband.

Mrs. Bessington was quieter – thoughtfully listening. The courage of this lovely girl, mother of a toddler and brand-new baby, having travelled alone to confront a situation such as this. Both thought her immeasurably brave; so poised and stalwart and alone. There was a strength about her and a sweetness.

Mrs. Bessington, for a moment, forgot her own deep grief and showed consideration for Eleri.

"Mrs. Garonne must be tired, dear. Perhaps you should show her to Serena's room," she added. "I hope there is no air raid. If so, I won't take shelter." She was crying again.

"I'll show Mrs. Garonne the basement, just in case."

He gently took Eleri's arm and led her to the cellar, now converted into a shelter with two camp beds, a table, a chair, emergency rations and clumsy crockery, a large container of water, primus stove, matches and an antiquated gardener's lavatory behind some makeshift alcove. He explained that the house had been damaged but not hit. It was up to her, if there was a raid, to join them in the cellar. He also said that after this tragedy he would probably leave his job and leave London until all this was over. There was nothing left to strive for.

He then took her to Serena's room after she had said goodnight to his wife. He followed the now normal routine of pulling the blackout curtains and switched on the light. He took this opportunity to ask her if she had plans for the funeral. Would she be taking her husband's body home?

"No. I decided on the journey to settle for the simplest dignified service, preferably in a crematorium."

The same thought had struck both. Before he rejoined his wife the decision had been made for one service – the sooner the better. He said he'd start telephoning to make arrangements straight away. She thanked him, telling him how much this meant to her.

She looked around a very pink, very feminine room, dizzyingly young and frivolous. There was a doll dressed as a ballet dancer on a frilled chair, make-up, perfumes and tiny ornaments on the dressing table as well as a tinted wedding photograph of a beautiful bride and her young subaltern husband in dress uniform beside her, each gazing adoringly into the other's eyes. Eleri turned it over and placed her bag on top. It was too sad. On the wall was a painting of a lovely child, also in ballet dress. She would also turn this over. She thought of her own mint-new daughter and understood their grief. She hung her cloak in the large wardrobe. Serena's perfume reached her and some of her party dresses were still hanging within. There were hats and a selection of shoes.

Tomorrow there was a funeral to be planned. Neither she nor Alvar had made any pretence at religion so she did not consider that she was doing him an injustice. Her last thoughts before sleep overcame her were of Alvar and their life together, the ecstasy, the style. She thought of her now fatherless young children, of Pen Melyn, where there had always been such love, and how they would now need it.

She sank her head into the pillow of the girl who had died with him. Her presence was everywhere. Eleri wondered whether they had known each other in their mad whirl partying days. She may even have been one of the gilded girls who once frequented Campions. She was just twenty-seven years old, three years older than herself. On this sad note, the oblivion of sleep took over.

At four in the morning she was awakened by air raid sirens. Mr. Bessington tapped at her door. He said the bombing seemed some distance away, but they were going to the basement. Eleri was welcome to his camp bed – he would use the armchair. Gathering her cloak around her and carrying bag and clothes she followed him. His wife, completely exhausted, was already asleep. She longed to be home as she listened to dull thuds and whines. The house appeared to shake. She then slept.

At eight-thirty, she awoke alone in the basement. She had not heard the 'All Clear'.

She found Talbot Bessington in the kitchen, making tea. He had already been out and managed to find a bakery open, where he queued for bread and buns. His wife was still in bed. He asked Eleri to join them in the bedroom, the only heated room in the house, where, well-wrapped, they sat on the big ornate bed and finalised funeral plans. He considered this arrangement more intimate and easier for his wife.

The old Chelsea church where Serena had been christened and married had been bombed some time ago. They decided on cremation. Things were very difficult, but he had acquired a priest. The crematoria, however, were fully booked. They would have to wait until the following day, but they could be together. Eleri was relieved. These people had her welfare at heart. She dreaded waiting another day but there was no option. Later she would return their kindness. In the meantime, she would do what she could for them.

It is said that anyone can accept anything in twenty-four hours. They became a close trio as Talbot (they were now on Christian name terms) telephoned instructions for the removal of the bodies, the time of the service and other details. All wanted a simple service and they asked Eleri for her suggestions.

Instead of an oration the young priest would read Christina Rossetti's lovely poem ending in: "Darkness more clear than noonday holdeth (them), Silence more musical than any song."

It was not dreary and to Monica offered a gleam of hope. For herself and Alvar she chose Shelley's lines ending: "And so thy thoughts, when thou art gone, Love itself shall slumber on."

They had used this for their concerts, and both liked it. It gave her some comfort in the bizarre situation which seemed removed from reality. Monica Bessington asked for 'The Lord's my Shepherd', Crimond version, to be played on the organ. It had been used at Serena's christening and wedding. The rest of the day was an unwinding and a waiting. A strange calm had descended.

At eleven o'clock the next morning they left by car without mishap and decided to ask the driver to wait. They entered the chapel and sat together, Talbot in the middle, holding both their hands as the gentle music played. There was nobody else present. The coffins were side by side, each bearing an identical wreath of scented white narcissus. Eleri closed her eyes. No longer would she see the lift of one pointed eyebrow as he puzzled over something – no longer see his eyes following a lovely woman. Age would not have suited him. Growing old together would not have suited either.

The Bessingtons were numb with grief. She somehow felt their pain to be greater than her own. Her life lay ahead, her children were infants. There was a loving family waiting to encompass her; they had only each other.

The service was soon over. The poems had been read quite beautifully. The curtains closed as the age-old words were intoned. It was over.

She did not return to Chelsea; they parted outside Wellington Station. Both kissed her and promised to meet again. Eleri gave them her card, said she would await their letter to settle accounts. She also suggested that they keep their secret. They knew what she meant. Eleri thanked them, turned and waved and disappeared into the cavernous depths of a wartime mainline station.

After much difficulty and queuing she at last managed to telephone Briende. The line was cracked but Briende's relief showed in her voice. "I'm on my way home. Are the children well?"

"All is well. Quellyn is with me. Come straight here whatever time you get home."

"Yes, I will." She hung up.

The loathsome instrument must be alive with germs; the kiosk itself was filthy. She sought a place to sit, as the waiting room was a haze of smoke. The platform was teeming with uniformed men, all kinds of uniforms, couples clinging unashamedly, children hanging on. Somewhere, somebody had a gramophone and Vera Lynn's voice reverberated – "We'll meet again, don't know where, don't know when" – as many clung in the throes of goodbyes.

She and Alvar would not meet again but she had decided to keep her secret even from Briende. It was the last thing she would do for Alvar – keep his good name. One day, when she was too old to care, perhaps she would tell her sister. At the moment it hurt, hurt, hurt, hurt!

When the train eventually pulled in, she pushed with the rest. Her first-class ticket was of no consequence; first class was already commandeered, as it had been on the outward journey, by some government body she imagined.

Luckily, she found a seat, settled herself, tried to rest her mind. The last three days seemed like months, but she was going home, where she now longed to be.

CHAPTER TWENTY-SIX

Eleri's Wartime Charity

IT WAS ALMOST MIDNIGHT WHEN ELERI REACHED Brackens and Briende was waiting. She rushed to the door, hugged her sister, took her cloak and hat and led her to the fireplace. She tossed another huge log on the blaze. "Get warm while I fetch a hot drink."

Briende handed her a steaming cup, drawing up her armchair opposite, as she had so many times before. She scrutinised her pale beautiful sister, red hair cascading onto her shoulders, glinting in the firelight. There was an uncanny stillness about her.

"It is Alvar, is it not? Mrs. Sullivan said he had taken the car. There's been an accident."

As if in one sentence her sister answered, "He was killed in Wednesday's air raid. He was in a taxi going to a friend's flat. They phoned me at three in the morning from

St. Bernard's. The journey was unpleasant and long, the walk to the mortuary at St. Bernard's endless. He looked asleep," as if in one breath. Briende's unease of the last few days had anticipated some accident but not death. The shock to Briende was considerable. She felt the large hot tears falling. She relived her own loss. There were now three fatherless children. Her tears rolled faster.

"You went alone! Did it all alone! You phoned from Chelsea – said nothing of this." She could not control her tears… memories of Ralph, her own grief, a mixture of emotions.

"At the hospital I met a couple. Their only daughter was killed in the same raid. They took me home with them to Chelsea."

"The funeral – you had to arrange to bring him home?"

Her voice was barely audible as her heart wept for this indefatigable young sister. "He was cremated this morning. The Bessingtons, that was their name, stayed with me and I with them."

"The service? Who…?" Briende, stunned, could not find words.

"They had 'The Lord's my Shepherd', Crimond version, and Christina Rossetti's poem about darkness and light. You know the one. I asked for Shelley's "Music, when soft voices die, vibrates in the memory". It ends "love itself shall slumber on". We've used it many times at the concerts."

Eleri stood to comfort Briende, held her head against her breast. Briende was trembling. "The estate, the concerts, your projects? Such a lot to think about." Briende was almost voiceless.

"I had a long, miserable journey, both ways. I've done my thinking. No more new staff when the present ones retire, afforestation of the land and, when peace returns, renting Campions – a school, college, hotel, hospital – anything. It is not mine, it is Quellyn's, in trust, until he is of age."

Briende marvelled at Eleri's composure; she seemed impassive. Shock perhaps? Or acceptance? She had known since Wednesday. "Does his sister know?"

"No. You alone know. It will be tomorrow's task. I have everything prepared. I wrote the obituary in rough. I think I'll go to bed now."

She seemed unreal.

They ascended the stairs together. Briende tucked her in and twice during the night checked on her. Her sister was an amazing person – strong, brave, resolute, honest. How deeply she felt for her.

Next morning there were sounds of delight from Eleri's room. Briende found Quellyn and Maeve in bed with her. Her sister's spirit was unquenchable.

While they breakfasted, Eleri, who was not hungry, wrote a letter to Reverend Britt. The sad news as related to Briende could be announced from the pulpit at the service. They would mail it at the vicarage on the way to Pen Melyn. They would not stop. Everyone would be profoundly shocked, and sympathy would flow towards her. That would be the hardest part.

Although they never went to church, the Garonnes had always been generous benefactors throughout the generations, even though they had been suspected of being Catholic at heart.

The two sisters and two children drove to Pen Melyn before Mrs. Blethyn had left for the service. She knew as soon as she saw them that there was some dire news to disclose. On being told she wept bitterly. Nobody had ever seen her weep; it was as if fate had struck at herself and both daughters, while they were in the flower of life. With Uncle Gil she marvelled at Eleri's spirit and strength – may she always so remain, was their innermost hope. Mrs. Blethyn then chose to walk to her sister's home to tell them the sad news. The walk would calm her. She suggested that Eleri spent the day with her children. The diversion would be some sort of healing. Briende decided to accompany her to The Lodge.

After a bath, fresh clothes and a simple meal, Eleri was prepared for the heartbreaking tasks ahead. Briende said she would take over the children adding, "I think it would be wise of you to drive to Alvar's office in the big house. This door knocker will bang continually all day, believe me."

"I'll write the obituary and start off on the list of people to be informed. I'll take his address book; tomorrow I'll phone for the cards. Today I'll start on short letters after writing to his mother. That will be the most difficult letter I've ever written."

"I'll phone his sister and our relatives."

"Thank you, Briende – I dreaded doing that."

On odd moments that day, while the children played and Mrs. Sullivan helped, Briende would parcel and box Alvar's clothes to be given to Mrs. Britt to be distributed on the mainland, in the bombed cities. His small personal possessions would be locked away in the safe for Quellyn. As she had with her own husband's photographs, all pertaining to Alvar were packed away with Eleri's approval except for the splendid portrait of Alvar on horseback. That would remain at Campions.

Eleri had already decided against a memorial service; it would have been hypocritical and she knew that he would not have approved. She was being true to him and to herself, but his staff and many acquaintances would be shocked. This she anticipated. Bearing in mind the mores of llandia, she donned a simple navy dress and set off for her dismal tasks, pondering on the short drive that her best tribute to him would be to carry on what they had together begun. Minus his charm and aplomb there would not be the same glamour, but the committee would undoubtedly replace him with a well-known local as compère, one for each season, but for the first concert she would take over the duty herself. To discontinue would be churlish and self-indulgent, as well as depriving many people of pleasure and charities of revenue. The Campion musical events had become an institution, every fifth Saturday when the big house was unoccupied.

Fortunately, she had learnt to manage the estate but there would be substantial pruning. Without her husband she did not plan to revolve her life around Campions.

Suspended in some sort of vacuum, Eleri attacked the important issues pending, the most painful being her letter to Lady Bettina, whose smiling portrait, beside that of her son, gazed down on Eleri as she wrote.

Eleri, who loved her mother-in-law, wrote tenderly

and tactfully, describing the whole sad saga from her miserable journey in a state of shock to the gruelling experience at the hospital. She comforted her regarding the manner of his death without suffering and gave an account of the quiet dignity of the funeral. She ended by writing that throughout she had felt close to her in spirit as she did at the time of writing.

Alone in his own domain it was pleasant to reflect that together they had achieved something worthwhile. Until his marriage he had been a remote figure and completely unknown in the village. Together they had brought glamour locally and revenue to worthy causes, though he was seldom seen away from his own property. The Blethyns were known, part of the community, and Eleri's bereavement was something deeply felt. Apart from visiting city families on respite, and Dr. Skiroski's orphan refugees, Brymadoc had been untouched by the war and Alvar Garonne was the first casualty. For Eleri it was a poignant situation; for a while it would be best for her to remain secluded. The kindness and concern were overwhelming but each expression of sympathy would be graciously answered.

Her balm had always been her work. During the next month or so she determined to seriously paint. Her subject would be Maeve. At almost ten her features were formed. The chaise longue would be conveyed to the studio, the child clad in a loose pale blue dress, her knees curled under her and red slippers peeping beneath her long gown. Her long pale hair would be swept back to rest on her left shoulder. Her only fear was that she would fail to get the expression in her wonderful eyes, a look of kindness and understanding beyond her years. This work would be part of Eleri's escape and healing.

Each morning would be set aside for her children and conscientiously for one afternoon per week she would concentrate on duties pertaining to the estate.

Every afternoon after school became a favourite time when Maeve arrived to pose patiently. The child was so perceptive, more vital than her mother, and she was the first person to make Eleri realise how like Mrs. Blethyn, her own mother, she herself was – energetic, courageous, brave. On reflection Eleri imagined that given the same circumstances Mrs. Blethyn would have reacted as she had and faced things alone, though there would have been a proper church burial. Eleri also realised for the first time her own mother's early widowhood and was charmed to hear from Maeve, via the aunts, of how an enviable suitor was rejected.

The village ironmonger, a Mr. Pryson, had been supplied with stock by a prosperous Mr. Pollitt, who came occasionally from the mainland to check on his visiting salesmen. Mrs. Blethyn, used to managing an estate, was a favoured customer of the said ironmonger. The tall, slim woman with chestnut-brown hair in a neat French twist at the nape of her neck had immediately engrossed Mr. Pollitt's attention. His written proposal had been politely declined, in a copper-plate hand, thanking him for his admiration, but there had been only one man for her and when her day was done, she hoped he would be waiting for her.

It was the first time Eleri had really laughed since her harrowing experience and this child was responsible. She was not laughing at her beloved mother but at this fey child's possession of the secret. Neither she nor Briende had heard the tale.

There was one thing she did not have in common with her mother or sister. She needed a man in her life and was unlikely to remain eternally attached to the memory of one. This child though, she doubted; there was something about her of the steadfastness of her mother and grandmother, both chained by the memory of one great love, the entire universe encapsulated in one man. Eleri fervently hoped this would not be Maeve's fate.

As she worked at her canvas, she was reminded of the unfinished portrait of herself. She still planned to reclaim it this summer from the vaults of Nations Bank. She smiled at the memory of the great seduction, when she had loved without being asked to love, but she felt no shame. It would be some time before she once more braved London and the raids seemed unceasing. Perhaps dear Juliette would reclaim it for her when the time arrived if armed with a letter and photograph. An authenticated legal letter if necessary, then Dr. Skiroski could convey it. She would have liked her husband to have seen it and learn of her part in its execution; she surmised that he would have smiled. He had never stinted himself when it came to physical satisfaction.

Such were her sentiments when, alone in her charming bedroom that evening, she once more accepted the full realisation of her widowhood. Never again to reach out for

Alvar Garonne, to be transported to realms of boundless bliss. She would never cease to rejoice in having fascinated him and captured him. Both had accepted a challenge, but one was a veteran of long experience in the sexual arena. Now he was gone.

From her bed she gazed out at the undulating lawns and gracefully grouped trees, the silver-edged church spire in the near distance poised on a cloud, the thin setting May sun outlining the red chimneys of Campions. The rosy reflections of the distant hillsides, the winding drive to the big house. Together they had often perused this scene and rejoiced in their manifold blessings. The memory of Alvar Garonne would always be sacred to her. She would not have missed one hour of his devastating attraction, always conscious that with her at hand no other female would ever have posed a threat. The five years of knowing him were worth giving a lifetime for. She had been transported to the world of the senses; she had lived, even if she never again bathed in the rays of daybreak. She had his children and his death had strengthened her beyond all other experiences. She would live again and again and again.

Three weeks later, on a magical June night, the scheduled concert went ahead as planned, except that this particular event would be a tribute to Alvar Garonne, incorporating his favourite pieces of music. Eleri's contribution was to act as commère and engage the fiery Constantia Solera to sing the Carmen arias Alvar had found so exciting; when together they had heard her sing at the Royal Opera House.

On entering the hall Eleri had been confronted with a bank of flowers in front of the stage, new lighting effects and rows of new suitably stackable chairs, newly purchased as a surprise. Truly, this was a tribute to the Garonnes' combined venture in forming the musical events, now an established feature of island life. If nothing else had emerged from their few years together these musical evenings, managed by a superb committee, would improve and continue. Nothing in llandia compared with this success and the constant increase in attendance signified the need for such. On this particular night the once-handsome drawing room and hall adjoining were filled to overflowing; from the sparsely populated island over a hundred and fifty people had made an effort to attend.

As Eleri ascended the stage there was a spontaneous standing ovation. She surveyed the assembled audience, most of whom she knew, and inwardly gave thanks for their warmth and encouragement.

Briefly she thanked them and the committee, swiftly reiterating the sad events as she had written them for the vicar's announcement. Needless to say there had been much embroidering of the facts. She then introduced Constantia Solera. Eleri, cool and elegant in black, a contrast to the gypsy-like Constantia in the crimson, theatrical dress, created by Eleri, seemingly so long ago. Perhaps it was her Carmen dress.

The whole evening was an outstanding success, the delight overwhelming. After the close of proceedings and the politeness and compliments which followed,

Eleri chose to wander alone in the gardens. She envied Constantia's excitement at being escorted back to The Lodge by Benito Androtti, that superb tenor who had graciously given his services as a tribute to the Garonnes and their effort to bring music to llandia, against, what seemed at the outset, insurmountable odds.

The unutterable beauty of the moon and stars echoed that night almost a year ago, when with Alvar she had roamed these same glades. Hetown void dreams added to the solemnity of how she felt. The shores of reality, however, reminded her of that far-off evening, the end of a day of devastating news of lost friends. And now Alvar was no more, the ache within her was almost unbearable and the vibrations within her were as powerful as any music. She had her dark-eyed Miranda as a memory of that night.

The roses, in tight buds, glistened in the moonlight. Roses, ah roses! One day she would return to that crematorium's newly planted rose garden to read the memorial plaque on the stone wall and be uplifted by the beauty of a rose flourishing from the combined dust of Alvar and Serena. It would have to be the most exquisite of blooms.

Summer faded into autumn and Eleri abided by the stringent programme she had set herself, though she recognised the ache within her, a chasm of loneliness, a longing, a sense of wastage. She, who had established a successful business before being thwarted by circumstance, accepted that she was making splendid headway running the estate. However, she also realised that this was not what she was meant for – she had creative talent lying dormant and personal happiness being sacrificed. Though cosseted and admired by her loving local relatives, each was a woman alone. Gilbert Madoc was becoming frailer, her cousin and brother seldom visited, as each was occupied with his own world. Frustration was, for the first time entering into her psyche and she wondered whether her supreme efforts were leading to satisfaction.

Ryan Cordell, the foreman, became her prop, her advisor and encourager. She dreaded any idea of his retiring after many years in the service of the Garonnes. Together they traversed the property on horseback. She had not had the heart to sell Alvar's superb stallion, which now replaced a noisy, antiquated, small truck as the conveyer of the portly Cordell. Together Eleri and her manager attended the All Counties Fair, did their buying and selling and gathered information. It was planned that within two years the stock would be disposed of and a massive afforestation plan embarked upon. The few remaining staff would be retrained for this ambitious project. Timber, rather than animals, would spell the future.

London visits, which had been her escape and fillip, had lost their magic. Though the air attacks were becoming fewer, the drabness and absence of any kind of replenishing of the bombed areas remained. Conscientiously she kept up a correspondence with friends on the mainland and had *The Times* and favourite periodicals delivered, which in a way added to her frustration, as she had nobody with whom to discuss the current issues, especially in the world of the arts. Letters from Egypt and Dubai had ceased, as had those from Bellan and Lawrence Britt. Lawrence had been reported missing after the fall of Thermylopae, the ancient place having made a valiant stand as in days of yore. She knew that if Lawrence had been involved, he would have acted as nobly as some of the ancients he had loved and studied with such delight in his scholarly days.

On a particularly gloomy night early in the autumn, at another popular concert arranged by the committee, she met Dr. Skiroski. His duties had lessened somewhat as more doctors were recruited from their medical schools a year ahead of normal qualifications, to alleviate the pressure of work in the London hospitals. The good doctor planned to come home more often to check on his adopted family, his property and all it entailed, see the Blethyns and Garonnes and try to relax.

Eleri felt heartened, more so because accompanying him was a London architect, who had arrived to plan an extension of Fentons – or a modification rather, as Rachel Mann needed and deserved her own private quarters. Until the present she had endured uncomplainingly rather spartan conditions. Eleri immediately invited Amos Skiroski, his visitor and Briende to supper the following evening. She longed to hear 'real news' of the outside world, to feel alive, interesting, eager.

Phillip Headingly was just under six feet tall but seemed shorter on account of his stocky build. He had a thatch of black hair, which endearingly fell over his forehead on one side, and which he constantly pushed back with one hand. His wide smile revealed very white teeth, and horn-rimmed spectacles shielded his dark blue eyes. His habitual dress seemed to be a tweed jacket with leather elbow patches on the sleeves, corduroy trousers and heavy brogues. There was a manliness about him which Eleri found attractive and the light in his eyes as he beheld her did not pass unnoticed by the good doctor, whose dapper appearance made Phillip Headingly a sad contrast in elegance. These special evenings were for dressing up as much as for the music and there were a few raised eyebrows at the shabby newcomer, of whose story they were unaware.

Supper the following evening was a plenteous feast compared with what London restaurants were offering. During the supper they learnt that Phillip was in the throes of divorce proceedings. His wife, a nurse, suffered shock the night of the bombing of St. Bartholomew's. That same incident terminated a much-desired pregnancy, followed by discontent, moodiness and quarrels. Their house had been damaged and she had refused to move, so she continued nursing. In the meantime, a subaltern on embarkation leave was admitted to hospital, having been struck by appendicitis. A new love ensued.

Phillip Headingly had since bought for a low price an enviable Georgian house near the church in Horsham, after the West End practice of Frost and Kimble had relocated to the suburbs after severe bomb damage. The ambitious young architect had visions of a glorious, new, gleaming London, to compare with the best of Regency days, when hostilities had ended, and he planned to be at the helm.

Eleri delighted in his confidence and enthusiasm and

when Amos Skiroski suggested that Eleri show him the island he was delighted.

Deciding to take Quellyn with her she suggested the following day. She knew little about architecture, though as part of her art course she had learnt to recognise a variety of styles. This man was interesting, he appreciated paintings and sculpture and was particularly well-informed regarding the Impressionists, disliked the Pre-Raphaelites and collected Cruikshank, Rowlandson and Gillray cartoons.

The older houses were visited and Pen Melyn interested him far more than Fentons or Campions, or indeed several others. Its 'rounded' corners and variety of building materials, the differently styled additions throughout its long history, fascinated him. The motifs around the huge front door, depicting unrecognisable animals, kings and giants, the edges sufficiently storm-weathered to resemble a surrealistic art creation, intrigued him, as did the antique carved wood furniture within, which seemed like Welsh craftsmanship, the flagstoned floors and huge fireplaces.

Their third outing, again with Quellyn, was to the Stones. Like many others he vowed one day to discover something of their history or purpose. Eleri laughed, listing the many legends already connected with them, the awe and fascination.

Sadly, but not unexpectedly, she realised that he was falling in love with her. She began to curtail their meetings, stating work and duties as an excuse, and thereby giving him the opportunity to plan the work he had been employed to do at Fentons. His company would soon expect results.

To once again dine out with an attractive man in Trevere or Limorrnah was exciting and rejuvenating. She felt her own spirit reviving, her vivacious self becoming a semblance of what she used to be. To once again have real conversation on a variety of topics was to sparkle anew, but she determined to see him less frequently, perhaps to give herself time to adjust and not allow her loneliness to cloud her judgement.

After one particularly charming night, he suggested a walk in the grounds before he departed. The moon was full, the sky cloudless. To disappear indoors seemed almost a sin. It was satisfying to feel a man's protective arms around her, to be aware of his tweediness, admire his confidence and masterful command. He could so easily be in awe of her, but he had his own confident brand of masculinity. Beneath a massive oak, now leafless, he suddenly took her in his arms, kissing her tenderly then hungrily. To be once again in a man's strong embrace was pleasurable, to be hungrily desired by a desirable man was an almost forgotten delight, but as his lips pressed hers she opened her eyes to survey the heavens above, trying to lose herself in the magic of the beauteous night, but the stars did not spin in a demonic dance and the moon looked on complacently. The soft whispers of the garden did not commune with her spirit, the impatient twitterings of a disturbed bird became a warning rather than an encouragement. She released herself. "Sorry, I am not ready."

There had been no revolution of the emotions, that mysterious excitement, that whirling temptation that nothing matters but this moment. In short, the alchemy was missing, for she had been to heaven and this was merely the soft comfort of a lonely existence.

"May I hope, Eleri – even a faint hope? I have fallen deeply in love with you."

"I suppose friendship would be out of the question, unfair to you, but I will miss you, would not have missed knowing you."

"To be with you and not be allowed to love you would unman me, completely destroy me. I pride myself on being strong but a mere escort I could never be."

"You are attractive, manly, talented, ambitious but I have a lot of healing to do."

"You are so beautiful, Eleri, as well as warm and endearing. You are probably searching for a replica of what you lost; another, wealthier, smoother, more privileged than I," and with a broad sweep of his arm, "and you have all this."

"All this is not mine. It is in trust for my son. I look for none of the things you listed. When I find the right man, I will know immediately. Wealth will not come into the equation, nor social status, nor nationality."

"You must have had a wonderful marriage."

'We had a five-year romance. I doubt if it could have survived ageing, reduced circumstances or illness. Our vows were hollow. It was sailing on a cloud. No yesterday, no tomorrow, unreal, never to be repeated. So, you know what I mean by 'healing.'"

"Goodbye, Eleri. I'll never forget you – in fact you'll haunt me. I actually wish we had never met."

He seemed to be seething with anger or emotion. Momentarily she was frightened as he gripped her fiercely, thought better of it, then stormed off into the darkness of the trees.

To compose herself she sat on a cold stone seat in the shadows until she heard his rackety car whirring off into the night. She felt empty but honest, doubted whether she would ever again meet anyone, never again sail into paradise. Phillip Headingly had all the essential ingredients; his divorce mattered not, nor his humbler station, but that spark within her did not ignite. But for a moment his ardour had registered fear.

Sadly she returned to her lonely room, drew the curtains against the wasted moonlight and the splendour of the heavens and for some reason placed a heavy chair beneath the doorknob, as there was no lock or bolt. She was aware of her vulnerability, the power of her sexual attraction almost a danger. Floating into her consciousness came the far-off memory of her ambitious Arab admirer and dear Hagar's warning. She no longer smiled. Tonight, she had been alarmed at the potential passion of a healthy man. A lesser man would have crushed and possessed her. She was tired of treading carefully, tired of being unprotected.

She rang Mrs. Sullivan in her attic flat on the pretence of asking where something was and enquiring after the children, though she knew them both to be asleep. She hoped she was not losing her confidence and succumbing to uneasy fears. She would welcome morning, welcome happy household sounds, be ready for her many duties.

Once again only ardent activity could salve her loneliness – not a physical loneliness but a loneliness of the spirit, the hollow emptiness of unrequited passion.

CHAPTER TWENTY-SEVEN

Eleri Meets Simon Peerless

THE BLEAK WINTER SEEMED ENDLESS UNTIL A SUDDEN telephone call in February from Amos Skiroski summoned her to a party. He was home for a brief visit and had with him two American servicemen, newly arrived in Britain, bewildered and lonely. Neither had wanted to leave his own country just as he was becoming established in employment. The little gathering was meant to enlighten the winter gloom politically and in other ways. Rachel Mann was preparing German and Polish food within the confines of availability. Briende had also been invited and Dr. Skiroski and the Polish airmen, Hendryk, Ulric and Saas, longed for the reunion.

The night was frosty and very cold. Clad in a white angora jumper, a pink tweed short skirt and her white high-heeled boots with an army of buttons marching up the sides, those boots bought seemingly years ago in an extravagant moment in Bond Street, she awaited her sister. She drew her faithful cloak around her as she walked to the approaching car. Briende, after depositing Maeve with her grandmother, shared her excitement as it was their only outing that season with new company.

After a long drive, the welcoming silhouette of Fentons was a relief. Laughter and warmth seemed to radiate from within as they approached, and a happy hum of voices soon greeted them.

Divested of their outer garments the young women readily mingled. The older girls, still on vacation, swelled the numbers, the younger ones were in bed. Among the dozen or so present, a few of the men were in uniform. One turned and looked towards Eleri and, in that electrifying moment, all others ceased to exist. Neither waited for an introduction as automatically each moved towards the other. The almost imperceptible movement did not pass unnoticed. As if in unison of thought, Amos Skiroski and Briende had both noted the attraction.

The tall American, a thatch of dark blonde hair and amber eyes flecked with green, tanned, solemn looking, moved his glass into his left hand and extended his right hand to Eleri. "Simon John Peerless."

"Eleri Garonne. Welcome to llandia."

The touch of his hand like a magnetic force transported her to a realm beyond the present. She saw and heard nothing of the activity around her and it took Anya's accented voice, bringing her a drink, to return her to reality.

Rachel Mann seated the couple next to each other at the long table loaded with German and Polish dishes as promised. Amos Skiroski, in welcoming his closest friends, requested that they spoke not of war or of the recent grim news. *Repulse* and *Prince of Wales* had been sunk in December, Hong Kong had surrendered, and the Japanese were victorious in the Dutch East Indies. Instead he wished them all to relax and enjoy themselves, forgetting the outside world for a few hours. He himself had seen a surfeit of horrible injuries in recent weeks, and his heart ached for the uniformed young present.

The atmosphere was riveting, the presence of servicemen the only salutary note. Anya, a medical student at Cardiff, expounded on her recent experiences in the Welsh valleys, the warmth of the people, the small, terraced houses, the overcrowding, the typical ailments resulting from these conditions. She talked of silicosis among the miners, the overworked wives.

The Poles talked of their escape, first from the German invaders, then the Russians, and their adventures through unheard of regions on the fringe of Asia to Tashkent, to Iran, to eventually reach the refuge of Britain. Now they were fighting in the Royal Air Force with immeasurable pride. They accepted that they would never again see their homeland; the exiled Germans did not want to return to theirs; the Americans were already homesick. Simon, with sincerity, lauded America and what he owed to that land.

Drawn into the conversation, Eleri's natural sparkle was soon evident. She vainly tried to dismiss from her awareness the man beside her. She was charming, responsive, her own brand of vivid intelligence registering everything. Her practical logical self would normally dismiss the idea of 'love at first sight', that well-worn cliché, but she was undoubtedly attracted.

Briende, opposite her, watched her sister. She instinctively knew that her sister was seriously smitten by the heightened flush, the bright eyes and a sort of suppressed excitement. It was almost a repeat of that morning when the young Eleri had arrived flushed and excited after her encounter in the Dell with Alvar Garonne. But this was no Alvar Garonne with his cushioned wealth and suave sophistication, nonchalant and aimless in ambition. Here was a soldier, a doctor, a captain in the USAAF, an immigrant to America, who had known poverty, depravation and adaptation as a child followed by a striving for professional qualification throughout youth and young manhood. The whole scenario unfolded before her. Eleri's future was going to be punctuated with complications, perhaps agony, for this man was going to war. Briende was aware of his background, having already spoken at length to Dr. Skiroski on the telephone, when he elaborated on the guests he'd invited. He seemed to instinctively champion such people; the intelligent, persecuted, Jewish or lonely. His judgement was usually acute.

It had been the most enjoyable of evenings, so real, so contemporary. Even though seemingly bewitched, Eleri contrasted the present assorted gathering with the elitist gatherings of the near past, when everyone had seemed so similar. The two Poles who had fled their homeland, the two Americans of Polish descent, the German Jews, doctor, near-doctor and orphans, the two attractive widows, were all indirect victims of politics or war. Though llandia was relatively unaffected by war, the present company were all beings affected by war or racial prejudice. It occurred to Eleri that the present company spelt reality, things as they were. Each person had 'a story', a unique background because of external pressures. She herself, in spite of early widowhood, seemed to be the cosseted one, the most privileged, the one Fate had treated least harshly. All this had invaded her thinking throughout the meal. Though dominated by her attraction to Simon John Peerless, this had been a memorable evening, enough to make ordinary outings seem insignificant.

A glance from Briende signified that it was time to leave. They alone had a journey and duties next day; the rest were on holiday.

Amos fetched Briende's coat and in his unique fashion directed Simon to fetch Eleri's cloak. "Which way?" came his American drawl.

"Turn right towards the kitchens. Rachel put it in the big airing cupboard – said it was damp."

Strategy, of course, for Eleri accompanied him to show the way.

The slatted wooden linen-bearing shelves along one side, the girls' outdoor clothing hanging on the other, this was not the most romantic of venues. Simon tenderly placed the cloak on her narrow shoulders, his hands trembling as he did up the frog-loop fastening at the neck. Their eyes met, and though her warm instinctive self longed to throw herself into his arms, she maintained her dignity. Had she not recently read of the way British women were already flinging themselves at American soldiers though they had merely been in these islands for a few short weeks? She did, however, venture to ask, "How long?"

"Three days," he replied, "unless recalled."

"I'll be home tomorrow from mid-morning."

She did not bother to say where or how far, this she left to him. Deep within her she anticipated that her future lay with this man. Her instincts were usually correct. Though constantly aware of her attractiveness to men, rarely did a man attract her. This man did.

She was strangely quiet on the journey homewards – preoccupied, pensive. The mist had lifted, there was a faint covering of pristine snow on the narrow winding road. The stars hung large and low over the vast heathland. Lazy flakes of soft snow fell intermittently, an occasional flake radiating a prism of colours, like a miniature falling star. Briende broke the silence. "He is not married, I hope."

"No, I asked him."

Briende remembered the relief in that far-off moment when she had learnt Ralph Maine was unattached.

"Before you say anything, I'm aware of the enormity of what I'm about to embark on. I will see him tomorrow."

Briende had dearly desired another marriage for her sister but had never remotely considered a soldier, an American and a medical man of Jewish blood – a further complication.

They drove on, quiet, though their thoughts were twinned. Eleri remarked that the night was the most beautiful she had ever seen. The snowflakes seemed to escort them like mischievous sprites, disappearing as they touched the warmth of the car. Briende mused that her own brief love affair had been as a snowflake – growing into beauty, sparkling and fading away. Her heart ached for her sister.

After delivering Eleri at The Lodge, Briende drove home with an acute sense of loneliness. She wished Maeve was at home, some anchor to all that mattered. She undressed by moonlight, parting the curtains wider in order to gaze at the splendour of the night; might as well have something lovely to enjoy. She had accepted that sleep would evade her. Eleri, in contrast, climbed into bed bathed in the beauty of her moonlit room, prepared for a night of blissful sleep and consumed by a happiness she had never expected to experience. There was not an iota of doubt; love had touched her, enveloped her. She had no intention of using caution, discretion or self-denial. If Simon came on the morrow, and she knew he would, it would also be her engagement day, to be followed by a speedy marriage. She had never felt happier. Like petals unfolding from a tight bud, in the warmth of the sun, such was the way she responded to this new experience. She smiled at her own imagery.

Saturday was the day she had least to do. She breakfasted with the children but had earlier arranged by telephone for Briende to collect them after mid-morning. She wanted Simon to see them, more natural, more honest. Meeting them was important, as hereafter they would be a part of his life. How confidently free from doubt she was, how secure in this new-found joy.

When the doorbell rang Quellyn was painting and Miranda sitting on the hearth, unravelling a ball of wool. She quickly secured the child's reins to a chair before walking to the door, every nerve acutely tuned, as she listened to her own heartbeat.

Face to face at last. She was not mistaken. He bore an armful of spring flowers, crudely bunched, several bunches actually. She received them, her eyes upon him. "Promise of spring, thank you for coming."

He removed his hat and with American informality tossed it onto the nearest chair, while she led him to the fireside and introduced the children. Quellyn, already the miniature gentleman, solemnly shook hands, while Miranda stared at the tall stranger.

"I'll put these in water, while you get acquainted." She was shaking.

In the kitchen she grabbed the first vessel at hand, an earthenware jug, and quickly put the flowers in it before placing the whole on an already laid tray except for the coffee pot simmering on the hob. This she also put on the tray. In a matter of seconds, she had rejoined them, as her sister and Maeve arrived for the children. Briende quickly moved the precarious jug of flowers to a window ledge, greeted Simon warmly then, in a flurry of activity, the family left. Briende knew better than to linger.

They were alone, divided by a small table holding the tray. She poured and passed the coffee. There was no time to play the charming hostess, no point in domestic pleasantries. She was conscious of his eyes upon her, conscious that every moment was precious.

"You found the way easily?"

"I asked in the village, when I bought their entire stock of flowers in the greengrocery store next to the mail office. About four ladies seemed dumbstruck. One told me to go to the end of the village and turn right as far as the iron gates, saying Campions, and another repeated it exactly so. It was really weird."

Eleri smiled as she visualised the scene. "You were straight off the screen of the Rialto cinema. They had no doubt that you were a film star and had come to offer me a film part. By the end of the day they'll have us wed."

She raised her eyes to his. He drained his cup and placed it on the table and stretched his hand across the hearth to reach her hand. 'Will you marry me?"

Unhesitatingly she said, "Yes." Neither had a doubt.

Hands still clasped, he raised her to her feet and tenderly kissed her. Thus positioned, they shuffled to the nearest sofa. "You want time to think? If there is time?"

"No. I have done my thinking," she replied, her eyes radiating a clear honesty.

"Do we go to that church today?" indicating the spire above the distant trees. He was so charmingly casual. She shook her head. "There are banns to be called for a church wedding."

"What are banns?"

"Banns – a notice of marriage, an Anglican church rule." He pulled her towards him and passionately kissed her. "I feel as if I'd always known you."

"I feel the same."

Once again there was a revolution of the earth

and a motion of the sea, but then the telephone rang stridently.

"Ignore it," she breathlessly whispered as she clung to him. "It could be for me," he said.

He immediately became a man awaiting orders and rushed to pick up the receiver. "I have to leave early this afternoon to report back to base by midnight. Ulric took an urgent message this morning before I left. I had to see you."

She grasped his hand. "We'll go to the vicar now, make arrangements. Come."

Both were trembling.

The jeep throbbed its bumpy way along the narrow road on the short distance to the vicarage.

Charles Britt appeared stunned when he saw them, more so when he heard their mission. "Come into my study." He seemed incredulous. They followed him and sat at his desk opposite him. "We have to talk this over. It is my duty," he began.

Eleri held up her hand, palm outwards and moved it slowly to and fro. She did not want to hear.

"Your mother?" he ventured.

"You know the answer to that." She smiled wryly.

"You have to see her… promise."

"I promise."

He took out a sheet of paper and proceeded to write. Eleri's details he knew, he had christened her, but this stranger – he seemed to have no creed, thought he was a good part Jewish but was not overly concerned about such data. Charles Britt decided to leave the space blank.

He called his wife and introduced Captain Simon John Peerless.

"They have to leave, Jenny. The captain has been summoned back to base. We know all about that, don't we?"

Jenny Britt smiled as she remembered their own wartime days, almost twenty-seven years ago.

The betrothed couple boarded the noisy little jeep, leaving a bewildered and concerned vicar and his wife.

He drove the toy-like vehicle up the winding drive of Pen Melyn to the front door. Eleri jumped out, pulling him by the hand up the broad steps.

"Mama," she shouted from the familiar hall.

There was no reply. She called again and heard steps approaching from the far cold pantry. 'What is it?"

Mrs. Blethyn appeared from the recesses in a snowy apron with bib front and capacious pockets. She must have been concocting something, Eleri thought.

She stared at the newcomer in a fancy uniform. Eleri could not decide whether her expression registered fear or shock. This daughter had ceased to surprise.

"Excuse me," she said, retreating backwards towards the pantry. She quickly removed her apron before returning in her buttoned-up neatness and stiffly shook hands. "You'd better take a chair and have—"

Eleri interrupted her. "No time, Mama. Simon has to report back on duty, but I promised Charles Britt I'd call to introduce Simon to you."

'Why Charles Britt?"

'We are getting married, as soon as possible."

"Married!" She kept her eyes on the foreigner in uniform. "And when did you meet?"

"Last night. Come, Simon."

"Last night," she replied unbelievably, as she went with them to the door. She extended her hand and said, "I suppose it is goodbye and good luck."

"Thank you, ma'am. It was real nice meeting you."

She was almost speechless and Eleri felt vaguely sorry for her as she brushed her forehead with a kiss. Her mother watched her climbing into the jeep. *That skirt is far too short*, she thought.

Back at the front door of The Lodge Eleri clung to him. "Please come in – just for a while."

"I dare not. To tear myself away would be even more painful. I'll write each day. If you do not hear you will know that it has been impossible."

He placed his forefinger beneath her chin and gently tilted her head back. "The war news is very grim – you do know? And my country is more and more committed."

"Yes, I know." She knew and understood. He crushed her to him, kissed her and released her; he drove off, stopped, reversed, sprang out, kissed her again.

"You are the loveliest woman I've ever seen. I know we are meant to be together. There will never be anyone else for me."

She could find no words. She turned and, still in her poncho-styled coat, sat alone at the fireside. The bounding flames seemed to crackle in sympathy. The warmth of his kiss was still upon her, the pressure of his arms around her, she felt more bereft and lost than ever before and all amounted to a crushing sadness. She dreaded being alone in the echoing house. She would run through the wintry gardens and take the path through the meadow. The wind, tearing at her hair, whipping at her clothes with a demonic howl, would bring her back to reality as she decided to return to the vicarage, to try and make them understand that this was no whim, that she was certain that she was right and would not swerve from her decision.

Reverend Britt was already at the door. "Come in, come in. I was just coming to see you. Jenny, she's here." He seemed relieved.

Jenny took her coat, stared at her paleness and dishevelled hair. "Let us talk it over, Eleri," she cautiously began, as they sat together.

"It is barely nine months since Alvar died and you have not given yourself time to adjust, just thrown yourself into more and more projects, and you are lonely, you adore the children but are desperately lonely."

"You believe I'm on the rebound. Were that so, the respectable and desirable Phillip Headingly would have sufficed."

"You have known Simon for less than twenty hours. He is on his way to war. As a doctor he will not be far from the action. Give yourself one week to reconsider. Charles will withhold the banns."

"Jenny, you know me well enough to know I'm spontaneous and instinctive about many things, but I am not governed by emotion regarding serious issues and am never out of control. Call the banns tomorrow."

Charles Britt took her cold hands in his and gently

chafed them. "Jenny will fetch some tea. Relax a while and I'll drive you home. We can fetch the children, though perhaps it would be better for you to remain at Briende's tonight."

Ever the pastor, ever the friend, but she would be at home eagerly awaiting Simon's call.

He called before he left Fentons late that afternoon. The next call came just after midnight when back at the base in East Anglia. The next days were to be spent equipping American hospitals in Britain and immunising troops as they arrived. His letters on PX-issued stationery came daily as promised. As yet they were uncensored.

His letters told of American medical school and his training, what he had witnessed in the cities, a horrendous assault on the senses. But all was as nothing compared with what he was experiencing in a variety of British war hospitals.

The USAAF medical men of all ranks had been sent to gain first-hand experience of what to expect. Britain had already been at war for well over two years. The officers had to liaise with British hospitals in order to equip the American hospitals being constructed at an alarming rate. The British system was already established – Oxford for heads, Basingstoke for maxillofacial, Liphook for chests, Stoke Mandeville for spines and limbs. Simon, in his letters, wrote of how impressed he was by the discipline maintained in all the drabness, the tenacity of grievously wounded men, the remarkable human spirit displayed.

From his letters Eleri learnt of his early history. His

Jewish mother, daughter of a master tailor on the outskirts of Warsaw, had, against parental wishes, married a half-Jewish humble junior school teacher, not sufficiently rich or educated to be something more. The pogroms in Warsaw were increasing in severity and the young couple bravely decided to emigrate to America, while there was still some hope of escape. A sparse collection of money and available jewels was amassed from relatives. Their prayers accompanied them. A passage on a laden ship was acquired and with heavy hearts they departed, knowing that it was forever.

He was six years old when they eventually arrived on Ellis Island, to be offhandedly sorted along with many hundreds more. Simon was ill after the prolonged and unhealthy journey. A kind assistant, a young immigrant recently arrived, went forth to buy some throat lozenges for the child; it was the first kind act in a new land.

On hearing the clerks wrestling with impossible names his father asked the young man if they could take his name. He was flattered, hence the name John Peerless. It had a good English 'ring' to it and Shim Joel Polanski became Simon John Peerless as he made his debut in the United States. At least the initials were unchanged.

The first accommodation in the Polish sector of Brooklyn was soul destroying; the new world had to have something better to offer. The new Mr. Peerless sold sufficient possessions such as rings and an antique watch to purchase a ticket as far west as they could afford. A few weeks later they ended up in Pennsylvania then to Erie on Lake Erie, poor but eager. Simon went to school to suffer greatly on account of having no English, his mother secured employment in a factory making all kinds of work uniforms, his father worked in a foundry.

They were poor but had that peculiar quality of Jewish energy. Within a few years they had their own tailoring establishment and had purchased what was called a split-level ranch-type house on the outskirts of the city.

Their initial poverty was such, in spite of help from the Jewish Temple, which his mother sadly had to revert to, that fear of another pregnancy became an all-abiding governance of their lives. They drifted when his mother became aware of his father's eyes feasting on a comely neighbour. She worked overtime and found a cleaning job. She salvaged her meagre savings and saw an unscrupulous doctor, who was also a Jewish immigrant. Instead of tying the fallopian tubes, an operation already current, he advised a complete hysterectomy, which not only placed her in debt but necessitated a long period of recovery. Simon remembered her striving, though in a weakened state, to keep working for him and vowed if he ever became a doctor, he would be an honourable one.

In his maturer years, as a newly qualified doctor, had the man still been alive he would have exposed him for his callousness. He had already witnessed that the temptation to make money was irresistible to some doctors. The bitter lesson remained with Simon. The one radiant gleam was the survival of his parents' marriage. He was still very close to them, his only relatives. The European relatives had probably died in the death camps, news of which was reaching the West, although treated as rumours rather than fact. His love for his new country and profession became paramount.

From his letters, Eleri also deduced that the Far East would be his ultimate destination. The Japanese were victorious. Hong Kong had succumbed on Christmas Day before the arrival of the Americans in Britain, the Japanese were winning in Burma and the Americans in the far-off islands making little impression. Unheard of places were in the news and formerly humble men were enmeshed in the theatre of war. Singapore had also surrendered in February and, in a mild, tactful way, Simon was warning his beloved wife-to-be of what to expect.

When reading of the latter catastrophe in Maeve's scrap book she recollected a poignant memory. The Argyll and Sutherland Highlanders had blown up the Causeway. She clearly remembered re-tying that label on Major Johnstone's luggage when leaving the ship, noting his regiment. He, though wounded, was one of the ninety survivors out of almost nine hundred, and his name was listed among those picked up by a hospital ship, several sea miles away. She related the incident to Maeve. In her clear script the serious child added a note below the cutting and underlined his name.

CHAPTER TWENTY-EIGHT

Eleri's Marriage

ELERI SET HER WEDDING DAY FOR THE END OF MARCH. Like many others hers was to be a rushed wartime marriage, the only guests being family and close friends. Delightedly the Bessingtons agreed to make the journey from their temporary home in Wiltshire. They would stay with Briende. There was no time for elaborate planning. Simon desired her to wear white, which was not exactly suitable for a second marriage. To Eleri it mattered not – had she not worn green the first time? Her aunts suggested a pale blue silk sheath beneath the full-skirted family lace dress, the waist, which was slightly too high for Eleri, disguised by a wide softly pleated cummerbund from the same material as the underlying dress. Aunt Deborah, in failing health, helped briefly in its construction. Mona Lamoine would once more prepare the lace and would weave a rope of pearls in Eleri's ample curls, the style resembling a Medici or Borgia painting. Maeve, once more a bridesmaid, would wear the blue dress she had posed in, which was by now at calf length, giving her a waif-like appearance. Her pale hair was drawn back into a wide plait with tiny spring flowers among the weave. Once more the church overflowed with the villagers, and spring blooms decked every available space, their delicate perfume blending with the distinct odour of old churches.

Mrs. Blethyn suffered a turmoil of unrevealed emotions as once more she watched a beloved daughter being united to a soldier she barely knew. His olive-green jacket and what Mrs. Blethyn considered pink trousers appeared very strange. To her mind Simon Peerless and Ulric, his friend and supporter, seemed very foreign. The only conventional thing this daughter had ever done was to marry a rich local landowner almost six years ago. That wedding she understood.

Once more, to her delight, the family dress was worn at the same altar, except that it now looked like something she had never before seen. Eleri had agreed to dress and leave for the church from Pen Melyn, which Mrs. Blethyn supposed was a compliment to her. Uncle Gilbert, too doddery to escort his adored niece up the aisle, was overcome to see his son, a younger replica of himself, performing the honour. It was Eleri's final compliment to him. Her own brother agreed. The practice struck her as silly, but she hardly relished walking alone up the aisle.

At the Pen Melyn reception there was a general feeling that this could be the last family gathering. The world was changing at a headlong pace. The large dwellings would fade into insignificance. llandia would lose its isolation and Mrs. Blethyn visualised her grandchildren all over the globe. Eleri, of course, would lead the way if this dear man survived the war. His casualness and easy-going charm, and what Mrs. Blethyn considered a lazy way of speaking, would always make him seem a stranger. He had even turned up at the church in a jeep and it was only after great debate that Eleri agreed to ride home afterwards in Mr. Byatt's big car. The Bessingtons, Dr. Skiroski and his bevy, the Reverend and Mrs. Britt, in addition to the family, gathered in the large dining room. Greetings had arrived three days earlier from Simon's parents in Pennsylvania. Mrs. Blethyn's wry comment was, "At least he has a family." This made him somewhat more understandable. On hearing the buzz of foreign voices around her, all on llandia because of her daughter, she wondered anew how she could have spawned the beautiful and original being blending so effortlessly among these strangers, and again searched for a family likeness, as if trying to convince herself that she was really hers. How often she had wished for ldwal's appraisal of her. Perhaps he would have understood.

With Simon at the wheel of Eleri's car the couple left in wind and rain in the late afternoon for their honeymoon destination.

The honeymoon was spent at Loch Shee at the northernmost point of the island. The wild seas around, the low constantly moving clouds above, the small hotel, with its Irish fare and peat and wood fires in every room, a humble and happy contrast to her first honeymoon in Paris, seemingly aeons ago. She now had a man she had no fear of growing old alongside. Her fervent wish was for his preservation. She now understood her mother's and sister's all-abiding passion for one man. She had found her happiness, her emotional security, her lifelong companion, her realised dream.

They decided to spend the last four days of his ten-day leave at The Lodge with the children. They belonged to their life together, the real life, the memory he was to carry with him to the hell he had no doubt lay ahead. It was a hell he hoped to endure, emerge from undamaged, stronger, nobler and worthy of the land he loved, the country later to be graced by his beautiful and free-spirited wife. the country for their children.

Those were memorable April days with the world wearing a newly painted look, a sun interspersed with showers and a daily rainbow. The bouncing moon in a cloudy night sky, the forty-degree rain, the occasional creeping rays of an afternoon sun, the damp chilly mornings, created an ethereal atmosphere. Together they revelled in the world's beauty, the beauty of their devotion to each other and Eleri's trusting certainty that he would return to her. There was a sense of the absoluteness of this destiny, whatever lay behind the curtains of their future.

On their last day they ambled to the Stones, well-wrapped against the elements, blissfully happy with no thought of the past or future. The towering giants glowered, the sea beyond raged, the wind whipped around the brooding structures. Simon had never experienced such residues of history or nature. He had never undertaken such a gruelling trek or seen anything remotely like these threatening monsters. Instead of the expected awe, his delighted laughter, echoing on the hilltop, was taken up by the wind and its peals drowned in the gale. They clung together in the fierceness of the elements, pledged their love and made a date to repeat this experience on his first wintry leave. Later in humidity and sweltering heat, in mosquito-riddled swamps and relentless sun, he would remember this day.

They returned along slippery, barely surviving paths, crossing numerous newly birthed streams rushing to some collective destination as they headed to their own haven at The Lodge to enjoy a steaming bath and tea in the nursery with the children, then an early retirement to a prepared room she had not shared with Alvar Garonne.

This was a new chapter, a wonderful chapter, a chapter of agony and ecstasy, mostly agony. Each now knew that his destination would be the Far East, but this night was theirs, its magic a sustenance for the coming uncertain months. Eleri kept the news of her pregnancy a secret until the final moments of his departure. He left with a singing joy, foreseeing a vision of a radiant future in his beloved land. What a dream to carry with him into the unknown, as the little jeep bore him northwards, then eastwards back to base, to confront whatever hell lay ahead.

The daily loving letters soon ceased and when Miranda's birthday was remembered, at the end of April, a prearranged greeting dutifully sent, she knew that Simon was in the Far East. When, on Quellyn's birthday in June, a card already purchased at the PX also arrived, her husband's thoughtfulness touched her deeply. It was his way of showing her that these children were accepted as his own.

That summer was to be the grimmest in Eleri's life. Immediately after Simon's departure her beloved Deborah died. She had for some time been a patient at a nursing home in Trevere and shortly before Eleri's wedding dismissed herself from the clinic. With tenacious willpower she braced herself for the joyful event, though in delicate health. Her delightful, adored niece was meant for happiness. She never questioned Eleri's sudden and unexpected romance and sent for her in her final hours to tell her of the joy she had given her aunts and happily she was leaving this world, knowing that Eleri had found happiness.

Though Deborah had been ailing for some months the reality of her death was still a cruel shock. When Psalm 88 was read at the funeral it was the deepest sadness Eleri had ever experienced. "You have taken my companions and my loved ones from me: the darkness is my closest friend."

She tried to find some comfort in the service but failed. Her comfort lay in the love shared over the years, the fascination, the amusement, the delight she had given her aunt. She clung close to Editha, behaving as expected with quiet dignity.

This funeral became a rehearsal for another two weeks later, when Uncle Gil, who had always enjoyed perfect health, though frailer of late, had a sudden heart attack. He was found dead in the garden, still clutching an unplanted rose, which was later planted on his grave.

Mrs. Blethyn, stalwart as ever, managed both sad events, considering it her duty as the elder sibling. With her usual thoroughness and dignity, she selected the same readings as for his sister but chose his favourite hymns, rousing rather than sad.

Eleri was devastated, far more so than she had been by Alvar's death. These stanchions of her childhood, her companions and devotees, were gone forever. Her only happy thought was their knowledge of her new pregnancy, her delight in telling them that they were the first recipients of her news. She could still see him wiping a happy tear because he knew that she was so deeply in love. He gently chided her for not first telling her mother. How he had laughed when she gave as her reason for not telling her mother, the expected accusation that she had rushed into marriage. They had laughed together. Mai Madoc Blethyn was dearly loved but her stern code of conduct had frequently made Eleri and Uncle Gil feel like sinners of the first order.

There was gloom over the entire village. A tremendous unity ensued. Elderly inhabitants could not remember a time when Gilbert Madoc and his sisters had not been around. The Madocs were as old as the village which bore their name. St. Petroc's churchyard bore witness, with its many indecipherable memorials – many horizontally forming lichen-covered paths.

May, June, July and no news of Simon's whereabouts. His commanding officer merely stated that he had gone to New Guinea with his unit. He said that one communication from the unit had listed the names of men killed in an ambush, those whose names were known. The rest were numbers taken from their identification discs. There was no record of any prisoners taken, nor had there been any confirmation of the captain's death or that he was missing.

Eleri's remarkable, luminous personality sustained her. She had a deep certainty that he was alive, an absolute confidence that he would return to her and this gave her a buoyancy of spirit, a feverish determination to keep the candle of hope burning. As ever, work, effort, a giving of herself, became her motivation. She would spice up the VAL efforts for the benefit of visiting evacuees or locals in need of help. She would commère two more concerts in spite of her pregnancy. She would visit Fentons regularly with her children, occupy the girls in art or sewing, get them baking and making for their own charity. She would ride, as long as she could, attend the summer county show with Cordell and continue with the forestry project. As often as possible, Quellyn and Miranda would accompany her. Children, she was convinced, learnt by being involved rather than by remaining in the nursery with a nanny, however well qualified.

Laughter and beauty would never desert her and in her bedroom at night, the lateness of the hour, the moonlit beauty of the garden, the impassive moon, helped her in her conviction that he was somewhere thinking of her. Popular sentimental songs were a flimsy comfort: "Day by day we see the same blue sky, and each night we see the same old moon go by". He was, of course, in a different hemisphere, but it mattered not. He was alive, she felt it. On this optimistic note she would sink into sleep – "sleep that knits up the ravell'd sleeve of care". The Bard was always a comfort. Without what most called religion, she considered that every pleasure had to be earned and effort had its own merit.

Then, using her usual sleep potion, she would mentally list the myriad blessings she had known. Tomorrow was another day. Her diary was as crowded as it had ever been.

CHAPTER TWENTY-NINE

Simon Peerless Alive

THE TENTACLES OF WAR WERE REACHING LLANDIA. Royston, straight from Eton, had no inclination to endure the crippling boredom of his father's law firm and with his English peers joined the Air Force – his goal, of course, to be a fighter pilot.

He revelled in his new calling, excelled in his zeal and earned the nickname of 'Killer Garonne', his middle name. After a DFC and bar he became more daring than before. His exploits were legendary, and his plane being downed in flames in 'the drink', a heroic end.

The local paper gave extensive coverage, complete with handsome photographs and accounts of his daring and heroism.

Eleri, who hardly knew Cecile, his mother, went to see her. Royston's parents, remarkably calm, had expected such an outcome. He died as he lived, irresponsibly. Once in the air, he became careless of self and had on more than one occasion exceeded his mission. To chase off a Luftwaffe plane was not enough; he would pursue it to the enemy coast. He was fêted for his success with women and machines – always being toasted in the mess, accepting a dare, or betting on any issue, a careless, handsome, swaggering, popular specimen.

An attractive, much desired curvy girl, a civilian serving in the mess, had become a dare. She was a Jehovah's Witness, from a strict family, quiet and unassuming.

None had managed to date her until Royston bet on the challenge. Lisa Marsden, flattered and overcome by the dashing pilot, succumbed.

A few weeks after Royston's death, his remaining co-fliers, perhaps with some iota of conscience, contacted his parents. The poor girl was pregnant, her parents devastated. She had asked for nothing and knew nothing of his friends' awareness. It was typical of Eleri, when she heard of this, to contact the girl and arrange for her to visit and hopefully meet Royston's parents; her own had planned to banish her to a distant place.

The Burnettes hesitated. The girl sounded too humble, hardly seemed the right type to have attracted Royston. Eleri persevered until Cecile and Howard Burnette agreed to meet Lisa Marsden. They liked the girl. She fulfilled a yawning fissure in their lives and when they met the child a few months later and the dark Garonne eyes looked at them, they had no doubts. Lisa came to live in llandia; Cecile and her husband had another reason for living and

Lady Bettina had a grandson and great grandson under five years of age. The maternal grandfather was more convinced than ever that God moved in a mysterious way.

July came and went dominated by Eleri's ripening pregnancy and a surfeit of work, each day more hectic than the previous one. Another July morning dawned all around, a glorious promise of a lovely summer's day, when the telephone rang earlier than was usual. A familiar voice. "Eleri, he's safe, please come over. I'm in some sort of spin."

Elehi hesitated. Instead of, "Which one," realising it was a son she tactfully asked, "Where is he?" The caller was Jenny Britt.

"Still in the Amazon. There's a letter and photograph. Do come."

She knew it was Bellan, the botanist, her dear friend since earliest childhood. "Wonderful news, Jenny. Here I come."

The letter had been travelling for seven weeks, a survivor from many lost letters. She longed for cheerful news. Gathering her children, she let each choose a rose, which Eleri wrapped in scarce silver paper saved from cigarette packets. With picot scissors she made a stiff white enclosure for each flower. These the small children presented to Jenny Britt, and Quellyn really enjoyed seeing each rose being placed in a wine glass on the mantlepiece.

The letter stated Bellan's good health and some progress in his work, contact with Oxford was much interrupted but the studies continued. The big news was in the enclosed snapshot, which depicted a dusky maiden with long straight black hair past her waist, so black the sunlight left white patches on the crown and along the sweep of hair. She wore a longish sarong hitched up in a knot on one side. Her arms crossed her chest in a sort of modesty or submission, reminding Eleri of the poem, 'The Beggar Maid': "Her arms across her breast she laid; she was more fair than words can say". Perhaps she was bare-chested and had been asked to cover herself, one could not tell from the small snapshot. She was very thin and standing in a boat, her height could not be guessed.

The letter informed that she was about twenty years old but nobody really knew. She was of mixed blood, Portuguese, Spanish, Indian. Her language was impossible to understand but her name was, or sounded like, Umblah. Bellan was enraptured by her sweetness and knowledge of the jungle and its plants. He decided to call her Eleri, which she would not manage, so she became Ellie. He had arranged for her to go to a convent in Rio to learn English and whatever language she had some semblance of. The good nuns accepted the sweet girl so there was no more working on the boats carrying goods to rough settlements up and down the river. Being honourable, Bellan searched out her father, who had no qualms in handing her over; in fact, he offered another sister as well.

He concluded by saying he would not be able to bring her home so his dream of an Oxford post, someday, was over. He would apply for a South American university.

How excitedly they read and reread the letter! How bright the world suddenly became! How charming to have attempted to call her Eleri!

That Sunday Eleri would have to go to church, along

with most of the villagers, and join in the tea and cakes afterwards, organised by Mrs. Blethyn and a few stalwarts as a celebration of his safety.

Inwardly, Eleri thought this the first gleam of gold beyond a weak rainbow. The day continued but a rosy glow suffused everything. She felt comforted by renewed hope and when she retired that evening, the same time as the children, she settled to her usual pattern. She avidly listened to every news bulletin on the wireless and read anything pertaining to the American forces in the Far East she could find in her collection of bedside magazines or newspapers. Her ever-present map was scrutinised for islands and places she had hitherto never heard of and these names became as familiar as Trevere and Limorrnah. This night, however, sleep overtook her before she had read one page because the day had been the happiest for several months.

Just before four o'clock next morning she was woken by the shrilling tones of the bedside telephone. The memory of the last time this had happened jerked her into immediate consciousness. She was unafraid; her instinct told her this was good news. Nobody would send bad news about a serving soldier at such an unearthly hour. Excitedly, she listened to the thrilling message.

The United States Embassy via Capetown had telephoned the base five minutes ago. Captain Simon Peerless was on a New Zealand ship heading for a British port. It was a cargo ship conveying meat, cheese and butter to Britain. With one other he had been picked up near a South Pacific island and was seemingly well though suffering from exhaustion and malnutrition. The voice informing her had a treble of joy running through it. It was so wonderful to convey good news in all the gloom. Eleri's vocal cords seemed to have frozen.

"Are you there, ma'am?"

"Yes. When will he arrive? Where?"

"In a few days, depending on whether there's a clear passage. I cannot divulge where."

"Shall I meet him?"

"No. He'll be officially met and taken to base for a medical and debriefing for a minimum of four days. We never know what condition they are in or what information they have to disclose."

"He's alive," she heard herself stupidly say. "Yes, Mrs. Peerless, and bless you ma'am."

In a whisper she thanked him.

Her heart was pounding, the babe leapt, she was lightheaded, like waking from a disbelieving dream. She took a few deep breaths before bounding out of bed, wrenched the wardrobe door open, threw on a woolly jumper, raced to the downstairs cloakroom, slipped a mackintosh over her nightdress and put her feet into flat shoes. The morning was drizzly, but she could not run in wellingtons. She considered waking Mrs. Sullivan but decided against it. She longed to herald the news to the world, to echo his name to the hills and trees, to dance, to laugh, to run. Where to? To Briende, of course, to arouse her from her bed by throwing small stones at her window. She did not wish to disturb Maeve.

How sweet was the early morning. The mist and soft rain were as a healing balm. How effortlessly her feet carried her, how silent the world! The whole village was asleep, and each echoing footstep along the country road carried the good news: "He's safe. He's safe." There was never a sweeter dawn beginning to percolate through the drizzle, there was no hymn or prayer or poem to match her emotions. Every blade of grass, every closed flower in the hedgerow, the veined leaves, the diamond droplets – all took on a new significance. Coleridge on laudanum, De Quincey on opium, William Morris at his most observant could not have seen more clearly than she the intricate patterns and blended hues.

Breathlessly, she gathered her small stones beneath Briende's window. Three throws were sufficient. Her accuracy amazed her. In a twinkle her sister descended in her nightgown, threw open the door and enclosed Eleri in her arms. The look on her face was sufficient to convey her news. If anyone could be said to have an aura about her, Eleri had it in that moment.

They sat together on an item of wooden furniture known as a skew, the origins of which term nobody seemed to know. This cushioned, wooden seat, which opened like a trunk, was usually set beside the old kitchen range. Briende stirred the coals into a flame and shared her sister's joy. Steam arose from the wet mackintosh, which Briende gently removed. Later, Maeve laughed when she saw them thus seated in nightdresses and jumpers, Eleri's damp curls encircling her head like an elaborate halo. Instinctively the child knew that the news was good, her sensitive nature aware of her mother and what she was undoubtedly reliving at that moment.

Maeve sat squashed between them, as she had when little.

Eleri left when dawn was streaking across the sky. The rain had ceased, the sun was bursting into a million rays, a rainbow still hung tenaciously above the church spire and its familiar old clock with its age-old message, "God be with you". She would share her happy news with anyone she met before greeting this new day with her children. She would take them into the garden to see the timid rainbow, listen to the boisterous birds, gather flowers for the breakfast table.

There was a sort of reverence breathing over the whole expanse enveloping her and the little ones – Quellyn running among the shrubs, Miranda toddling through the heather clumps like newly escaped seeds from some confining husk. Or was this her own free spirit, shed of anxiety and doubt after months of crippling suspense? What a celebratory gathering was promised for the coming Sunday morning! There was no tonic to compare with shared joy.

When, some days later, Simon telephoned from Liverpool, her spontaneous self longed to travel to greet him. He would be home for an extended leave in two weeks' time. In the meantime, it was to be rest and observation, medical tests and interviews. He was not expected to work or travel. Needless to say, they were in constant contact, by telephone. He had lost a considerable amount of weight and his sleep was interrupted by unpleasant dreams. While in hospital he witnessed the ravages of war as the injured arrived from distant battles. And these were the fortunate ones, having acquired a passage to England. Simon longed to be working, helping, consoling; the tedium of being useless, ordered to rest, was frustrating in the extreme. Henceforth what he had experienced, and what he now daily witnessed, would have a profound effect.

When he did arrive in the green haven of llandia, in a brand-new uniform and 'official' car instead of the draughty little jeep, Eleri's joy was measureless. She cancelled all her engagements and devoted the entire sixteen days' leave to a domestic routine, living as a family, as they hoped one day to live on a permanent basis. Her happiness was complete.

In the meantime, Simon's bitter-sweet experience was not something he intended to share with anyone. Except in sketchy detail, Eleri was unaware of his island prison. He had, however, kept notes.

After a severe ambush in a Sumatran jungle, which involved the destruction of a casualty clearing station and loss of colleagues and equipment, three medical officers and a sergeant, after noting the identification numbers of many dead they did not know and writing the names of those they did, hopefully for some future reference, accepted that their own capture or destruction was imminent.

To the sound of heavy firing, Japanese, they thought, they boarded one of their own unit's abandoned boats. Lieutenant Clement Holt from Kansas had a bullet wound in his thigh and Captain Joss Wattenhew from Ohio was sickening with fever. Both would be a hindrance, but both considered a watery grave preferable to a slow jungle death or capture, which would, of course, mean certain death, by their primitive captors, who they realised were victorious.

The foul-tasting water and primitive sanitation which had been their inheritance, since the destruction of their facilities, had already killed a number of men. The lack of letters sharpened their wretchedness. By then they had accepted that the Japanese soldier was cast in a different mould. Forgiveness was unknown to him – nothing made any difference.

Packing as many emergency supplies as possible, including medical equipment, flares, the sparse amount of clean water in the emergency bottles, leather-covered notebooks, newly issued biros, pills and biscuits they stole away on a smooth sea. They drifted southwards, they thought, for three days. By the third night Wattenhew was dead and Clem Holt feverish and in pain. To remove the bullet could have set up uncontrollable bleeding. It appeared to be pointing downwards but lodged chiefly in the muscle; without X-ray it was difficult to make a judgement.

On the fourth day, sunburnt, fragile and dehydrated, when all had given up hope, they were spotted by a fishing boat with about ten men on board. Excitedly some of them jumped overboard and swam to the foreign craft. They appeared friendly and concerned and with much jabbering tied the American boat to their own craft and took the Americans on board.

The exhausted captives were fed sweetened water and covered from the sun. They seemed to realise that these were soldiers from the war zone. With outstretched arms they pointed to a near-distant island, "Atu, Atu." Whether this was the name of an island or a word meaning 'home' the Americans knew not.

Communication seemed impossible beyond smiles and much head-nodding. Once on land, Simon showed the bullet wound and said the word, "Jap." They understood the message but not the word. In response, with a stick, the natives drew a cartoon-type Jap on the baked ground, complete with slit eyes, protruding teeth and spectacles. They then scribbled over it, stabbed at the image and ground their feet over it with much emphasis. Simon repeated, "Jap," they repeated, "Jap," and there was some communication. They, too, feared the Japanese.

The Americans were placed in their own hut with woven beds slung like hammocks. This could have been the guest house. The chief came to visit with his wife and maybe the eldest son. The men wore a sort of mayoral insignia, made of what looked like animal teeth and a sphere the size of a golf ball, the chief's decoration being slightly larger than his son's.

Help was summoned for Holt. They brought fruit and leaves made malleable like a poultice and placed this on the wound. Though a doctor, Simon could offer nothing except antiseptic ointment and painkillers; these they had already used to no avail.

Over the next few days Sergeant Maurice Filton and Simon closely studied the natives. Under different circumstances, this would have been a fascinating experience, an anthropologist's dream.

They all looked alike, with wavy rather than curly

black hair and skin varying from coffee-colour to khaki, denoting some interbreeding with neighbouring islanders. They had fine physiques, good teeth and skin, the whites of the eyes yellowish, the pupils extra-bright. Physically they matured at a young age. The young girls were very beautiful, mothers at twelve or thirteen, then showing a definite tendency to obesity. Their social and cultural patterns were a mystery, although they noticed that the men visited the women's huts but not vice versa.

By the fifth day Clem Holt was showing signs of septicaemia. One day in the open air he begged Simon to remove the bullet. They had their basic surgical equipment and a small quantity of well-packed anaesthetic. The men, only, gathered to watch this wizardry, the unconsciousness, the stitching and binding. It was too late. That night Holt died. His weakened physical condition and strange diet had not helped.

The disposal rites were like something from a Hollywood film. The bier was quickly and deftly made of what looked like liana, the body covered by a blanket of large leaves, where the central vein seemed elongated to form a sort of string which was used as a binding lace. After carefully watching the heavens, around midnight, Simon guessed, the body on its woven bier was slid into the sea. Filton had heard of the Eskimos doing a similar thing. He remarked to Maurice, "Clem would have approved of this," which they did not understand.

A circle was formed on the shore, a particular cross-legged way of sitting with arms linked in a sort of elbow lock. There followed a low chant in monosyllabic words, then in a certain wavy line, a sort of dance, they returned to the village and a feast.

By trying to eat as the natives ate, whether cooked large insects, which tasted not unpleasantly like a sort of cereal, and enough fish, the two men survived. Their insides sometimes rebelled, perhaps because of their weakened state or maybe because of the unfamiliarity of the diet. They became very thin.

They ate communally around a fire in a pit – a fire which was never extinguished. During the frequent rainstorms, a roof was placed over the fire and part of aspiring manhood seemed to be fire guarding; there were always a couple of boys on duty.

Depression inevitably set in after the third day. The Americans could see no means of escape. Were they trapped forever? Their field glasses showed an endless watery desert; no ship had passed but an occasional plane flew overhead.

"We have our guns, Sim."

"Yes, it will be out into the sea and simultaneous firing. Don't let me down."

They shook hands on this. Simon thought grimly that all his studying and striving and near-poverty, as an immigrant child who had escaped persecution, had led to this. Both sought relief in recognising the kindness of their hosts but saw no hope of themselves rejoining the world they had once known.

One morning, there was excitement outside their hut, which the islanders never entered uninvited. They motioned to a ship on the horizon, they said, "Jap," then nodded vigorously in the negative. Perhaps they had checked earlier that morning. They pointed to their own vessel and made motions to hurry. Quickly the Americans packed the original four bags and followed their hosts.

In less than an hour they were alongside a New Zealand cargo ship carrying meat, cheese and butter to austerity-stricken Britain. It was heading for Capetown, then Liverpool.

All rejoiced. Except for the guns the previous contents of the four bags were distributed to their island friends, as well as a metal food tin with their own names, addresses, units and numbers, just in case fate would reunite them via other visitors from the outside world. There was an interlocking of elbows and warm smiles of good will.

It was with immeasurable relief that the two soldiers clambered aboard that ship, but the human warmth they had experienced would always act as a salve whenever human ugliness or cruelty threatened. Innate goodness and innocence was something they had witnessed, and would never forget.

CHAPTER THIRTY

Life Anew

Simon and Eleri Peerless relived that August in letters throughout the sadness of autumn. That holiday had become the template of their future life. For the first time Eleri's days had not been dominated by duties. Reality had exceeded expectation during those glorious days. Together they did the normal things families indulged in, driving to the limit of petrol availability, picnicking, swimming in the new pool, surrounded by shrubs, which now occupied the land once owned by the Day family and instigated after a committee decision, led by Briende, after four young swimmers had been dashed by the waves onto those inhospitable shores. It had been an accident often expected. Quellyn, taught by Simon, had learnt to swim, a red letter day in any child's calendar. The only shadow was the contemplation of Simon's next posting. He had no doubt that it would be the Far East again, as the Japanese were still winning and American forces were becoming more and more committed.

There was one more leave in September, when they consciously decided to accept the present as a gift. She recollected some homily that 'the present is a gift, that's why it is called the present'. A gift it became, the balm when future moods of hopelessness set in, the proof that "in short measures, life may perfect be".

They were immeasurably happy and longed for the days when their present delight became normality. Simon hoped to be back for their child's birth, even hoped to deliver the precious newcomer, but doubted such luck. If a son, he requested that they call him Branson, after a woman teacher, Irish, he thought, who had treated him with kindness as a small child, before he had mastered English.

Eleri liked the name. Even shortened to Bran it had a manliness about it and a Celtic flavour. Yes, she approved and promised.

The perfect interlude ended. The wrench was more keenly felt than at their previous parting, the unknown yet again hanging over them like the sword of Damocles, but Eleri had determined to be brave, and she wished him to remember her smiling, not weeping. He had optimistically decided to part with a promise: "I'll be with you for Christmas, hopefully to deliver my son." Both knew the unlikelihood of this, but gloom never helped; instead she determined to ask Venetia and Juliette and their children to visit her. It would be a tonic for all concerned, for children and mothers to get reacquainted after so many diverse experiences.

They had a splendid reunion and relived the past with laughter. Her friends found the island entrancing and vowed to come again.

During the remainder of that cold gloomy autumn nature seemed in sympathy with the grimness and privations of war. Yet through the miasma of doubt, her ever-bright spirit assured her that he would survive. Somewhere deep within her psyche was a font of glowing happiness. It had ever been thus; there was always a pot of gold at the end of her personal rainbow.

As October faded into November and into December letters regularly arrived. By December Simon was en route to the Far East and for the sake of morale letters were left at ports, whenever possible, to be flown home or aboard another vessel. By the second week in December letters had ceased. Simon, she deduced, must be in a war zone, probably Guadalcanal, where the conflict was bitter. She had never heard of the place until recently but could now pinpoint its location on her atlas without hesitation.

Maeve, her fellow war student and sympathetic listener had, in September, become a weekly boarder at her mother's school, as Briende could not bear a six-week separation between visits home. The slight child, with her usual fairness, mature and independent, had become a familiar personage on the ever-ploughing ferry. Her mother would dutifully meet her every Friday evening, otherwise alternative arrangements would have been adhered to. Her cousins, senior to her, were already boarders at Dewary School, so to Maeve it was no wrench. Scholastically Maeve was unusually promising, which fired her mother's ambition; she herself had been so young facing motherhood and later completing her studies with an iron discipline and much inconvenience.

In the meantime, Eleri, delighted with her pregnancy, did not let the condition hinder her. She recollected a day in the summer when she, who never did any shopping, called at Lewis, the butcher, to collect two dressed capons as a spontaneous gift of appreciation for Bridget and Mrs. Sullivan for their solicitous care of her and her children. Suddenly she was riveted by an overheard conversation in a lilting Welsh voice. The expounder was an older Welsh woman, attired in a shawl and plaid flannel skirt, although the day was warm. She had an enthralled audience of about six women and even Mr. Lewis, cleaver in hand, seemed transfixed.

"Wonderful girl, that Ceinwen. There will never be two of her, brought her up myself mind, her mammy being dead. Determined to have that Rhys she was, he the boyo all the girls fell for. But he married her, proper like, delivered that babba all by herself she did, tied the cord twice so neatly and cut. Takes courage mind.

He came home to a meal in the oven as usual, tired he was, did not notice her new shape till the babba cried.

'Duw mawr,' he said. 'Old Dr. Pritchard's done a quick job today.'

'No,' she said, 'I did it. I delivered your son.'

'A boy, too,' he said. 'There's a clever girl my wife is. Mind you, I would not have wanted a girl.'"

The unique conversation had 'lived' with Eleri. It was like a piece of modern theatre. She concluded that Peak Powys farm on the outer West Cliff must be theirs and what a splendid farmer's wife this Ceinwen would make!

A few days later, when attending the summer agricultural show with Cordell, she heard the same sort of lilting voice near the cattle pen and saw a very young girl, with shining hair scraped back and tied, an open honest face and her sturdy compact little body clad in an immaculate white Tobrolco dress with pink spots. Eleri knew immediately that this must be Ceinwen. Eleri approached and introduced herself. The girl replied, "And I am Rhys's woman." She did not even give herself the dignity of a name; what charming humility! Eleri thought her entrancing and offered the experienced Cordell's advice, if they ever needed it. That piece of land was not exactly productive and ever susceptible to the elements.

"Thank you, madam, but proud he is, see, my Rhys will make mistakes and learn from them."

On a miserable Christmas Day, cold, cloudy, dismal, interspersed with rain and a lazy wind, unable to decide whether to gust or retreat, Eleri smiled at the reaction of that summer's day at the agricultural show.

The Madoc family had gathered as usual for Christmas at Pen Melyn but Eleri decided to spend her 'free' day in bed. She would read and listen to the wireless, map at hand, and wait, wait, until her body made its decision. She was sure that the day would be her baby's birthday. She had faithfully promised to contact the family if any problems arose. She was not hungry, and her restricted movement would not have made a family day pleasurable. They had promised not to telephone.

Mrs. Benson, the midwife, had also extracted a promise from Eleri that the least twinge or anxiety would mean her availability, Christmas Day or not. "Christmas never stopped a ripe baby arriving. I'm used to being summoned."

Ripeness indeed! Eleri compared herself in shape and succulence to a ripe pear about to detach itself from its supporting branch. Her slim arms and legs seemed surplus to requirements; she was merely brain and baby. She smiled to herself, longing for Simon as she surveyed her preparations for the birth.

The rubber sheet, old calico sheet, small basin of sterilised water, small scissors and two neat strips of linen. Beneath the bed an enamel basin for the placenta – someone said this should be kept for examination by doctor or midwife. The baby bath, jug of cold water, electric kettle, were all at hand. Beside her a baby basket for Simon's child. She felt vaguely intoxicated with this delightful thought. Her beautiful, romantic bedroom had been converted into a delivery room. Feeling slightly audacious she curled up with a book and waited for something to happen.

Being well and strong and with a great respect for nature she would not hesitate to deliver her own child. Victorian novels had always infuriated her, even as a girl. The mystique of childbirth, the ten-day confinement, the prolonged bedside scenes of death or illness seemed stupid. Except for rare complications a doctor was unnecessary.

She would only use that telephone in dire emergency. She gave birth easily, why should this delivery be any different? Her first little girl was in her thoughts but that traumatic experience had been the result of a cruel accident and the perpetrator of it was also dead. No, she had no fears. None.

The lonely day, punctuated at first by mild twinges and then stronger contractions, drew on. The bare branches of the trees looked like primitive graffiti on a grey background. There was no sound except an occasional gust of wind whipping the window. The pains were becoming vice-like. Again, the thought of Ceinwen gave her courage. She, Eleri Madoc Peerless, had so much by comparison, a telephone beside her and several pairs of eager hands ready to reach her, encompass her, help her. How dare she have a shred of anxiety!

The clock struck four. Yes, the pains were more evenly spaced and quite vicious. In between, she coped. She was unafraid. The day was lightening. Lazily, clouds drifted aside to reveal a friendly sun, whose great shaft of light wafted towards her and for a brief period lit up her bedroom like a message from Simon. Another cruel contraction – she held her breath. It passed.

The telephone rang. It was Mrs. Benson. Mrs. Blethyn, unable to bear the suspense any longer, had telephoned the midwife for news. She was not breaking a promise as she had not telephoned her daughter. She had an uncanny feeling that Eleri would indeed deliver her child alone. There was no guessing what that girl would not do. Always a law unto herself.

The shrill ring continued and Eleri could barely reach the receiver. "Hello! Your mother phoned me, said you'd put her off. How are...?"

The midwife sensed the situation as Eleri could barely reply. There was an almighty contraction. "I'm all right," then, breathlessly, "I think the baby's arriving."

Mrs. Benson minus uniform speedily drove to The Lodge. As she climbed the stairs, she heard Eleri's penetrating cry. The head was already presented. Eleri had almost succeeded in being her own midwife, and actually felt disappointed that the job was not completed. It was a boy.

There was jubilation at Pen Melyn, shrieks of delight from Quellyn and a triumphant new mother at The Lodge.

CHAPTER THIRTY-ONE

Joyful News

AFTER MONTHS OF SILENCE A LETTER ARRIVED FROM Australia. Later the same day a letter arrived from the military. This time there was no polite telephone call, just a message. Both contained the same joyful news. Simon had just arrived in the American hospital in Sydney. His letter told the full story. He had been tending wounded on a carrier, or hospital ship, when an SOS from a destroyer in the same region begged for help for serious burn victims after an attack by the Japanese; the fires were under control but there were many casualties. Simon and another doctor were selected to be conveyed to the *Armitage* and bring back the wounded to the carrier. As they arrived on the destroyer there was another attack, and along with others the doctors became rescuers. As Simon pulled a sailor from beneath a blazing structure, part of it fell on the back of his neck and he became one of the casualties conveyed back to the carrier. The burn was extensive, the deepest part over the atlas vertebra, the thick hair was burnt, and his clothing melted into his flesh over his back and shoulders.

An agonising day later, when Vaseline gauze and sulphonamide powder, acriflavine and saline packs, the standard treatment, had proved ineffective for many victims, the ship pulled in at a small island, where a Dakota, specially adapted for stretcher cases, was waiting to convey the many wounded to Sydney. Simon, among the walking wounded, ministered to the patients as far as he could. He, with others, was now awaiting transport to England via Cairo, where many wounded from the allied desert campaign would also be picked up.

Once more Eleri could barely contain her elation. Surely this must signify the end of the war for Simon. He was alive, his injury would heal, of this she felt convinced; her ever-optimistic nature giving buoyancy to her hopes. He should be home within weeks.

It was four weeks before they met. She travelled to the East Anglian Hospital, when once more their ecstatic reunion abolished thoughts of war and suffering. He looked ill but her strength flowed into him. While she was with him he visibly improved, and though a patient he longed to back in harness. After much treatment himself and witnessing the treatment of other burn victims he considered specialising in this field. Eleri approved and understood, though it would mean further studying.

When later in the spring he arrived at Brymadoc he

was fascinated and overwhelmed by their sturdy son. At barely five months he already had an abundance of heavy fair hair. "Just as well," his father commented. "Mine will never again grow at the back of my head." In fact long fronds would be swept back to cover part of the scarred neck and bald area, giving Simon a rather 'arty' look. Forever more he would have to be extra-cautious in summer and remain with head covered but this was a small price to pay for the future happiness he anticipated. He vowed never to complain if in pain or ever distress his wife with data of the injuries he would encounter in his work.

During his service in the war zone he had seen many burn victims. Men glowed in ghostly fashion because of phosphorus burns as they were brought to the casualty clearing stations before being transferred to hospital. The only treatment for the deep destruction of tissues seemed to be continuous antiseptic irrigation, the limb usually encased in waterproof sleeves then known as the Bunyan-Stannard envelope. Patient nurses on hourly rota bathed damaged eyes and saved the sight of many men. Those soldiers convalescing helped with the simpler tasks.

At Park Previtt near Basingstoke, Simon had observed the work of Sir Harold Gillies and Sir Archibald McIndoe, constructing new noses, eyelids, lips and separating sealed fingers in badly damaged hands with patience and skill. He was sufficiently inspired to decide finally on plastic surgery as his own specialty. He determined not to do cosmetic surgery for the sake of vanity but to repair the damage caused by nature or accident, particularly among the poor or maimed.

During these months he considered himself privileged to be among the first American doctors in England to witness the power of a new miracle drug, penicillin, and even hear first-hand of Alexander Fleming's visit to North Africa to try out the new drug. The sun-scorched troops had decided that the visiting man, white-kneed beneath khaki shorts, must be of some importance. In the meantime, Simon's own burnt flesh was healing, apart from the one stubborn patch over the atlas vertebra, but he accepted that this would always be a delicate area – something he would never be able to completely forget about. On the positive side it would always serve to remind him of the damaged human beings he'd encountered and be a constant reminder of his own vocation.

No longer expected to serve overseas, he continued to work in American military hospitals. Casualties from the North African war continued to arrive from the joint Allied invasion; as well as war wounds, many had sheer physical apathy and mental sluggishness. Many had serious desert sores, which had been oases of succulence for the myriad flies. All filth was manna to these parasites, sunset the only relief from their buzzing and swarming. For a newly fledged doctor there was an endless supply of new experience away from the lecture hall and the academic approach. This was real doctoring, demanding energy, courage and devotion. The task already seemed insurmountable yet the advance through Italy and D-day were pressures yet to come.

Eleri and Simon became typical of other wartime couples. They met when they could, relished the moments, planned the future. Sometimes they met halfway across England but usually he travelled to llandia. It was a memorable time and their happiness surpassed their utmost expectations. Eleri pledged her support for his future ambitions; her financial standing would be their security while he achieved his aim.

Towards the end of the year, American troops were beginning to return home. Simon was still being treated for his injury, but his workload had lightened when more doctors arrived, to cope with the influx of casualties from the continent. As a veteran, Simon found himself in an administrative situation. In addition to the battle casualties, the incidence of venereal disease among United States troops had risen by seventy percent. The newly arrived doctors had their baptism dealing with the problem and the organisation of this programme became Simon's respite after months of ceaseless ward work. It also released him to see more of his family and plans were already afoot for settling in New England. The tide was turning in the Allies' favour, though slaughter continued in Europe and the Far East.

Eleri was already documenting what she wanted to take with her, arranging storage of special items from Campions, doing her part arranging the adoption of the Garonne children by Simon Peerless, to simplify their entrance into the United States, and selling her London property to Mrs. Levi. It had escaped destruction but had blast damage, which the government would aid with repair when the war was over. She had almost forgotten the elation of purchasing the sweet place and setting up her own business. It seemed another era and present contentment was more than recompense for the fiery ambitions less than six years ago. She no longer needed the intoxication of commercial success and recognition. Instead she relished the expectation of a new way of life and found the idea of a nation her husband so appreciated exciting and challenging. When he talked of his homeland her ardent gaze made it clear that her desires and expectations were in tune with his. The old world had been hindered by traditions; she was all for the new, the experimental. His longing to go home had a soporific effect upon her and her overwhelming love for him could demand any sacrifice on her part.

In the meantime, Captain Peerless was offered a passage home. Priority extended to the one hundred and fifty thousand wounded in British hospitals. The *Queens* and the *Aquitania* were among the ships taking thousands of men per month back home. Simon declined to go. He would wait, until he had made arrangements for his family to leave. This necessitated a visit to the American and the British Embassy, an account of which, in a letter, amused Eleri. "Some deadpan let me in, a sort of receptionist dressed like an undertaker. He did not exactly ask me to step on the welcome mat." British formality still amused him. On another visit he had informed the "imposing chap at the desk, looking as though he must break if he moved" that he "could not leave the Garonne kids behind and whisk off their mother". He found the formality of trying to adopt the Garonne children beyond belief. And this was wartime!

During the summer of 1944 Simon attended as many lectures as were on offer at his base, or in London, pertaining to the new 'miracle' drugs. He again heard at first-hand how Professor Fleming came to test his new drug the previous year in Constantin Plateau, North Africa, trying it on a man with gas gangrene, specially selected, as the man was sure to die. He recovered. A patient with an appalling wound of the buttock was another, selected as the least likely to live. He recovered. Deaths from sepsis were in future reduced to a low level. But the drug was expensive and at first reserved for the front-line troops in the Mediterranean arena. America and Australia stepped in to help with production until the great discovery became available to every soldier. Simon longed for the day when it became generally available. He also longed for the day when further study had granted him the satisfaction of a career in his chosen field, his rainbow's end.

Simon, along with other American doctors, was assimilating papers, now regularly arriving from the States, pertaining to the exciting work being done on the new antibiotics, including the massive efforts of Waksman's team working on streptomycin in the search for a cure for tuberculosis. While he was attending lectures, writing reports and practising medicine, Eleri had another contract from her publishers: would she prepare another Christmas calendar depicting current events, in short, a war theme. The child Leah became her inspiration and the large-eyed bewildered child was depicted in the foreground of a long line of orphaned children approaching a ship in the distant background. Each pathetic child had a full-named label – the foreground child just her first name. It became an instant success and there were several reprints. Dr. Skiroski's pride in Eleri was measureless; he had never expressed such emotion.

Eventually, in the final days of war, after a memorable Christmas at Pen Melyn, Simon left without his family to arrange his future career and prepare a temporary home for them. Choosing their permanent home together would be part of Eleri's acclimatisation to America. With thousands of war brides she patiently awaited her passage. Amos Skiroski and four of the girls had already left for Pittsburgh; he to return to his original specialty, pulmonary diseases. Rachel Mann had been accepted at Temple University, Philadelphia, to complete her training, Anya was to marry a Welsh doctor from the Rhondda Valley, who trained with her and Mara, a secretary in Bristol, was to marry a colleague.

CHAPTER THIRTY-TWO

Goodbyes

ON A BRAVE SUMMER'S MORNING ELERI UNLOADED the three children at the entrance steps of Pen Melyn. The sun had concentrated its brilliant light on the imposing front door highlighting Arthur, Lancelot, griffins or dragons, unicorns and headless saints in the surrounding stone. Had some master mason aeons ago given his apprentices free scope? Or was there a story or moral beyond the ciphering? To Eleri they made no more sense than they had ever made but in the white sunshine the images were more endearing than ever.

The door was open. Quellyn rushed in, followed by the stately four-year-old Miranda, towards the approaching footsteps. Eleri followed, carrying Bran. "Hello, Mama. We've come to see you before we leave. I don't believe in goodbyes."

Her mother took the toddler from his mother's arms after hugging the others.

She sat on the capacious sofa, Quellyn beside her chatting animatedly about the coming journey, Miranda plumping up the cushions before arranging herself. "Go and water my garden but don't get wet," was their grandma's kindly command.

This was a treat, that hose was an exciting piece of equipment. The boy rushed off, Miranda slid smoothly off the sofa and sedately followed him, Bran was given a box of coloured sticks and placed on the sheepskin rug.

"I hear that you've let Campions."

"It's leased for twenty years, Mama, to Ivory Life Insurance. It is to be a training centre. They have also purchased the heavy furniture and carpets. Ryan Cordell will look after the grounds until they take over; he will continue to manage the plantations."

"I see. And The Lodge?"

"It is to be let half-yearly to a Mr. Fergus Frazer, who's a soil scientist working with a colleague in deepest Africa – some agricultural project or other. He takes the summer off, his partner the winter. Mrs. Frazer, who lives in Scotland not Africa, will join her husband here."

"I understand Powney and Morag are to be the solicitors in charge. I always found them reliable."

"Of course. They chose Mr. Frazer, I've not met him."

"I must say that you are organised."

"Where do I get that from?" She lightly brushed her mother's cheek.

Her mother turned to the child on the floor. "You have

beautiful children. I hope they inherit your optimism and cheerfulness; there have been times when I've almost wished to be more like you."

To Eleri this was a surprising confession. "Mama, we are more alike than you give me credit for. Alvar's death struck me deeply; Miranda was less than three weeks old. I faced it alone – a nightmare memory. Only one other person would have had the same courage. It took young Maeve to point this out."

"That child's as old as the hills, she idolises you. It used to worry me. You are sailing from Liverpool, I hear. How will you get there?"

"I'm driving. Alvar's car is already sold, the agent will meet me on arrival in the dock. Cars are precious, quite unobtainable. I've been paid more than it is worth – far more. Simon assures me that I'll get a smart American car for a fraction of the price."

"And the other car?"

"A surprise for you! Daniel, Bridget's nephew, who does your garden and other gardens, loves cars; he is to be your chauffeur. He will convey you anywhere now that Star is dead and your phaeton a relic. Incidentally, Mr. Byatt wants to buy it – for tourists or honeymoon couples. He is looking ahead and sees tourism as llandia's future. This island will become fashionable; just wait."

"You think of everything. I will not get another horse, that's for sure. Thank you. It is a surprise."

Eleri had expected objections. Her mother continued, "Everything is changing. High Beeches a school, Fentons an orphanage, Campions an insurance mansion and

Leybourne is to be a country club, whatever that is. Pen Melyn will be the last of the big houses but it will remain a home as long as I'm around. Editha may consider joining me here – there's enough space to maintain our independence." She gave a toss of her head.

The children returned with wet feet, much to Miranda's disgust. "I'm uncomfortable." Eleri ignored her.

"I'm off to see Aunt Editha before I leave. She has promised to visit us next year. I'll telephone Briende, a personal parting may upset her. I'm off now."

She hugged her mother, who reached into a cupboard. "Here's a box of gingerbread men and small griddle cakes for the journey." She lifted the lid to reveal deftly packed layers of cakes divided by greaseproof paper. "I suppose it is goodbye then."

"I don't believe in goodbyes! The Atlantic will become like a road to Limorrnah – quite accessible."

They all kissed her. "Change these children's footwear on the way." Her mother was her usual controlled self.

"I will." She bundled them into the car and waved as she sped down the driveway. The worst was over. Aunt Editha would share in her adventure, find it exciting and look forward to visiting them but would quietly cry when they had gone. She would sorely miss them but moving to live with her sister Mia was a doubtful prospect.

Next day's journey to Liverpool, with several stops and run-arounds en route, was pleasanter than anticipated. The children slept on and off during the journey and Quellyn saw little of the grim evidence of wartime in several places. Eleri was not sorry to be starting afresh. She had her own sad memories of the war years as well as happy memories of the local charities she had established. Her work would continue and gain in prominence, of this she was sure. She sighed to herself – only six more days before she would be in Simon's arms and she visualised the pride on his face as he beheld his vigorous, intelligent son. Only six more days. A shiver of expectation coursed through her. Confidently, she looked ahead.

The agent in Liverpool was waiting as arranged. They exchanged documents on somebody's upturned trunk, shook hands and he wished her success. In his eyes she saw surprise and admiration. Such efficiency on her part had not prepared him for this startling beauty.

The dockside and adjoining buildings with many alcoves seemed a sea of people. There were wails and sobbing, excitement and sorrow, shouts of commands, "Write straight away", "Come home if you're not happy", "Good luck", "Take care" and some humour, "Give my love to Clark Gable".

It was a veritable human circus. She seemed the only one alone as she shepherded her children to a sleazy café, already overcrowded. She queued for whatever was on offer, which was not much. Mercifully the toddler slept but was a weighty burden. Miranda was bored. "Is this America? I don't like it."

Quellyn was excited. "Will all these people fit on?" She patiently answered each query.

Boarding at last… documents, allocation of cabins, a friendly crew and a smiling 'welcome aboard'. They had been trained to try and be hospitable to these new

Americans. Eleri's family shuffled along with an army of others. The allotted cabin, when they eventually reached it, seemed a temporary haven. They unpacked, ate some cakes and prepared to await instructions as the chaos outside continued.

Soon they adjusted to the crowded mealtimes and variety of accents. She was impressed with the organisation and thought the children well catered for. Quellyn was considered sensible enough to explore the surrounding area and chat with other travellers and he seemed to revel in the excitement and strangeness of it all. Miranda seemed to think Simon was somewhere on board and kept searching for him. "You'll meet him when the ship stops," Quellyn informed her.

Eleri had to agree that this was some adventure! Ever adaptable, she spoke to as many as possible. What a chapter of history was being written! Some of the women hardly knew their spouses. Many had no idea of where they were heading to beyond the shores of America, no inkling of the vastness of the United States.

A huge wall map, already much used, dotted with flags, marked the regions for the new brides. A Connecticut flag marked Joan stood neatly beside a New Jersey flag marked Sue. "Oh look. We'll be close. We can visit."

Eleri felt sorry for and ashamed of many of her fellow travellers. Few had any idea of the distances involved and some were not even welcomed. Nothing was sadder than a message from the erstwhile lover – "Please Sally, don't plan to stay". There had been mistakes. There were tears and regrets and already some talk of begging the fare home as soon as they arrived. Homesickness was already rife; England from the middle of the Atlantic Ocean seemed snug, secure and far away but no doubt most would eventually settle.

In her new life Eleri determined to set up some organisation, starting in her own locality, for these new brides. She was already planning action. It could flourish. Among the passengers she met two other doctors' wives, who thought along the same lines. One was going to Colorado and already had a job arranged, the other was going to Vermont. From what she deduced by mixing throughout, most of the husbands already had jobs, some were to continue with their studies on a post-war grant. Those already employed had more lucrative jobs than their counterparts in England and the post-war boom was already in full swing, the mines, factories and oilfields contributing to full employment. Several of the women she spoke to were eager to find employment, especially the nurses, teachers and secretaries. There was a healthy optimism, a freshness, a hope. Battered England was beginning a long convalescence.

Six days later she did not clamber on to the decks with the excited hordes who became intoxicated with expectation as they approached the shore. Wisely Eleri hung back until the final trickle of immigrants were about to disembark. Simon, patiently waiting, surmised that this was exactly what his wife would do and made no attempt to scrutinise the first passengers ashore.

She had already extracted their arrival outfits from the luggage and during the heady excitement all over the vessel she remained in the cabin and dressed the children and herself. She wished to glow with joy.

Many women expressed disappointment at the first glance of their men out of uniform. Many still visualised a dashing soldier in smooth well-tailored khaki – the image they had carried with them. Suddenly they seemed ordinary. One woman was crying, probably overwrought, feeling that there was a stranger waiting for her. Some had nobody waiting, the distances being so great. It was a strange and bewildering atmosphere – all human emotions exhibited – a microcosm of a macrocosm of all humanity. The experience registered; she would always remember her arrival in this new land.

Then she saw him, in a cream linen suit, standing erect and expectant, calmly surveying the surrounding throng. Her heart gave a leap. She picked up Bran and held him aloft. He saw her, radiant as ever, oh her effervescent capacity for joy, her magic undiminished. With great swift strides he hurried towards them – enveloped them. "At last my love, at last. Welcome to our country."

They drove to New Canaan, where he had rented a large furnished house. It was an elitist village, quite the Mecca for emerging architects, like Frank Lloyd Wright, prepared to give full flow to their slightly curtailed imaginations because of the war. It seemed a beautiful place to a new arrival. Even Miranda approved; "I don't mind this America," as with her brother she explored the property. Simon and Eleri both felt that this was their happiest day. Having been granted two weeks off duty to settle his family he had already decided to take them all to visit his elderly parents in Erie, Pennsylvania. He would show them the familiar sights of his poverty-stricken young boyhood and spend a whole day on Presque Isle where, as a child, he had often forlornly roamed. They should see the Great Lake Erie, large as an ocean, they would picnic among the pine trees at sturdy log tables, catch some fish and cook them. They would stay at the Lawrence Hotel, a place he had once yearned to stay at but thought he would never afford. They would spend just one whole day with his parents because three small foreign children would overwhelm them. They had never really ceased to be foreign themselves and both retained a Polish accent, as Simon explained to his wife. He tried to prepare her but had no fears as to her adaptability.

Three days later after a long but exciting journey over the Appalachian Mountains, decked with pink laurel, the state flower of Pennsylvania, and through small towns with village greens and wooden churches, they eventually arrived at the split-level ranch-type house in the suburbs of Erie. Everything within and without was charming and immaculate and it was with enormous pride that Simon introduced his wife and son. Their pride in their own son was evident. Simon's photograph was everywhere, the one in the most elaborate frame depicting a small boy, bewildered and poorly clad. The next photograph was of a confident schoolboy, then a student in a white tuxedo, then the graduate. Next a further graduate, an enlarged snapshot of a doctor in white coat and stethoscope busy at his work and finally the Army officer in full uniform at his wedding. The old couple spoke in low voices and were beautifully dressed. There was about them a humility and gentleness, plus a sense of gratitude and the satisfying breath of success. Hard work crowned with reward was now their hallmark.

Eleri loved both instantly and Simon's pride in her was obvious. The grandparents sensitively tried to give attention to all the three children, but their eyes devoured the handsome toddler, their own new American citizen. This was a day they had lived for, dreamt of and Simon deeply felt their joy. What a wonderful day – the culmination of years of dreaming. Such complete happiness seldom touched a mere mortal.

CHAPTER THIRTY-THREE

A New Home

It was winter when they first beheld their chosen permanent home – an old Connecticut farmhouse adapted and readapted, the original stone sheep walls bisecting the garden, dividing the stream from the lawn and orchard, sloping to the narrow road ahead. Behind lay the sea, a moody grey on that bleak morning. The marvels of the yet unseen garden lay beneath the snow, the bare branches of the fruit trees pierced the low cloud. But all were delighted – it was what the devoted parents had painstakingly searched for. Each side of the elongated building had an extensive wing, which Eleri and Simon immediately claimed as their own domains. Eleri considered the light before deciding on her own patch, as it would be for her studio. The opposite side would be Simon's office and study. Quellyn, who already showed an interest in art, would have his own miniature easel sharing her space. The basement would hold a playroom and utility room, the surrounding land would be their own special haven. The house stood on a country road leading south from Westport. Their neighbours in the well-spaced zoning would share the same front road and back sea view. The minute man always on guard was the closest landmark.

Already Christmas lights were twinkling around the homes and many a stalwart snowman stood guard. Eleri had never witnessed such extravagance.

The deserted beach immediately beckoned them and during the unloading, the men following the instructions clearly annotated by Eleri, they all went walking along the shore. Both parents desired a sea location with easy access to open country.

The children soon adapted and within a month were part of the community. Carol singing with neighbouring children and afterwards sipping cocoa, with pink and white marshmallows sailing on the top, in many diverse kitchens, became part of the programme. Sledging, snowman building, skating on garden ponds or frozen lawns added to the delights. Life seemed like a dream unfolding.

Suddenly, after much hindrance of connection, there was a happy telephone call from Briende, who gave exciting news just received. Lawrence Britt was coming home, having, after much difficulty, acquired a passage home from Crete. Before this he had been hidden by a family in Athens, earning his keep by teaching English. Dressed as a peasant he had escaped from Thermopylae on almost the last over-laden boat. He was now engaged to marry Leila, the daughter of the house, and was negotiating to rejoin his university as a tutor. Everyone in Brymadoc shared in the joy.

Eleri was elated by the wonderful news and immediately telephoned Janet Britt. Christmas had a new meaning. Happiness was infectious, and the Atlantic no barrier to the heart's affections. After the one-day Christmas vacation normal life continued.

Commuting to New York became Simon's daily pattern. He had his hospital work and he continued with his programme at Columbia. Their lives became typical of the lives lived by their neighbours and contemporaries, except for the sports clubs. Simon had no spare time and Eleri, who had never been remotely sporty, instead became involved with the schools and charities.

Together they had settled the school plans. Simon's loyalty to America decided his intention to use the local schools for Bran and any further children; Eleri would use the charming local schools for the Garonne children for the early years. Bettina Grayling, with her excess wealth, had extracted a promise that she would be allowed to finance her grandchildren's education. Her Lancashire acres had been purchased by the government during the war, her Garonne inheritance and the prosperity of her present marriage over-filled the coffers. Eleri agreed – she had no desire to deny her children an exclusive education chosen by their grandmother. Once settled the subject was closed. It would be interesting to compare both systems.

The pressure of work meant Simon spending long days and sometimes nights away from home but Eleri rejoiced in his devotion to his chosen career. While together he was hers exclusively, the joy of their marriage unfading, the attraction to each other still magical. In deference to his time with her, his work was temporarily slotted away. He had decided at the outset that he would never distress his beautiful wife with details of his daily experience, some of it horrendous – just as he had vowed never to talk of his war exploits. In fact, he tried to erase the latter from his consciousness, even though frequently troubled by his stubborn injury, which still necessitated periodic treatment, much of it directed by himself.

Proximity to New York became an added bonus for Eleri. Precious time together frequently meant replenishing a breadth of interests. They attended concerts, theatre first nights and previews at art galleries and Eleri recaptured much of what she had once enjoyed in pre-war London.

Punctuating the contentment there was the occasional hiccup. Quellyn announced one day that he wanted to go to church like Leroy Flynn. "Yeah," said Miranda, "and I want a Madonna like Rosalie's."

Simon was unusually sensitive when it came to religion, knowing the agony and cost of Jewishness in his own Polish background. Eleri had never made a pretence of believing all which was traditionally taught, yet both conscientious parents recognised the importance of the spiritual element in life.

After much deliberation they decided on unitarianism, from their reading purporting to be the fastest growing church in the United States; to their understanding embracing an amalgam of lapsed members of other denominations. Westport had such a church and it was thriving. It suited the Peerlesses and became an anchor for their children over the years, providing much satisfaction and enjoyment. It had been one of their happiest decisions.

The snows of that first winter melted into a short spring. Simon, who had never had a garden as a child and Eleri, who had never shown much inclination for gardening, found themselves interested in the variety of plants, many strange to Eleri, revealed by the disappearing snow. The great red robins and colourful jays were welcome visitors, the sea birds along the shore an added interest for the children.

Ever the organiser, Eleri established a club for war brides but soon left it in charge of an able committee. She had more interest in children's charities and quickly founded a medical charity for children whose families had little or no financial means. It flourished, and her imagination was limitless when she chaired the committee for fundraising ideas. Everything she arranged became an occasion. "It's strawberry time, we'll have an English garden party. All must wear pink and white. Wendy, you choose the date, Marian, you get the press involved, Teresa, make enquiries regarding the cream and strawberries. You may find the farms and food shops competing."

"Who'll do the posters?" came a question. "What about you?" She agreed to do the posters.

A school pageant was next on the agenda. A big fancy dress party in the park with Mayflower arrivals, Puritans and preachers, redskins and redcoats and cowboys galore.

Youngsters carrying beribboned baskets circulated among the spectators, collecting contributions. The high school cheerleaders added colour and skilful gyrations. For the parents there was the inevitable concert under the stars, a chance for all to dress up and feast. Eleri was happy, she was fulfilled.

Her happiness brimmed over when, at a New York function, she accidentally met Simon L. Seznick, whom she had met in London so long ago. As expected, she remembered his name and mentioned that she still had his card. The outcome of this was an introduction to the producer of Noel Coward's *Blithe Spirit*, currently being planned for Broadway and an invitation to be in charge of the costumes. She was delighted to accept, already mentally visualising the research, the fabrics, the styles and so much more. Once more she was invited to Hollywood, but she was brimming over with present all-round happiness and could imagine nothing to supersede this. What more could she possibly want?

Her unquenchable spirit never ceased to amaze Simon, her strength and vivacity a constant pleasure along with her implacable sanity, so whole, so true.

To Eleri, a turn of his head or the beginning of a smile could send her heart racing. His patience and good humour never wavered and his devotion to home, work and family was constant. Though in possession of a formidable intellect and recognition within his field, his humility was endearing. Amos Skiroski, their old refugee friend, who saw them twice a year, thought their meeting his most beautiful achievement.

Blending into their lives from the time of their arrival, Dolores and Silas Clay, the home help and gardener, became permanent fixtures, much loved and cared for. The easy-going pair lived in a neat frame house in their own part of town with their two gently and lovingly cared for children. Dolores sang Negro spirituals as she went about her work; sometimes Silas's rich booming voice would join her in chorus. Both sang in the choir of the local Baptist church. Eleri, non-domesticated as ever, could never have managed her rambling house and lively family without them; she was free to contrive with her manifold interests, her current life not unlike the life she had lived in llandia, except for the easy access to New York, which was a luxury because the journey to London had always seemed endless.

When, the following summer, Briende, Maeve and Aunt Editha came to visit they found a happy established family. The relaxed household and much open-air living interspersed with trips to New York was a breathtaking experience. All wished grandmother had come but she was indomitable as ever, though in excellent health compared with Editha, who seemed to need frequent rest. Simon suspected a heart condition, though as yet not too hindering. He advised caution and frequent medical check-ups, even arranging an appointment with a colleague, but Editha refused to comply. Eleri determined that the following summer she would visit Brymadoc with Quellyn, who would be old enough to accept that Campions would be his inheritance, and it was right that he became acquainted with his future responsibilities.

By that first summer Eleri had become pregnant, to the delight of all, and the birth of Deborah Editha Madoc Peerless as Bran's most special Christmas present, that second Christmas, crowned their happiness. This time Simon did deliver the child and then organised a seven-day retreat for Eleri in a quiet location with no telephone, no visitors, useless magazines as reading matter, chocolates, wine and fruit, rest and replenishing. The boredom became a punishment and great was her joy on the day of release before plunging herself back into a whirlwind of activity.

While Eleri continued with her version of the American Dream her beloved sister's battles with a beloved budding daughter were rapidly approaching a zenith of emotional agony.

The silvery Maeve at fourteen was a serious schoolgirl. A familiar crowd became part of the railway routine, the boys in navy travelling to Limorrnah Grammar School and Maeve, with her evacuee friend Lucy, finishing her schooling, both in green, going to Dewary Girls College. To the exuberant lads they became known as the Green Goddesses as they continued their journey on the ferry. They were different!

During the junior years they were remote, inconsequential, but by the time the Green Goddesses were fifteen, for the boys colour blindness had become a side effect of hormonal activity. The girls were not unaware of a group of four interesting boys, already in the science sixth form and heading for medical schools. Awareness turned to interest and polite interchanges began. The tall fair-haired one was particularly enamoured of the reserved Maeve.

It was a warm summer's day when Limorrnah boys came to play cricket in an end of term match against Dewary Boys College. Later the young people travelled home together on Sea Dame, the ever-plodding arthritic old vessel.

Maeve was on the deck when she espied Garth Protheroe hovering near and when the heavens kindly sent forth a shower of rain Maeve and Garth raced for shelter between tall barrels covered by a tarpaulin. Huddled between two of these they sat on the slatted deck and were gently rocked by the old ferry boat. To Maeve the nearness became discomfiting and when her bare thigh touched his white-clad thigh the electric current was immediate. She quickly placed an inch or so between them, but the excitement had registered with both.

Briende saw this unfolding relationship with trepidation. Would her daughter hold out until qualified? Would he lose patience? He was four years ahead of her. Briende saw her ambitions for her daughter crumbling. The barely susceptible flush on Maeve's pale face each time a letter arrived in his spidery handwriting did not pass unnoticed. His short letter undoubtedly spoke of his love; hers in reply were longer and probably beautiful. The girl could write. Briende, remembering her own youthful romance, agonised over the situation. There was nobody with whom she could discuss her fears. Dr. Skiroski and Eleri were far away. Her mother thought Maeve could marry at eighteen as she'd had enough education, and a doctor was acceptable, she supposed, as Dr. Phillpot had done well enough and was much esteemed. Her relatives in Limorrnah had their own problems. Niamh had become pregnant and married, university forgotten; her trapped life had become boring and disappointing and the marriage was unlikely to survive. Bethan, like her mother, became a harpist and toured with a philharmonic orchestra. They suspected many lovers in tow. As yet music mattered more than marriage.

Maeve was of a different mettle – genuine, steadfast, committed. No invitation could tempt her to waver from her loyalty to Garth Protheroe. Briende's distress went unheeded and Maeve at sixteen would remind her mother that she herself had been very young when Cupid's arrow struck.

Briende had gleaned that Garth was the only child of a widow in the neighbouring village of Hafod. His only books were necessary schoolbooks, his only serious conversation was with his teachers. His home, though respectable, was devoid of culture. It harboured no dictionary, atlas, Bible or reference book and a newspaper in the house was a rare occurrence. He was, however, academically good enough to acquire sciences at higher levels and thereby enter a medical school.

In frenzied letters Briende explained to Eleri her doubts and fears and Eleri, with American enlightenment, advised her sister to meet the young man, invite him home. Such a measure in llandia was tantamount to a betrothal.

Briende met the young man and liked him. He was decent, well-dressed, polite and rather quiet. He was certainly handsome in a clean-cut fashion – very Anglo-Saxon in appearance, tall and slim.

Briende observed the young people during the brief meeting. Physically they looked well together. It was definitely a strong attraction; their eye contact was constant, the atmosphere charged, they just longed to be off and alone. But Briende was pained to realise that he did not know her daughter – her depth, warmth, maturity and intellectual breadth. Her wide reading and questioning mind, her facility with the pen, her ambition to be a journalist, her sweetness of nature, were all inconsequential. This intoxicating, all-consuming, exciting affair was a physical thing between them, nothing more. Briende could only tactfully warn Maeve and hope her daughter had enough wisdom not to become too involved sexually. Niamh, her cousin, had been a promising mathematician, Briende reminded her.

When at seventeen Maeve was offered a place at St. Hilda's, Oxford, her mother was overjoyed. She would meet new people, become more involved socially with a variety of interests, become absorbed in her studies, though she had no doubt that Garth Protheroe would remain within her orbit.

At this juncture a heartbreaking conversation ensued.

"Mama, London University has offered me a place based on the early offer from Oxford. Garth is in London and there are vacancies in the rented house he shared. Would you mind overly if I accepted London?"

No crisis since Ralph's death had reached such an impasse. Briende was convulsed with worry and disappointment. For the first time ever, she became dogmatic.

"You are under eighteen. I've decided that you should go to Oxford. What an opportunity! How I envy you! You have led a sheltered life and had one youthful romance. Do you really consider that enough?"

Her own hypocrisy shamed her, remembering her nineteen-year-old self, but Ralph Maine was of better substance than Garth Protheroe, she excused herself. "Garth is at St. Mary's, Paddington; he has a heavy schedule. I would not see him constantly."

"You would see him every day and night undoubtedly, and both your studies would suffer."

"He claims the frustration of being away from me would be more likely to cripple his studies."

"In the meantime, you give up a first-class college with comfortable living accommodation in the most coveted city for sleazy living in a shared house in a bomb-damaged area – and probably the end of your education."

Briende withheld her observations as to the great differences between them, not quite knowing what her daughter's reaction would be. She seemed blinded by love, if such it was.

"I see your point. At the moment I'd feel more genuine following my heart." Briende's own heart ached as she remembered Ralph Maine, the agony, the ecstasy, the longing. However, she persevered.

"If he cares sufficiently, he will understand. Has it occurred to you that it is crass selfishness on his part to deprive you of Oxford? Your father would never have expected such a sacrifice from me had the opportunity arisen." Again, she felt herself on shaky ground.

She had never mentioned Ralph, just plodded on alone through every obstacle, willing herself to be strong but this was the severest test and she was aware of her helplessness.

"Shall I write to London and cancel their offer, or will you do it? I have the right to forbid this."

"Mama, you would not be that cruel. What I do I'll decide."

Heavy, miserable days followed that first chasm between them. Common sense reigned, and Maeve went to St. Hilda's as planned that autumn.

There was a tremendous unfolding as anticipated, she worked steadily, increasing her horizons, travelling, making new friends, gathering experience.

Garth, in London resented it if they did not meet at weekends, stressing that she had more money and a less taxing schedule of study. More demands were made on his time because of the necessary hospital experience. The conflict had begun.

Without this constant friction those early college days would have been fulfilling, exciting and a happy whirl of activity. Much of her delight was immersed in a glowing new friendship with a Welsh music student. She was Ceridwen Bowen Beynon, known as Ceri. Dark, petite, ever smiling with a charming lilting voice and the most perfect rendering of written and spoken English. She had her own column in a serious publication and was already almost an established music critic; she was much in demand at college functions whether for students or the academic faculty. Her harp, as tall as she, would travel with her and even on a train journey she would remain with it in the guard's van.

Her exuberance cheered Maeve after yet another tempestuous eruption with Garth. Ceri scolded her for not accepting more of her many invitations to dances, concerts, or parties. She should have been having an exciting time.

When Garth failed the fourth year and had to repeat the examination, he blamed her, said frustration had bedevilled his studies. She refused to spend weekends at the student house, knowing full well what the outcome would be. She refused to promise marriage as soon as he qualified; though she considered herself deeply in love, she hoped to complete her own degree course.

Dissension and impatience, also bitterness, was now creeping into their relationship, causing Maeve's own work to suffer and hope for the much-coveted first class degree was beginning to fade.

Garth had negotiated, in fact had been offered, his own small hospital in Rhodesia. It was well funded and he would be in sole charge, gaining experience and being well provided for, acquiring knowledge, especially of little-understood tropical diseases, a field in which he could perhaps specialise later. He was staggered that such an opportunity had come his way. When the final results were announced his first mission was to Oxford to see Maeve. The discord continued. "You cannot refuse to come. You are not likely to get the degree you wanted, anyway and you don't need it."

"I'm going to complete the course. It will only be a few months after your departure, take the job and I will follow you." She meant to do so.

Secretly he believed that once away from her he would never reclaim her – some richer, more privileged partner would win the lovely creature. He knew how men feasted their eyes on her and what used to be a sense of pride in claiming her affection had become a real fear. She was surrounded by worthier people than he, people more like herself. Or so he imagined.

That weekend, for the first time, she witnessed his violent temper. His bitter words intimated that she thought herself above him and was spoilt and elitist.

No woman who loved him could refuse to join him, when such a splendid opportunity arose. He was suffused with his own success and her independence rankled, her poise and quiet determination.

When her final year in college began, he was already preparing for the African venture. Their relationship, too volatile for comfort, was reaching its climax and when, that final Christmas, Maeve decided to accept her friend's invitation to Wales to escape the taxing discord of meeting him at home, it signified the end of their affair.

Garth went home and spitefully dated Hazel Corrie, Rosemary Day's pretty daughter. She was blonde, curvaceous, sweet-natured and pliable but an outsider to the faithful little group of schooldays; a girl from a totally different sphere of experience, no real education, no ambition and no old-established family. She was thrilled when in their first weekend of intimacy she became pregnant. It was an unexpected conquest. Decency demanded marriage. She revelled in her new status, fed his ego, pleased his mother, who always thought Maeve more learned than a girl needed to be and too 'precious'.

St. Petroc, Brymadoc, saw another pretty wedding. Lucy, now engaged to Dr. Daryl Hughes, of schoolday fame, was bridesmaid, and his friend Hughes was best man. In that intimate group of friends of long standing the only new face among them was that of the bride.

The young couple were honeymooning on their way to Africa while Maeve, home for a rest, was struggling to come to terms with the traumatic turn of events.

CHAPTER THIRTY-FOUR

The Unexpected

ON A CLOUDY LATE AFTERNOON FOUR WEEKS BEFORE Easter, three days after the unforeseen wedding, Maeve wended her way to the church. The transparent, colourless, plastic raincoat, the latest fashion, gave her an ethereal look, as, misty-eyed in the fading light, she approached the great west door. She would see the flowers before they were removed on the morrow, stand at the altar where she had expected to stand, weep silently as she sat for a while in the Madoc pew. In that peace she tried to assemble her thoughts. Alone with her conscience, because she could not find it in her heart to wish him well, she also accepted that she held no rancour towards Hazel, as she remembered the sweet, pretty child whose frequent absences from school were accepted. The whole family had been lax about attending school, even more so when they once owned a now-defunct busy nursery. In fact, Maeve felt a slight pity. After the first flush of new love would she be able to cope with the undoubted challenges which lay ahead professionally and socially? Would the shadow of Maeve Maine come between them? Maeve knew Garth Protheroe pretty thoroughly, knew something of his selfishness, conceit and ambition regarding the new opportunity which had unexpectedly come his way. He had even managed not to give two years to his country as a serviceman like his colleagues and friends. His expectations from a wife would be pretty gruelling. In fact, Maeve had already realised that snobbery had become a part of him. His lowly origins were already forgotten, his social ambitions had already taken root. A pretty woman on his arm, an important accessory to begin with, could in a short while become insufficient for his ego. Sophistication would be expected.

Such were Maeve's thoughts. Yet she vowed that never again would she become completely immersed in one man, to the extent that she'd become immune to any other, while in the throes of devotion. The poet may have written that it was better to have loved and lost than not to have loved at all but were the hurts of the past three years worth the suffering, the tears, the complete destruction of her secure comfortable self? The frustration, the endless self-denial, the psychological upheaval? Was it worth it, she wondered?

The great church door, which she must have left, open slammed with a resounding bang, as if to startle her from her reverie and signify the finality of what had been. It started to rain, it lashed at the delicate, ancient, windows and thundered on the roof like a Shakespearean stage setting to match her grim mood. She moved to the door. It creaked its protest as she pulled it open as if in competition with the thrashing wind. The rain and wind would cleanse her, invigorate her, battling against the elements would reduce her tension. She felt fragile but was beginning to realise that maybe he was unworthy of her. As the tears and the rain mingled on her face, she went to Pen Melyn; her grandmother's common sense approach would be the best tonic. As she stumbled along in the rain, she composed her farewell.

First Love
Ambling along a country lane
Climbing the heathered hills
Fair hair ruffled in the mountain breeze
Laughter lost in the wind.
And the time was always summer
And the days were always long
And the birds were always trilling
And life was an endless song.
Oh the turbulence of loving
The sleepless nights of longing
The watching and the waiting
The tempests and extremes.
There'll be nothing half as sweet again
As love's young dreams.

A stark lesson. She wiped her eyes, put a firmness in her step and resolved to be less susceptible in future. She would draw a sharp line underneath the poem when she'd written it. It would be her 'Amen'.

Daniel O'Leary was leaving as she arrived, having just driven Mrs. Blethyn home from Trevere. With surprise he greeted her. "Well, Maeve, hello! How grand to have you around again and looking so fine."

With rain-splattered face, misty eyes and stringy wet hair she had never felt less fine but his delightful Irishness could make any woman feel beautiful.

"Thank you, Daniel, and how are you?"

"Not good. My ma objects to my female company."

"Anyone I know?" she asked.

"Drusilla May Smith of River Cottages. I'm smitten good and proper this time."

"Tut, tut," offered Mrs. Blethyn, "a few weeks ago you were in love with Hazel Corrie."

"Almost. But she wanted marriage and lots of babies and I'm not ready for that. Anyway, she's spoken for, she wed a doctor chap from Hafod on Saturday. Imagine that."

He was obviously innocent of Maeve's involvement as Maeve had been away for some time. She cringed but went to hang up her wet coat.

"Must go. See you tomorrow, Mrs. Blethyn," and he was gone.

The kettle whistled. Maeve's grandmother disappeared to the kitchen and soon returned bearing steaming cups of tea and some cakes. She passed Maeve a cup and seated herself opposite in the old rocking chair, which had heard so many family confessions. She poked the fire vigorously, looked at Maeve. "You've been to the church, I suppose."

"I have and I stood at the altar and I wept. I also failed to pray for him so I'm not much of a Christian."

"You've been dashed to the depths, my girl. Young love can be extreme if the path does not run smoothly. You can do better, give yourself time. You need someone more like your father – cannot put a word to it – quality, I suppose. He had a beautiful soul."

"I'll never fall in love again. Next time I'll be more measured, it will be less all-engrossing. I was devoted to him for years. I never accepted the many approaches I had, I just was not interested."

"Don't be bitter. Enjoy your last term at college – never mind a first class degree. Make up for lost pleasures, within reason of course. Do not go overboard like Niamh, who's trapped with someone she would no longer choose. Bear that in mind."

"I think I've come to terms with things. Daniel cheered me up. What a splendid, uncomplicated lot they are! The good-natured, dark, delicious Delilah will soon tire of a callow youth, but she'll be wonderful for his ego."

"Reputedly she has gypsy blood. On Fridays she sings at a restaurant and plays the mandolin; also runs her parents' market stall on Saturdays, a gaily befringed affair. They grow fruit and vegetables to sell and they are very industrious folk. Her father works at the quarry and Mrs. Smith tells fortunes."

"I can imagine the chat." Maeve felt more relaxed than for some while; hearing of local doings was pleasant. She wished some of the authors she had studied had known Brymadoc.

"The Mrs. Grundys of the village say their living room is spick and span with flower-painted furniture and gay accessories, like the immaculate interior of a Romany caravan."

"I know someone who would enjoy knowing them."

"Quite. She would be down there with easel and paints, no doubt. Perhaps they would appear on a peacetime calendar or a book jacket. What throw-back to the past produced her I'll never know."

They both smiled, remembering the fascinating being. "Your mother will be worried. It is getting dark."

"True. I must be off, as I have loads of neglected work to catch up on. What are your plans tonight? Is there a play or reading on the wireless?"

"Not tonight. On nights like this I like my bed and my book. I'm reading a splendid book."

"What is it?"

"*Grapes of Wrath* by Steinbeck, a sensible work. America is not all Hollywood glamour. Such books should be compulsory reading in the schools."

"That's a good book. I know it well."

She kissed her grandmother, who seemed to have mellowed considerably, then donned her raincoat and went.

Relief showed in Briende's face as Maeve entered. She knew what was coming. "You've been with your grandmother. Before that you were at the church."

Maeve's face bore the hint of a smile. The clairvoyant Mrs. Smith would undoubtedly trade in her art for the psychic qualities of the Madoc women.

Among the correspondence awaiting Maeve when

she returned to Oxford, four days later, was one in an unfamiliar hand with a London postmark. Intrigued, she opened it to find a pleasant communication from a Dominic Witherslea, whom she had known vaguely since schooldays; she had been too young to appreciate his masculine, macho tendencies or be impressed by the girls in his wake. She had last spoken to him on the street in Limorrnah when he invited her to see the film of Lawrence's *Sons and Lovers*, then much in vogue. She, of course, had declined.

From the letter she learnt that Oxford had rejected him, though accepting his brother, and that he was at the London School of Economics on an ex-serviceman's grant. The gist of the letter was that he was exchanging his rooms for his brother's, for a week, as his brother was 'hot' for a girl at LSE, as he put it. Could he meet Maeve during the week? He had seen her photograph among his brother Brinley's party snapshots and thought how pleasant it would be to renew her acquaintance. The party had been in the rooms of somebody called Sefton Maynard.

She disliked the 'tone' of the letter but remembered the said party, though she did not know his brother.

After a discussion with Ceri, who thought it might cheer her up to meet somebody from home, Maeve thought, *why not*? Apparently, his brother had negotiated his presence at a few functions, plus a theatre outing, instead of himself. Maeve duly met him, attended the theatre, went punting, went to two parties and on a bus to a neighbouring village to see *Spring in Park Lane* starring Anna Neagle and Michael Wilding – something light and romantic to lift her sagging spirits, she imagined. The spring weather was unusually warm.

She enjoyed the flirtation for what it was, as he was splendid company with many amusing anecdotes to relate. He had an easy charm, almost too confident, and a swaggering conceit she found slightly repellent but kindly labelled 'immaturity'. He smoked and drank to excess, she thought, having probably perfected these pastimes while in the services. He was no better and no worse than many others and it was pleasant being escorted by a handsome young man, so light in spirit, tinged with irresponsibility and enough personality to make his presence felt among people he had not met.

On the fifth day of their friendship he had two functions planned, a sherry party at Christchurch instead of his brother and his own small party in his rooms at three-thirty. In between, Maeve had a lunch date, having been invited by Cynthia Forrester's parents to lunch at The Randolph. Cynthia was heading for a first class degree and was her special literary friend. They worked together and read each other's essays before submitting them. The latest had been an essay on the rival claims of art and life as perceived in Jane Austen and Eliot. Maeve had worked on this while at home. The current essay was on modernism, with 1922 as a key date. This they were both struggling with, combining information and opinions.

Maeve dressed suitably for both functions, wearing a pale blue knife-pleated skirt and matching cotton knit top with short sleeves, a demure square neckline and her string of pearls. It promised to be a warm day and to aid her in keeping cool she wore what were then known as French knickers, a loose-legged, comfortable garment in delicate silk. She had to scramble in drawers for a suspender belt to hold up some scarce nylon stockings sent by Eleri – luxurious for their scarcity. She slipped her feet into what they called Cuban-heeled white shoes. Thus attired, she was formally clad for The Randolph and casual enough for the sherry party.

At Christchurch she remembered drinking three sherries, hugely enjoying herself after months of a nun-like discipline. A small group detached itself from the main party and wondered off by invitation to the Oxford Union. It was Maeve's first visit. The haze of smoke and cigarette smells, mingled with beery odours, on first acquaintance made it seem more like a pub than a renowned place of debate. The scruffiness and dark ambience had a tinge of austerity, which she excused as a remnant of wartime, perhaps. Most places seemed 'tired' and in need of refurbishment. The framed yellowed pictures along the corridors depicting noted debaters of the past were interesting but she alone seemed interested. Sefton Maynard had purchased five bottles of wine, which were rapidly becoming depleted. They hailed her to hurry and join them, which she did, and had her glass surreptitiously refilled as soon as it was half-drunk. She sipped more slowly. Argument raged pertaining to money and an assertion that any man had a right to do what he liked with his own cash. To illustrate the point, he lit a cigarette with a pound note. Maeve tried to appear neutral, offering no comment, though secretly disgusted and convinced of his immaturity. This was not her type of crowd and she was grateful that she had an excuse to leave.

Before leaving the merriment of the Union, Dominic reminded her of his own small party in his brother's rooms at three-thirty. She had looked forward to this coming luncheon and wished she had not gone to the Union beforehand and been soured by the exhibitionism indulged in. It was like a page from Evelyn Waugh's *Brideshead Revisited*; some dinosaurs from the twenties still seemed to be breeding. She wondered whether they did any work.

The luncheon was elegant as she expected, her hosts charming. Maeve sipped the excellent Merlot slowly and with an ample amount of water. Cynthia guessed the reason for her caution and admired her poise. It proved a tasteful, pleasurable, interlude in a hectic day and as she charmingly thanked her hosts, she said so before leaving for the next gathering.

When she arrived at the rooms in St. Aldate's a small party was already in progress. Wine flowed liberally but she was now happier to join in, with caution. If this was what was meant by getting the most out of student days she was making up for lost time, at the same time grateful that she had not lived at this place for three years. Having grown up in a household which never served wine and having a grandmother who restricted it to very special occasions, Maeve was unused to such liberal consumption. She had to admit that she was slightly shocked but to own up to such thinking would, among this lot, appear unsophisticated. She cautiously measured her own sipping.

A short while after her arrival, miraculously, the other three couples left, pleading other commitments. With their departure, Maeve, for the first time, could survey the shabby room. There were two single beds against opposite walls, lopsided curtains, photographs of girlfriends at wonky angles, the usual sagging bookshelves, a tallboy consisting of six chipped drawers, a table, two utility chairs and a stove. Dominic had placed a few flowers on a new teacloth on the table and provided a tray of clumsy sandwiches and biscuits. Once the table was cleared, the bottles ensconced in the waste basket, the room had a semblance of neatness, though the drabness remained.

Feeling unusually lightheaded and tired Maeve gratefully lay on one of the beds. She was not aware of Dominic hanging a 'Do not Disturb' notice on the door. It lay on the chair quite openly. Perhaps it was of joint ownership, part of the custom when they had a visiting girlfriend, or if they needed peace to study, or so Maeve generously assumed. She felt weary, relaxed, slightly hazy. Could she possibly have no tolerance of three sherries and four glasses of wine throughout the day? This feeling was new, a never-before feeling. It must be the wine. During the past years two lingering glasses had been her maximum. Of course, she had travelled to llandia and back a few days before and was tired.

She did not object when she felt Dominic beside her, caressing her, murmuring compliments, holding her with vice-like intensity. Suddenly she took herself in hand, thought clearly, tried to extricate herself, to no avail. She begged him to release her, but he was deaf to any request, as if some demon had possessed him. His hand was on her thigh, the other tugging at her bra. The truth dawned on her too late. A panting, sweating, grunting monster had possession of her, ruthless, rough, impatient. She could have been anyone, or some inanimate object. She was no longer the elegant, controlled Maeve Maine, reserved and non-assertive. She was nothing, nothing.

The horror of it temporarily paralysed her. She could not move or talk, she heard her own racing heart beneath a still, heavy, statue. She extricated herself by using her knees to dig into him, using more physical strength than she had ever used, ruthlessly pressing until he rolled over in a repulsive lump. She slid off the bed, picked up her shoulder bag and wrestled with the ill-fitting door. He resurrected and rushed over to her, looking ridiculous in his undignified state. "I'm sorry, Maeve. I could not help myself." The heavy old door yielded, and she raced down the stone stairs. He called again, "It's not the end of the world. Please wait, please."

With a husky sob she was gone, around the corner of the stairs, out of sight.

Shock and disbelief were the two issues she had to come to terms with. She crossed the road, feeling faint and soiled, towards a clump of sad-looking bushes at the entrance to the Broadwalk across Christchurch Meadows, and, shielded from the road, she was violently sick. She had never vomited or felt so ill. Like the other delicate-looking Madoc women she had enjoyed superb health. Feeling fragile and vulnerable she decided not to return to college via the Broadwalk but to cut across Bear Lane to the High and dice through traffic and people, noise, normality. Disgust enveloped her, the fact that she had not willingly surrendered, her only comfort. But was she blameless? Or just naive? She had stayed behind when the others left, she had lain on the bed – where else? She had actually seen him hang the notice outside the door, but she had not expected such an outcome. The most painful suspicion was the fact that he had planned the seduction. Perhaps they were in league, his friends and his brother. Did they do such favours for one another and think nothing of it? Was it commonplace? Such thinking assaulted her normally sound conceptions. Though her tears came and went intermittently as she walked, she felt resilient enough to promise herself not to be psychologically damaged by the outrage, because it was a mere 'bodily' thing after all. Her mind was uninvolved. She nevertheless determined never again to trust anyone. Her precious, pure, trusting self had been violated. Perhaps she did not know the rules – lying on that bed could have signified a willingness. The greatest agony was remembering Aunt Eleri's frank sexual discussions – "Make sure that your first experience is with someone you adore, whether it lasts or not, because the memory of the first time will always be fresh." Her tears flowed liberally.

Garth, whom she had adored and now remembered with longing, had been denied what had been stolen. Tears welled again as she blindly walked towards the college. Memories tortured her, memories of scrambling over the crags and scree as they'd climbed towards the Stones, the luminous cushions of heather and lichen; granite seats covered with creeping silver weed, its starry yellow flowers competing with those of the nipplewort along the base. The spiky brown bracken and emerald niches along the stream and Garth's patience as he heeded the final 'no'. She wished with all her heart that she had been less virtuous, less precious, more natural. The outcome would probably have been unchanged – she would not have abandoned her degree. Eleri's words stung more than ever. Her artistic make-up would not have allowed for self-denial and at this moment the vital and adorable Eleri was the only person to whom she could have confessed. She considered discussing it with Ceri but decided not to burden her. It was she who had encouraged her to see him, meaning well, of course. No, Maeve decided, she was alone. She would have to convince herself that it was meaningless and had to be magnanimous enough to believe that he had not planned it. With the same strength of mind, she would somehow stoically arrange an illegal abortion, if she'd been impregnated. Remembering Eleri's lonely courage, as she went to claim her dead husband's body, gave Maeve strength.

She fumbled for her keys and let herself into her room. In the shared bathroom she ran the hot tap immediately. For once she could excuse herself for being selfish and using up the available hot water. A passing glance in the long mirror surprised her – the fact that she looked as she usually looked, a bit paler perhaps, nothing more. She flung her underwear into the wash basin and, after throwing an abundance of bath salts in the bath water, immersed herself. Her long blonde hair, washed the previous night, was again shampooed and she several times immersed herself completely in the climbing water, the ensuing, singing, bubbles almost comforting. She re-emerged to mercilessly rub herself dry with a rough towel. A fresh towel was wound securely around her head. Suddenly the flimsy nightie seemed distasteful, too feminine, too baby-dollish. She extracted a simple, sleeved, cotton garment from the drawer and, thus attired, crawled into bed. She had no idea of time, no memory of whether there was something on somewhere that evening or on the morrow and did not care if she missed anything. She would, so to speak, sleep it off. It was not the end of the world, as he had gallantly informed her, but it was certainly enough "to put rancours in the vessel of my peace" and teach a bitter lesson in caution, and for the first time in her life she felt a tinge of something resembling hatred.

CHAPTER THIRTY-FIVE

The Morning After

THE LONG NIGHT WAS OVER. IMMEDIATELY ON WAKING Maeve recollected the previous day's agonies. The comfortable sounds of morning seemed all around, birdsong blending with gurgling pipes, footsteps, low voices, sliding locks. She reached a long arm to scrabble among objects on the nearby dressing table to find her watch. It was a quarter past seven. She had probably slept for over thirteen hours, deeply, undisturbed by bad dreams. The head towel had unwound itself, but her hair was dry. Sitting on the edge of the bed she felt faint but realised that she was hungry. She seemed to have endured a long fast and was physically bruised and battered, though she looked as usual, judging from the mirror opposite. This seemed to surprise her anew.

The day looked promising. She brushed her hair until it gleamed, put on a touch of rouge to alleviate the paleness, which was normal for her, and walked towards the hall. A murmur of young female voices reached her as the students planned their day. Many looked fresh and pretty in summer dresses in honour of the unfamiliar stretch of warm weather. She greeted a few before joining Ceri and Cynthia at the table.

Ceri was engrossed in a church music programme, which was almost meaningless to her friends. Though Maeve loved music and played the piano reasonably well, she was not a 'natural'. Ceri intended going to the cathedral – would they join her? Marvellous selection of pieces on offer and the choir was excellent. The young women agreed. Maeve had already decided not to spend any time alone that day. Church music transported Ceri to realms none could reach and her tears usually moved Maeve to tears, affected by Ceri's emotion as much as by the music, until the whole exercise became like a catharsis, which today Maeve could do with.

Providing it was still sunny after the service they would stop for tea or coffee if they found a place open, then walk along the river before lunch in hall. That afternoon Cynthia's friend at Somerville, also reading English, had asked Cynthia to tea and to bring Maeve, whom she had met a few times. Maeve was pleased, as the day promised to be quiet and restful. As Ceri was to be occupied with music in the afternoon, Cynthia and Maeve decided to find a secluded corner in the gardens and do some reading. By the end of the day Maeve's spirit had revived and the ugly episode was put in context. Intermittently, the thought of it crossed her consciousness but she quickly rallied.

On Monday morning, when gathering her letters, she temporarily froze to find one from Dominic. His bold artistic script in black ink hypnotised her. Revulsion made her loth to touch it. Instinctively, she knew that it was an apology, yet something she had not expected. She tore it open.

"Dearest Maeve,

Forgive me, I could not help myself. You, who had always seemed unattainable, were on a bed, looking incredibly beautiful. My impatience was inexcusable and my lack of tenderness boorish, but I had been drinking. You seemed so upset when you left.

I hope you did not take it to heart too much. It happens all the time. It started in the Garden of Eden and still goes on. I long to see you tonight, as planned, as it will be my last night here. Sorry you did not make today's 'do' at Sefton's. I'm recovering from a hangover as I write.

Incidentally, they call you the ice maiden. Apparently, you've been remote and unsociable but one and all would relish melting you. I found myself a much envied chap.

It's been wonderful being with you, such reserve, such style. Until tonight at seven, in the usual place and I vow to behave myself, I really do. You are a lovely woman – a truly lovely woman.

Dominic."

She read it twice and memorised it. In a flash she saw a

future politician, charming, handsome, popular but thick-skinned and with zero conscience. Yes, the nation would hear of him one day but not in flattering terms.

She tore the note into shreds. Had she a fire she would have relished seeing it burn. If she ever became a writer such a letter would serve admirably for the rogue-hero's communication.

That night he waited in vain outside the college. Maeve spent the night at Somerville, giving a persistent boyfriend as an excuse. The truth she kept to herself.

The next day brought a charming letter from Eleri. It was racy and bursting with information. At a New York function she had met a charming man, "about my age" as she put it, an executive with an oil company, who travelled widely as a business assessor. He had been educated at St. Andrews, then Harvard; his schooldays had been spent in London as a day boy at St. Paul's. While his parents were in London they had kept their only child at home. He was much travelled, attractive, modern in outlook and a lover of art and music. Eleri had met him at a dinner following a preview. She had been invited to help him choose three paintings at the Summer Exhibition at Burlington House. They were for his recently acquired office on Thameside and the company policy to champion new artists meant that they would pay. Eleri felt honoured to be asked to help him choose, as she would be visiting Britain on that date. Alas, she could not come – the family as usual took precedence. Miranda was a star in the school play, her first, and she had been chosen to play the Sleeping Beauty, which admirably suited her; she just lay on a couch looking beautiful for ninety percent of the action. She had already objected to the leading man chosen, Roy Parsons, who was too short. She would only be the opposite of Luke Meyers, who was tall. As usual her will predominated. For a laid-back child, not particularly serious about study or anything else, it was amazing how she conquered and got her own way in almost anything. For a dress she'd purchased a gold brocade curtain in a Salvation Army charity shop and designed a long-sleeved dress with a skimpy top and miles of skirt to drape over her couch! She drew the design for Eleri; there was something of her mother in her but not much. Sadly, any perseverance or energy was lacking. She cared not for reading or studying and was usually a silent onlooker, though poised and well-mannered for her age. Would Maeve, her finals being over, meet Eleri's friend instead? Eleri's invitation was duly enclosed. Eleri would, of course, be writing to him explaining things; Maeve would hear from him. "Incidentally, his name is Percy Edgar Pennistone-Craig. If that does not remind you of *Wuthering Heights* what will?" So the letter ended.

Maeve had never been to Burlington House and this was a tremendous honour. She wondered what Percy Pennistone-Craig was really like. Delightedly she raced to Ceri with the news.

"I envy you but cannot see you with a Percy," she teased.

"It was good enough for Shelley, should be good enough for me." Ceri laughed. "I wonder who you can imagine me with?"

"Let me see. Not Keats, too mellifluous, too

inexperienced, certainly not Byron – you would not be that stupid – too experienced, not Wordsworth, too dull, Tennyson could inherit the 'black moods'; I know, it would be a Disraeli or a Browning – intellectual, romantic and just right for taking you to all the concerts. Verona, under the stars, La Scala in Milan."

They laughed together, promising to give the question further thought.

Maeve heard from Edgar Pennistone-Craig within days. He had heard much about her and if she cared to come to London on the 25th he would be delighted to meet her in the foyer. He would be wearing a dark suit with a yellow rose in the lapel. No doubt others would sport a carnation and he wanted no confusion; in any case he'd given Texas the honour of a yellow rose. He would be returning from Houston that day. He added that he did not consider that his days were 'in the yellow leaf', though he was twelve years her senior. He looked forward to meeting her. In the meantime, he wished her a happy Easter, which he would be spending in Saudi.

That Easter Ceri accompanied Maeve to Brymadoc. Her beloved harp had been left in the care of her tutor and Briende had arranged the loan of one because Ceri was to participate in the concerts once founded by Eleri and now held in Trevere Town Hall; splendidly expanding and flourishing and by now an island institution. It was to be the last short vacation of the student years before final examinations and celebrations and seeking employment.

Maeve attended several parties after the conclusion of 'schools' but declined the revelry afterwards. Succumbing to the self-chastisement of considering herself 'prissy', her honest, sensitive self deplored the all-night drinking and often debauchery along the river and in the quads. Hers had been a salutary experience a few short weeks ago – affairs with students were not within her ken. She thought of her mother, grandmother and Eleri. Maybe, like them, her fate lay with an older man. Immature behaviour and raucousness embarrassed her, maybe even frightened her. Perhaps, being nurtured as a fatherless only child among gentle, intelligent, women had established her code of behaviour; the ladylike all-girl school had sealed the rest. She had gossiped and giggled with the girls and dearly loved her friend Lucy but neither had slept around, as the term went, or experimented with strong drink. Appropriately, the mores of llandia were meant to be triumphant.

At last the final farewells were over and job applications took precedence over partying. Maeve had decided on the world of publishing and was currently applying to a variety of publications for a niche; she saw herself as a reviewer, later a columnist. In the meantime, she looked forward to meeting Percy Edgar Pennistone-Craig.

It was "a beauteous evening, calm and free." Wordsworth would have approved of the contented Thames as it ambled its way past the Foresters' house in Chelsea. Cynthia and Maeve were unusually excited; Maeve because she was preparing to meet Pennistone-Craig and Cynthia because an older cousin she was besotted by was taking her to see the musical *Oklahoma*. Deciding what to wear dominated the conversation, as Maeve's trunk had already been despatched home. She had one, rather formal, navy blue dress. Cynthia also decided on a navy blue silk sheath dress; Maeve's was of taffeta, sleeved but with a low neckline. Both borrowed Cynthia's mother's jewellery. Mr. Forrester would drive them to town. Both parents were amused by the excitement of the young butterflies but both young women had to promise to return by taxi before midnight.

Maeve was delivered first. The smart, sophisticated groups were already ambling towards the entrance. Maeve, walking alone, felt slightly tremulous but trusted Eleri's judgement implicitly. Once inside she stood in a corner to the left of the entrance and took time to assess the gathering as she searched for a yellow-rosed lapel.

Her escort, waiting in the diagonally opposite corner, his way blocked by a chattering group, knew her immediately and was struck by her calm beauty. Simon Peerless had referred to the Madoc women as steel magnolias, delicately beautiful but strong. In Maeve he quickly saw a fleeting resemblance to Eleri, but Eleri would have been radiant and already striking up a conversation with anyone around her. Maeve just stood unaware of admiring glances, of which Edgar was already aware. He negotiated his way to her through the growing crowd and held out his hand. "I'm Pennistone-Craig, my friends call me Penn."

"Hello. How did you know me?"

"How could I not know you? Your description, plus a hint of Eleri."

"I was frightened in case you did not manage to find a rose."

He smiled at her warmly then took her by the elbow and gently led her to where the celebratory champagne was being served. As he looked at her over the rim of his glass, he thought her exquisite. In appearance she seemed an icy top-class model, everything about her perfection, but she was young, rather nervous, over-cautious; he would have to tread carefully. She, in turn, saw a confident, attractive man just under six feet tall, brown hair cut straight above the collar, pale blue intelligent eyes which spoke volumes. He had a straight nose and a dimpled chin and a smile which revealed even teeth except for the left canine, which was slightly unaligned, the side on which his mouth went up as he smiled. He breathed success.

Together they judged the pictures. One modernistic effort captured him, a million dots which somewhere in the centre arranged themselves into a never-ending spiral, wide at the onset, then moving off as if to infinity. He found it interesting, Maeve found it disturbing. She was happier with quiet landscapes or fine portraits. They agreed on one only, a fantastic apple blossom tree in a magical background. That would be a cert, he pronounced as he smiled, that lifted smile she found so attractive. The excited chatter and perfume and well-dressed people milling around signified wealth and confidence; the chandeliered room, the uniformed attendants, the variety of splendid works of art, produced an intoxicating experience. Penn excused himself briefly to make the necessary negotiations, and quickly returned to her and the apple tree picture, which seemed to have captivated her. He suggested leaving for a nearby restaurant he knew well, admitting that he was too tired to travel far; one reason for having booked in at Brown's in nearby Albemarle Street, where he had arrived in the late afternoon and tipped a waiter to snip a yellow rose from any display in the hotel. He was also hungry and eager to leave the now-crowded room.

The cosy Italian restaurant, with light romantic music full of the usual heartache, was charming, gay in red and white cloths and curtains, flags and raffia bottles as the usual décor, real red carnations on the tables and, of course, candlelight. They found a quiet alcove and she was delighted to find that the waiters knew him. It made him seem less of a stranger. He seemed to know the menu, so she asked him to direct her.

During the meal they chatted about Oxford, about the preview, about his work and, of course, about the Peerless family. He had had dinner with them in February, found them charming and unusual and obviously in love. The elder children had been allowed to join them. He said that Miranda was beautiful and silent – the world was a boring place! Quellyn was interesting, lively, imaginative and already excitedly intoxicated with the world of history and art. Maeve felt so happy and Penn was the most relaxed and delightful company, with an air of being able to cope with any situation. Maeve felt completely at ease and quietly hoped that he found her interesting. Many women must have been attracted to him, yet at thirty-two he was unmarried. She longed to discuss this with him but of course would not on such early acquaintance, though she honestly felt as if she had always known him. Comfortingly she assumed that his work, which he revelled in, was enough. The evening ended too soon.

As he negotiated their way through Piccadilly's traffic to find a taxi, he held her hand tightly. With every step Maeve hoped he'd want to see her again, half-fearing that she was too young, too inexperienced, too cosseted, perhaps. She sensed his admiration for Eleri, who had achieved so much. But then, everyone was dazzled by Eleri; with all the glamour and opportunities which had come her way she had still chosen reality. Her manifold talents had become a sideline, a diversion, a stimulation when required, but Simon and the children were real and ever-satisfying.

A taxi drew up. As he handed Maeve in, he slightly squeezed her hand as he looked into her eyes. "It's been a lovely evening. Thank you. I will write." Then, giving directions to the driver, he waved her away. Throughout the rest of the journey she thought of him. Her attachment was genuine as she contrasted him with the young men she had half-heartedly dated during the past few weeks. Never before had she enjoyed an evening so thoroughly, with an attractive man of absolute confidence, minus conceit or the desire to prove anything, and she parted from him with a warm glow, a sweet relaxation, which remained with her on the short journey.

The obedient Cinderellas arrived back simultaneously, which invited some teasing from Cynthia's doting parents, who, clad in dressing gowns, had stayed up for them. The young women were invited to quickly don their dressing gowns and join them for a homely cup of cocoa around the electric fire, in order to hear an account of their evening. At such times Maeve almost envied the presence of a father and felt a pang of sorrow for her mother's long loneliness, during which she had conscientiously borne the mantle of two parents. She tried to imagine what her own father would have been like; would he have gazed at her with the rapt adoration with which Mr. Forester now gazed at his excited bright-eyed daughter? Maeve snapped out of her melancholy and she told them of Penn, how it was a blind date, how worldly and commanding he appeared compared with their Oxford boyfriends, and heard herself admitting that she hoped he would write. They said he certainly would, that he'd be foolish not to. Maeve thought Cynthia singularly blessed in having such sweet parents.

The girls continued with their analysis of the night's events in their twin-bedded room, made gay with dotted lights bouncing off the river on the opposite shore, interspersed with an occasional long beam from some passing vessel. In the intimacy of that room Maeve aired her fears regarding the age difference, wondering whether she had given the impression of being naïve, and Cynthia wondering whether the fact of their being related would make her cousin hesitate. Regardless of doubt, for both the evening had been a memorable success, a highlight both would remember, a fitting climax to their Oxford years. Soon Maeve would be travelling home to unwind, to fill out application forms, to plan some sort of future – in London, of course – to reach forth in some sort of creative writing. llandia, after exposure to a different tempo of life, would be too stifling even if work was available, though the kernel of her being would always remain on the island, infused with the beautiful tranquillity of her secure childhood. The resistance to change made the whole beloved place seem like an afterthought to the main tenet of modern progress.

She discussed this with Cynthia, who already had a situation in the advertising department of a major publisher, dealing with new authors.

CHAPTER THIRTY-SIX

BRIENDE WAS AT THE PORT AWAITING HER DAUGHTER. The beloved child was coming home before starting another chapter.

The ferry banging into the well-known landing stage, that familiar banging and scraping, the crash of the gangplank, the whistling and shouting, orders shouted in French, English and Welsh, were noises so familiar to Briende since early childhood.

She spied her daughter, cool, slight, self-possessed. She had not changed much from the five-year-old who carefully, mentally measured her space as she walked behind the bride at Eleri's first wedding. She was faint with emotion at the culmination of years of single parenthood, as she saw Maeve cast her eyes around for her car. Briende rushed out to greet her and hugged her warmly. There was no need for words; Maeve sensed her mother's emotion.

As Briende sat behind the wheel Maeve bent over and

kissed her lightly. "I know what you are remembering. You were right, of course. Thank you."

Briende smiled at her through watery lashes. "Someone better will come along. You are still very young and very beautiful. I never told you that."

"Thank you but I am older than you were, Mama."

"Granted, but I was less self-possessed, less educated, less confident. I forced myself to become qualified after having a child, just as Niamh is now doing. I did not want that for you. It's highly unlikely that you'd have completed the course if you had gone to London. I felt your pain as much as you did, perhaps more. But I am not sorry. Incidentally, there's a letter for you. I don't know the writing."

In the twilight Briende caught an expression – of relief? Hope? Just something barely perceptible on Maeve's face. That letter was important. She would ask no more.

Once inside the door Maeve tore open the letter. Briende watched as a slight flush was followed by a lightness of expression. She exhaled softly then went up to her room.

She came down within minutes to see their supper laid on two trays. She sat opposite her mother in front of the old kitchen range. So much of their thinking was in unison – each knew that the other was thinking of Eleri, the morning she rushed down at dawn to say Simon was alive. There were tears in Briende's eyes. Maeve thought she'd divert her by revealing the contents of Penn's letter and telling her of him. She had previously been afraid to mention the Royal Academy evening in case it had been a 'one-off' thing.

"I guessed there was something when I mentioned that there was a letter."

"You miss nothing, Mama – just like Grandmother."

"This Pennistone-Craig made an impression on you. Tread carefully, I'd hate you to be hurt. At least he wants to see you again. Read it again to me, if it is nothing private."

She read:

"Dear Maeve,

The evening of the 25th was exceptionally delightful. I can honestly say that rarely does an evening measure up to such expectation. I have since thought of you awaiting examination results and feel confident that the outcome will be better than expected.

I am sorry that the evening was not longer, though wisely you had to be back in Chelsea before midnight. I was too tired for a dinner dance, which would have been more of an evening out, though the summer Art Exhibition was an experience.

I will be in London for a mere four days for meetings the last week in July but, as I have not taken my full leave, could take a further week in England. If you would not find me an inconvenience, I would like you to show me Oxford, which I do not know at all. On second thoughts, perhaps you will be too busy job-seeking, may even have one by then. Also, it is a long journey for you, though no doubt one very familiar to you.

Let me know something of your thoughts on

this. Thank you again for a very special evening. I have already written to Eleri to say all went well and of course mentioned the pictures.

Yours, very sincerely, Penn."

"You want to see him again, of course, but he is cautious and has put the onus on you. Would you like to ask him here?"

"Not until I've seen him again and reassessed."

'Wise as ever. You know, Maeve, I am very proud of you, and constantly feel that you are what your father would have wished."

"Thank you, Mama. Compliment for compliment – you look too young at forty to be my mother. The girls took you for my sister that time you visited the college."

Briende smiled. "I can rely on you to answer that letter in like tone, but I think you want to see him."

"I do, I do, and I want your impression of him."

"Eleri would not have arranged a date with an unscrupulous type, we can trust her judgement."

"Exactly. That's what I thought while waiting for him."

Companionably they ate supper and discussed an amalgam of topics, from local affairs to family, to job-seeking. They both retired early, as Briende had an early morning meeting next day. In all her working years she had never taken a day off sick. Luckily, Maeve had been an exceptionally healthy child.

Maeve decided to retire with a light novel of her choice, something outside the syllabus. A newly earned luxury; but first she would tactfully answer Penn's letter.

A carefully worded letter was duly sent, stating charmingly that she would see him in Oxford as she was not likely to find employment before the end of August. In the meantime, between job applications, there were driving lessons and enjoying her mother's company, as she had seen little of her during the past three years.

Much of her thinking revolved around meeting Penn again as she impatiently awaited the last week of July. As July expired the hot weather arrived in time to meet Penn in Oxford. She planned to spend the previous night in Oxford, where Ceri had lodgings, Ceri who had musical engagements throughout the summer. It was important for Ceri to get herself established and the income was a necessity. She had also fallen in love with Emrys Pugh, the emerging Welsh tenor, much in demand. She was elated when talking of their plans for the future. Both were suffused with music.

On a warm summer's morning Maeve, in her Liberty-printed dress, an angora short-sleeved cardigan on her shoulders, awaited the train from London. Dressed in a light suit and soft shoes, Penn alighted, stood still and looked to both ends of the platform. Then he saw her emerge from the waiting room, so pale, so fair, almost ethereal, he thought. They shook hands. 'Well, Maeve, lovely to see you, and thank you for coming. You are the leader, I'm in your hands." He smiled, then competently took her elbow and led her towards the exit. Her turn to smile.

Her itinerary was planned, her knowledge scant but sufficient to make most things interesting – the quods or grounds with their splendid gardens, the chapels, the Ashmolean Museum, the bridges and meadows, the statues and Maeve's gathered snippets of information about a variety of eccentrics. Most of all she relished walking along the riverbank and having coffee in the shade of the trees while consulting the guidebook. She was determined to show him the Shelley memorial at University College and *The Light of the World* painting by Holman Hunt at Keble College.

They lunched at the Randolph. Maeve tried to erase from her mind memories of that day, the last and only time she had lunched there. She again realised how happy and at ease she felt with this man. She did not want the lunch to end and dreaded the day's ending in case he would not see her again. They talked of Oxford and what they had already seen.

"Where next?" she asked. "Anything in particular?"

"Please," he said, "the Grinling Gibbons carvings at Trinity College Chapel. I've heard Eleri talk of them."

By the time they reached Trinity they were holding hands. After admiring the extravagant carvings, they rested for a while in the cool and quiet. She wondered what his thoughts were. Hers revolved around a strong desire to see him again. Surely, he would see her again, she prayed fervently.

Over tea in a pretty little patisserie, he thanked her for a splendid day. Could she spare another day soon? In London if possible? The next two days would find him in Holland, but these were working days and would not interfere with holiday time. This was the sort of peripatetic life he lived.

Maeve did not feel inclined to impose herself on the charming Foresters for three days, though they would have welcomed her, and she felt disinclined to spend days alone in London, so she told him she would remain with Ceri and travel to London in three days' time to save her the long journey home. He held both her hands and looked into her eyes. No words were spoken.

As they arrived at the station, each realised they did not want to say goodbye. He insisted that she did not wave him off. Instead, he hailed a taxi, placed her within, paid the driver and rushed to the train. He cast one backward glance as he reached the station entrance, waved and disappeared. Maeve was desolate.

The taxi slid into the mainstream of end-of-day traffic. Her thoughts were of Penn as she gazed and saw her own face reflected in the taxi window and in the windows of passing vehicles and in the shop windows, as if her own doppleganger was warning her to tread carefully and not become too involved too soon. She realised this was a reflection of her own insecurity. A short while ago an endless empty horizon had lain ahead, a non-world, a lost world. She was beginning to be amazed that the sudden impact of Garth's desertion could have taken such a toll. She, who was not a flirt, could so easily have dated anyone of her choice, but it took a man of Eleri's choosing, twelve years her senior, to regain her self-esteem and make her actually enjoy living. Over and over she convinced herself that he was superior to any man she had met and felt privileged that he loved being with her.

Disappointingly, Ceri was not at home when she

arrived at the lodgings. She rushed upstairs to see if the harp was in Ceri's room. It was, wrapped in a sort of heavy blanket of rough Welsh wool, intricately woven in geometric designs – an article Ceri called a 'carthen'. Apparently, it was tough, almost waterproof, and exclusive to a mid-Wales factory owned by the British Legion, employing injured ex-servicemen. Ceri had been there and said she would take Maeve next time. Maeve longed to purchase such a quality article for Eleri to use as a throw over the sofa in a room they called the den. She had many times watched Ceri put the cover over her harp and deftly pin back the corners with outsized safety pins, such as those usually seen on kilts. Maeve smiled with affection. The girl was a wonder.

She went to her own room to await Ceri's return. It was a typical room in suburbia, dark carpets, dark paintwork, a small iron fireplace with hearth tiles adorned with flowers unknown to botany. Beside the fireplace was a meter to feed with shillings when the three-bar electric fire in the hearth was required. On the mantlepiece sat two china dogs, glassy-eyed and complete with chains. The single bed had a pretty blue satin eiderdown, which gave a touch of luxury to the otherwise drab but clean room.

Maeve counted her shillings. After a warm day it had become distinctly chilly and she slipped on the angora cardigan she had carried all day. Tonight Ceri would share her fire, but in the meantime, Maeve rested under the eiderdown and remembered every word spoken, every gesture, every smile since the arrival of the train that morning. She also realised that such a day would have been wasted on Garth and admitted to herself for the first time that the first love affair had been purely physical, an early awakening, an excitement and nothing more. It was tempestuous, extreme, born of the body, carried to dizzying heights, then a dashing to the depths. Her present sense of freedom and quiet pleasure was pleasing. She had sometimes been in an agony of impatience to see Garth but there was always an undercurrent of dread weaving through her desire and the clashes of the past year had been more akin to hell than heaven. She also acknowledged that sexual frustration had been at the core of their problem. Added to this, her independence and desire to be a qualified person in her own right was beyond his comprehension.

Her musings were disturbed by Ceri's cheerful voice announcing her arrival to Mrs. Dayton, the landlady. Maeve rushed to meet her. Together they ascended the stairs to Maeve's room. They sat on a sofa, wrapped in the eiderdown, awaiting the delicious-smelling meal. They would save the shillings for later, as they would not linger over supper, the other lodgers not being conducive company. One was a student, catching up on a neglected term's work, living in lodgings because his parents were abroad. The other was a retired tutor, regularly visiting to recapture what was past – the Oxford he'd known, superior, of course, to today's gracelessness. He'd spice any pronouncement he made with an appropriate line of Latin – irritating if one's Latin was more or less dead. They were pleased to escape *Memento ergo sant.*

In Maeve's room, with the meter well-fed, the young

women relived their day and chatted throughout the long evening; enough was still unsaid when they parted for bed. By then Maeve had realised that her student days only began when she was leaving. She would always regret the years of tension because of her involvement with Garth Protheroe.

Three days later, in London, Maeve met Penn at Browns for coffee. The day's itinerary was already planned. They would use bus or taxi and do the things neither had done before. They would stand on the meridian at Greenwich, travel up the Thames to Westminster, visit Poets' Corner and Henry Vll's chapel, walk up Whitehall to Trafalgar Square to the National Portrait Gallery, get a bus to Madame Tussauds waxworks, lunch at Lyons Corner House, Marble Arch, something Maeve had always longed to do because the Corner Houses were so popular with her young friends. Penn smiled and obliged. The salad bowl restaurant, with its check tablecloths and elegant orchestra, was a happy pleasure. Penn had never ventured into the Corner Houses but had heard of them. He was pleased to see Maeve unwinding; she seemed to be too much on her guard for one so young, and certainly lovely. The day was hectic, but Penn found it exciting and different, as he had almost forgotten how to relax, forgotten how to be young. He felt quite rejuvenated and had not even given his work one thought. That in itself was a tonic.

London had not lost its drabness. There was ample evidence of wartime bombing in many destroyed buildings; the remaining structures, like jagged teeth surrounding an unsullied patch of wild flowers, re-establishing themselves. Some bombsites had been made into rough car parks, some were still surrounded by scaffolding. As they walked, they could see a new London growing around them. Normally neither would have taken much notice; together they drank in the new awakening of a blasted city.

They returned to Browns for tea and to retrieve Maeve's case, both loath to see the end of the day. They taxied to Paddington, and this time, as they parted he encircled her in his arms, kissed her cheek tenderly and thanked her. With her head on his shoulder she murmured her own thanks. Both promised to write as he placed her in a corner seat and waited until the train left. She turned, waved and already the longing to see him again crept like a wave across her consciousness. She felt bereft, almost panicky. What if he did not write! He was a man of his word, surely, she had already established this. Such was her unease.

Several hours later, when the pale shades of evening were gathering around the old port of Limorrnah, Briende was waiting. Maeve's timekeeping was always dependable. Her mother had no qualms when Maeve took the wheel to drive home. Her cool head, her caution, her powers of concentration struck Briende anew; anyone could entrust their life to her daughter in any situation, and more and more she was reminded of Ralph Maine. How he would have adored her, marvelled at her, enjoyed her; how cheated they had both been by the power of an unidentifiable bacteria in a miserable Indian outpost. He had certainly 'wasted his sweetness on the desert air' – wasted, and for what? Sassoon's sad line "too young to fall asleep for ever" punctuated her thinking. Her daughter probably knew the poem but Briende was silenced by her own tears. She willed herself to think of happier things and certainly all her happiness was bound up in the lovely being beside her.

Before bedtime mother and daughter had decided to invited Edgar Percy Pennistone-Craig to visit. By what name was Briende expected to call him? Maeve suggested they all kept to Penn. Like Ralph Maine, he had but one relative, which made Briende warm to him. Unlike Ralph Maine's aunt, Penn's mother was a bridge-playing committee lady, living in a smart London flat in a block called River Mansions. Penn saw little of her but never missed visiting when he was in London. She sounded a sophisticated, liberated woman, the sort Mrs. Blethyn would not have approved of. Another Lady Bettina attached to the family would be more than she could ever tolerate, although Mrs. Blethyn now drove her car around her home area and felt unbelievably released, though slightly decadent.

CHAPTER THIRTY-SEVEN

PENN DID ARRANGE THE HOLIDAY OWING AND ARRIVED in llandia on a blustery August day. Maeve was at the port awaiting him, slightly nervous, inwardly troubled in case things did not work out. Entranced with what he saw of the island, he was reminded of the southern part of the Isle of Wight, or one of the Orkneys, and longed to explore the place.

Maeve was pleased to arrive at Brackens, where Briende's warmth and sweetness would hold sway and lighten what Maeve thought of as her responsibilities, for that is how she felt. She was anxious for him to like the place and her people – what was left of them.

Over a delicious meal they talked of Oxford, of Eleri, Briende's work, his work and travels. That they liked each other became apparent as they chatted. Maeve was greatly relieved; the morrow would be easier.

When they arose next morning Briende was already

gone and Maeve found herself shyly playing hostess. He realised her dilemma and suggested packing a picnic and going into the hills and along the streams, exploring with her this new Arcadia.

Together they worked to pack canvas shoulder-bags, with food and a Thermos of tea and set out for the Stones. He was fascinated, not only with their ancient mystery but with their interweaving with Madoc family events over several generations. The Celtic forest motifs with enigmatic beings intertwined adorning some of them made him wonder if the carvings were made years after the implanted stones. Maeve talked of her grandparents secretly meeting among them, of Eleri's old admirer, the architect, who was confident he could with research unravel their mystery. She talked of her own father's dream of settling in the island and devoting his time to research and much else, she talked of his many ideas and aspirations, his love of writing and studying, all of which she had, of course, gleaned from the few who had known him. She told him of Eleri and Simon, whose American lack of reverence had called the Stones "A heap of old rocks, real spooky", which had made Eleri laugh, considering the awe in which most people held the strange edifices. In llandia one did not laugh at legends.

After lunch they ambled back to the village, Maeve longing to be taken in his arms, Penn longing to do so but wary of her reaction. They drove to Limorrnah and were back in time for Briende's arrival home by Mr. Byatt's taxi, as she had generously lent the young couple her car. Penn helped them prepare a meal, for his bachelor status had long equipped him for usefulness. For him there were days when evenings alone were preferable to hotels or restaurants and dreary business talks. He was remarkably organised, and the joint effort soon produced an appetising meal, over which the trio relaxed. Briende even produced some wine, a very rare indulgence.

The next day was spent touring the island, Maeve pointing out the impressive Campions, The Lodge, the Park and Plantations. In the afternoon they drove to Fentons, now a school, Maeve relating Dr. Skiroski's strange, true, story and his impact on the area with his refugee housekeeper and six orphan girls, this rest home for Poles and for American Polish servicemen, when they could be home for a few days. One of these turned out to be Simon Peerless, she exclaimed.

That evening they attended a concert, a relic of Eleri's imagination in wartime, as Maeve explained. The charity now helped island causes, a new concert hall in Trevere, a new village hall in Brymadoc and an occasional scholarship. Maeve and her companion were warmly welcomed. Penn had never experienced small-town intimacy and continued to be astounded by the number of people who knew Maeve and her family. The warm greetings from so many hindered the start of proceedings and, like many others, Penn was gradually being seduced by the charm of the place.

Before he left, three days later, he requested another visit to the Stones. The day was dry, though the clouds were lowering, the sea impatient, grey and angry as they stood above the cliffs, staring out at the endless expanse, unable to decipher where the sea ended and the sky began in the distant murkiness. Though not cold there was a threat of thunder and the Stones were an intimidating presence. Maeve once again made him listen to the intense whispering as he placed his head against the most ominous of them which, according to Eleri, on a different sort of day, was where Maeve's father had proposed to Briende. For that obvious reason it had always been Maeve's favourite stone and as they leant against it, Penn made his declaration of love. He took her in his arms, and she was consumed by a warmth and desire, a melting of self, a security, a delight. Everything except being with him ceased to matter. "Let us go," he whispered. He was still wary of her and of his own passionate desire.

They arrived back at Brackens to find a letter from Guthrie and Patton, the Limorrnah publishers, offering Maeve a position in the editorial department as a features editor, anything interesting pertaining to the island worthy of inclusion in the pages of *Island Heritage*, a quarterly publication. It was a new venture. Maeve's cup overflowed and she would, of course, accept the position until circumstances decreed otherwise.

Penn took her in his arms and kissed his congratulations. She felt a release of all tension, a contentment, a peace. This was her man, her prop, her shield, her love. Together they went to see the Reverend Britt, stopping at the old family plot to give Penn a further insight into that ancient clan she sprang from. He was fascinated as she related more and more of their island story. She talked of Eleri's two marriages and the saga of the innocent white dress, which Eleri had changed to smart chic. She even told him of Eleri's little Faye and the subsequent history of Royston Garonne Burnette and his brilliant wartime record.

For the first time Maeve learnt that Penn had also given time to his country, in 1941 when he worked at a radar communications centre in the Orkneys, and what excellent training it had bee, because radar was in its infancy. He progressed to being a petty officer (radar) on the *Belfast* and had spent seven months on the *USS Yangtzee Kiang* in China. He been baptised into many horrors as bodies daily floated by; the poverty, and lack of humanity evident, disturbed even the ruthless.

"Let us not talk of war. Show me the church."

As they sat with hands clasped Maeve recollected the last time they had sat in a church and how she had longed to hold his hand. This time she did not hesitate; they clasped hands and kissed. How daring she felt!

It was with despondency that she drove him to the port next day. The following week he was scheduled for Bahrain, where his next assignment happened to be. They seemed to be at a high pitch of intensity while they stood waiting for him to board. He held her tightly with nervous urgency.

"Get organised quickly, have anything you want but please wear that white dress. A lovely tradition. My only request will be my mother, who will probably bring her current escort." He kissed her tenderly and bounded to the ship.

It was late October when they next met, for their

harvest-time nuptials, just as on Eleri's day. Maeve duly wore the dress Eleri-style but over a white sheath and with a white cummerbund. She carried pink, mauve and white heather, the idea suggested by Ceri, who had grown up in the shade of the Brecknock Beacons and had an ongoing romance with those hills, so like those of llandia. Her attendants were Eleri's three children; Quellyn, in a miniature tuxedo to match his father's, was man enough at thirteen to sit beside his parents. Miranda and Eadie, in pale pink taffeta dresses designed by Eleri, were competently escorted up the aisle by Bran, in black trousers and silk shirt. Simon's pride in them was reflected in his face as he held Eleri's hand throughout. Many in the congregation had witnessed several Madoc weddings. Those villagers present at Eleri and Simon's were invited to the Rectory afterwards. It was Simon's planned special gesture to his wife, in league with the Britts, a complete surprise for and a special tribute to Eleri, and briefly attended by her American family before they'd left for Pen Melyn. Eleri's own special radiance was at its peak among old friends, people who had known her all her life.

By the time they reached the Pen Melyn reception the guests had become acquainted, thanks to Briende's skill as hostess. Mrs. Pennistone-Craig and her escort had blended in remarkably well, delighting in this wedding, where all the people seemed to know one another more like a family than a galaxy of guests, so unlike the London functions. Two of the Limorrnah young were abroad and two of Dr. Skiroski's six girls were absent. Leah, the only one to revert to Judaism, was working in a kibbutz in Israel, another had examinations in America, but two of the students accompanied him. He was, however, delighted to have a reunion with Anya and Mara, Anya now married to her Welsh doctor friend of student days and Mara, whose secretarial work with the Bristol Authority had led to marriage with Desmond, who managed the office.

Disappointingly, Rachel Mann, now a paediatrician in Pennsylvania, was on urgent duty replacing another doctor. She had married a Jewish immigrant, Moab Brent, who owned a bakery. Both his parents had been prosperous bakery owners in Hamburg, and both had died at Dachau. Moab – another Jewish orphan – was fortunate to escape but had arrived almost penniless.

The dear Bessingtons came; they had never lost touch with Eleri and had become friends of Briende and Mrs. Blethyn. Ceri's intended and her parents, also Cynthia and her parents, had made the long journey. Her beloved childhood friend, Lucy, and Dr. Hughes were not invited. Briende understood. The whole party became a grand reunion. After the wedding breakfast Ceri played on the harp and her sensitive rendering gave a new dimension to the familiar ballads as the harp emphasised the emotions engendered. There was absolute silence, then a crescendo of demands for a repeat. Ceri had translated the haunting Welsh lyrics beforehand to increase the enjoyment of the audience.

Brymadoc emerged from its closed chrysalis. Pen Melyn, Brackens, the Hermitage, the Limorrnah homes were filled to overflowing. Needless to say, the best rooms of Pen Melyn, at a special request from Maeve were given to Ceri's parents. Maeve loved those people, their warmth and hospitality reminiscent of her grandmother, whose circumstances were so different. Mrs. Blethyn had an immediate affinity with them. She had always been convinced that the early Madocs were from Wales, though they had been domiciled in Brymadoc for over four centuries.

Penn, at the close of proceedings, was aware of Maeve's loveliness as she stood beside him, taking leave of their guests. With disbelief he found himself studying her – the earnestness of her attention to one and all, her treasures of patience with the lingering ones. As she stood beside him in her slender whiteness, she seemed reminiscent of a lily, her head bowed in modesty or shyness, still, fragile, vulnerable. A suffocating sensation gripped him. May he never fail her.

Such was Maeve's perfect day and Penn's overflowing bewilderment that he had found such a woman from such a place. No place in the world could ever again compare with this paradise and he determined to purchase a property on the island and one day live there permanently.

In late afternoon, when they eventually departed for their honeymoon, where Simon and Eleri had spent theirs, the aura around them seemed infused with a supernatural glow. Maeve felt removed from reality. With him she could cut out the entire world; it was like living in a garden, permanently sunny, tall white flowers around them, a stillness abiding, complete detachment from the small monotonies of life. Encircled by his arms no other should enter her universe, yet she felt intensely alive as she wondered what his silence signified. As the autumn landscape shared its magic, the setting sun its glory, the island its peace, the patterned heather spread like a carpet, he was overwhelmed by the inexplicable joy which pervaded the scene. There was a deep contentment, the absolute climax to a few short hectic months.

Soon the crashing of the sea against the rocks could be heard above the throb of the car engine and the lights of the precariously perched hotel reached them through the mists of evening. He stopped the car, held her close and kissed her. A few hundred yards or so and they would be ensconced within the fortress-like walls, lost in each other.

CHAPTER THIRTY-EIGHT

Six American years elapsed, six eventful summers and six replenishing winters. Simon and Eleri's fascinating brood flourished, an endless source of delight. Eleri was aware of the fact that she had hatched three contented, graceful, manageable swans and one insular preening bird of paradise called Miranda.

Quellyn, a freshman at Yale, majoring in art, history and architecture, after a successful five years at Harriman Glade College; Bran, an outstanding pupil at high school, definitely, much to his father's delight, heading for medicine; and Eadie, a delightful eleven-year-old with a fascination for all living things, possessing an unending curiosity and the patience to read and research beyond her years. Undoubtedly her future lay with the natural sciences. Their father's book-rich study was a familiar haven to both children and Simon's pride in his all-American offspring was evident.

Miranda, however, was an enigma. Poised, beautiful, good-natured, reserved but non-academic, her only reading shallow magazines, her only music light romantic, or popular songs. A typical product of the Henrietta Rolle Academy for Ladies, complete with a light voice, a slight breathlessness in speech, she was just what the HRAL girls were meant to be. To Simon she was a source of amusement, to Eleri, a source of wonderment or bafflement. Her siblings loved her but never expected her to join in with them in any activities. From a distance she seemed a replica of her mother, the abundant red curly hair, the white skin and slenderness, until she turned her dark Garonne eyes upon one, which held a different light from her mother's eyes. Her mother despaired of and admired her in equal proportion but her paternal grandmother in Palm Springs, Florida, considered her perfection and the zenith of her ambitions, a depository for her wealth.

From the age of thirteen the girl had regularly flown alone to Florida. Her grandmother, now known as Mrs. Rupert Grayling, was a society lady of the first order, moving in exclusive circles. She had purchased a large beach-side house for visiting families, her husband's and Eleri's, but Miranda always stayed with her in her own grand house. Mr. Grayling's wealth, in addition to her own inheritance through the wartime sale of her Lancashire lands to the government, plus the Garonne portion, pivoted her into the foremost social circles. The Garonne children and her great-grandchild in Limorrnah also became future recipients.

Eleri heard the click-clack of her daughter's footsteps,

platform-soled mules, the latest fashion. She heard her open the refrigerator and pour a glass of milk. At her mother's call from the living room, she came and sat beside her, sipping her milk from a long, elegant glass. She looked at her mother and waited. Something was afoot. "There's an official-looking letter for you – am I to be told?"

"It is from my agent, giving directions for tomorrow's interview."

"Agent? Interview? Tomorrow? What's all this, a summer vacation job?"

"At the graduation, the photographer picked me out, said I had potential, he took many photographs with Miss Armitage's permission."

"Yes, I know about the portfolio he made. But agent?"

"Oh, I paid for the portfolio, insisted that the copyright was mine, and I chose Grant Elkins as my agent. He's good, I believe you know him. His daughter was at school with me."

She looked at her dome-glassed cocktail watch. "Excuse me, Mama, I have to see Mavis. We have decided to wear sarongs for Saturday's pool-side birthday party."

She sallied into the kitchen, rinsed her glass as trained and click-clacked down the driveway.

Eleri awaited Simon's return with impatience. He would have to have a word with Miranda. He had slightly, very slightly, more influence than she did.

She heard his car draw up and rushed to greet him, her warmth and delight in him unchanged. She kissed him and took his case, led him to the living room, mixed him a highball on the marble-topped side table and sat on the arm of his chair, her head on his shoulder.

"You have a problem, my love. Is it Miranda again?" He seemed tired, stressed.

"Please talk to her, Simon. She has this modelling interview tomorrow in New York and has secured an agent for herself."

He laughed, in spite of himself but realised it was serious.

"She's a smart, sophisticated madam, removed from reality in that fancy academy. Exactly as I feared."

"She would have been no different, she's a trendsetter, the bane of some mothers. I have phone calls complaining. Men's formal striped shirts, tied around the waist with men's ties and boots even in summer and a hat – that's the latest and some of the youngsters cannot carry the style."

He laughed again. "I heard that you were once bizarre."

"I was – shocked a good many, but I had been to art college and was qualified, even considered talented. She has done nothing. Draws tolerably well, a reasonable pianist, a deft way with a garment to make it different and beautiful writing – nothing else."

He kissed her lightly. "See to the young ones, I'll have a word with her."

An hour later Miranda dutifully reappeared for the evening meal. Good manners meant punctuality. Simon hailed her. "Before dinner, a word in my study," then with a smile, "please."

Without a word she swayed her way to Simon's study, arranged herself as taught, knees together, long legs to one side, feet tucked back, and waited.

His inadequacy made him awkward.

"First of all, I love you. You've been mine since you were nine months old and I do care." His words faded awkwardly.

"I'm waiting." She gave an elegant shrug.

"This interview, for God's sake, you are only sixteen. One of us must accompany you."

"Do you think I'd go alone? Stephanie will come, she's a smart cookie, been around," she drawled.

"You think you are smart: an experienced man could easily take advantage of you. This is madness." He tried to sound angry.

"Do you think I'd ascend in an elevator to some creep's glossy office alone? Steph will be outside; I'd insist."

"Not every time you'll be alone, you could be overpowered."

"I'd know exactly how to kick, grab and twist; Mavis's brother is an expert teacher of self-defence."

Simon was speechless for a second, then, "Your grandmother had hopes of Vassar or La Salle."

Miranda laughed cynically. "It would be HRALs all over again – academic sham, and I'm no academic."

Secretly he agreed with her. The interview ended. As she coolly sauntered away, she turned. "Of course, I'd only allow my likeness in the exclusive publications and no nudity. Woe betide any hood who would steal a picture. Mama never capitalised on her beauty, but I will."

Simon's scholarship experience and daily dealings with all manner of people, in all sorts of situations, had not equipped him for dealings with Miranda. They would have to trust her.

Three more hectic years elapsed and Miranda, a successful model, became a well-known media figure and an exceptionally wealthy young woman. Escorts galore appeared and disappeared. Most were 'for the camera'; she cared for none. She followed the path her mother could have taken but had rejected, but like her mother she cared not for Hollywood – in fact she was not tempted, though countless offers had come her way. Before she was twenty, she was married to an oil-rich Texan, Jake M. Pointing III. He was also a substantial landowner who dabbled in real estate, along with other business angles.

Their society wedding in New York had coast-to-coast coverage in every aspect of the media. Her grandmother's dreams had become a reality. Florida had played a part.

Perfectly happy and fulfilled within her criteria Miranda retired to a normal married life, devoid of any ambition and with no qualms at all regarding her choice of partner. Cool, poised, seemingly divorced from any extreme of emotion, she became a beautiful possession, a trophy wife, who within her experience knew perfect contentment.

Quellyn graduated from Yale, passionate about his interests, already immersed in his plans to become an art dealer and promoter of new artists. Frequent trips to Europe, Italy in particular, had already sealed his ambitions. He saw Campions, one day, as the ideal art gallery of the future and the end of the lease was approaching. His enthusiasm overflowed. His mother, an icon central to all his ideas, encouraged him at every step.

His first project on leaving university was to hire the

Bell-Vue ballroom in New York and, with his London contacts, plan an outstanding exhibition of British and American portraiture from the last twenty-five years. He was a lesser artist than his mother but had far more scholarship, more travel, more education. With grants from the city authority, some industries, and sponsorship from several large stores, which would also advertise the coming exhibition, he was impatient to get started.

He had already asked permission to exhibit Eleri's painting of Maeve and was actively gathering works from known artists in America and Britain, as well as from present or recent students. Professionalism was to be paramount. Full-sized photographs of several paintings, tastefully framed, were to serve as advertisements and placed in shop windows, cloakrooms, hotel foyers and restaurants, with many small photographs in magazines and newspapers – all in colour. The costs would be considerable, but he sensed great success and comfortable profits. The artists were to be responsible for conveying their own works personally, or whichever way they chose, and a working team was arranging accommodation, insurance and presentation. He himself was to prepare the glossy brochures to be sold at the opening. His main English contact, Susannah, would be the liaison and he constantly talked of her and to her. Her name had become familiar to them all and Quellyn appeared enamoured of her. All longed to meet her.

One evening he arrived home tired, excited and fulfilled, and, while all were still seated at the dinner table, having just completed their evening meal, he handed his mother the first glossy brochure. His openness, so reminiscent of his mother, made Simon smile. He had the same blend of honesty and tact, sensitivity to others and a lightness of spirit. Eleri's eyes glowed as she took the catalogue, then, for a moment, her expression changed. The cover bore a replica of the portrait of a striking, exceptionally beautiful dusky woman in yellow, and Eleri recognised it immediately. She had once glimpsed that painting for a fraction of a second on the mantelpiece of a scruffy London studio, seemingly aeons ago. It had registered then, never to be forgotten. Quellyn sensed the impact but Eleri's quick reaction smoothed the moment. "She's lovely, reminds me of one of Sir Gerald Kelly's women." She opened the cover but Quellyn, so attuned to her every nuance of thought, it seemed, asked, "Do you know her? She's Susannah's mother, painted by her father before Susannah was born. Look inside."

She did not have to look, but did, and read, "Soo Lin, painted by her husband Spenser Fortesque 1935."

Quellyn continued, "I insisted on having it. She was a student of his at Ondine's, probably before your time."

"Yes, I heard about her. We all knew of her." He glowed with delight.

The moment passed and Eleri turned more pages, as Quellyn excitedly commented, "What a small world!" Eleri quietly thought, *this will take some thinking out.*

Simon, who had been amused at the little drama, rose from his chair and went to put his arm around Quellyn's shoulders. 'Well done, son." He then placed an arm around Bran and Eadie. Quick as a flash her skinny arms were around his neck. "That's my gal, what about some piano practice before bedtime? Just half an hour?"

"Twenty minutes," she bargained.

"All right, twenty minutes. We are not ambitious regarding examinations, just for your own pleasure later on." He smiled at Eleri.

"And you, Bran?"

"Lousy chemistry formulae – what else?"

"No escape I'm afraid, a necessary slog, son," as he clapped him on the back.

"I'll be in my office, Eleri, for at least two hours. You know I try not to bring work home, but there's a new treatment pending. I have to be familiar with the tests. A lot to read." He brushed a kiss across her head and disappeared into his study. The family dispersed.

Eleri was alone, yearning to feast on that catalogue but strangely confused; shocked would be a more appropriate word. She cleared the table and haphazardly stacked the dishwasher, mentally hearing Dolores's comments in the morning – "I'se tol' Madame afore 'bout loading" – but Eleri's casual housekeeping was an accepted factor of her personality.

She then laid the long pine breakfast table, matching crockery but each family member with a different primary coloured set. She liked a cheerful start to the day. She laid out the cereals, checked the bowl of peaches in the refrigerator, then with a guilty smile opened a large can of prunes and placed these in a glass dish. She visualised her mother's horror at tinned fruit in summer, or at any time! Ah well, this was America. Throughout these menial tasks, particularly menial to such as Eleri, she was wrestling with what to tell Quellyn. Susannah was coming to stay with them during the big exhibition!

She sat in the rocking chair in the corner of the large kitchen, sinking into its Navajo Indian weave cushions. That chair was an article of furniture never used but the children were aghast when she considered abandoning it, remembering the early days when they'd found it comforting. She tried to assemble her thoughts. Would Susannah recognise her father's style in the painting of Eleri? Would they both turn it around and see the scrawl on the back; "Eleri – The Awakening, Summer '36." There was no signature.

She impatiently moved around, trying to clarify her approach to Quellyn, saw her reflection in the window and momentarily glimpsed Miranda. She would telephone her later. Miranda had achieved what she had set out to achieve, a splendid marriage. In this mother and daughter had succeeded, for in both, ambition had been stifled, but she doubted whether Miranda was capable of her depth of affection. Quellyn was different. Her thoughts revolved with this new dilemma.

She went into the den, catalogue in hand, read again about the painting on the cover, scanned the other works in miniature inside. Briende had parted temporarily with the painting of Maeve. Hagar could not be included as the work had been exhibited in the past. She listened to the half-hearted tinkling of the piano, yearned to hold her young daughter close. She failed to concentrate on the issue at hand – what could she tell Quellyn? Guile was foreign to her nature. To keep a secret and hide a fact was one thing, to lie was something alien to her.

The reluctant tinkling ceased, Eadie appeared. Eleri held out her arms. The pretty thirteen-year-old looked ten or eleven, small, like Briende and Simon's mother. The child cuddled close to her mother. "Do you want to see Quellyn's catalogue?"

"If you want me to," Eadie tactfully replied.

Eleri cradled her as they turned the pages to find a replica of the painting of Maeve, whom she knew and loved. It was the only thing of interest. She skipped away to nag her brother for a game of scrabble before bedtime. He usually obliged.

"Before you go – where's Quellyn?"

"He's writing a love letter."

Eleri laughed. "How do you know?"

"He told me."

A few minutes later Quellyn joined her, bathed in enthusiasm, bright-eyed and excited. "Well, Mama, what do you think?"

"It's a lovely production and the event should be an outstanding success."

"You'll meet many artists at the opening, some from London. Susannah is physically bringing some portraits. Her father helped to pack them."

"Did he teach Susannah?"

"No, she went to St. Martin's School of Art, a breakaway from her parents. Her father retired early from Ondine's, arthritis, I believe."

"How old is Susannah?"

"About a year older than I. Twenty-three, I think."

Eleri quickly calculated that Susannah was not the baby of 1936.

"Will her parents come across for the opening?"

"No, there are two younger children still studying, I don't think they could afford it."

Eleri, suffused with relief, decided to enjoy that preview, in fact long for it, proudly revel in it, with Simon beside her to share their pride.

Quellyn was about to retreat when his mother chimed, "I have other news for you. Susannah's father also taught me."

"I don't believe it! What a coincidence!"

"Not really. He has taught hundreds. In your world of art, you could meet many ex-students of his. One hundred per annum entry, three hundred students over three years, if my arithmetic means anything in twenty years that makes six thousand pupils. Not so much of a coincidence."

"I must add a PS to my letter to Susannah."

"Wait. Another surprise. Soo Lin, her name sounds like the breeze through the palm trees, was not the only young woman he painted." She smiled her radiant smile, her eyes full of love for the handsome youth. He looked aghast. "You mean he painted you? You actually posed?" He was breathless with excitement.

"No, I was sketched unawares. He was always sketching."

"Did you see the finished picture?"

"I see it every day."

"Not the one in Papa's study? The unfinished one? He gave it to you? It's incredible!"

“It was in Nations Bank’s vaults for years. The war intervened then a friend claimed it for me, and dear Amos Skiroski brought it home. A Jew with a German accent would have made them hesitate, so Juliette signed for it.”

He was delighted then took her hand. “Let’s disturb Papa.”

He related the exciting news, re-examining the work.

“I always wanted it completed,” said Simon, “but your mother liked it as it is.”

“I do,” said Quellyn. “I agree with Mama.”

“Reminds me of my unfinished self,” said Eleri.

Quellyn dashed to finish his letter. Simon pulled Eleri onto his lap. “How blessed we are.” He turned out the light. Hand in hand they called in to the children’s room to say goodnight. They left Bran still studying.

Eadie, still in her T-shirt, was already in bed, probably had her trousers on as well because her nightdress was neatly folded on the chair. Well, it was not worth making a fuss about. The child was eager to resume her reading – a new book on volcanoes.

“I’ll ask you all about it tomorrow,” said Simon with a broad smile, then kissed her.

They departed to their own bedroom as the night closed around them. Nothing would ever shake their devotion to each other. Their relationship was as fresh and new as on that pristine night they met and their appetite for each other was insatiable. As he held her, she had the sharpest echo of the long-ago car journey home with Briende, saw the stars, the frost, the snowflakes melting. Tomorrow she would write to Briende and ask her to recollect the magic of that night, interspersed with her fears for the impetuous Eleri, and she would re-emphasise her complete happiness with Simon. Her instincts were usually correct.

CHAPTER THIRTY-NINE

The Past Invades

As Eleri was being confronted by her own past escapades – it would not merit the exclusiveness of being called anything else – the ethereal Maeve, three thousand miles away, had her own serenity invaded.

One fine August day, while Penn, Maeve and their two infant boys were staying at their newly purchased holiday home in Limorrnah, a phantom from the past was strolling down Main Street, hoping to recapture school days with a friend or two. Both were unavailable when he telephoned, much to his disappointment.

Dr. Garth Protheroe, home from Rhodesia, en route to Rice University, Texas, to a convention, had become disenchanted with his own village of Hafod, where he had briefly visited his proud mother, and decided to spend his last night at the Guinevere Hotel, Limorrnah. He had taken his mother to dine there but she was miserably unhappy and concerned about the expense, which reminded him of his humble origins, much to his discomfort. He would stay there alone, an old impossible dream realised. Financially well-equipped, with a steady career and some recognition in his field, the world was his to conquer. Except for domestic fulfilment he was a success!

He ambled down the high street, which led to the familiar beach, pausing at shop windows, savouring his relaxation – then he saw her. She was in the form of a photographic image, in a gold oval frame on a wavy sea of green velvet, the only image in the bay window of a local photographer's premises.

Temporarily stunned, all around him became an indistinct haze as he stared at the image. The same warmth in her blue eyes, the long straight blonde hair shorter than of yore but just as sleek, the tiny freckle near the corner of her left eye which moved when she smiled. He stood transfixed, for the photograph in the frame was of Maeve Maine. He had heard that she was married and living in London, so why was her photograph here? Would she have returned here? If so, what would her husband be doing? A real estate agent? A doctor? A teacher? Business colleague of her relatives here? The exquisite Maeve, could she really be back here in this backwater?

Shaken and bewildered, he continued to the beach, where he hoped the spicy sea air would restore his senses. He settled outside a niche in the rocks he remembered since schooldays and thought of how he could find her. He surveyed the familiar cave behind him where, as a careless youth he and his friends would pass around the forbidden Woodbine, and talk of girls – who had the best bosoms, the best legs – and how they ribbed him over his crush on the reserved Maeve, until the chat moved on to the science examination pending, would it be dogfish, rabbit or frog to sport or the cinema. They would then mount their two-wheeled steeds and Limorrnah beach became the Californian desert, where Roy Rogers and Gene Autry held sway. They would soberly re-enter the town to stop and marvel at the smart cars and smarter owners cruising in and out of the Guinevere, which was, of course, outside their sphere.

Garth smiled at the memory and wondered anew at how far he had travelled. He had to find her, however futile the exercise. She had remained a lovely memory, almost a sanity he had clung to throughout his miserable marriage, though it had begun sweetly enough. Some measure of caution had prevented him entering the photographer's studio, as he did not even know her married name. To call her relatives here would solve nothing, as they would undoubtedly first contact her, and he could guess her response.

His blonde hair further bleached by the African sun, his tanned skin, and six feet two inch frame had not passed unnoticed by a few parading females along the shore, but for once he was unconscious of them. Instead he determined to return to the photograph and make some enquiries.

He ascended the rickety stairway to a cluttered studio, stepping over snaking cables and avoiding the usual props as he tapped his foot for attention. A fashionably dressed youngish man emerged from behind a screen. Clad in a wide-striped shirt, cravat and cotton-cord trousers of the latest style, he looked expectedly professional. "May I help you?"

"Yes, if you will. The young woman in the photograph in the window is an old school friend. I wonder if you could give me her address."

To himself it sounded hollow; the photographer also had his doubts. He hesitated, as one would expect.

"I'm sorry, I don't know her address. She called for the portrait. It was a present for her husband. She agreed to let me use the replica."

Garth sensed a reluctance to reveal anything else, so he produced his card – Dr. Garth Oliver Protheroe, FRCP (Lond.) Senior Medical Officer, Missions Hospital, Barimboaz, Rhodesia – and asked for her married name.

"It's Pennistone-Craig. They will not be in the directory as they've only recently arrived here."

"Do you know where she lives?"

"No, sorry," though Garth sensed that he did know.

"Why not try the estate agents? They know of recent purchases. Turn left at the entrance; Jarden, Tapley and Brown would be the most likely ones. These back of beyond places are becoming fashionable." Garth thanked him, bounded down the stairs and turned left.

Mr. Jarden, smooth and affluent in a dark pin-striped suit, in spite of the warm day, smiled broadly when Garth made his enquiry. Two young women operating the duplicating machine nudged each other. Garth Protheroe was an attractive man with an aura of success about him. Mr. Jarden surmised likewise.

"Ah yes, the Pennistone-Craigs, a charming couple, a matter of three weeks or so since the purchase. You'll find them on Vision Hill Lane, a winding road to the cliffs. Their house used to be called The Heights – it was so named for over a century – but they call it Lemons." He chuckled. "Lemons – charming, really charming."

"Is it far?"

"If you drive, be careful. We have our own local idiots, who tear down these winding lanes."

"I intend to walk. My car is at the hotel."

"It will take twenty-five minutes, but it is a delightful walk. Would you like to telephone from here and announce your impending visit?"

"Thank you, most kind of you, but I'd rather surprise them. On second thoughts, would you kindly telephone them and tell them to expect an old school friend. Say nothing else."

"Delighted. Have a pleasant walk."

Garth graciously thanked Mr. Jarden and went towards the cliffs and soon found Vision Hill Lane, on the left, with its steep challenge.

Excitement building within him, he began his uphill walk in the now-blazing sunshine. A new energy kindled within him. For years he had not felt so exhilarated.

The mid-afternoon was perfection. The overgrown hedgerows on either side seemed rampantly fertile, laden with their own succulence. The white wild roses, still lingering along the banks, shone like daytime stars. The brazen upright rosebay and slender stems of convolvulus, waving in search of a secure hold, all bore a new magic after the heartless African sun and the bold flora. Petals hung suspended in delicate cobwebs, as there was no breeze. How often had he walked such lanes with Maeve and never noticed? All was peace and promise, the whole of unkempt nature aching with desire, almost like an omen. Yes, he had done right to walk, he needed this respite, he needed to reflect but he accepted that Maeve was lost to him, that he was indulging in a punishing whim. He also accepted that, had she known he was coming, it was likely that she would not be at home.

Soon the tall gate-pillars of Lemons appeared, first one, then the other. The newly painted iron gate was shut. He tentatively pushed it open and its reluctant squeak alerted an attractive man, clutching a bunch of rooted plants, who emerged from the large rockery's summit of flowering shrubs.

"Oh, hello, you must be our visitor. I'm Pennistone-Craig – Penn." Garth introduced himself and the name registered.

"I cannot shake hands," he said, indicating his state, "but ring the bell. I'll clean up and join you presently."

He rang and waited, every nerve end strained, his heartbeat audible, as he heard her quick footsteps approach. She opened the door, paused but did not flicker. "Hello Garth," as if he'd been expected. "Do come in."

Poised as ever, he thought to himself, proud and unflappable, exactly what used to infuriate him.

In a cream-coloured short linen skirt, crisp white

blouse, her narrow waist cinched in a wide woven straw belt which matched her sling-back shoes, she was as desirable as ever. A decade had, if possible, increased her attractiveness because with it had come a confidence, an awareness of her sex appeal. She was as classic as he remembered her, but the damnable pride had not left her, her intimidating reserve was intact. For her there had never been wild abandonment.

Such were his swift thoughts as he followed her through a large hall, dominated by a round table tidily laden with books and periodicals. A cursory glance at the walls showed evidence of travel and a large painting of Maeve in evening dress. He ached to hold her and confess his undiminished passion. Instead he accepted a seat in the long sunny drawing room while she placed herself opposite. The curtains beside the open French windows flapped politely and a faint breeze reached a huge display of fern and wildflowers in the ornate fireplace.

Neither spoke and both were relieved when within seconds Penn appeared in a fresh checked shirt and immaculate pale trousers. Her light voice, little changed, addressed her husband. "Give Garth one of your status malts or similar. You will have one, Garth?"

Penn reached into the drinks cupboard, below a side table, and poured a generous measure.

"The usual mixed Martini for you, Maeve?"

"Thank you, Penn. Their eyes met. "Well… cheers." She raised her glass but did not look at her visitor. Penn took a sip, then, "Look, I have to post this pile of stuff. Get a paper and some stamps. I'll be back in less than half an hour. You two will have enough to talk about. See you later, and stay to dinner, Garth, it will only be us." He sensed the unease but considered himself surplus. Better to leave them alone.

"Thank you, but I will have to retire early, as I'm off to Texas tomorrow. You know what a trek it is from here to Heathrow."

"Understood. See you when I'm back."

Maeve dreaded his leaving them. She had nothing to say to Garth – nothing. They sipped in silence. Her small boys' voices as they played at the pond with Sylvie Corbette, their nanny-companion-friend, were a solace. Sylvie was a friend's daughter from France, perfecting her English during the vacation; Penn, a close friend of her parents, had been at her christening at Rouen Cathedral.

Garth commented on the heat of the day but a relief from the African sun, just to fill the silence. His eyes were drawn to a solitary bird trilling away on a nearby branch. "Would you like to see the garden?" *Anything better than this*, she thought. She was devoid of any feeling for him. How could she once have been so obsessed, so wounded?

They walked down the meandering path, a yard or so apart, the concealed children's chatter the only sound. He showed no curiosity.

"How many children have you, Garth?"

"A boy and a girl. Anita is ten, Marcus eight. Hazel's new man is a wealthy hotelier in Durban."

Maeve sensed that the memory was painful but made no comment. She remembered the pretty, curvy, uncomplicated girl, wondered whether life in East Africa had changed her.

The garden was almost tropical in its lushness. Far away the sea moaned quietly; the tide was out. The maze of paths, some bordered by lavender and rosemary, were heavy with the scent of summer. Majestic trees rose proud and commanding into the blue sky and in late afternoon the stillness was almost uncanny. In silence they moved amid the extravagance, then a steep descending path wound to the lower-most level where the ancient chastised garden met with the wild heathland. Gorse and heather invaded the boundary to surround a nest of giant boulders, moss-covered and eternal. A tall wire mesh fence along the border with the cliff had been completely concealed with foliage. The unkempt cliff top wildness had encroached into the low meadow, the extremity of the property.

They leant against a boulder, warm to the touch, though she carefully kept her distance as they gazed back at the house. They had nothing to say; she wished he had not come. Then suddenly his arms encircled her, and he pressed her to him as he searched for her mouth. She averted her head towards his shoulder and remained perfectly still, paralysed with fear. She fitted into his arms as neatly as ever and was aware of the familiar pulse in his neck. Momentarily she was back in that shabby room in Oxford with another man and was genuinely alarmed. She found her voice. “Please release me, Garth. Please.” She had not expected this.

The pressure eased, she wriggled free. “Let us go back.” Her voice was hardly audible. She was visibly shaken, he, pale beneath his tan.

The sweet perfumes of the garden, the gurgling brook,

the solitary thrush melodiously singing, seemed removed from reality. The couple were both in some distant world, Maeve because she was nervous, Garth because he was overwrought, frustrated, domestically unhappy and dwelling on what might have been. He had never fallen out of love with her and quietly despised himself for allowing her ghost to undo him. She had remained a lovely memory, through every high and low of the shattered years, something to savour whenever sorrow or disappointment, delight or success came his way. Yet in the magic of these lovely surroundings he accepted that to her he must be a remote memory. She was happy and how he envied, almost hated, Pennistone-Craig.

They reached the car in silence. "I'll get the keys and take you back to the hotel." She calmly walked into the house.

She opened the passenger door for him from within. They drove off in silence. The quiet lane seemed endless, but at last the main road and a meandering drive to the hotel entrance. They had not spoken.

He seemed to be fumbling with the door catch. She reached her left arm across to release the catch. He grasped it, thought better of it and released her.

Tremblingly, "I hope you find happiness, Garth. I have. Goodbye," were her last words.

In the mirror she saw him enter the hotel foyer. A gorgeous woman was emerging; he held the door for her. Maeve wished him luck.

Ahead she saw the distant hills crowned by the setting sun, the ending of a day when he had hoped to rekindle a fire which in her case had been extinguished. She dwelt on the whole strange episode. His conceit was undiminished, his method of seeing her almost trickery.

Feeling deeply distressed, uncomfortable, shocked, she continued down the driveway, her knuckles white on the steering wheel. At the first bend she pulled into a clearing among the giant rhododendrons, placed both arms on the steering wheel and, with her face buried in her arms, she wept. The tears, part anger, part shock or belated sympathy for her own innocent, vulnerable, youth, acted as a catharsis. She faced reality again, reached into the glove compartment for her compact and lipstick, repaired the ravages to her face, donned sunglasses to hide her inflamed eyes and drove home to the only man she desired, to security, stability and love.

Penn was not yet back so she walked to where she heard the children singing some French nursery rhyme which sounded amusing. It appeared to be about chickens having a race across a field.

"Quand les poules sont dans le champ
La premier est maintenant devant
La seconde est maintenant premier."

She did not know it; Sylvie would have to teach her as well. It seemed to be endless – the race went on and on.

She called them to her, told Sylvie to have the night off as she'd had them all day. While Maeve prepared supper they could look at children's television then Sylvie could view television in her room, telephone home, read – do anything. Maeve would see to the children's bath and bedtime story. She had to be occupied.

A while later, as Maeve passed Sylvie's bathroom, a delicious aroma of bath scents filtered under the door. She was really luxuriating. *Oh, for a girl*, Maeve thought, and this girl was a delight. She hoped she would join them next year. She would telephone the Corbettes later, a friendly gesture.

Maeve then dressed with care while Penn supervised the cooking of the prepared meal. She appeared in a blue silk trouser suit, beaded on one shoulder and the top of one sleeve – an Eleri design. She wore long earrings. Her long silky hair was up, secured by a circular comb. Penn thought she was making a statement.

He was making his own statement, having moved the circular dining table into the bay, where, with the window slightly ajar, they could hear the night sounds of the garden and the incoming tide. He had lit two tall candles and placed the wine and a bowl of salad on the table. The steak and baked potatoes were waiting on the hotplate. All was perfection and, as she reached across for the salad, he held her hand and kissed it.

"It's been a rotten day for you, and you did not want your friend to stay for dinner."

"I would rather be with you. I outgrew him long ago."

"Interesting job, were you not curious? An article for the island journal?"

"Interesting job but not an interesting man and he had a nerve to visit. I've thought of the article and passed on the idea. I have no desire to write it."

"I agree, but the temptation to see you overcame him. Incidentally, how did he find you?"

"He saw my photograph in the Quentin Studios window and followed up." Penn laughed. "Sounds like a novel."

They both laughed. How comfortable and secure they were with each other, how devoted and blissfully happy.

An hour or so later, when the last of the shadows had left the garden and the birds had gradually stopped singing, they ascended the stairs together – Penn to their bathroom, Maeve to the bedroom's large bay window to gaze down across the garden to the sea. She undressed in the pale moonlight, swept along by a warm flow of emotion, detached and at peace in the soft expectant night. There was no stir in the garden and the slow-moving sea was silent. Motionless and nude she savoured the unsurpassed loveliness. The moon looked immense, but the sky was almost starless except for one brilliant star rapidly twinkling, as if competing with a twinkling lighthouse on some distant shore. The reflected moon seemed to be chasing her across the slowly moving waves, the solitary bright star following as if in pursuit. She hoped to hold the image and maybe use it in prose or poetry.

Mesmerised by the solemn beauty she was unaware of Penn approaching until she felt his arms around her. "My exquisite wife," he whispered in her ear. "So beautiful, so perfect."

In one smooth motion in the silvery moonlight they slid onto the silvery rug and made ecstatic love as the magical night folded around them and they became lost in a luminous timelessness. The chill of the dawn had seeped into them before they glided to their bed, consumed with wonder at their undiminished devotion to each other.

CHAPTER FORTY

THEY WERE AROUSED BY A SHRILL RINGING OF THE bedside telephone. That early, it had to be her mother, who rose with the sun. "Hello, not up yet. It is to be a fine day, why not visit? Editha is fading. Seeing you and the little ones, however briefly, would cheer her."

"All right, we'll picnic on the way, on the riverbank as already promised, so we'll see you at teatime."

Penn, with no family life as a memory, relished belonging to this fine old clan and had an enormous sense of belonging to them. Most of all he respected and enjoyed Mrs. Blethyn. "I'd employ her any day" was his finest compliment. Her acute, uncluttered mind and keen business acumen did not seem to tally with her deep religious conviction. He found this fascinating. While his children played in Editha's garden during Maeve's visit he would visit Pen Melyn. Her astringent conversation was challenging and amusing.

The island had cast its charm upon him. The river, its tributaries, every knoll and range had become known to him, and a picnic on River Landia that bright noonday with his beloved young family a bonus he had never imagined. Sylvie had chosen to spend the day with a French au pair friend – a day using her own language. Maeve had agreed and helped her prepare their own picnic that morning.

The door of Pen Melyn was partly open but he banged with the great knocker, a sort of unicorn. Mrs. Blethyn appeared, neat and elegant as ever, in a blue-spotted dress with white cuffs and revers and the inevitable pearls. "Oh, it's you, Penn, take a seat." As he did so, "You like the ginger rather than the elderberry. I'll join you." She never wasted words.

She disappeared into the large cold pantry and re-emerged bearing a bottle in one hand, while the other hand held glasses, by their long stems. She poured the delicious amber liquid into each and handed him one. He was about to toast her when she raised her glass. "To you and yours – well, all of us." She continued, "You realise Editha's final days are here and, while on the subject, there will be two more places in the family plot. One will be mine, the other for Briende, and that will end the Madocs at Brymadoc. They have done well."

He smiled. "Quellyn's coming back. Campions is to be an art gallery."

It was her turn to smile. "I cannot see these people clamouring to see art."

"People said that about Eleri's wartime concerts, and they are now the foremost cultural events on the island, spreading fast and attracting well-known artists and being seriously reviewed."

"Music seduces the emotions, more so than art. One has to know what to look for in the latter. Well, that's my humble opinion. When did you see Eleri?"

"I was in New York last February. I stayed in Westport for one night. It is only one hour from New York. Eleri is busy and deliriously happy."

"You think she should see Editha before our Maker calls, which will be within days if I'm anything to go by. Eleri's common sense will direct her to the living rather than to a funeral."

"I agree. Phone her today. She adores Editha and would prefer it that way."

He looked around the room; something was different. "I've just realised, where are all the old family photographs?"

"I got tired of their sepia smiles, seemingly calling me. After all, I was the eldest sibling. I'm not yet ready to cross the Jordan."

Penn found her an unmatchable delight. He next commented on the television, which had a white crocheted cloth draped over it and a bowl of fresh flowers on top. "That could start a trend – very attractive," he said.

"I could not bear that unseeing eye following me all day. I only use it occasionally – very selectively, I tell you. Incidentally, how's business? I see that the shares are up."

"We are doing well, expanding to the Far East. I'm in Holland next week at head office. I should learn more."

She looked at the clock. "You'd better head back.

Fifteen minutes with small children around is Editha's limit."

He got up, brushed her forehead with a kiss and she led him to the door, and waited until he had reached the end of the driveway, her courtesy intact as ever.

He mused on her likeness to Eleri, whose warmth and spontaneity were more to the fore but with the intelligence, the energy akin to her mother, as well as the honesty and generosity. What a superb family he had joined. Even his fragile-looking wife had the same sort of strength and intellect if more reticent. He, too, desired a daughter, a continuation of these gifted Madoc women, endlessly occupied and never ill; even in old age they never lingered in sickness.

Tea at Briende's culminated the day, the small boys racing to their mother's old room as a child – a sort of ritual.

Soon a tinny tinkling was heard overhead. "That's my toy piano," said Maeve. "I'd forgotten about it."

"So had I," said Briende. "I found it while searching for something else."

"Listen," said Penn, looking amazed. "It's that French rhyme they keep singing. What a turn-up if he's musical!" He lit up with excitement.

"Perhaps Sylvie's picked out the tune on the piano at home," said Briende, "though music could well be in them. Their great-grandmother and aunt were superb pianists. Both gave lessons to make ends meet."

Maeve looked surprised. "I never knew that. I know so little of his people. It occurs to me that I could do some research. Brymadoc seems to be my only heritage."

It was the moment Briende had anticipated. She knew that one day her daughter would seek some answers. She pointed to an elegantly shaped, much decorated vase on the mantelpiece and asked Penn to reach it for her. She dipped a slender hand deep into its bowels and extracted a tiny brass key. "The bureau in my bedroom, his letters and mine, some photographs and gifts."

A few moments later Maeve was sitting on the floor beside the open bureau, the letters on her lap, her tears falling rapidly on the neatly tied bundles – one with pale green bias tape, the other tied with pale blue tape. The pearls in a silk hanky and three or four small gifts, she left in the bureau.

Locked in her own thoughts she did not hear the rooks quarrelling in the apple tree or the small boys noisily at play. She had never considered herself sentimental or over-emotional but could not control her silent tears. Downstairs a slight toss of the head from the acutely perceptive Mrs. Blethyn had directed Penn to his wife. He sat beside her and rocked her gently and placed the bundles in the bag.

"I understand how you feel. Pull yourself together for your mother's sake. You'll find more pleasure than pain in these bundles, you may even have the kernel of a story. Let us collect the children, they'll bring you down to earth."

Their loud protests on being dragged from play dispelled the gloom. They clung to the banisters to prolong the descent until given chocolate drops – a rare treat.

Maeve, though rather pensive on the homeward journey, looked forward to the research ahead. Penn was eager to encourage her as absence from each other would soon recommence. He suggested that she begin at the British Library – the Maines' area of mid-England had once been prominent during the War of the Roses.

The small boys fell asleep in a corner, entangled in each other in spite of the ample space in the back. Sylvie laughed to find them so. All were weary, ready for a simple supper and an early night. For Maeve, the last two days had been particularly emotional. She was loath to part with Penn and Sylvie after a full month of family life. One more week and Penn would be on his way to Holland and Sylvie home to France. However, there was one more excitement ahead; Eleri was coming home.

Before leaving Westport the energetic, irrepressible, multi-disciplined Eleri had meetings to cancel, duties to swap with others, Eadie to be sent to friends each day until her father and brother returned each evening. Simon insisted that his son worked during the long vacation and Bran was a hospital porter at the local hospital, exactly the right job for one who was to embark on a medical career. Working in the vacation was a sound American practice Simon agreed with. Eadie he considered too young this year, but she was scheduled to work at a zoo or plant nursery the following summer. Eleri could manage just four days away from responsibilities and she would devote these to Editha. She had to return the following Monday as she was scheduled to take Bran to Johns Hopkins in Baltimore, a duty Simon had looked forward to but was prevented from carrying out because he would be conducting a seminar in Harvard that week.

Two days after the phone call Eleri's arrival in Brymadoc heralded much joy. Dressed in a pale green trouser suit with a beige shoulder-bag and round suitcase she arrived bearing three dozen half-opened red roses and her own special radiance. The family joyfully awaited her but soon dispersed in view of Editha's weakness. None would forget the love in Editha's eyes and the lightness of her face on seeing Eleri. They had kept the visit secret.

The rest of the evening was spent alone with her aunt, companionably perusing albums and letters. These Eleri would be carrying home with her. She strongly felt that Maeve would one day write the family story.

Editha suggested placing the laden coffers and wardrobes of clothes in storage. These ranged over eighty years – even their childhood clothes had been preserved. The beautiful garments, beautifully constructed, covered almost a century of costume history. Editha even considered that Campions could become a costume museum as well as an art gallery; Eleri would certainly be interested in exhibiting the clothes in Westport or New York. Some theatrical costumiers would certainly envy her the collection. Ideas… ideas… there was always a new chapter to Eleri's life.

While Editha slept next day Eleri saw Janet Britt. Together they relived the dark days of the war and the shared agonies and ecstasies when missing loved ones at last made contact. The closeness of those painful days had sealed their friendship. It was wonderful to rejoice with her in Laurence's marriage and children, and hear that Bellan and his Brazilian wife, Eli, lived in Houston where he taught and Eli worked in a pre-school nursery in the poor part of town. The good nuns had achieved his aim. Eli spoke English and Spanish haltingly and was known for her gentleness. The Britts planned to visit them the following year. At the moment they were settling into retirement in a modern house on the Pen Melyn grounds, finding space for the numerous books which were to the Reverend décor. Both enjoyed Laurence's children, who lived in Cambridge, where he had resumed his work and studying.

On Friday, at mid-morning Eleri left Myrtle House while Editha was still asleep. She placed one red rose on her pillow, kissed her and left for the port in Mr. Byatt's new taxi.

It was the last goodbye and a silent one. It was best that way. Then the long familiar journey to London. Claude and Juliette, now grandparents, met her and drove her to the airport. It was a long enough reunion to talk of friends. Venetia and her husband still occupied a wing of the old house; the rest was in flats. The two girls, one from each marriage, worked for UNESCO. The Havillands had visited Cairo the previous year and had a memorable time with Abdul and Prunie, who was the proud mother of four Moslem children.

Eleri made no attempt to telephone Brymadoc; she seemed to know what the news would be.

After a fond farewell to her dear friends, she hurried down the ramp to board her plane. She longed for Simon and her children in her American home. Her hectic visit had been a success and an effort, and she had added joy to the last days of a beautiful woman's spotless life. Editha would not wish her to mourn.

Early next morning Simon was waiting. He still caught his breath at a glimpse of her, the pale green suit, the cascading hair, the smile. Who would believe that she had travelled overnight? She raced into his waiting arms and hugged him, always conscious of the old injury as she did so. Oh, to be home again. Hands on his shoulders, she threw back her head and looked into his eyes. "It's all right, I know."

"We heard last night. She had smiled at your rose but soon drifted back to sleep; they checked at noon and she was breathing smoothly. They checked at two and she was gone."

"Yes, I knew at two, although I was not there." She changed the subject. "I hope the children are not expecting me to be unhappy; better to rejoice for her good life. Agree?"

"I agree. The children are cooking a special meal."

"I hope they are better at it than I am and not upsetting Dolores's kitchen. Good thing she's off today."

He embraced her and smiled. A one-off as he regarded her.

It was as she expected at the house; the children eagerly waiting, fresh flowers everywhere. Home! What a lovely day ahead. Firstly, she would telephone her mother, announce her safe arrival and send her love.

That evening, as they were all pleasantly unwinding, there was a call from Quellyn, who had been in London for a week on business pertaining to the coming art exhibition. He sounded happy, excited. Eleri quickly became attuned to his enthusiasm but the message was devastating – he was marrying Susannah on Thursday at Chelsea Registry Office. Two friends would be witnesses. Susannah was pregnant and, after a week in Italy, with just a backpack, they were returning to New York to live in Greenwich Village. All was settled.

Simon gave a quick glance at Eleri, and instinctively moved towards her and placed his arms around her. Her miraculous optimism soon reasserted itself. She sent so much love from all of them, told him it was exciting news. She could not reveal her heartache.

"Where are you staying?" she chirpily enquired, though inwardly anxious.

"At the Blondel, on the river, very lively, full of artists." Eleri was relieved.

He ended by saying, "Mama, call Grandma Garonne for me. You'll cope better than me. You know how ambitious she is, but I love her dearly. Please tell her so. Love to you all." Then he hung up.

With his arm around her Simon led her back to the long chintzy sofa to join Bran and Eadie. She smiled her brave smile, but each felt her pain, aware of the special bond with Quellyn, whose nature was so like her own.

"Too bad," said Bran, who had already caught the gist of things, "and he only twenty-two, with the world at his feet." He gave a low whistle. "I can imagine the rumblings in Palm Beach."

"Yes, and I've been asked to inform her."

"Go ahead, over with it. Then accept it."

Simon appreciated his son's maturity with a glance of pride towards him.

Eleri obediently went to dial her ex-mother-in-law, now friend, a dear friend. “Bettina, I have news.”

“Don’t tell me you’re expecting another baby. You are as ageless as Rider Haggard’s *She*. I’m getting ready for a concert at the Hempsons. They have this new violinist, Japanese, I think. So, what a celebration.”

Eleri laughed. “Would that it were so.” She paused. “Quellyn’s getting married on Thursday at Chelsea Registry Office.”

She seemed to hear Rupert dragging a chair for her. “Not the art tutor’s daughter? Surely not? He’s too much in demand. Senator Bailey’s daughter, his only daughter, is crazy for him, a sporty, healthy type, marvellous boyish figure… and the clothes! She’s Swiss finishing school, the lot. She could have anyone, Baileys the publishers, no less. This Susannah’s not pregnant, I hope.”

“She is, I’m afraid.”

“That should be no problem. Where is he? Give me the number, I’ll make a substantial offer.”

Eleri took a deep breath before replying. “He lunched with Paloma Bailey more than once in New York. He did not fall for her. He’s in love with Susannah, he’s at the Blondel in Chelsea. I haven’t the number,” but she knew the outcome. Bettina, the brittle socialite, was not dealing with Alvar Garonne. Quellyn was of a different ilk.

She heard her directing her husband to go without her.

“I could not tolerate tonight’s music if it became emotionally taxing. I know I’d have to leave. That boy means the world to me.”

Eleri thought she detected a sob in the proud, poised

woman's voice. "I'm sorry, Bettina. How do you think I feel?"

"Fight this, Eleri. Please fight it. A young life must not be blighted because of a fling. He deserves a splendid match."

"I'll call you tomorrow, Bettina. My thoughts are with you."

Eleri hung up and returned to the sofa. "Don't tell me," said Bran, "she wants to buy her off."

Simon looked serious; his whole universe was encompassed in about thirty square feet. Eadie sitting on the floor, her head on Eleri's lap, Bran, and he with an arm around Eleri – a sad tableau of devoted people.

Eleri broke the silence. "Let us drink to the dear ones and the newcomer. Simon, get the bubbly."

Without being asked Eadie dashed to load the Lazy Susan with its various compartments for cashew nuts, savoury crisps, cheesy nibbles and anything else she found.

Eleri sank her head into the pillows, her mind retreating to a scruffy Kensington studio. How scornfully would she have laughed at Spenser Fortesque and herself sharing a grandchild. Bran took her hand. She returned to the present and looked into his eyes – his father's amber eyes. "Not to worry, I'm unlikely to get trapped…"

She checked him. "I wouldn't begrudge the full experience to anyone crazy about a person but pregnancy and marriage should take some planning." She patted his hand as Eadie and Simon returned. Simon still looked thoughtful. Events were moving too fast for comfort. He hoped, in some way, his son was learning something from this. The world of the young seemed beset by traps; biologically equipped but not emotionally ready. His heart ached for Quellyn. Like Eleri, he hoped that they were deeply in love.

Before bed, in deference to Editha and as a salve for this new blow, they decided as a family to attend church in the morning. Don Westlake, the minister, always had an inspiring programme prepared, varying from spiritual readings to fine music, to excellent acknowledgement of whatever good work was being accomplished. The tree-trunk pulpit dedicated to Albert Schweitzer, or so they had heard, the glass-walled hall, the inspirational design of the whole building was an experience each time. It was a church that made sense and welcomed lapsed members of any faith. *Only America!* Eleri thought. This building shaped like a ship in a landscape of grassy sea, the two sides of the prow reaching into the air but not meeting, representing the ever-open question.

After the meeting the lively, sophisticated writers, professors, advertising types, businessmen, would gather in the foyer around a long table, drink sherry from dixie cups and catch up on local news, the business world and politics with friends and neighbours. How different from the British way!

The Peerless family would then walk in the woods or along the shore, their silent tribute to Editha and much thought directed to Simon's ageing parents, who were due to be visited after the week's seminar. Simon would check their insurances with Stan Ignasiak, a friend of his since schooldays and now an accountant. Simon's mother felt more comfortable dealing with 'her own kind', because Stan was also of Polish extraction and on the committee of a sheltered housing complex for Polish-Americans. But not yet, though one had to plan ahead.

Simon and Eleri held hands and marvelled at their serious leggy daughter, studying rocks, pebbles, seaweed, seeds, with intense concentration. What a quaint child she was, her shock of tawny hair seemingly too heavy for her slender neck, falling like a curtain around her face as she studied whatever she leant over. The parents visualised her later on as a quiet, elegant woman, intense and genuine. She had already decided on majoring in the natural sciences at Temple University, her father's alma mater, in what she considered his home state and the home of her beloved Polish grandparents.

The family had barely united at the end of another hectic week when a letter arrived from the French Riviera, where Miranda and Jake were combining business with vacation. It was written by Jake Pointing – a very rare occurrence – on company stationery, in disjointed sentences, giddyingly sloping as if written in excitement or in a hurry.

He had withheld informing them until the diagnosis was certain and they had just heard. Miranda was expecting twins in seven months' time. He sounded puerile in his ebullience, as though he alone had ever sired twins. Proud of his connection with this ancient family, he said he was purchasing Myrtle House via the agents. It was the ultimate compliment to his wife, for he seemed to have the Texas Railroad as an ancestor.

It was to be a vacation home, or for rental to future holidaymakers. He, too, saw llandia becoming a desirable haven. He also informed them in typical tycoon style that he had arranged photo calls and interviews with selected periodicals when the babies arrived.

Eleri was pleased about the house because, to her, it was brimful of happy memories. She doubted whether they would spend much time there. She also imagined the much-loved, languid, unflappable, Miranda basking in her own glory. What luck!

Miranda's contribution to the letter was one sentence in her beautiful script, saying she was pleased to have two at once, as she would only have to lose her figure once. She sent an abundance of love to all.

CHAPTER FORTY-ONE

End of an Era

IT WAS A GLORIOUS SUNDAY MORNING IN JUNE ALMOST two years later. No modern Arcadia would rival such perfection. What the Irish would have called a soft sort of morning.

The bells rang their call to church, the late pink and white May blossom concealed a choir of birds, the air was seductively sweet, with no breeze to drown the secretive whisperings in the hedgerows.

Mrs. Blethyn was preparing for morning service. A touch of powder and lipstick and pearl earrings and then her new dress of dove-grey, sprinkled with white lilies of the valley. Her gloves, bag and hymn book were on the table. Her car she had already parked at the great door. She ascended the stairs to fetch her summer hat.

Mrs. Blethyn was absent from church, and a sharp-eyed worshipper had noticed the car parked in its usual place because Mrs. Blethyn now drove to church. There was something amiss. She crept out of the church to call on Briende.

Together they arrived at Pen Melyn. The things on the table signified an intention of going to the service. An icy coldness possessed Briende. Summoning her courage, she crept upstairs to the bedroom calling her mother – softly, endearingly. She reached her room.

Mrs. Blethyn, hands chastely clasped on her stomach, her dress covering her knees, her noble face in repose, was lying on the bed. A faint blue tinge beneath the pale lipstick suggested a heart attack. Whatever occurred had been sudden. She had lain down, composed herself and awaited the inevitable. Or so it seemed. It was the passing, the dignified exit, Mrs. Blethyn would have ordered.

A week later, with curtains drawn at every window and a slow tolling of a muffled church bell, the hushed bier was being slowly trundled through the main street of Brymadoc. The family followed in cars. All had decided to return from distant places. A long column of mourners followed to pay tribute to a remarkable woman. Scores had been at the receiving end of her many kindnesses, unknown to any except the recipients.

It was a pretty day. The sun obediently shone between skittering light showers, which came and went on the breeze. The Reverend Britt had emerged from retirement to conduct the service. The same hymns and readings were used as those for her siblings.

As the coffin was lowered into, what was for the mourners, a family garden, Eleri was the first to notice the delicate rainbow seemingly hanging above the church spire. Memories flooded back of another time, a bright morning in grim times, when the rainbow had appeared in the same place.

She held Simon's hand, pressing her palm into his, consumed with love flowing like a warm breath around her. She felt a closeness to those gathered around the yawning grave and shared their loss of the wonderful, unusual being who had breathed her last breath as she intended in the chamber in which she had first met, but who had bravely accepted in recent months the changes she knew would come after her demise.

Eleri's other hand clasped Briende's, which was icy cold though the sun poured its kindly warmth around them. Briende would feel the wrench more than any other as she recollected the early days of Maeve's existence.

Eleri looked across at the dear frail Bessingtons, who had made a valiant effort to attend. Her eyes met theirs. Their thoughts had already met at a lonely, bleak chapel seeming aeons ago. The only hope and promise of that unhappy morning lay in the freshness of the twin white wreaths in the acrid atmosphere of a post-blitz morning.

Jake, with his arm around Miranda, seemed bewildered and deeply touched – this was so unlike the American way of death. He appeared quite foreign.

Mrs. Blethyn had seen them all; a handsome, sophisticated playboy, a quaint black-clad European Jew, pink-trousered American officers, Bethan's Italian tenor,

Niamh's immature student husband and as a finale a cowboy-hatted Texan with the strange name of Jake M. Pointing III and an irritating drawling voice.

She did not see Pen Melyn become a maternity hospital, complete with up-to-date facilities, or hear of the plans to build a splendid library in the remaining grounds; all to be leased to the local authority. Or see Campions become an art gallery of note, followed later by a costume museum and later still a natural history museum – all on the same complex and the chief future attractions for the whole of llandia.

Her sharp brain, in spite of her age, would have enjoyed Maeve's novel about the Maines, her paternal grandparents, woven into the historical mid-England region which had nurtured both. More so, how proud Mrs. Blethyn would have been to read Maeve's *The Madocs of Brymadoc*, commissioned by Guthrie and Patton and released with the periodical *Island Heritage*. For centuries they had made an indelible mark.

She did, however, make acquaintance with the cluster of spring babies the previous year; Quellyn had reclaimed The Lodge and brought his family. Maeve brought Maia, her daughter, to Brackens and Miranda had once brought the twins to Myrtle House. The glamorous invaders from Texas, with their ultra-modern accessories and professional staff, creating quite a stir in what Jake called "a cute kinda place."

Eleri squeezed the hand of her beloved sister, soon to be hostess at Pen Melyn for the final family gathering. The whole assemblage would be oddly disorientated without the matriarch, who had figured prominently in all their lives and in the lives of those around her.

The ancient church clock struck three as the final words of the burial service were intoned. All eyes were raised to its familiar face with its age-old message, "God be with you".

Mrs. Blethyn would have approved.

Matador